RANGERS
OF THE DIVIDE™

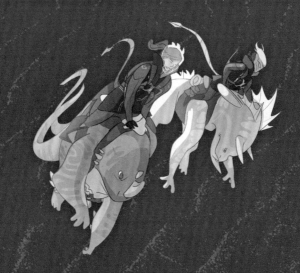

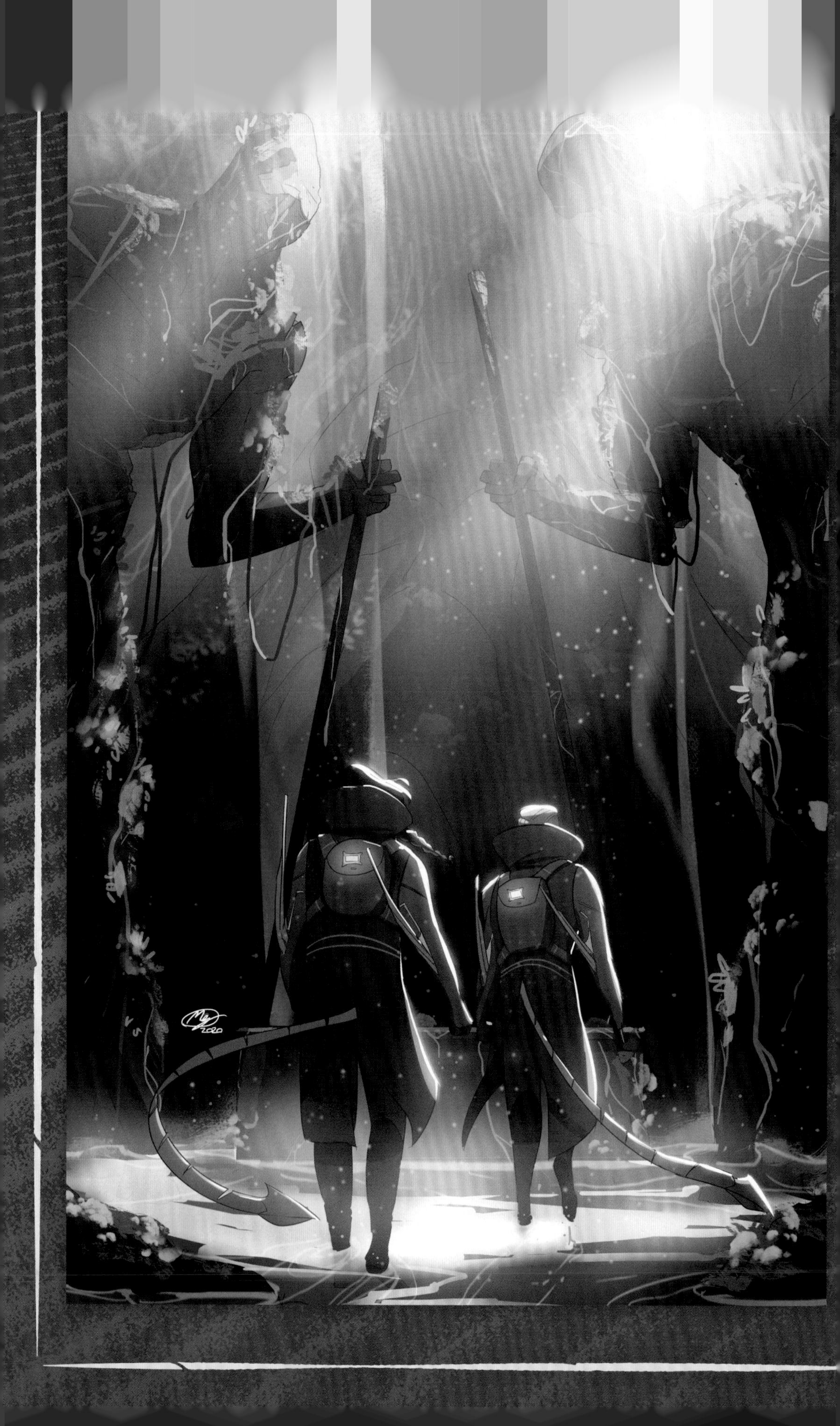

RANGERS OF THE DIVIDE™

VOLUME 1
FIRST ASCENT

Created, written, and illustrated by

MEGAN HUANG

DARK HORSE BOOKS

President and Publisher **MIKE RICHARDSON** | Editor **JUDY KHUU**

Assistant Editor **ROSE WEITZ** | Designer **KATHLEEN BARNETT**

Digital Art Technician **SAMANTHA HUMMER**

Neil Hankerson Executive Vice President | **Tom Weddle** Chief Financial Officer | **Dale LaFountain** Chief Information Officer | **Tim Wiesch** Vice President of Licensing | **Matt Parkinson** Vice President of Marketing | **Vanessa Todd-Holmes** Vice President of Production and Scheduling | **Mark Bernardi** Vice President of Book Trade and Digital Sales | **Randy Lahrman** Vice President of Product Development | **Ken Lizzi** General Counsel | **Dave Marshall** Editor in Chief | **Davey Estrada** Editorial Director | **Chris Warner** Senior Books Editor | **Cary Grazzini** Director of Specialty Projects | **Lia Ribacchi** Art Director | **Matt Dryer** Director of Digital Art and Prepress | **Michael Gombos** Senior Director of Licensed Publications | **Kari Yadro** Director of Custom Programs | **Kari Torson** Director of International Licensing

RANGERS OF THE DIVIDE VOLUME 1: FIRST ASCENT

Published by Dark Horse Books
A division of Dark Horse Comics LLC
10956 SE Main Street | Milwaukie, OR 97222

DarkHorse.com

To find a comics shop in your area, visit comicshoplocator.com

Library of Congress Cataloging-in-Publication Data

Names: Huang, Megan, writer, artist.
Title: Rangers of the divide / Megan Huang.
Description: Milwaukie, OR : Dark Horse Books, [2022] | "This volume
  collects issues #1-#4 of the Dark Horse comic book series Rangers of the
  Divide, published May-August 2021."
Identifiers: LCCN 2021026134 (print) | LCCN 2021026135 (ebook) | ISBN
  9781506725000 (trade paperback) | ISBN 9781506725017 (ebook)
Subjects: CYAC: Fantasy. | Dragons--Fiction. | Graphic novels. | LCGFT:
  Fantasy comics.
Classification: LCC PZ7.7.H84 Ran 2022 (print) | LCC PZ7.7.H84 (ebook) |
  DDC 741.5/973--dc23
LC record available at https://lccn.loc.gov/2021026134
LC ebook record available at https://lccn.loc.gov/2021026135

First Edition: December 2021
Ebook ISBN 978-1-50672-501-7
Trade Paperback ISBN 978-1-50672-500-0

1 3 5 7 9 10 8 6 4 2

Printed in China

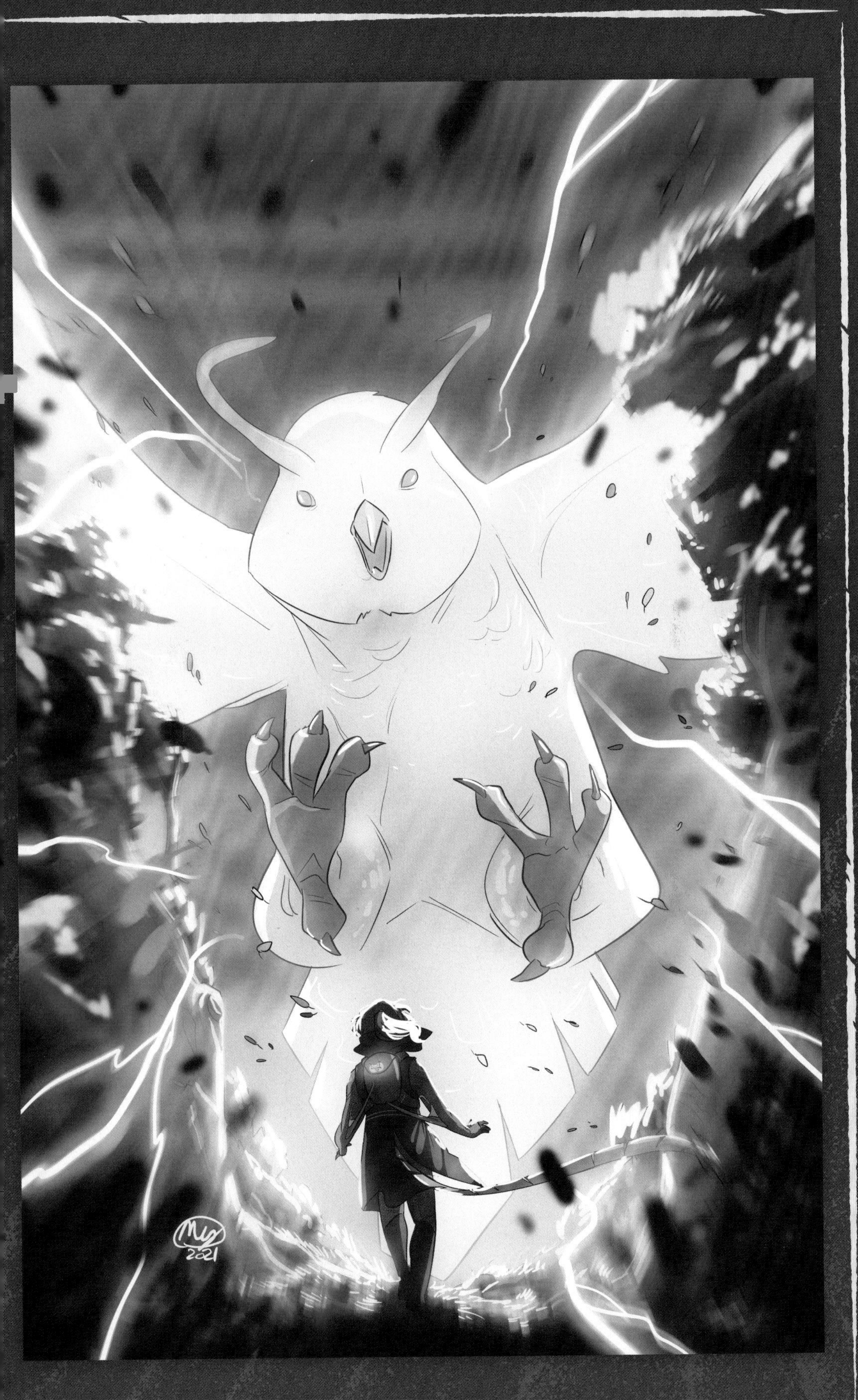

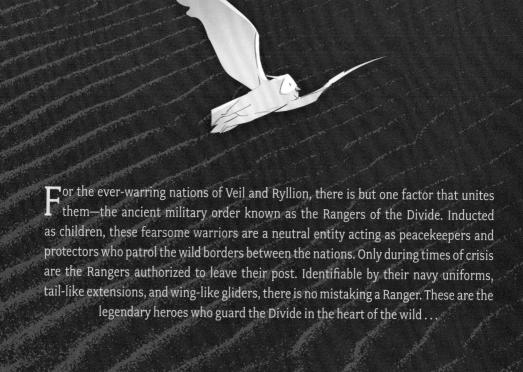

For the ever-warring nations of Veil and Ryllion, there is but one factor that unites them—the ancient military order known as the Rangers of the Divide. Inducted as children, these fearsome warriors are a neutral entity acting as peacekeepers and protectors who patrol the wild borders between the nations. Only during times of crisis are the Rangers authorized to leave their post. Identifiable by their navy uniforms, tail-like extensions, and wing-like gliders, there is no mistaking a Ranger. These are the legendary heroes who guard the Divide in the heart of the wild . . .

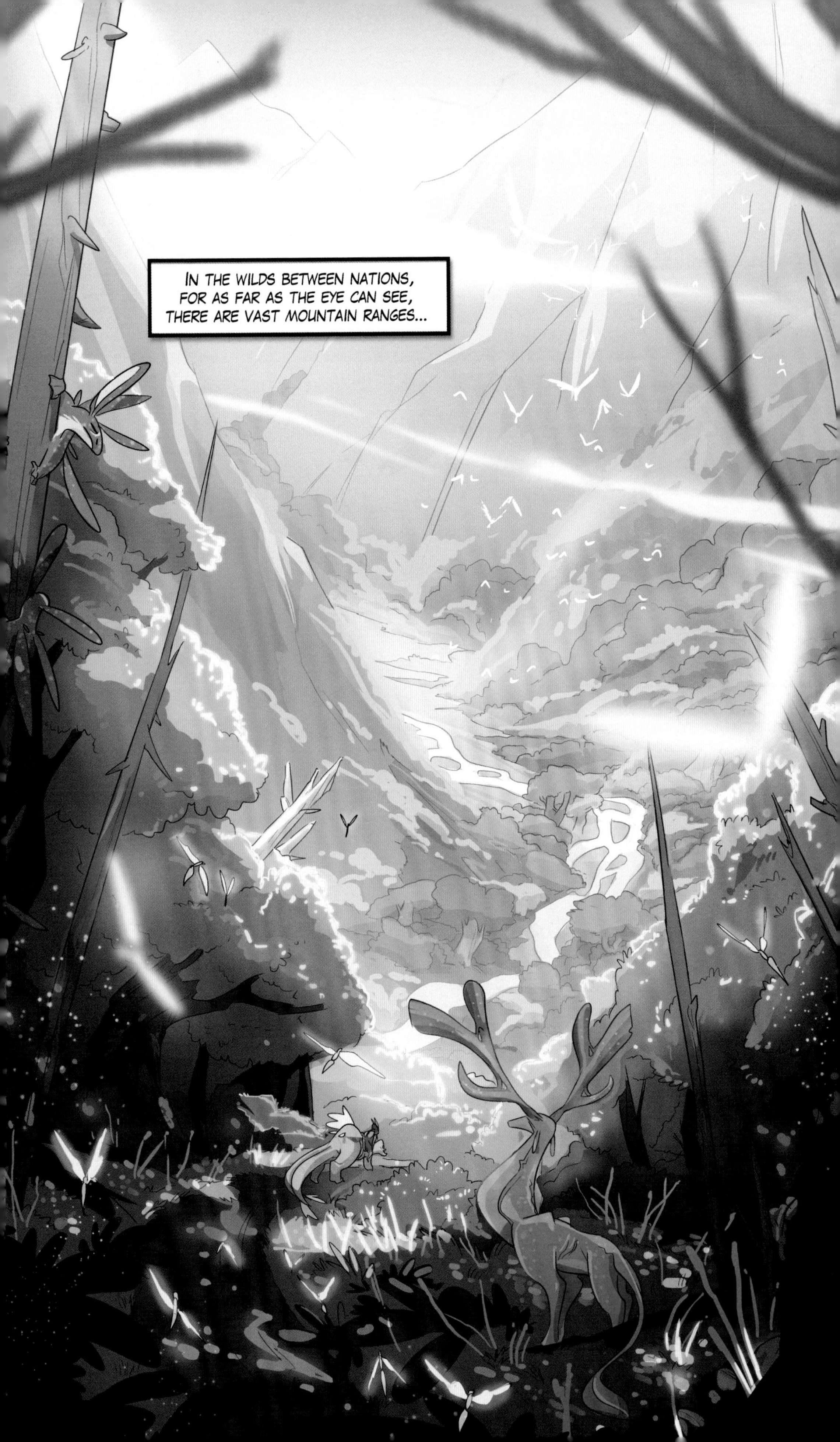
In the wilds between nations,
for as far as the eye can see,
there are vast mountain ranges...

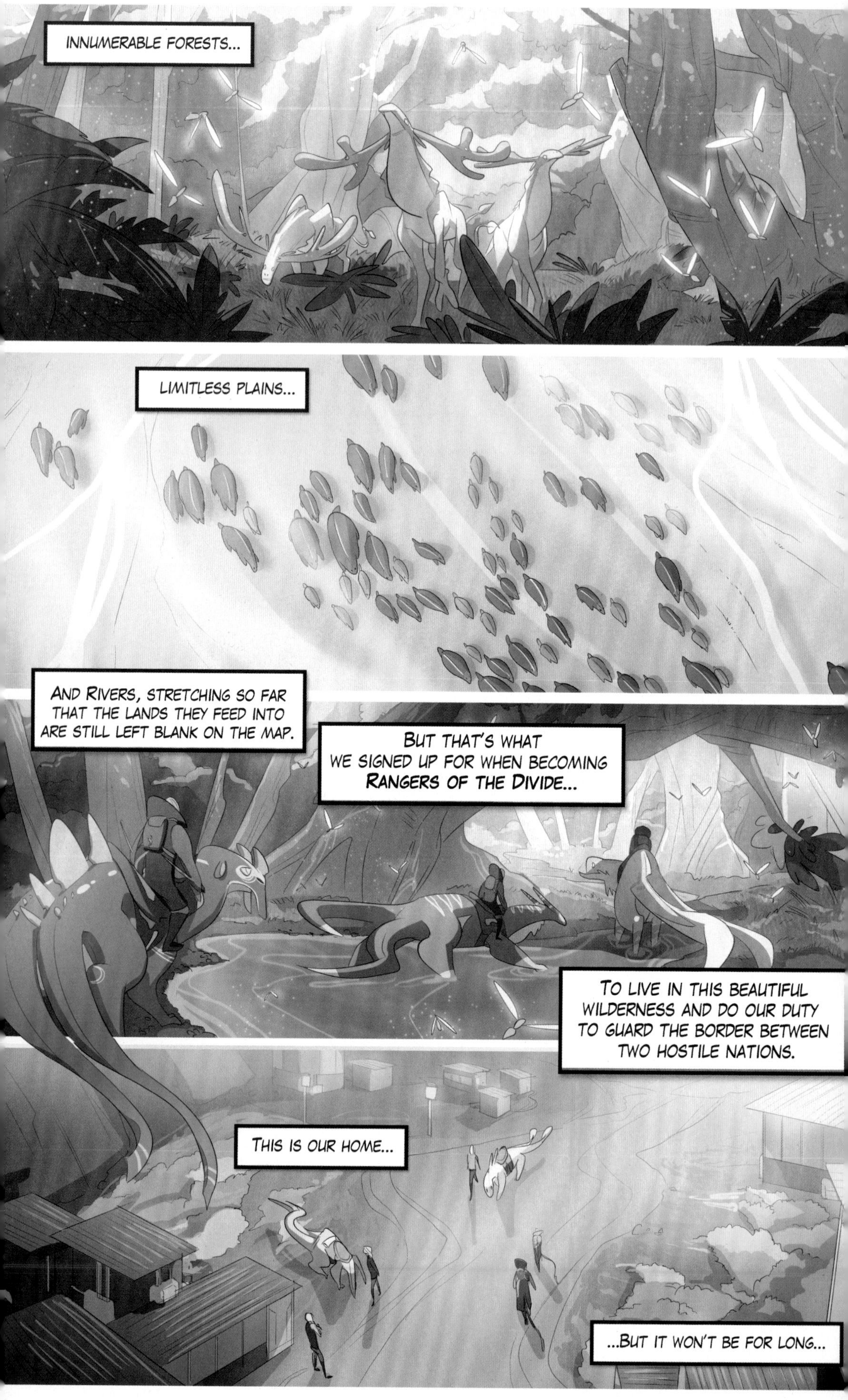
INNUMERABLE FORESTS...
LIMITLESS PLAINS...
AND RIVERS, STRETCHING SO FAR THAT THE LANDS THEY FEED INTO ARE STILL LEFT BLANK ON THE MAP.
BUT THAT'S WHAT WE SIGNED UP FOR WHEN BECOMING RANGERS OF THE DIVIDE...
TO LIVE IN THIS BEAUTIFUL WILDERNESS AND DO OUR DUTY TO GUARD THE BORDER BETWEEN TWO HOSTILE NATIONS.
THIS IS OUR HOME...
...BUT IT WON'T BE FOR LONG...

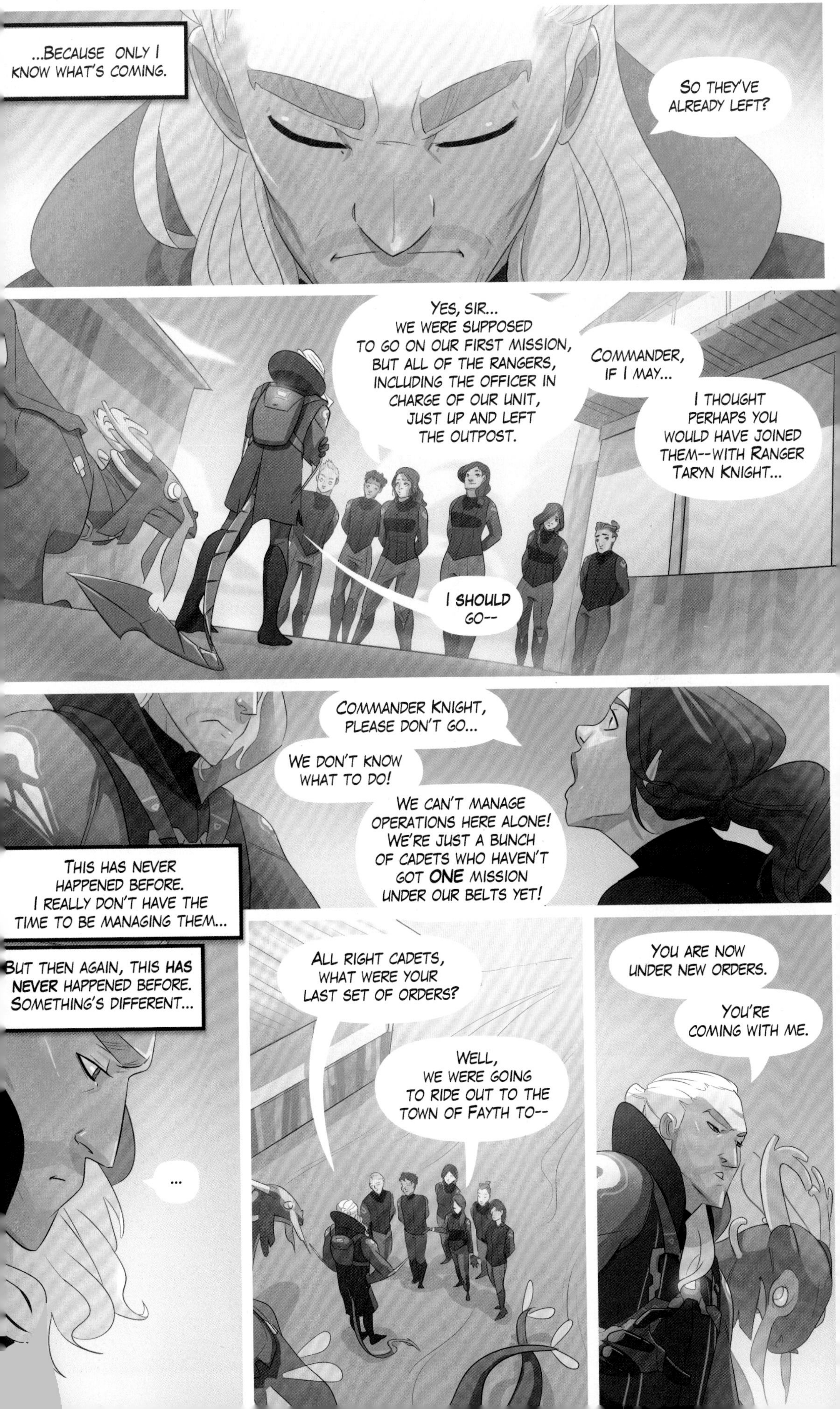
...BECAUSE ONLY I KNOW WHAT'S COMING.
SO THEY'VE ALREADY LEFT?
YES, SIR... WE WERE SUPPOSED TO GO ON OUR FIRST MISSION, BUT ALL OF THE RANGERS, INCLUDING THE OFFICER IN CHARGE OF OUR UNIT, JUST UP AND LEFT THE OUTPOST.
COMMANDER, IF I MAY...
I THOUGHT PERHAPS YOU WOULD HAVE JOINED THEM--WITH RANGER TARYN KNIGHT...
I SHOULD GO--
COMMANDER KNIGHT, PLEASE DON'T GO...
WE DON'T KNOW WHAT TO DO!
WE CAN'T MANAGE OPERATIONS HERE ALONE! WE'RE JUST A BUNCH OF CADETS WHO HAVEN'T GOT **ONE** MISSION UNDER OUR BELTS YET!
THIS HAS NEVER HAPPENED BEFORE. I REALLY DON'T HAVE THE TIME TO BE MANAGING THEM...
BUT THEN AGAIN, THIS **HAS NEVER** HAPPENED BEFORE. SOMETHING'S DIFFERENT...
...
ALL RIGHT CADETS, WHAT WERE YOUR LAST SET OF ORDERS?
WELL, WE WERE GOING TO RIDE OUT TO THE TOWN OF FAYTH TO--
YOU ARE NOW UNDER NEW ORDERS.
YOU'RE COMING WITH ME.

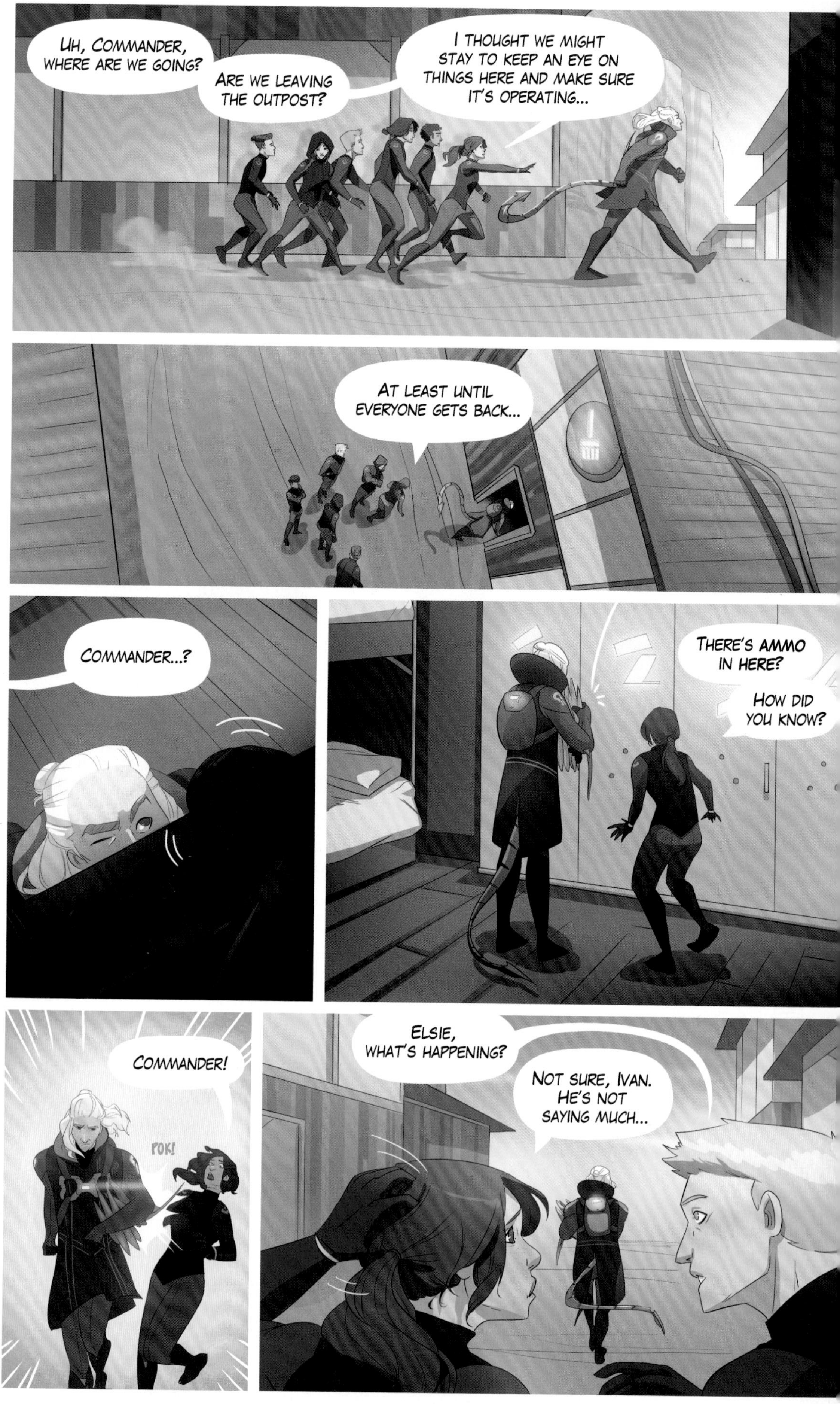

UH, COMMANDER, WHERE ARE WE GOING?
ARE WE LEAVING THE OUTPOST?
I THOUGHT WE MIGHT STAY TO KEEP AN EYE ON THINGS HERE AND MAKE SURE IT'S OPERATING...
AT LEAST UNTIL EVERYONE GETS BACK...
COMMANDER...?
THERE'S AMMO IN HERE?
HOW DID YOU KNOW?
COMMANDER!
POK!
ELSIE, WHAT'S HAPPENING?
NOT SURE, IVAN. HE'S NOT SAYING MUCH...

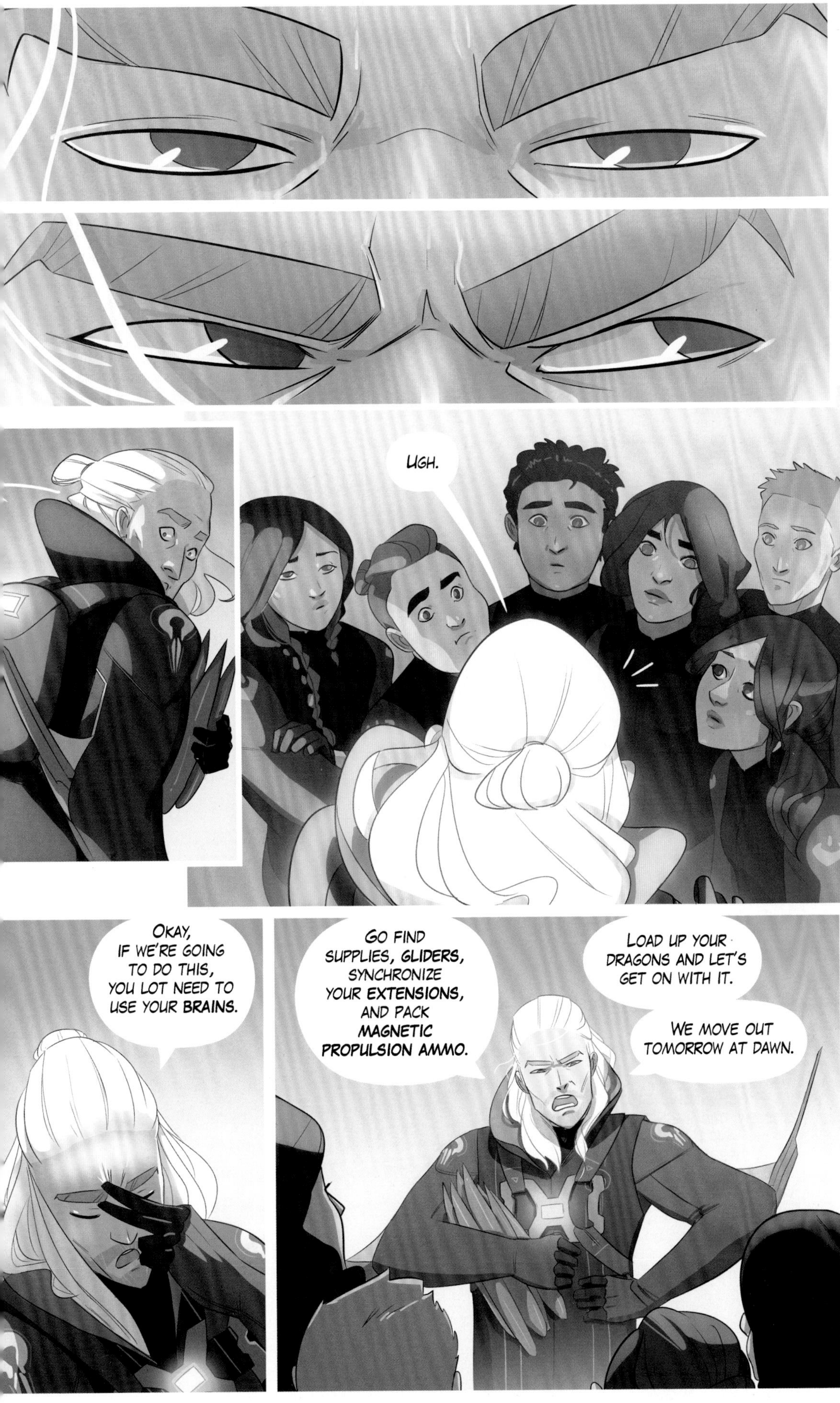
UGH.
OKAY, IF WE'RE GOING TO DO THIS, YOU LOT NEED TO USE YOUR **BRAINS**.
GO FIND SUPPLIES, **GLIDERS**, SYNCHRONIZE YOUR **EXTENSIONS**, AND PACK **MAGNETIC PROPULSION AMMO**.
LOAD UP YOUR DRAGONS AND LET'S GET ON WITH IT.
WE MOVE OUT TOMORROW AT DAWN.

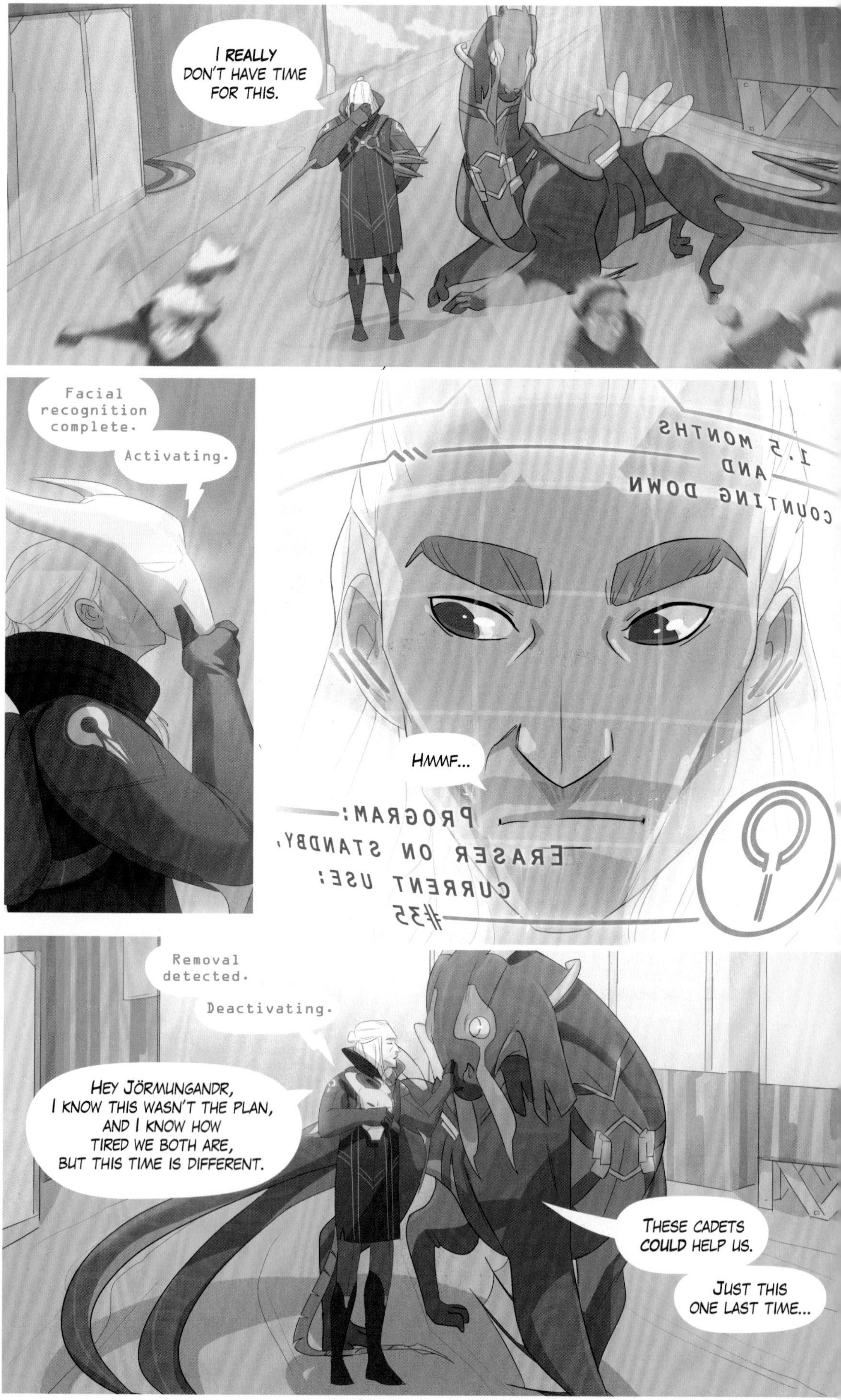
I REALLY DON'T HAVE TIME FOR THIS.
Facial recognition complete.
Activating.
1.5 MONTHS AND COUNTING DOWN
HMMF...
PROGRAM: ERASER ON STANDBY, CURRENT USE: #35
Removal detected.
Deactivating.
HEY JÖRMUNGANDR, I KNOW THIS WASN'T THE PLAN, AND I KNOW HOW TIRED WE BOTH ARE, BUT THIS TIME IS DIFFERENT.
THESE CADETS COULD HELP US.
JUST THIS ONE LAST TIME...

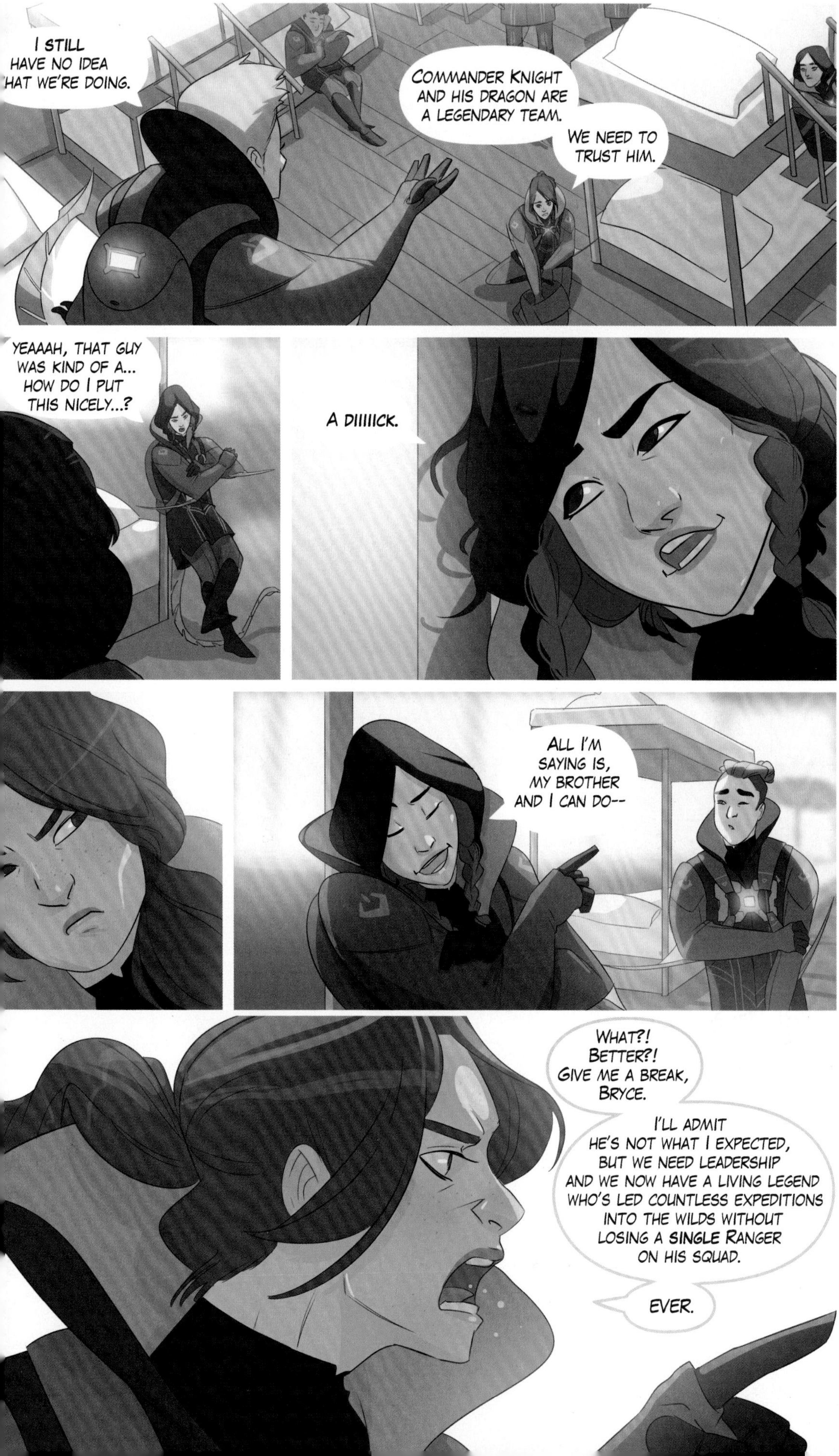
I STILL HAVE NO IDEA HAT WE'RE DOING.
COMMANDER KNIGHT AND HIS DRAGON ARE A LEGENDARY TEAM.
WE NEED TO TRUST HIM.
YEAAAH, THAT GUY WAS KIND OF A... HOW DO I PUT THIS NICELY...?
A DIIIIICK.
ALL I'M SAYING IS, MY BROTHER AND I CAN DO--
WHAT?! BETTER?! GIVE ME A BREAK, BRYCE.
I'LL ADMIT HE'S NOT WHAT I EXPECTED, BUT WE NEED LEADERSHIP AND WE NOW HAVE A LIVING LEGEND WHO'S LED COUNTLESS EXPEDITIONS INTO THE WILDS WITHOUT LOSING A SINGLE RANGER ON HIS SQUAD.
EVER.

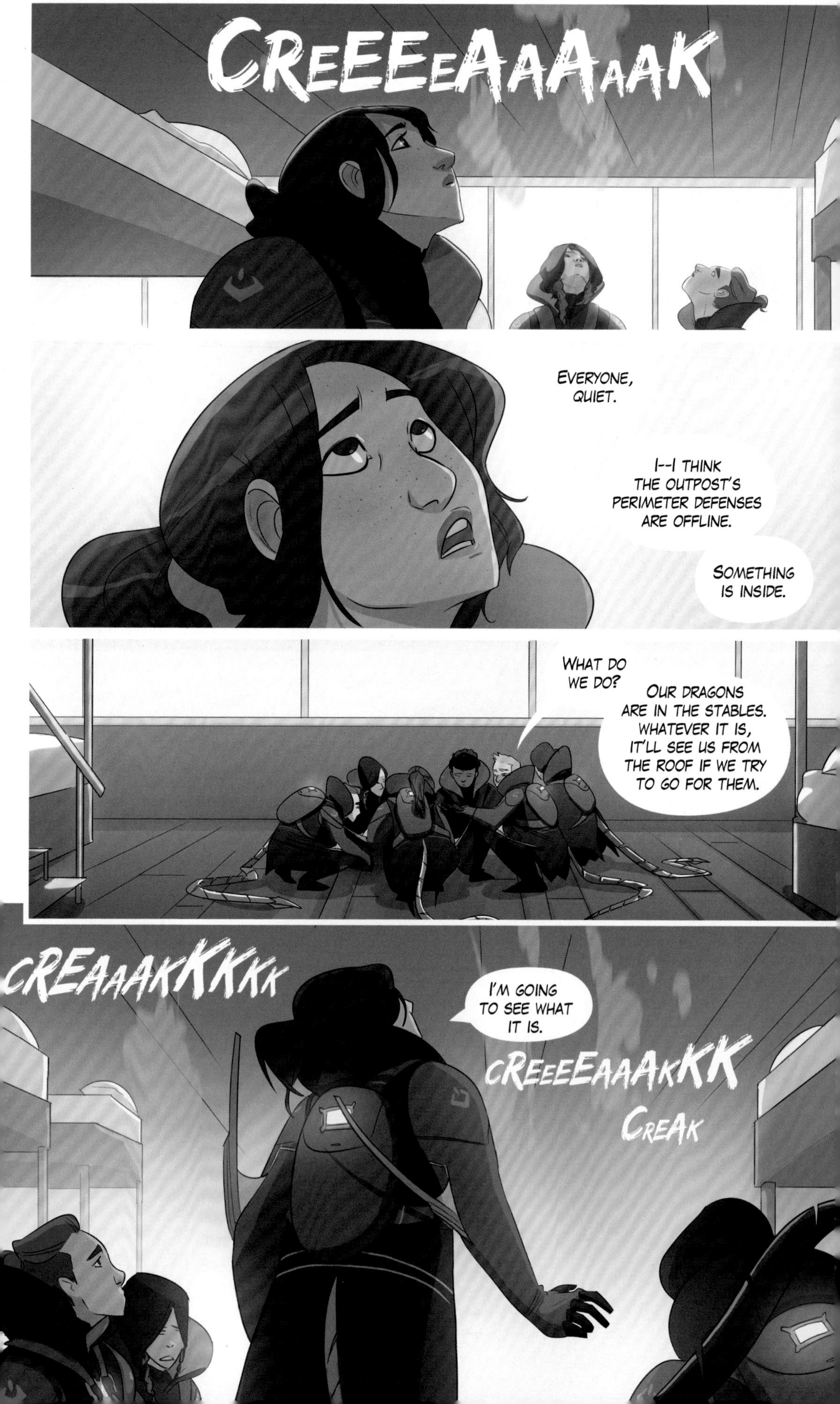
CREEEEAAAAAK
EVERYONE, QUIET.
I--I THINK THE OUTPOST'S PERIMETER DEFENSES ARE OFFLINE.
SOMETHING IS INSIDE.
WHAT DO WE DO?
OUR DRAGONS ARE IN THE STABLES. WHATEVER IT IS, IT'LL SEE US FROM THE ROOF IF WE TRY TO GO FOR THEM.
CREAAAKKKKK
I'M GOING TO SEE WHAT IT IS.
CREEEEAAAAKKK
CREAK

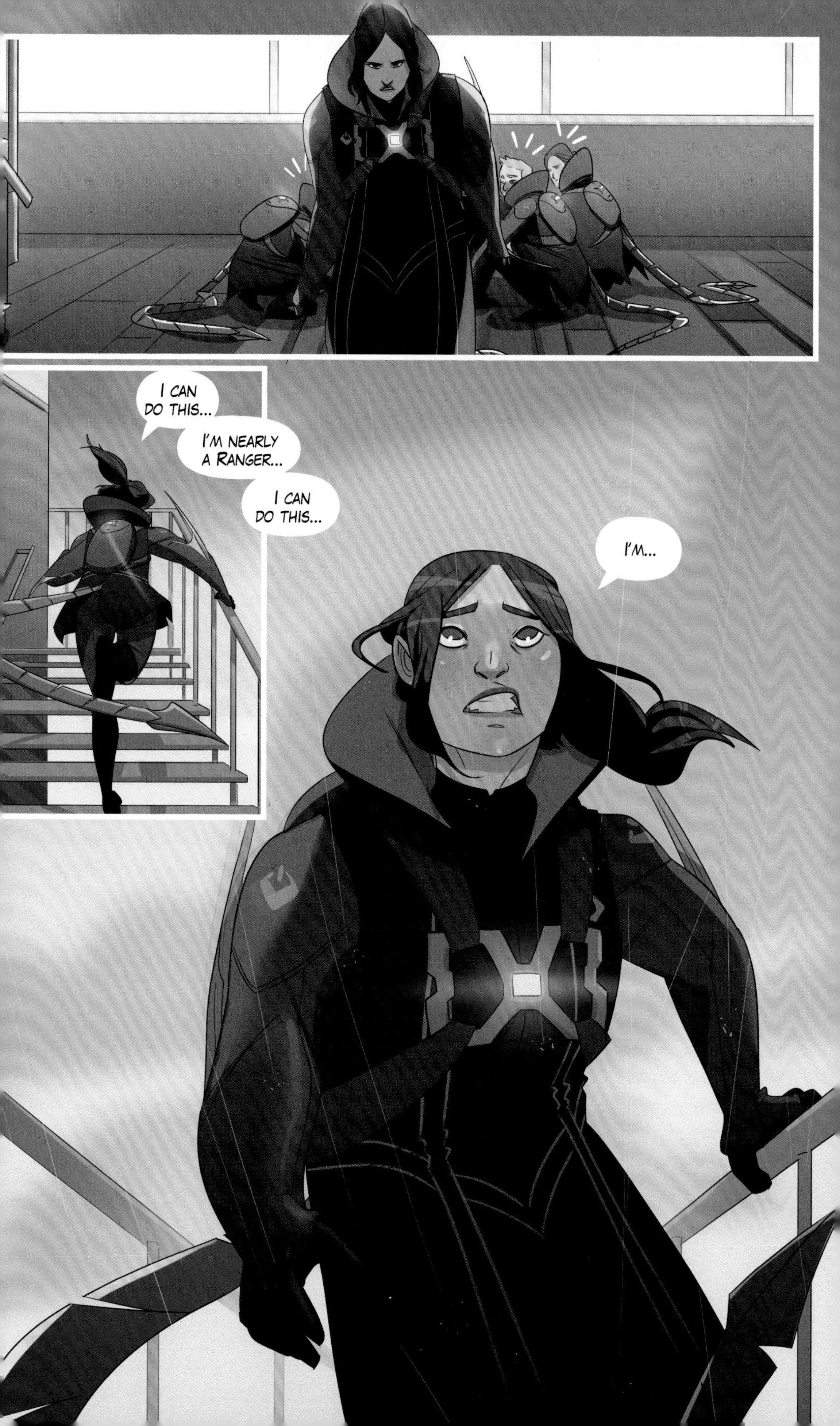
I CAN DO THIS...
I'M NEARLY A RANGER...
I CAN DO THIS...
I'M...

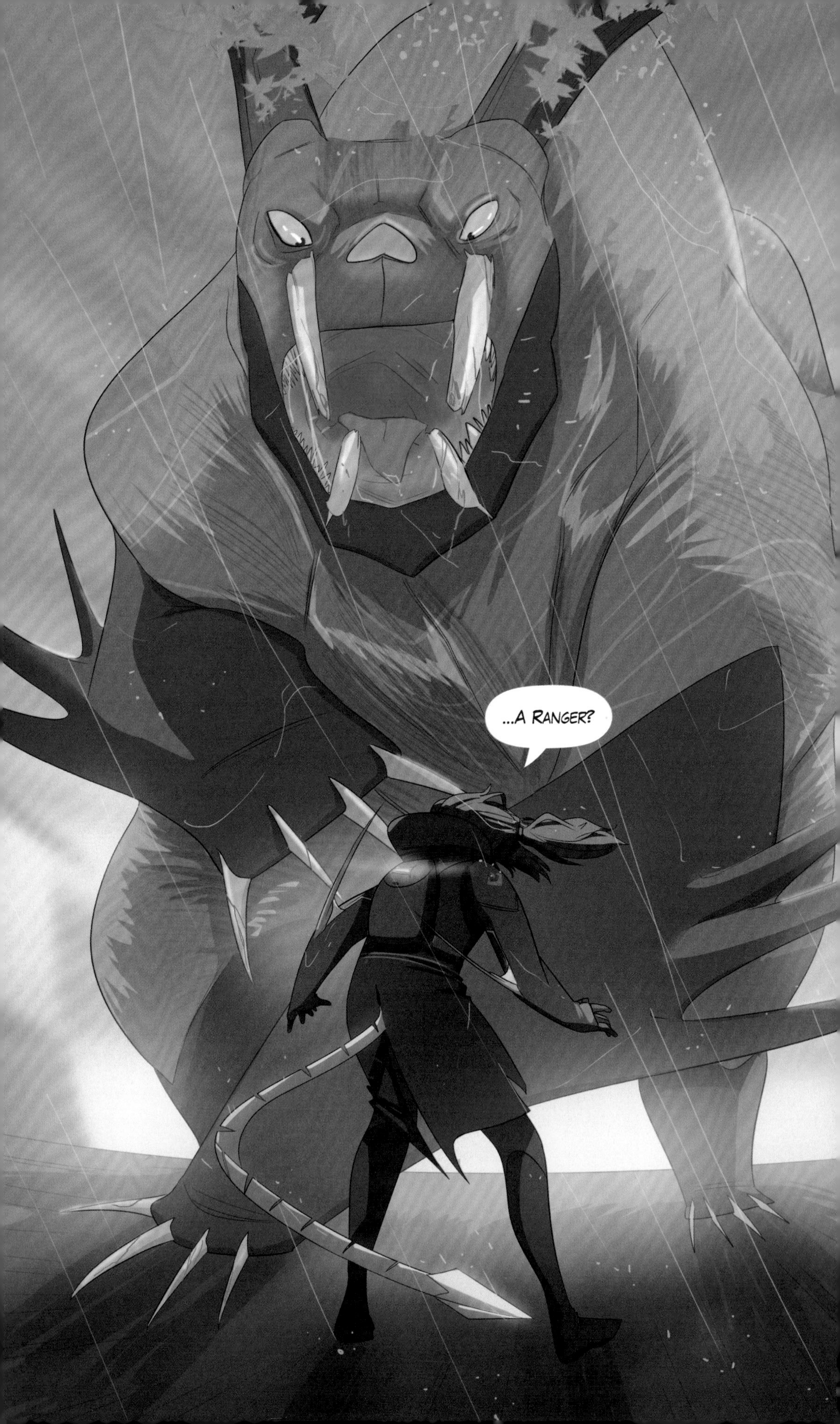
...A Ranger?

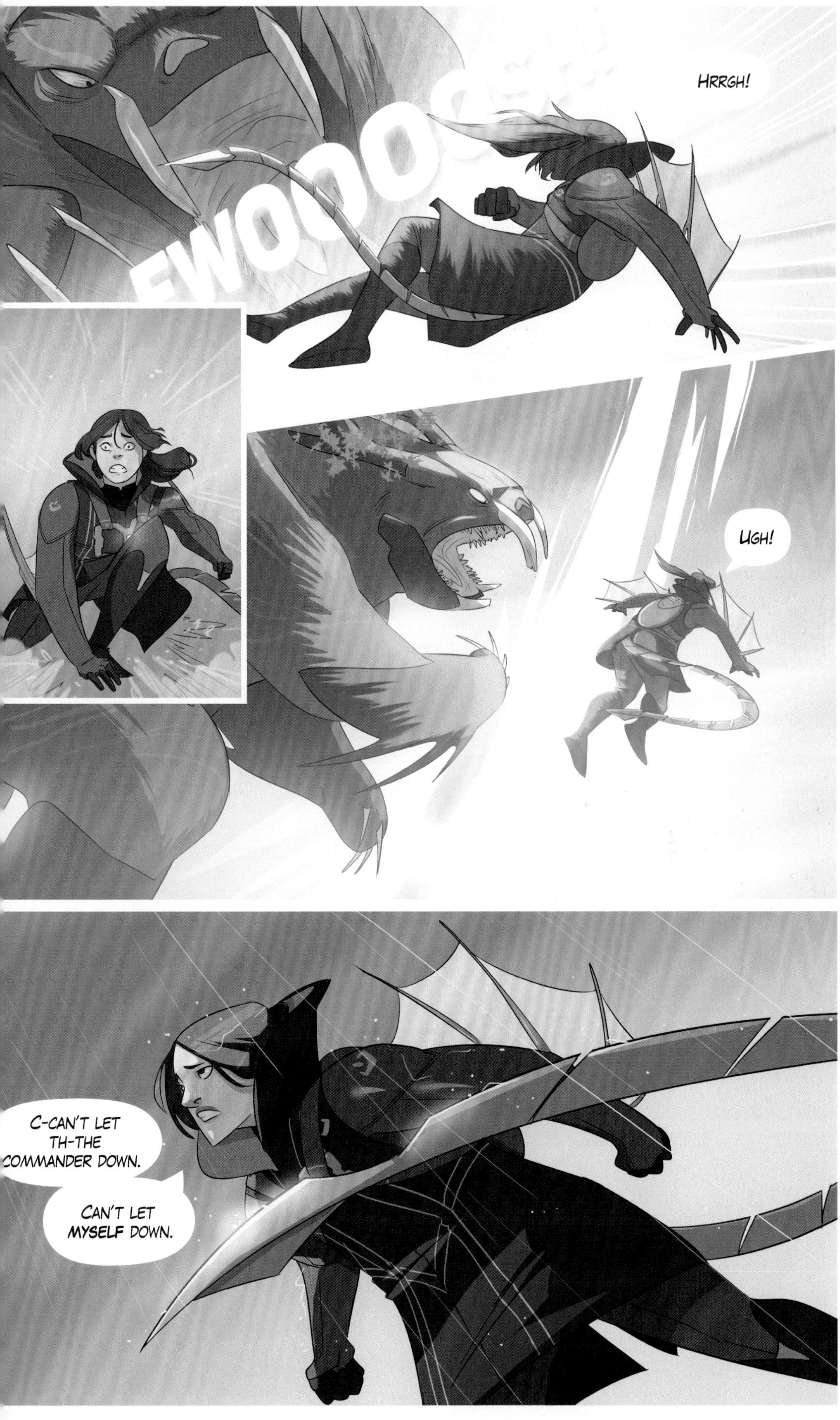
FWOOOSH!
HRRGH!
UGH!
C-CAN'T LET TH-THE COMMANDER DOWN.
CAN'T LET MYSELF DOWN.

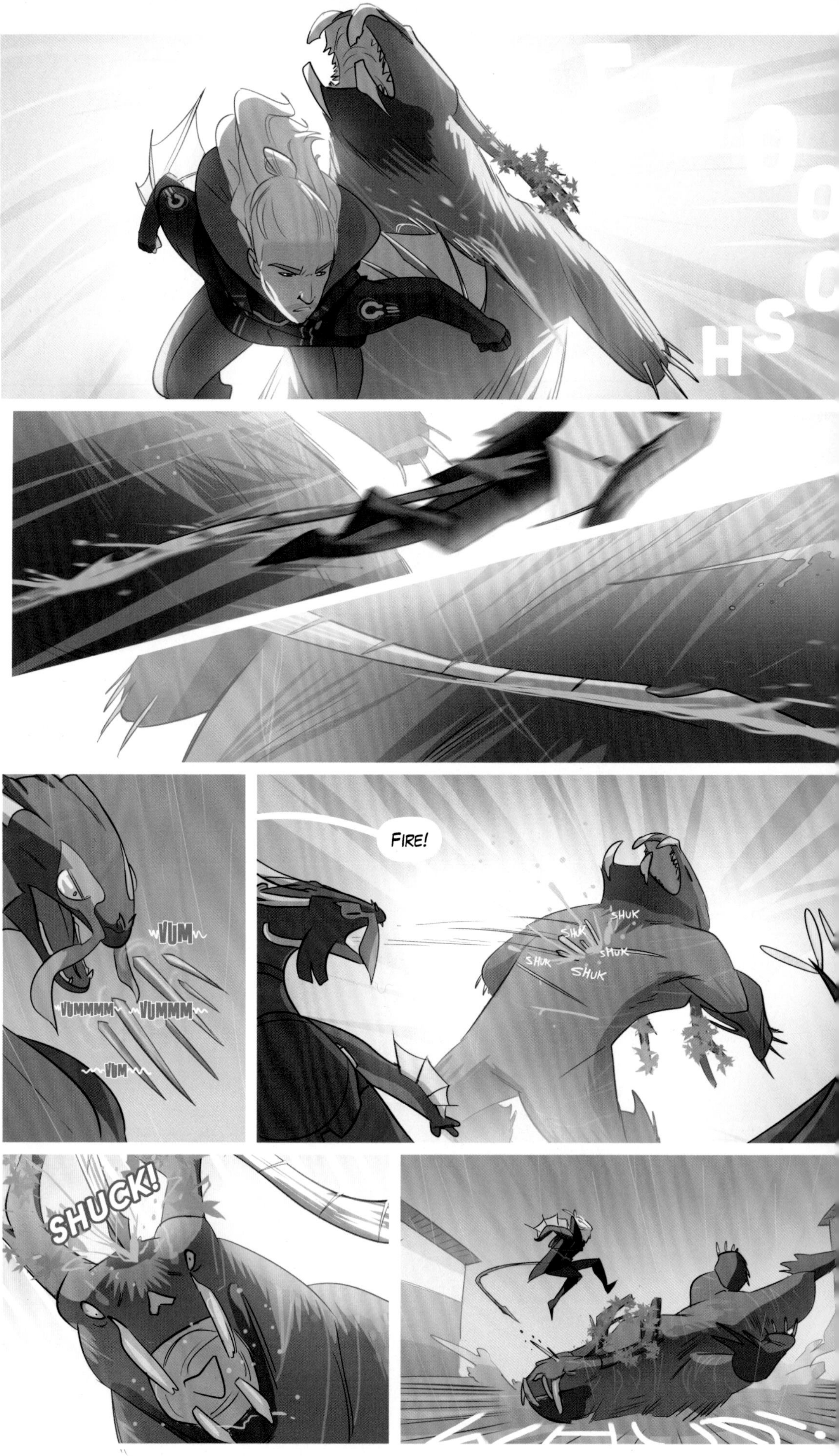
VUM
VUMMMM
VUMMM
VUM
FIRE!
SHUK
SHUK
SHUK
SHUK
SHUK
SHUCK!

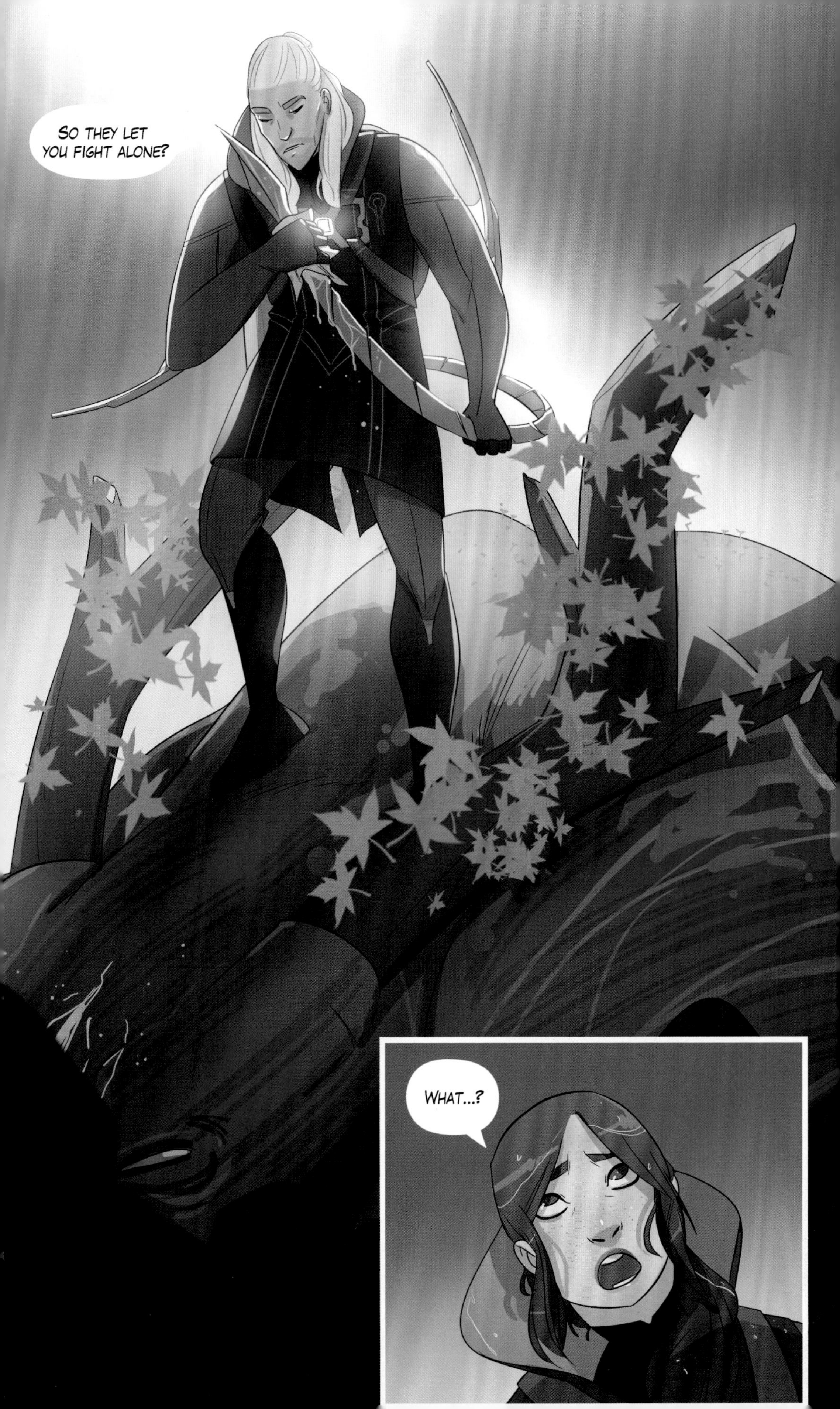
SO THEY LET YOU FIGHT ALONE?
WHAT...?

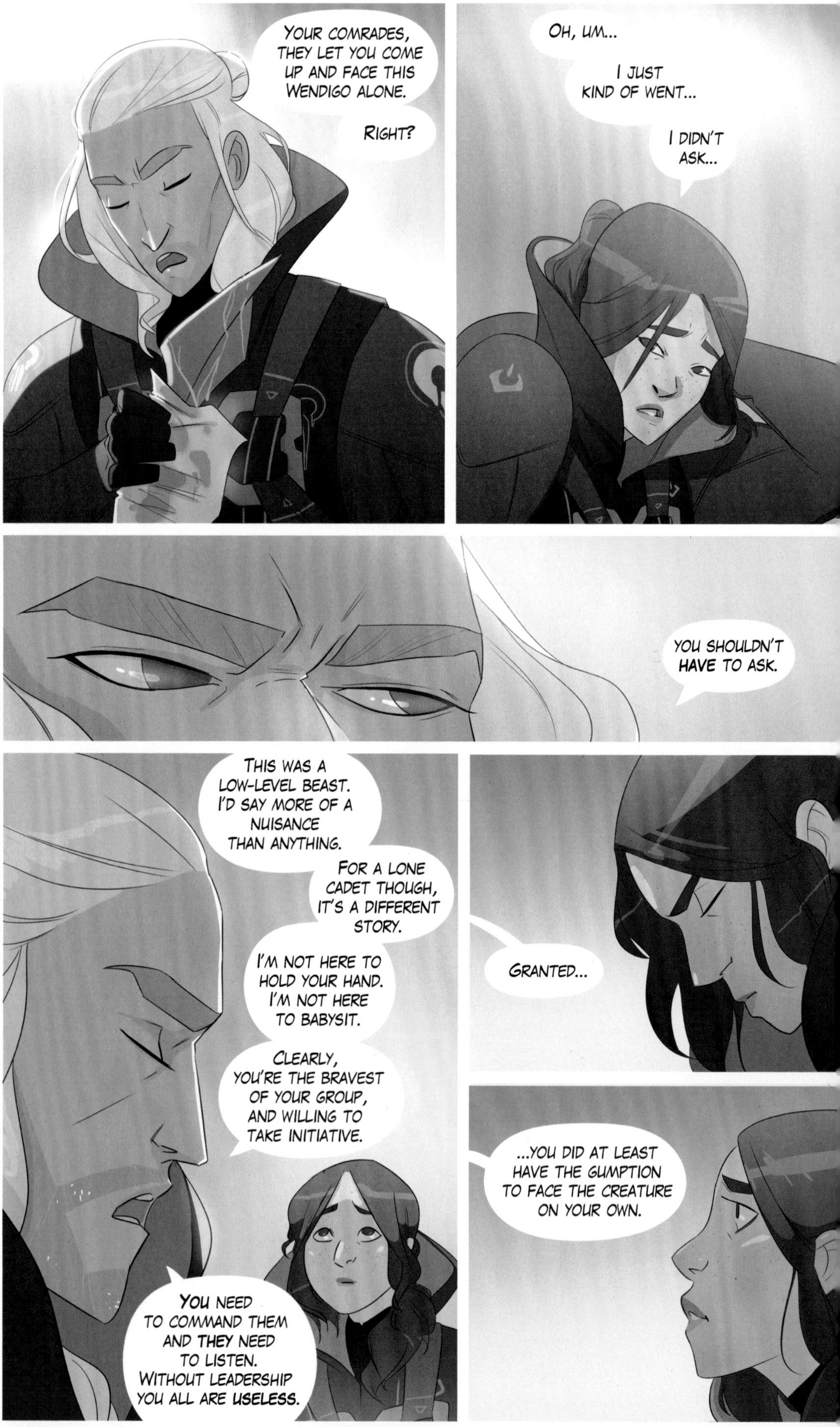
YOUR COMRADES, THEY LET YOU COME UP AND FACE THIS WENDIGO ALONE.
RIGHT?
OH, UM...
I JUST KIND OF WENT...
I DIDN'T ASK...
YOU SHOULDN'T **HAVE** TO ASK.
THIS WAS A LOW-LEVEL BEAST. I'D SAY MORE OF A NUISANCE THAN ANYTHING.
FOR A LONE CADET THOUGH, IT'S A DIFFERENT STORY.
I'M NOT HERE TO HOLD YOUR HAND. I'M NOT HERE TO BABYSIT.
CLEARLY, YOU'RE THE BRAVEST OF YOUR GROUP, AND WILLING TO TAKE INITIATIVE.
YOU NEED TO COMMAND THEM AND **THEY** NEED TO LISTEN. WITHOUT LEADERSHIP YOU ALL ARE **USELESS**.
GRANTED...
...YOU DID AT LEAST HAVE THE GUMPTION TO FACE THE CREATURE ON YOUR OWN.

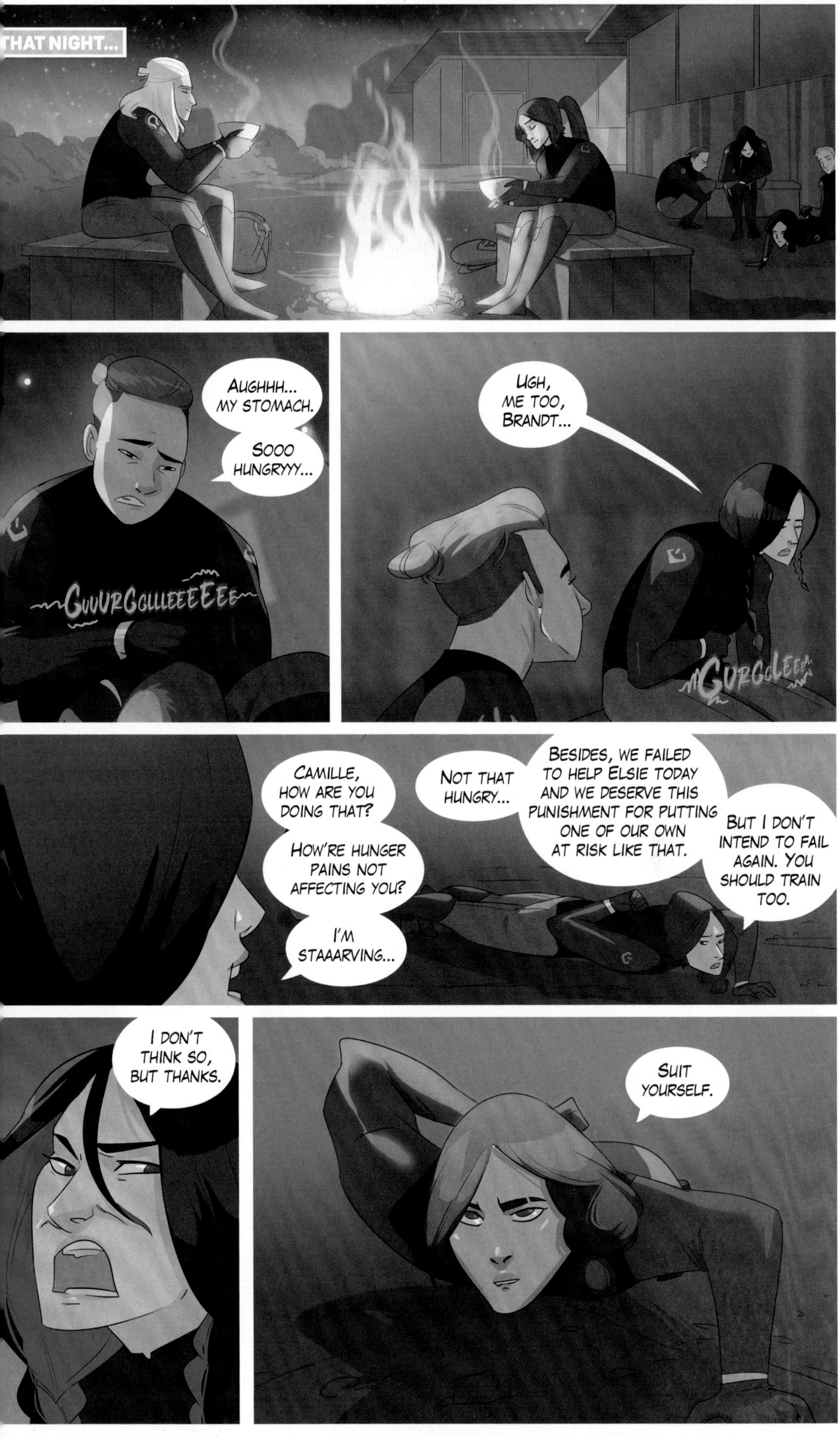
THAT NIGHT...
AUGHHH... MY STOMACH.
SOOO HUNGRYYY...
GUUURGGLLLEEEEEEE
UGH, ME TOO, BRANDT...
GURGGLEEE
CAMILLE, HOW ARE YOU DOING THAT?
HOW'RE HUNGER PAINS NOT AFFECTING YOU?
I'M STAAARVING...
NOT THAT HUNGRY...
BESIDES, WE FAILED TO HELP ELSIE TODAY AND WE DESERVE THIS PUNISHMENT FOR PUTTING ONE OF OUR OWN AT RISK LIKE THAT.
BUT I DON'T INTEND TO FAIL AGAIN. YOU SHOULD TRAIN TOO.
I DON'T THINK SO, BUT THANKS.
SUIT YOURSELF.

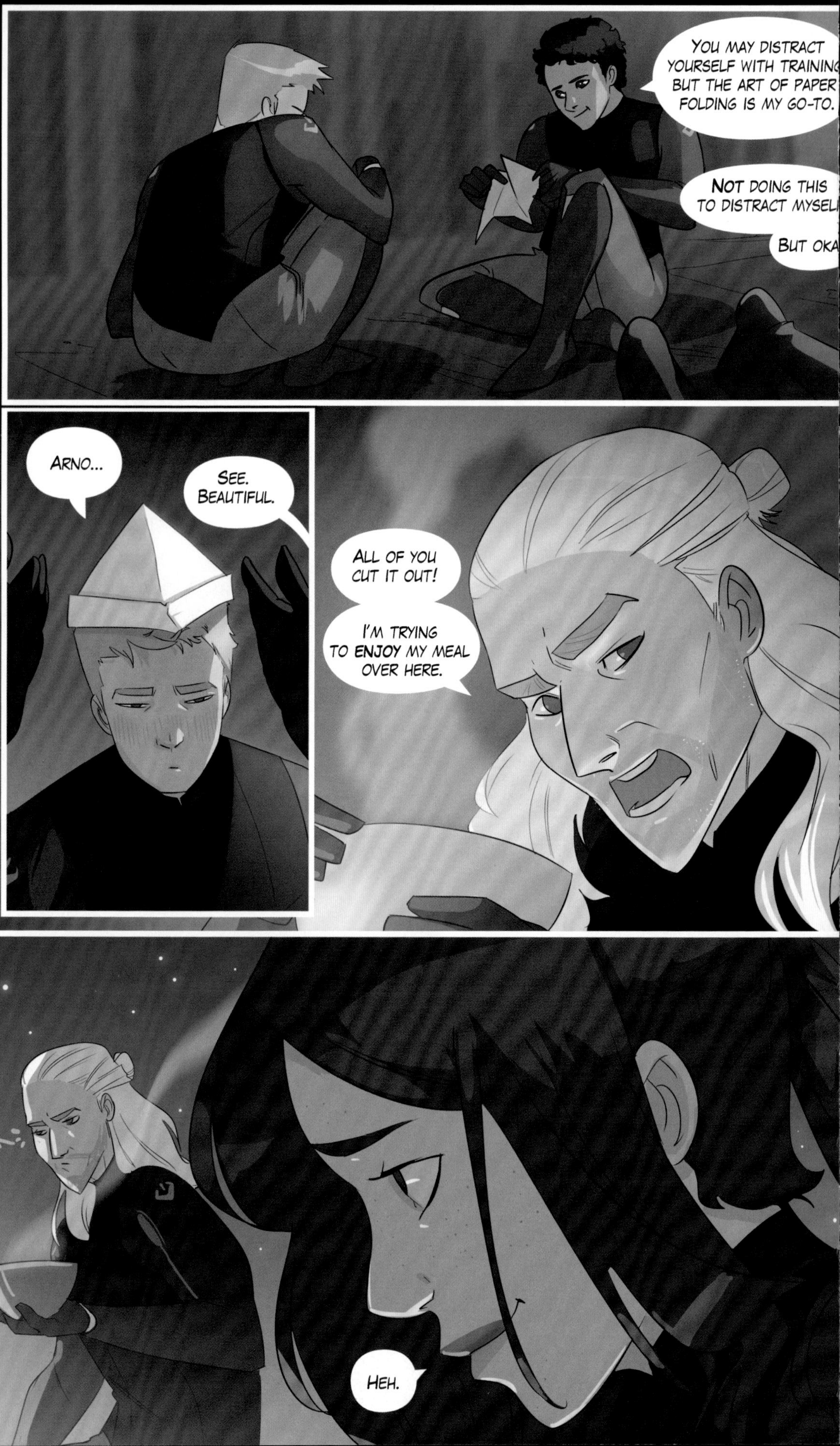

YOU MAY DISTRACT YOURSELF WITH TRAINING BUT THE ART OF PAPER FOLDING IS MY GO-TO.
NOT DOING THIS TO DISTRACT MYSELF
BUT OKA
ARNO...
SEE. BEAUTIFUL.
ALL OF YOU CUT IT OUT!
I'M TRYING TO ENJOY MY MEAL OVER HERE.
HEH.

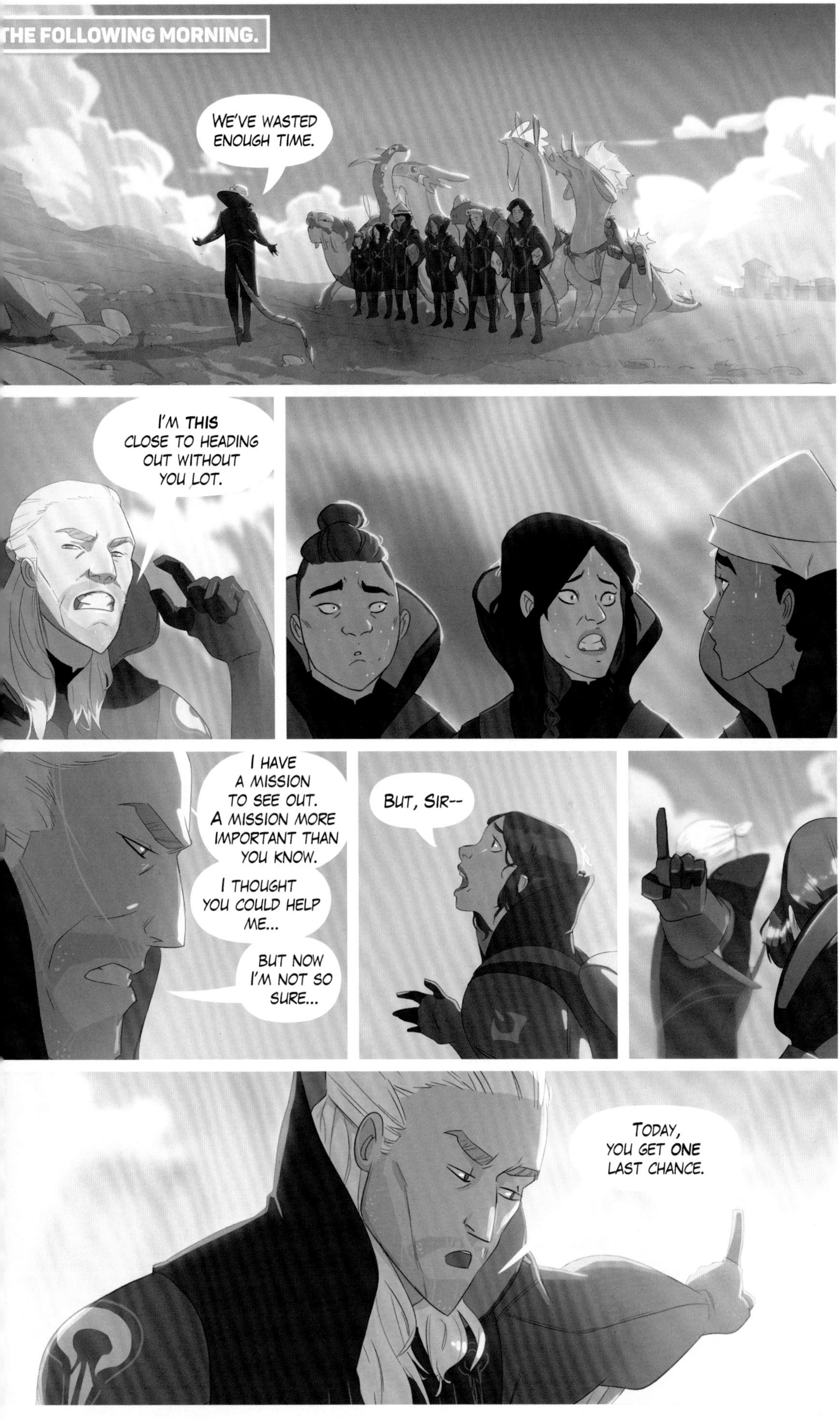
THE FOLLOWING MORNING.
WE'VE WASTED ENOUGH TIME.
I'M THIS CLOSE TO HEADING OUT WITHOUT YOU LOT.
I HAVE A MISSION TO SEE OUT. A MISSION MORE IMPORTANT THAN YOU KNOW.
I THOUGHT YOU COULD HELP ME...
BUT NOW I'M NOT SO SURE...
BUT, SIR--
TODAY, YOU GET ONE LAST CHANCE.

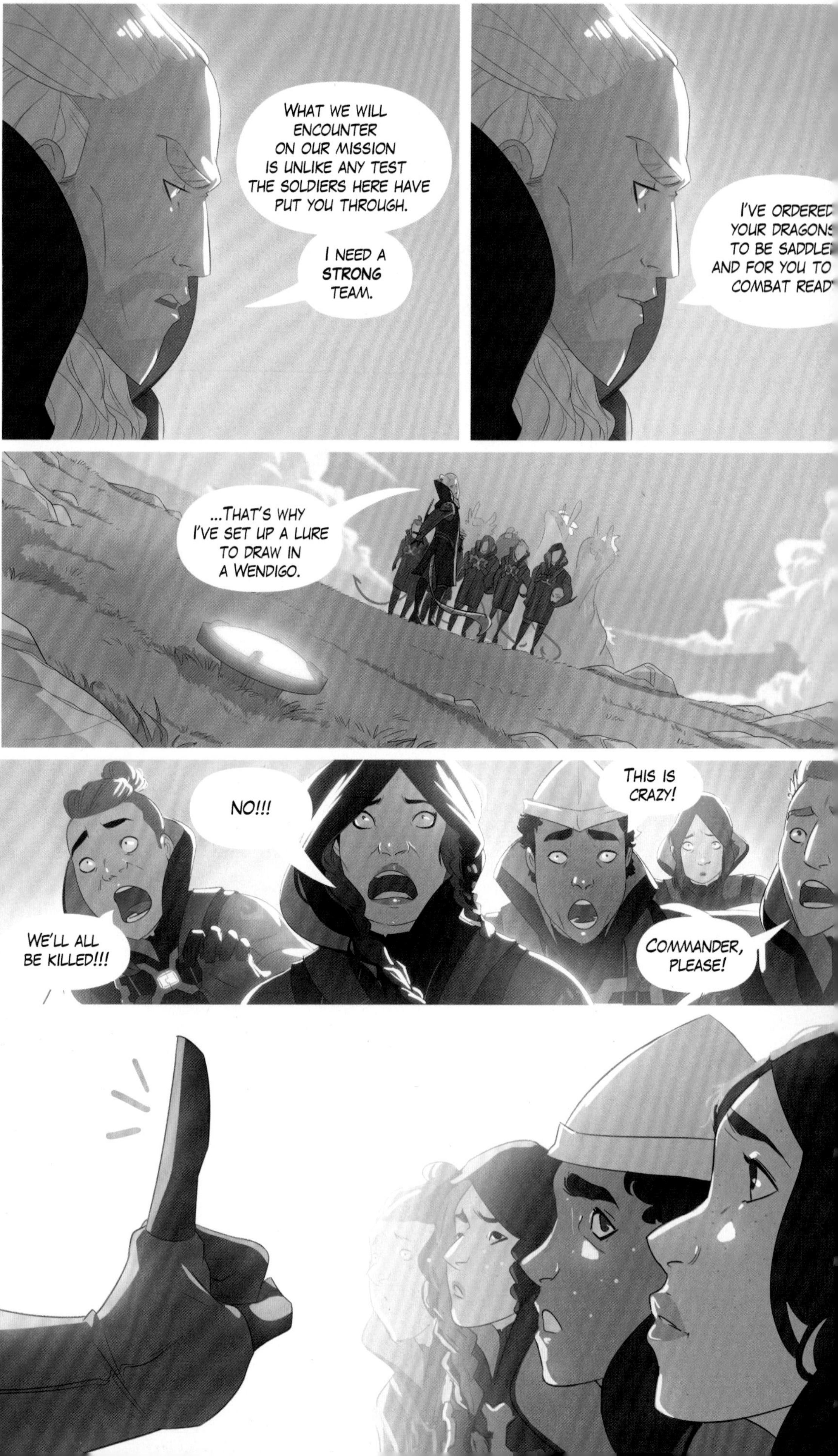
WHAT WE WILL ENCOUNTER ON OUR MISSION IS UNLIKE ANY TEST THE SOLDIERS HERE HAVE PUT YOU THROUGH.
I NEED A STRONG TEAM.
I'VE ORDERED YOUR DRAGONS TO BE SADDLED AND FOR YOU TO COMBAT READY
...THAT'S WHY I'VE SET UP A LURE TO DRAW IN A WENDIGO.
NO!!!
THIS IS CRAZY!
WE'LL ALL BE KILLED!!!
COMMANDER, PLEASE!

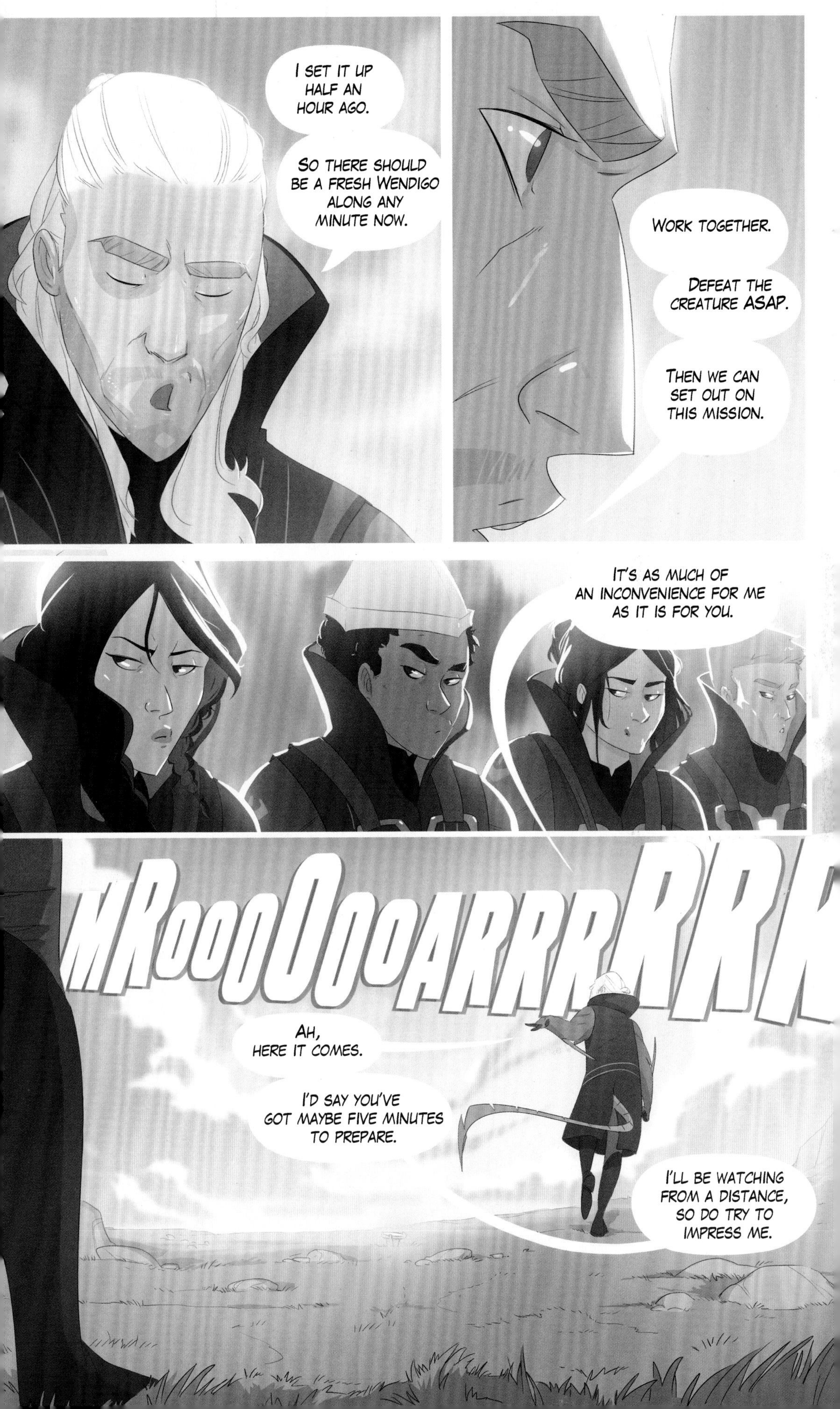
I SET IT UP HALF AN HOUR AGO.
SO THERE SHOULD BE A FRESH WENDIGO ALONG ANY MINUTE NOW.
WORK TOGETHER.
DEFEAT THE CREATURE ASAP.
THEN WE CAN SET OUT ON THIS MISSION.
IT'S AS MUCH OF AN INCONVENIENCE FOR ME AS IT IS FOR YOU.
MROOOOOOOARRRRRRR
AH, HERE IT COMES.
I'D SAY YOU'VE GOT MAYBE FIVE MINUTES TO PREPARE.
I'LL BE WATCHING FROM A DISTANCE, SO DO TRY TO IMPRESS ME.

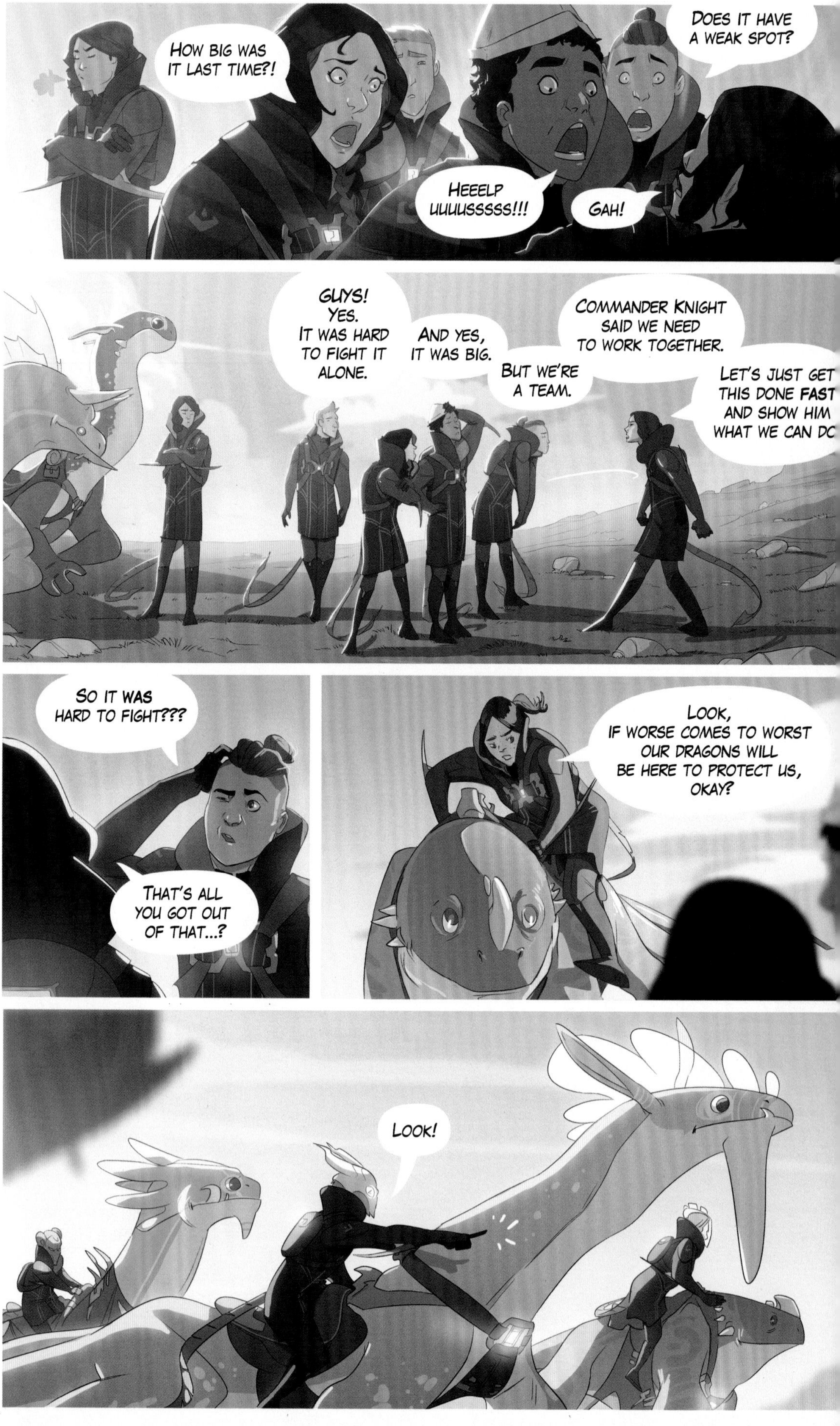
How big was it last time?!
Does it have a weak spot?
Heeelp uuuusssss!!!
Gah!
Guys! Yes. It was hard to fight it alone.
And yes, it was big.
But we're a team.
Commander Knight said we need to work together.
Let's just get this done **fast** and show him what we can do
So it was hard to fight???
That's all you got out of that...?
Look, if worse comes to worst our dragons will be here to protect us, okay?
Look!

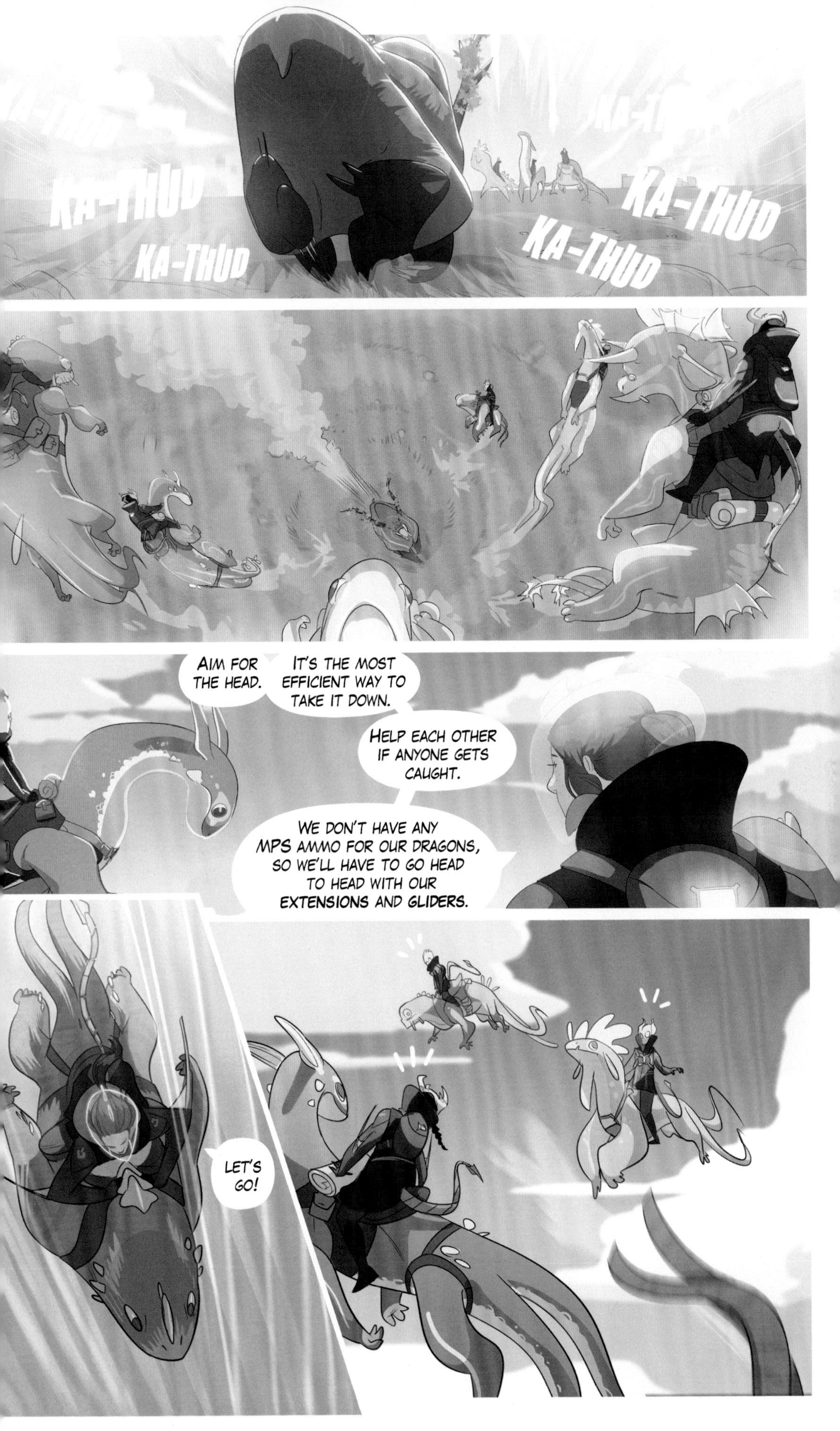
KA-THUD
KA-THUD
KA-THUD
KA-THUD
AIM FOR THE HEAD.
IT'S THE MOST EFFICIENT WAY TO TAKE IT DOWN.
HELP EACH OTHER IF ANYONE GETS CAUGHT.
WE DON'T HAVE ANY MPS AMMO FOR OUR DRAGONS, SO WE'LL HAVE TO GO HEAD TO HEAD WITH OUR EXTENSIONS AND GLIDERS.
LET'S GO!

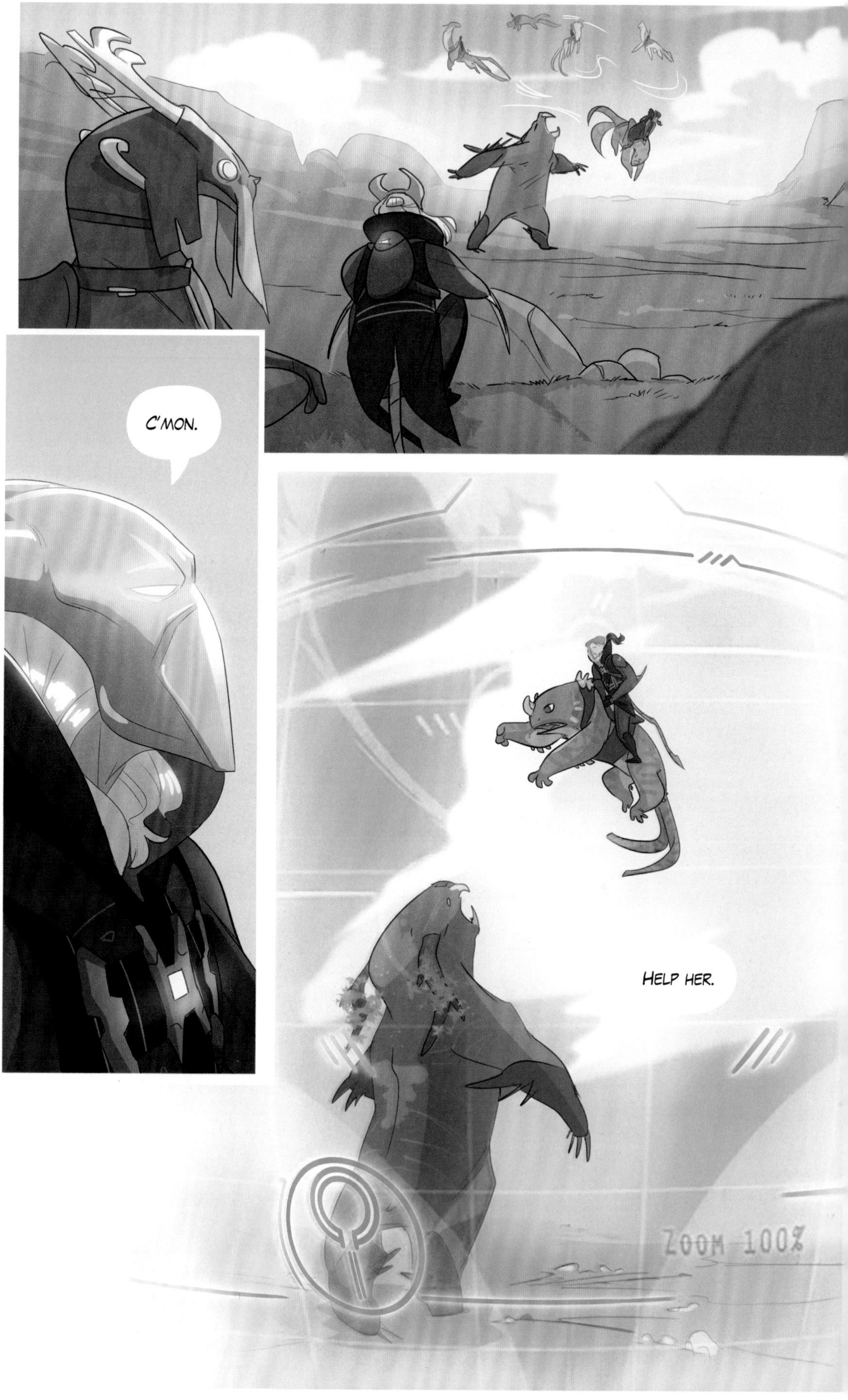
C'MON.
HELP HER.
ZOOM 100%

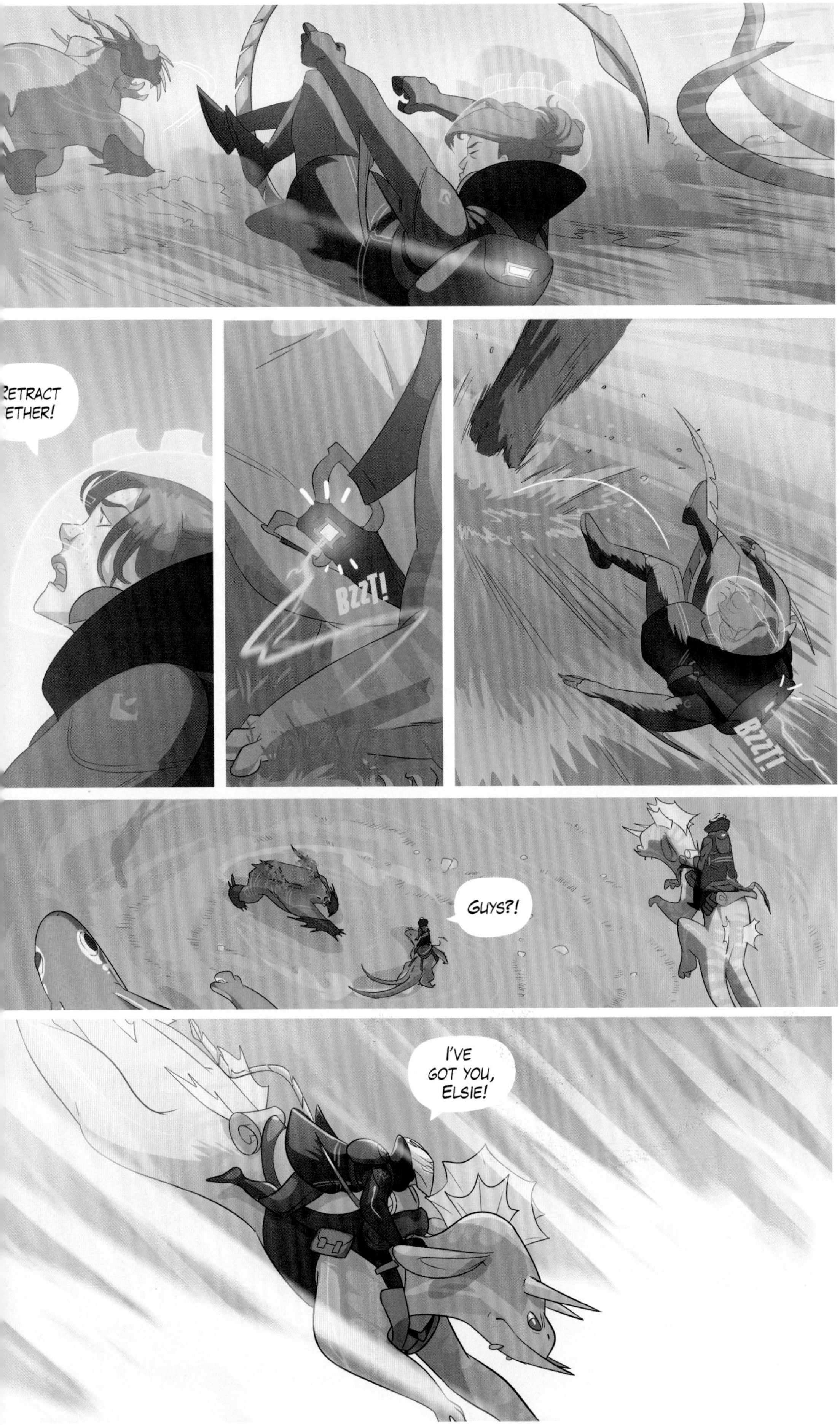
RETRACT
ETHER!
BZZT!
BZZT!
GUYS?!
I'VE GOT YOU, ELSIE!

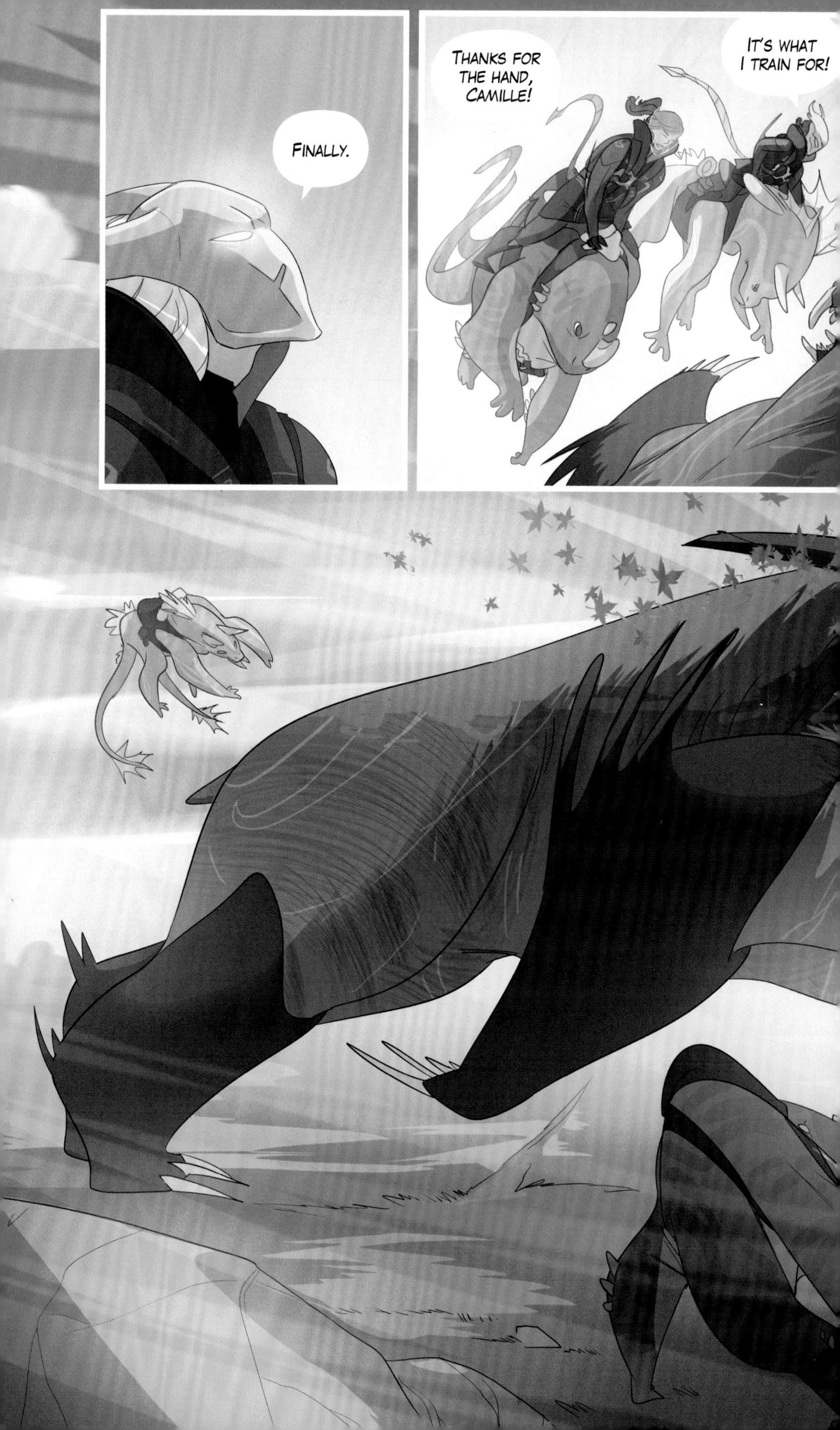
FINALLY.
THANKS FOR THE HAND, CAMILLE!
IT'S WHAT I TRAIN FOR!

WATCH OUT!

WHUD

I GOTCHA--

MROooOooARRRRR!!

SHUCK!

SHUCK!

WHOA, IT'S BRYCE AND BRANDT!

WHUMP!

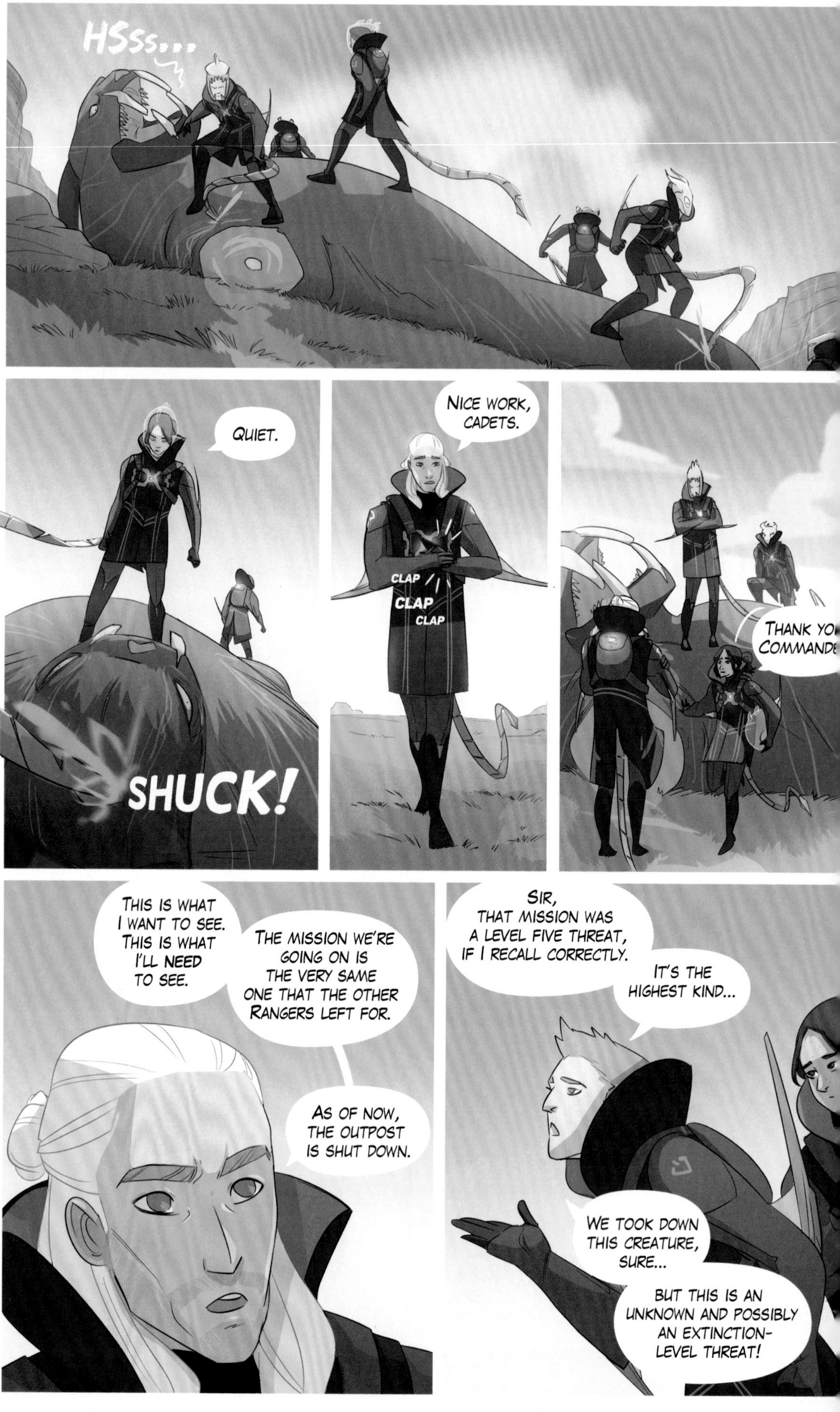
HSSS...
QUIET.
SHUCK!
NICE WORK, CADETS.
CLAP
CLAP
CLAP
THIS IS WHAT I WANT TO SEE. THIS IS WHAT I'LL NEED TO SEE.
THE MISSION WE'RE GOING ON IS THE VERY SAME ONE THAT THE OTHER RANGERS LEFT FOR.
AS OF NOW, THE OUTPOST IS SHUT DOWN.
SIR, THAT MISSION WAS A LEVEL FIVE THREAT, IF I RECALL CORRECTLY.
IT'S THE HIGHEST KIND...
WE TOOK DOWN THIS CREATURE, SURE...
BUT THIS IS AN UNKNOWN AND POSSIBLY AN EXTINCTION-LEVEL THREAT!

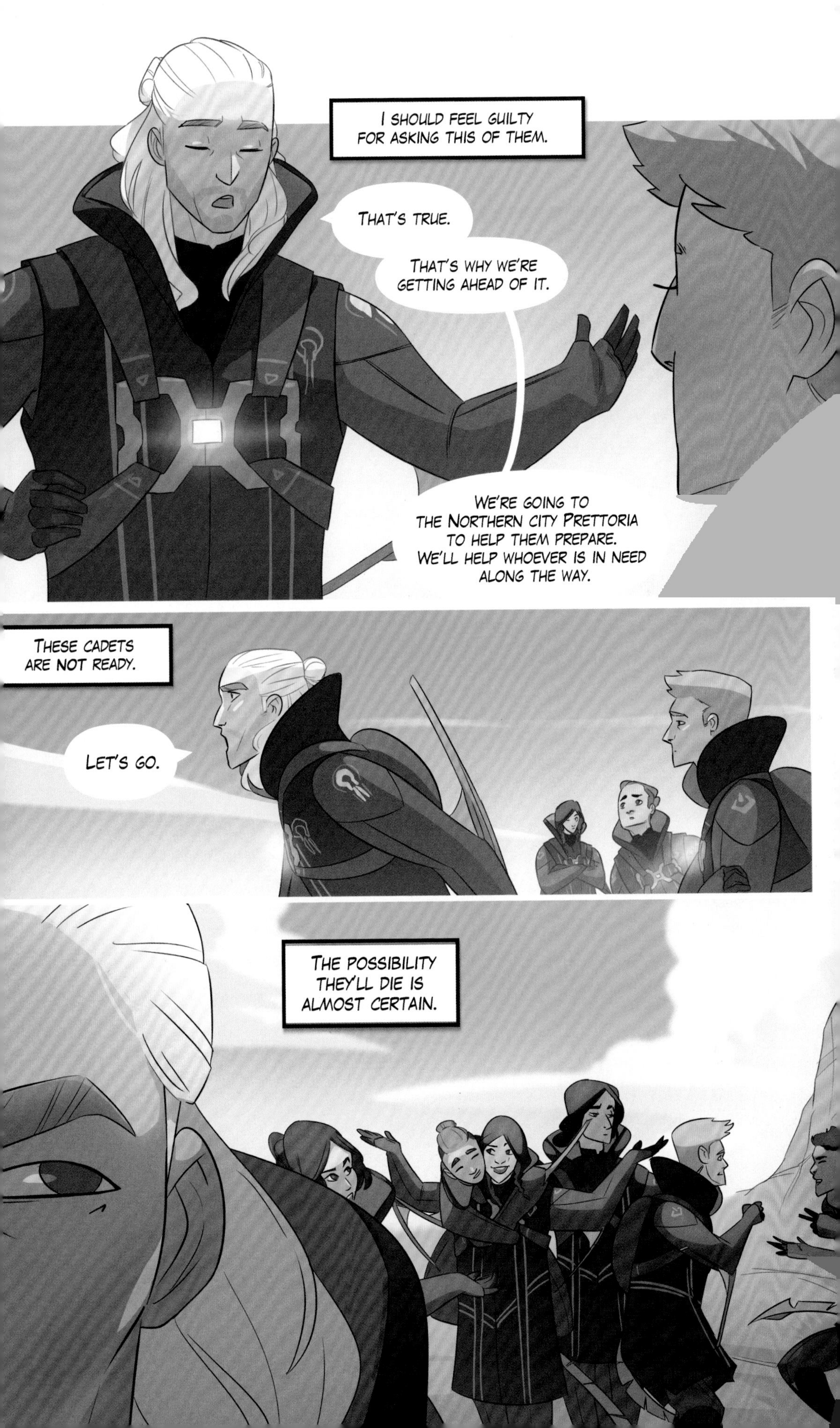
I SHOULD FEEL GUILTY FOR ASKING THIS OF THEM.
THAT'S TRUE.
THAT'S WHY WE'RE GETTING AHEAD OF IT.
WE'RE GOING TO THE NORTHERN CITY PRETTORIA TO HELP THEM PREPARE. WE'LL HELP WHOEVER IS IN NEED ALONG THE WAY.
THESE CADETS ARE NOT READY.
LET'S GO.
THE POSSIBILITY THEY'LL DIE IS ALMOST CERTAIN.

THIS TIME IS GOING TO BE DIFFERENT.
I'LL BE MORE FOCUSED.
MORE RUTHLESS.
I'LL SACRIFICE WHAT I MUST TO GET THROUGH IT-- HOWEVER MANY LIVES IT TAKES.
I WILL NOT FAIL. NOT AGAIN.

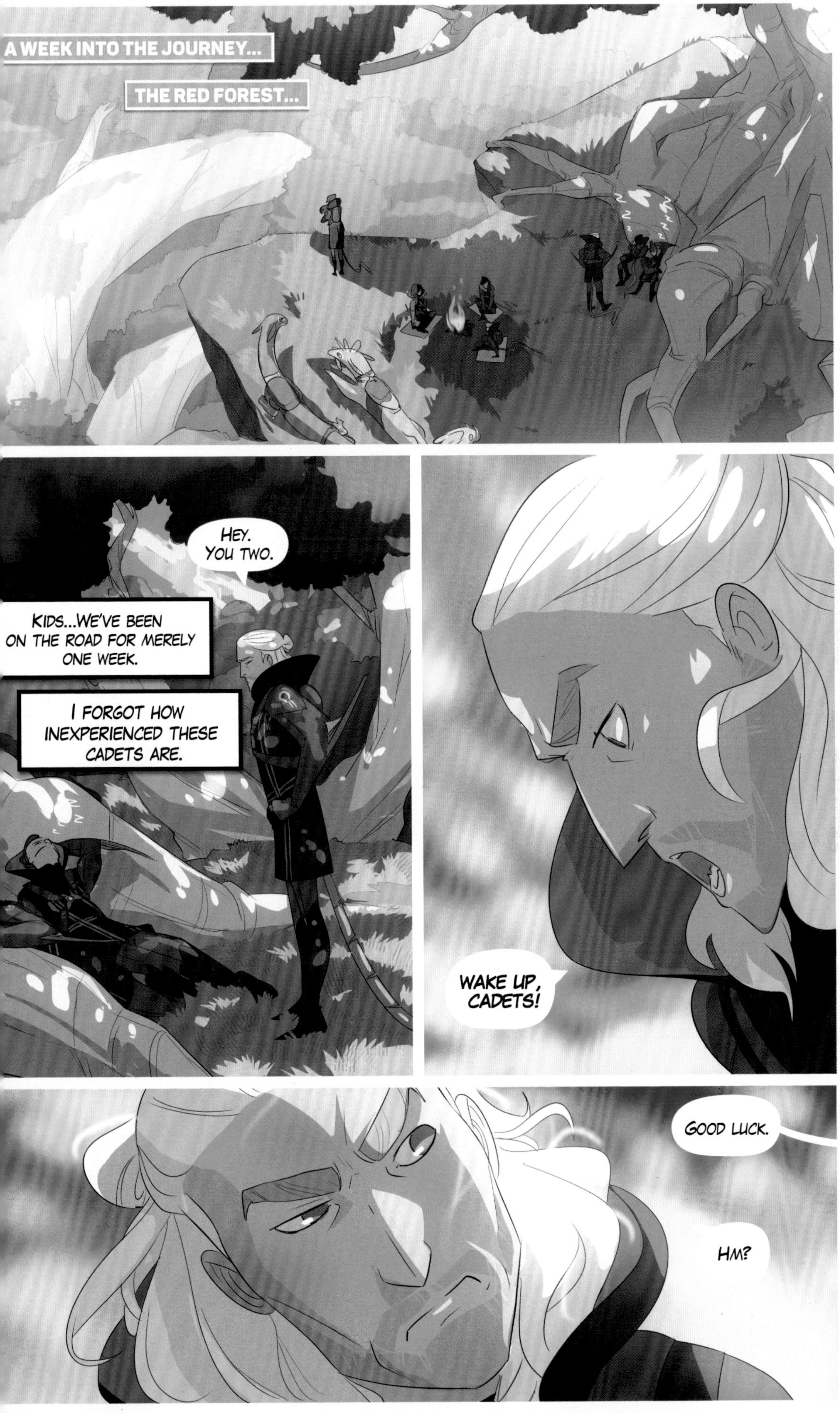
A WEEK INTO THE JOURNEY...
THE RED FOREST...
HEY. YOU TWO.
KIDS...WE'VE BEEN ON THE ROAD FOR MERELY ONE WEEK.
I FORGOT HOW INEXPERIENCED THESE CADETS ARE.
WAKE UP, CADETS!
GOOD LUCK.
HM?

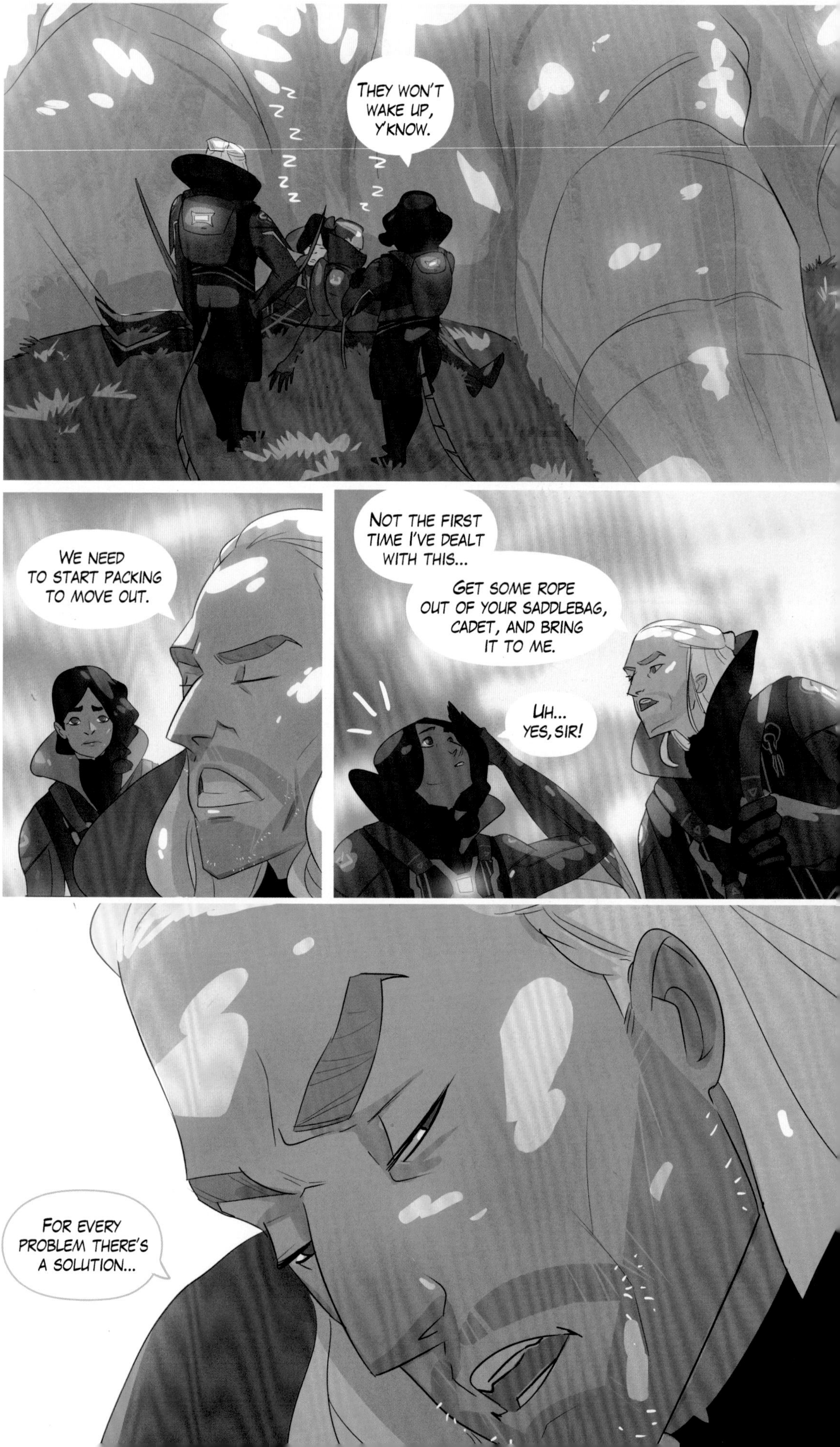

THEY WON'T WAKE UP, Y'KNOW.
WE NEED TO START PACKING TO MOVE OUT.
NOT THE FIRST TIME I'VE DEALT WITH THIS...
GET SOME ROPE OUT OF YOUR SADDLEBAG, CADET, AND BRING IT TO ME.
UH... YES, SIR!
FOR EVERY PROBLEM THERE'S A SOLUTION...

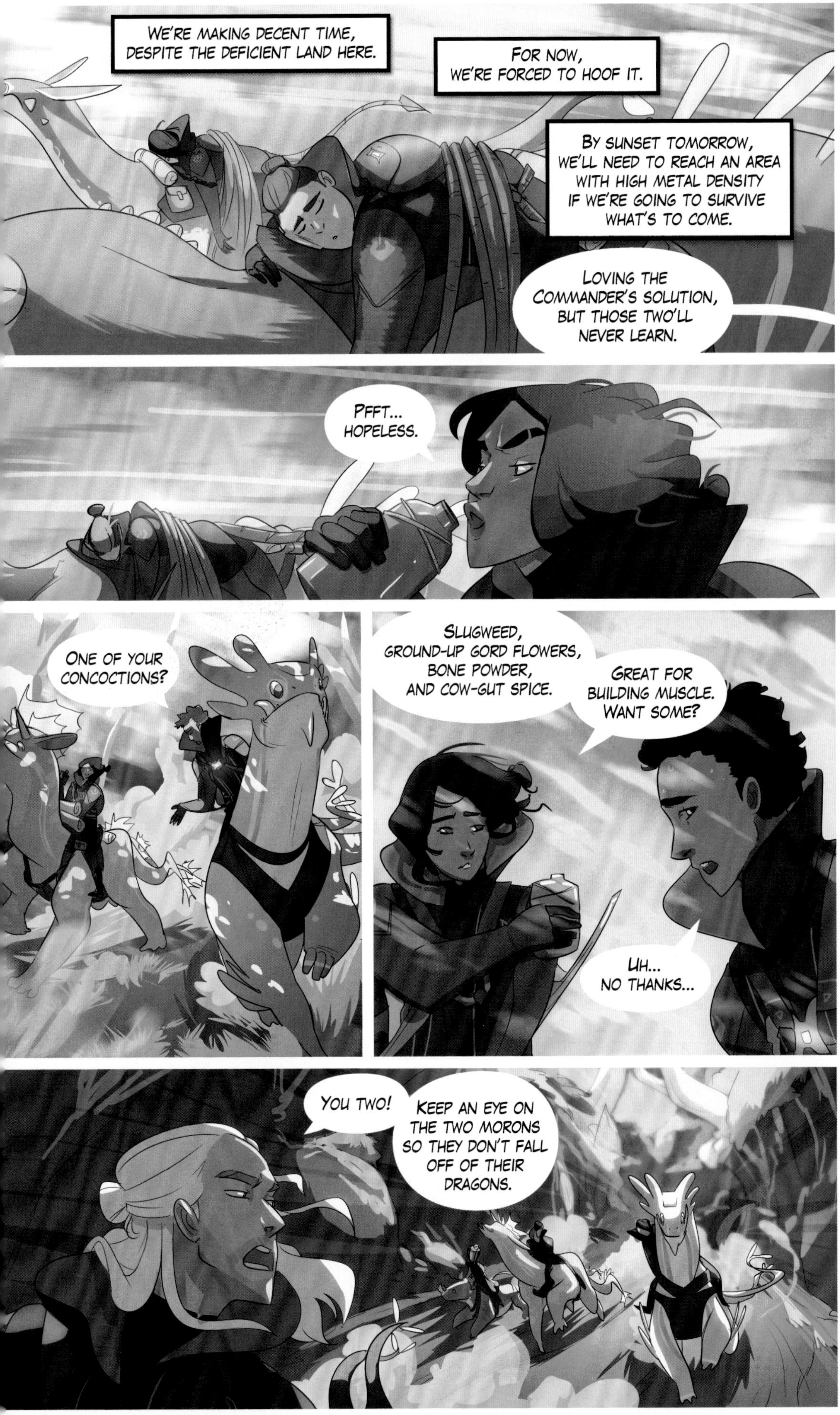
WE'RE MAKING DECENT TIME, DESPITE THE DEFICIENT LAND HERE.
FOR NOW, WE'RE FORCED TO HOOF IT.
BY SUNSET TOMORROW, WE'LL NEED TO REACH AN AREA WITH HIGH METAL DENSITY IF WE'RE GOING TO SURVIVE WHAT'S TO COME.
LOVING THE COMMANDER'S SOLUTION, BUT THOSE TWO'LL NEVER LEARN.
PFFT... HOPELESS.
ONE OF YOUR CONCOCTIONS?
SLUGWEED, GROUND-UP GORD FLOWERS, BONE POWDER, AND COW-GUT SPICE.
GREAT FOR BUILDING MUSCLE. WANT SOME?
UH... NO THANKS...
YOU TWO!
KEEP AN EYE ON THE TWO MORONS SO THEY DON'T FALL OFF OF THEIR DRAGONS.

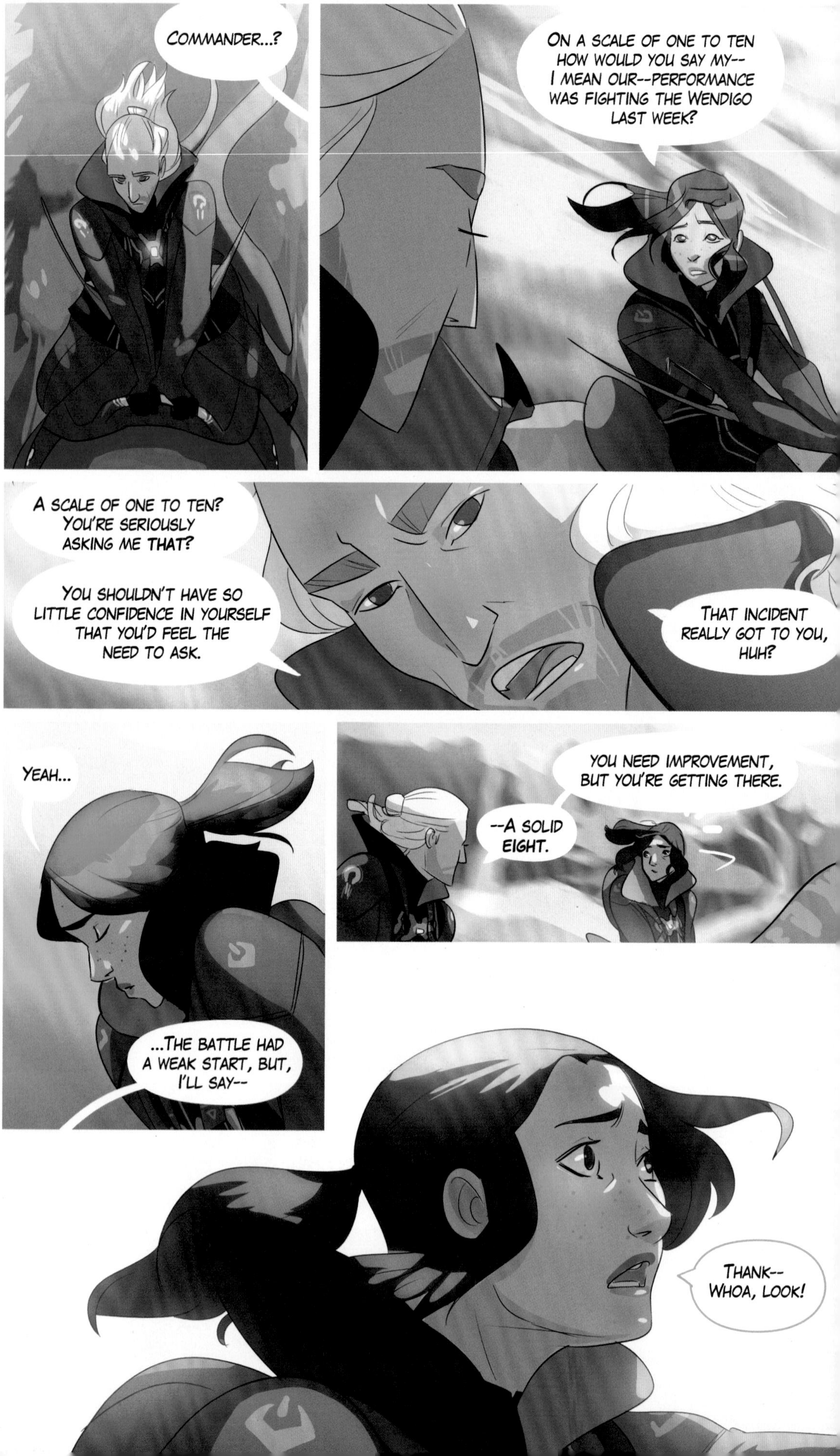
COMMANDER...?
ON A SCALE OF ONE TO TEN HOW WOULD YOU SAY MY-- I MEAN OUR--PERFORMANCE WAS FIGHTING THE WENDIGO LAST WEEK?
A SCALE OF ONE TO TEN? YOU'RE SERIOUSLY ASKING ME THAT?
YOU SHOULDN'T HAVE SO LITTLE CONFIDENCE IN YOURSELF THAT YOU'D FEEL THE NEED TO ASK.
THAT INCIDENT REALLY GOT TO YOU, HUH?
YEAH...
...THE BATTLE HAD A WEAK START, BUT, I'LL SAY--
--A SOLID EIGHT.
YOU NEED IMPROVEMENT, BUT YOU'RE GETTING THERE.
THANK-- WHOA, LOOK!

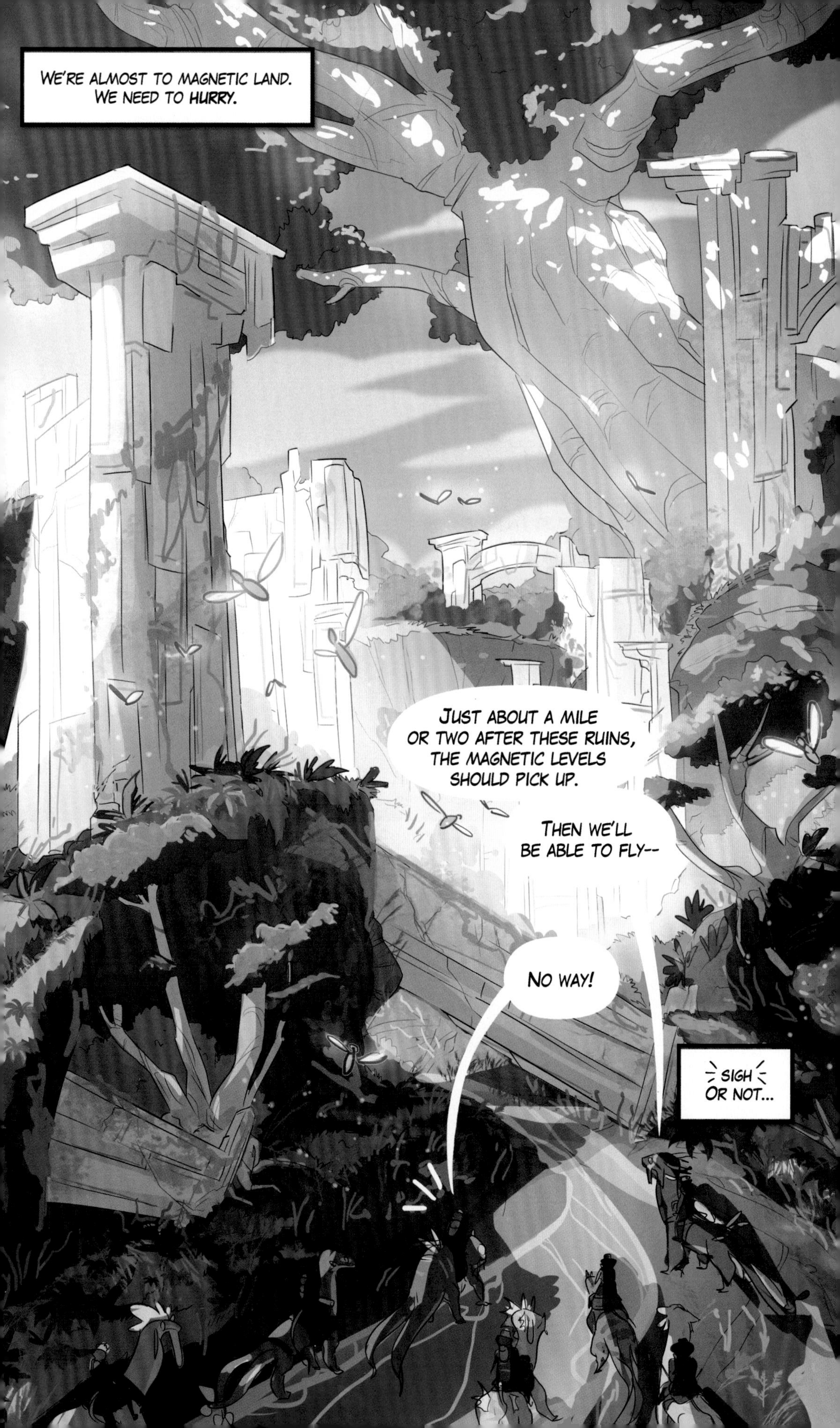
WE'RE ALMOST TO MAGNETIC LAND. WE NEED TO HURRY.
JUST ABOUT A MILE OR TWO AFTER THESE RUINS, THE MAGNETIC LEVELS SHOULD PICK UP.
THEN WE'LL BE ABLE TO FLY--
NO WAY!
SIGH
OR NOT...

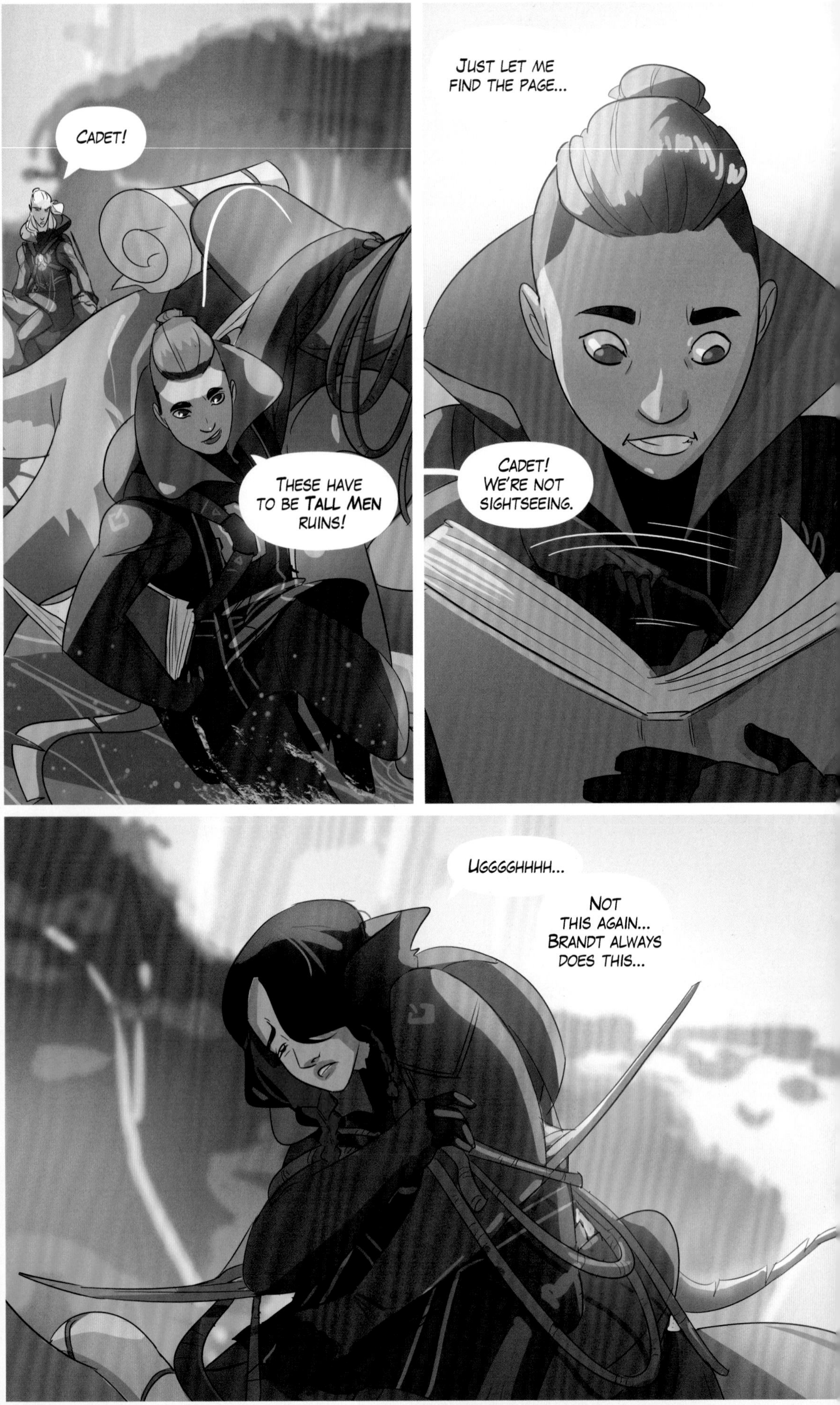
CADET!
THESE HAVE TO BE **TALL MEN** RUINS!
JUST LET ME FIND THE PAGE...
CADET! WE'RE NOT SIGHTSEEING.
UGGGGHHHH...
NOT THIS AGAIN... BRANDT ALWAYS DOES THIS...

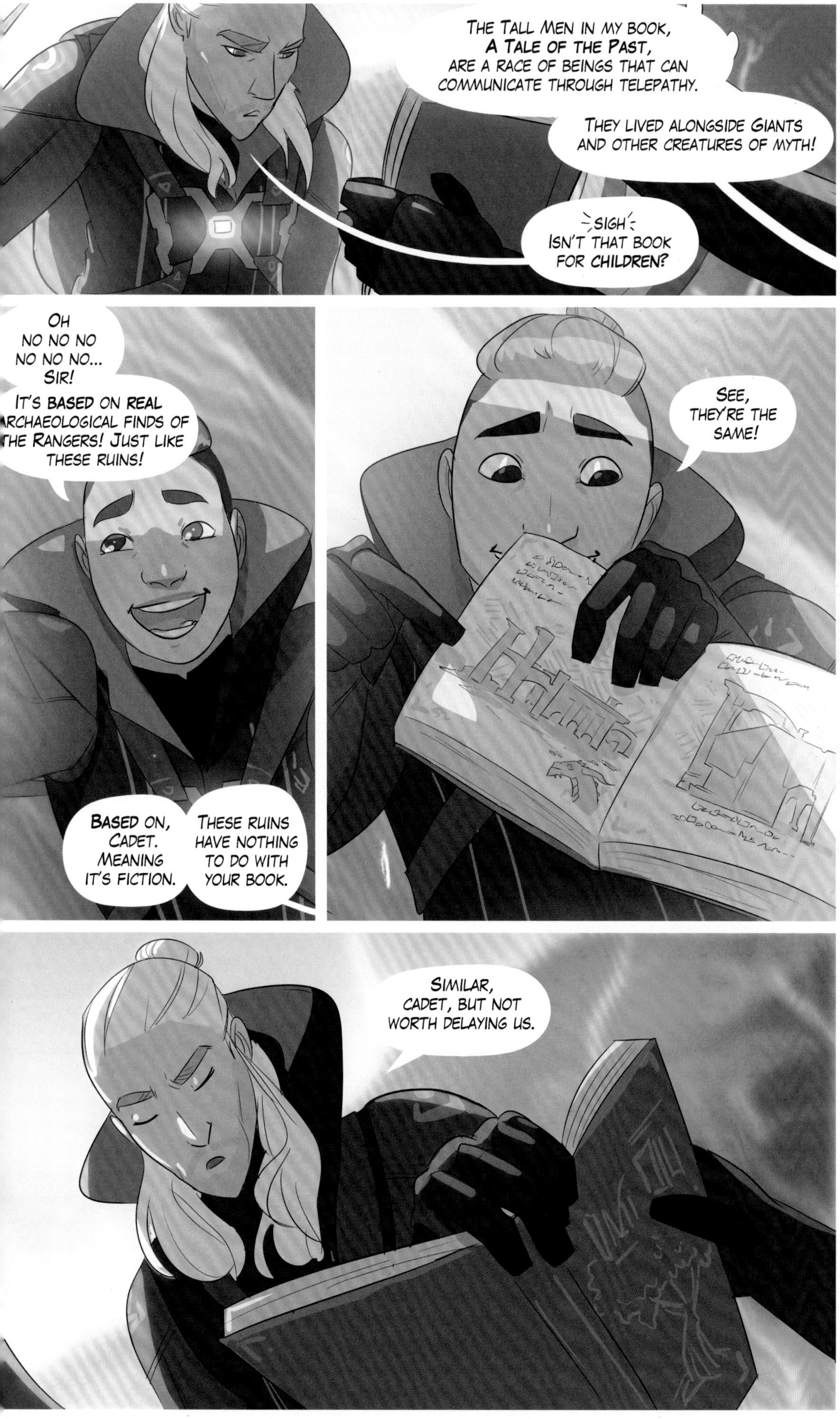

THE TALL MEN IN MY BOOK, A TALE OF THE PAST, ARE A RACE OF BEINGS THAT CAN COMMUNICATE THROUGH TELEPATHY.
THEY LIVED ALONGSIDE GIANTS AND OTHER CREATURES OF MYTH!
SIGH
ISN'T THAT BOOK FOR CHILDREN?
OH NO NO NO NO NO NO... SIR!
IT'S BASED ON REAL ARCHAEOLOGICAL FINDS OF THE RANGERS! JUST LIKE THESE RUINS!
BASED ON, CADET. MEANING IT'S FICTION.
THESE RUINS HAVE NOTHING TO DO WITH YOUR BOOK.
SEE, THEY'RE THE SAME!
SIMILAR, CADET, BUT NOT WORTH DELAYING US.

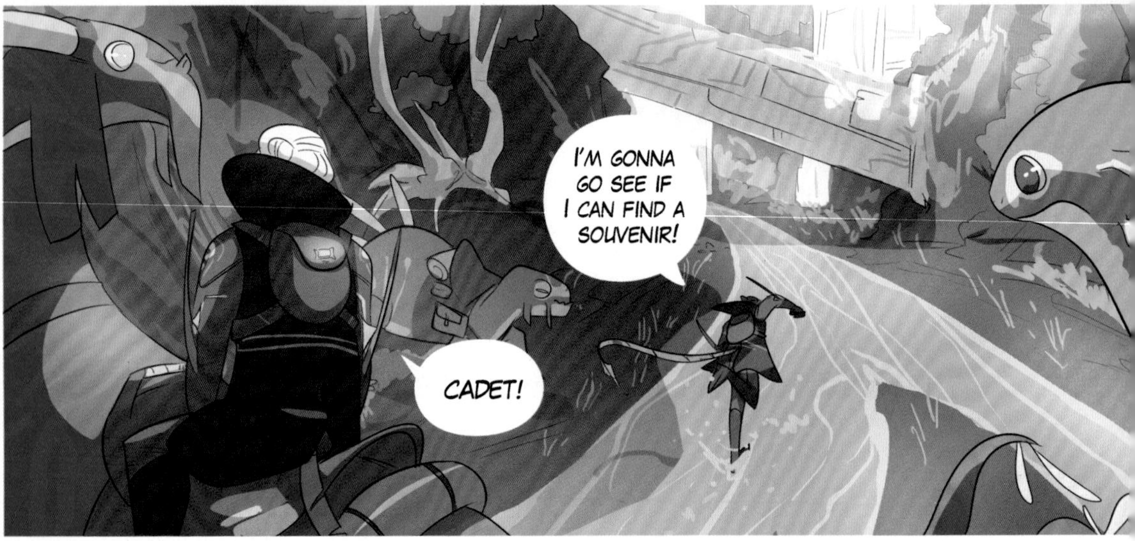
I'M GONNA GO SEE IF I CAN FIND A SOUVENIR!
CADET!

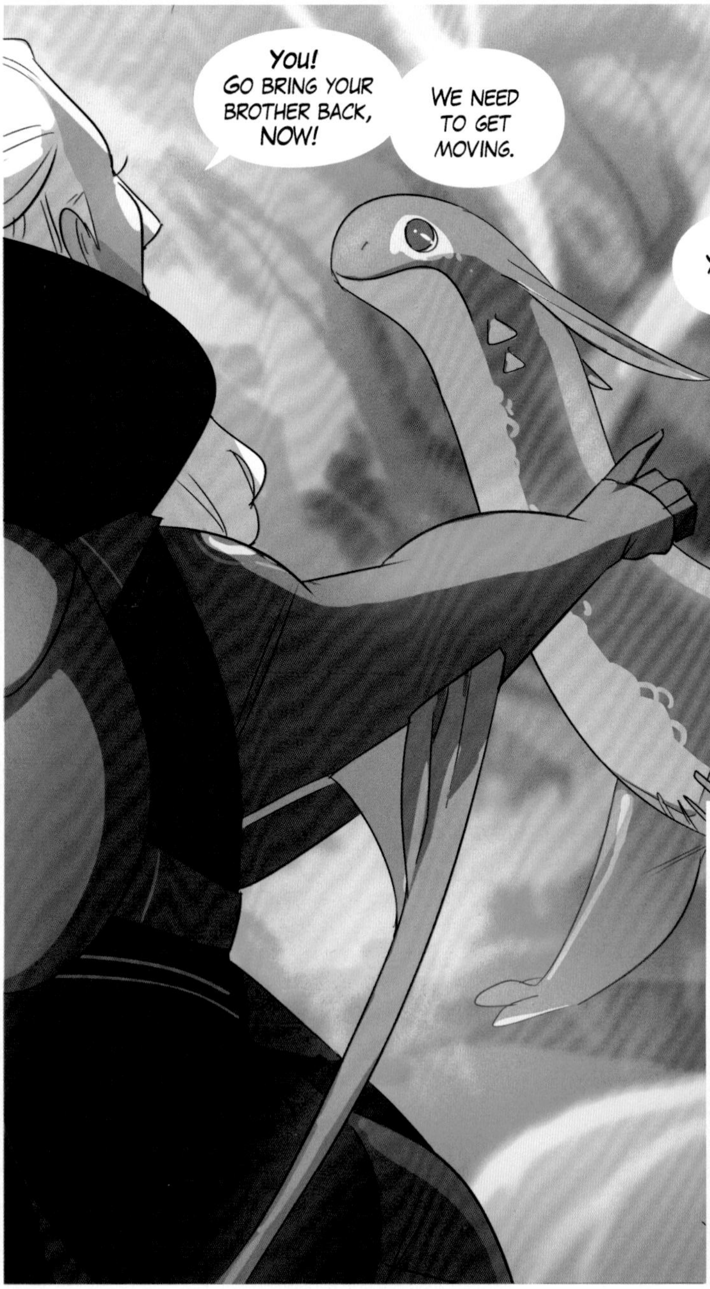
YOU! GO BRING YOUR BROTHER BACK, NOW!
WE NEED TO GET MOVING.
YES, SIR!

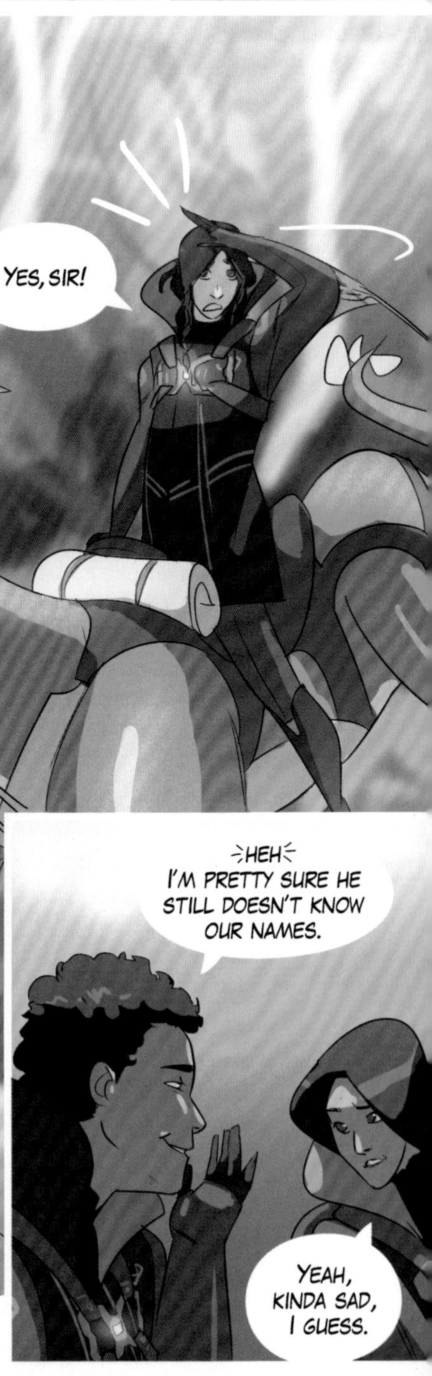
HEH
I'M PRETTY SURE HE STILL DOESN'T KNOW OUR NAMES.
YEAH, KINDA SAD, I GUESS.

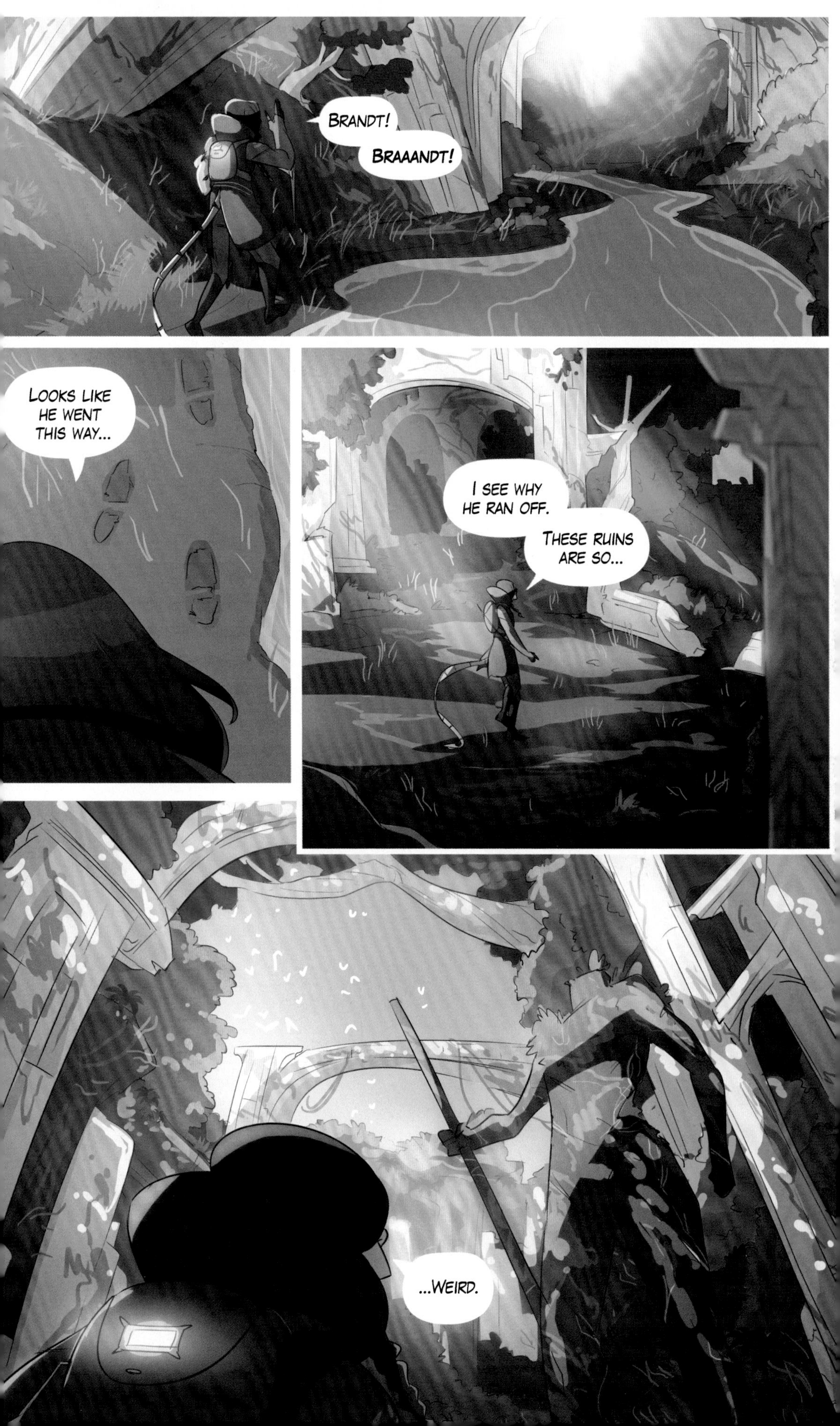
Brandt!
Braaandt!
Looks like he went this way...
I see why he ran off.
These ruins are so...
...Weird.

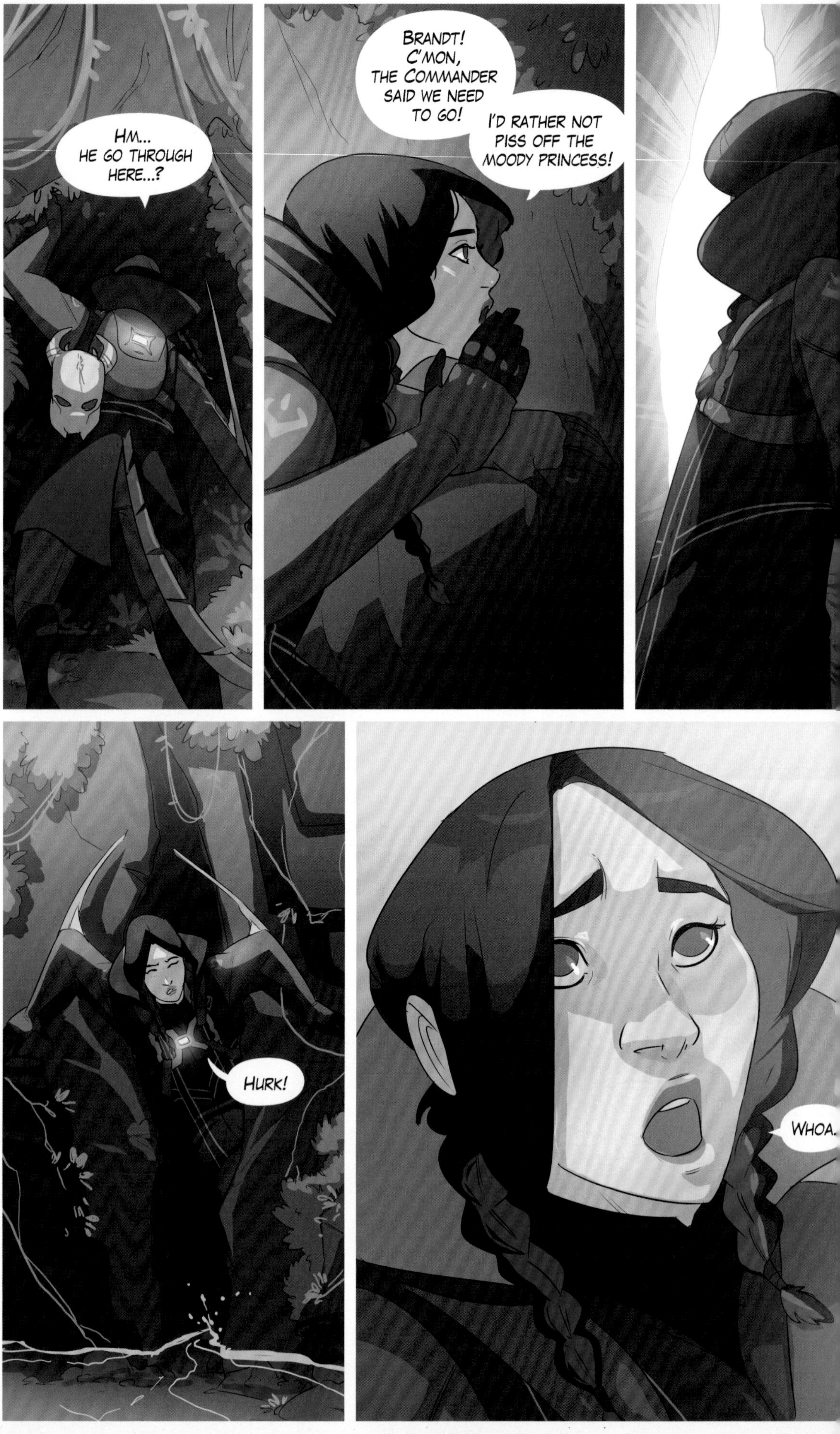
HM...
HE GO THROUGH
HERE...?
BRANDT!
C'MON,
THE COMMANDER
SAID WE NEED
TO GO!
I'D RATHER NOT
PISS OFF THE
MOODY PRINCESS!
HURK!
WHOA.

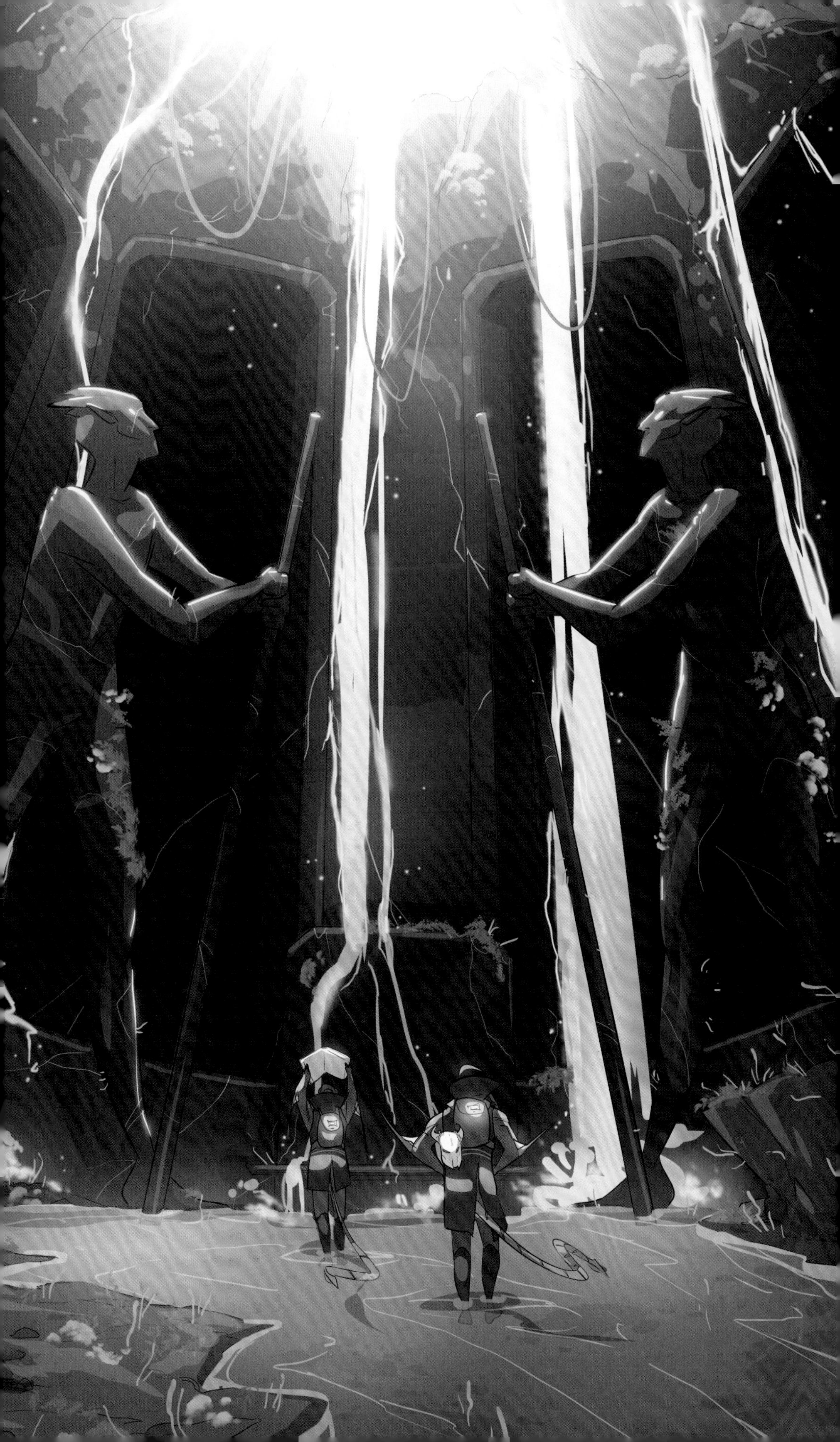

I GET THIS PLACE IS COOL, BUT EVERY SECOND THAT GOES BY, THE COMMANDER GETS MORE FED UP.

WE'LL HAVE OUR ASSES HANDED TO US!

C'MON.

HM... I CAN'T TELL IF THESE STATUES ARE TALL MEN OR NOT... MAYBE GIANTS?

BRANDT!!!

HEY, CAN YOU DO ME A FAVOR AND RECORD THIS PLACE FOR ME?

I LEFT MY HELMET IN ONE OF SLOG'S BAGS.

HMPH. YOU ALWAYS FORGET STUFF IN YOUR DRAGON'S PACKS.

IF I DO THIS, CAN WE GO?

YEAH.

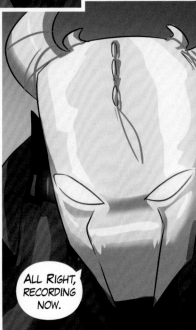

ALL RIGHT, RECORDING NOW.

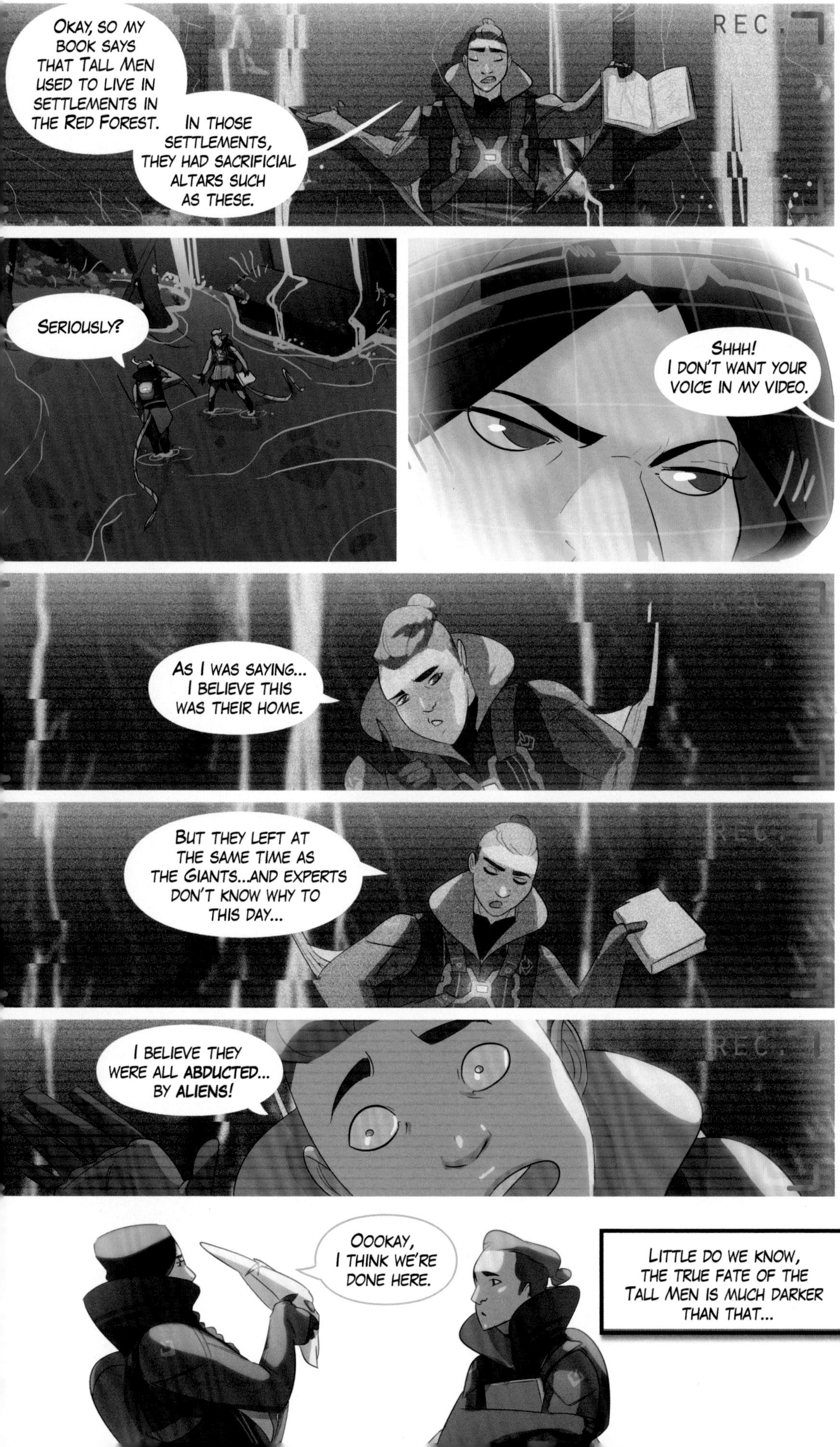
REC.
OKAY, SO MY BOOK SAYS THAT TALL MEN USED TO LIVE IN SETTLEMENTS IN THE RED FOREST.
IN THOSE SETTLEMENTS, THEY HAD SACRIFICIAL ALTARS SUCH AS THESE.
SERIOUSLY?
SHHH! I DON'T WANT YOUR VOICE IN MY VIDEO.
AS I WAS SAYING... I BELIEVE THIS WAS THEIR HOME.
BUT THEY LEFT AT THE SAME TIME AS THE GIANTS...AND EXPERTS DON'T KNOW WHY TO THIS DAY...
I BELIEVE THEY WERE ALL **ABDUCTED**... BY **ALIENS**!
OOOKAY, I THINK WE'RE DONE HERE.
LITTLE DO WE KNOW, THE TRUE FATE OF THE TALL MEN IS MUCH DARKER THAN THAT...

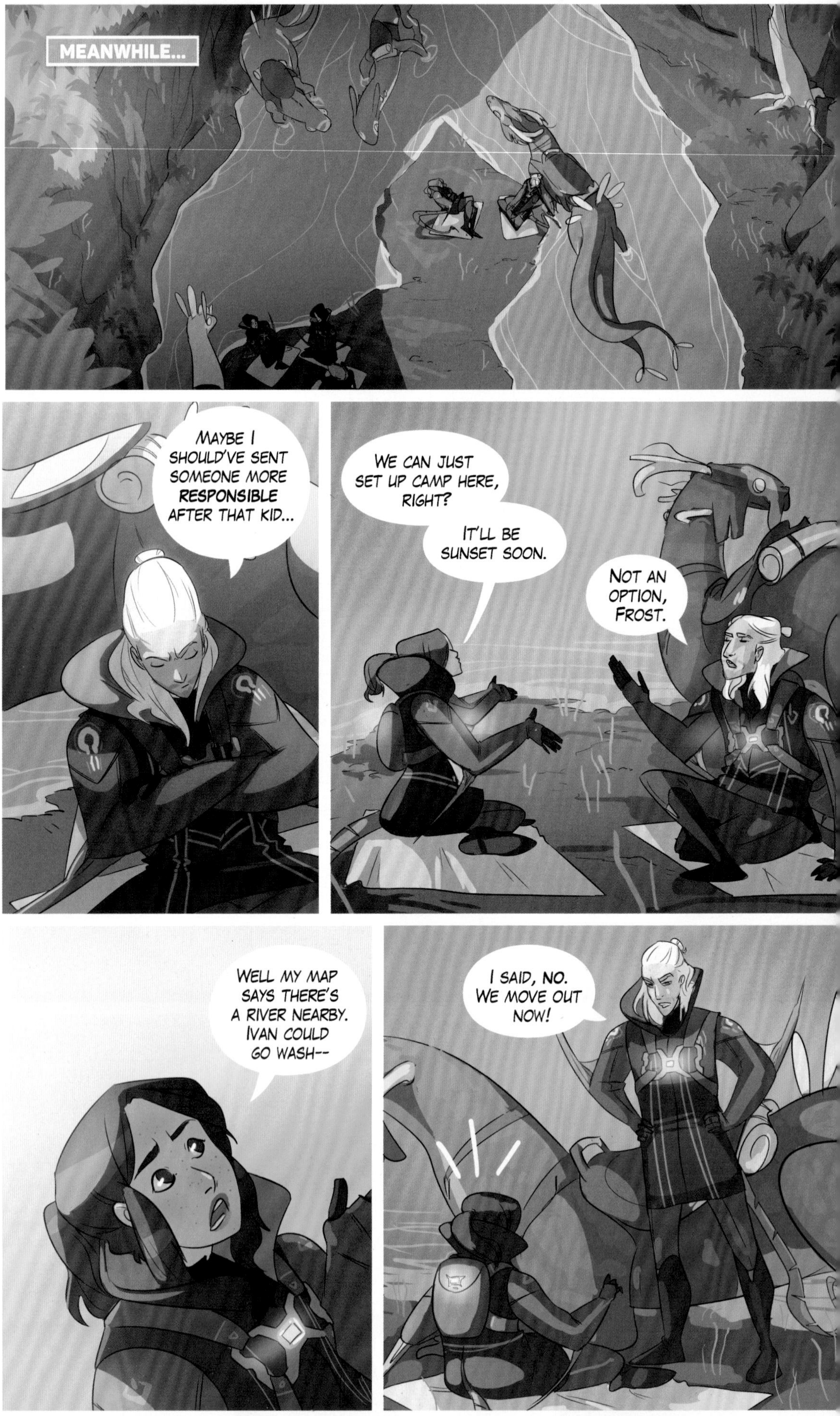
MEANWHILE...
MAYBE I SHOULD'VE SENT SOMEONE MORE RESPONSIBLE AFTER THAT KID...
WE CAN JUST SET UP CAMP HERE, RIGHT?
IT'LL BE SUNSET SOON.
NOT AN OPTION, FROST.
WELL MY MAP SAYS THERE'S A RIVER NEARBY. IVAN COULD GO WASH--
I SAID, NO. WE MOVE OUT NOW!

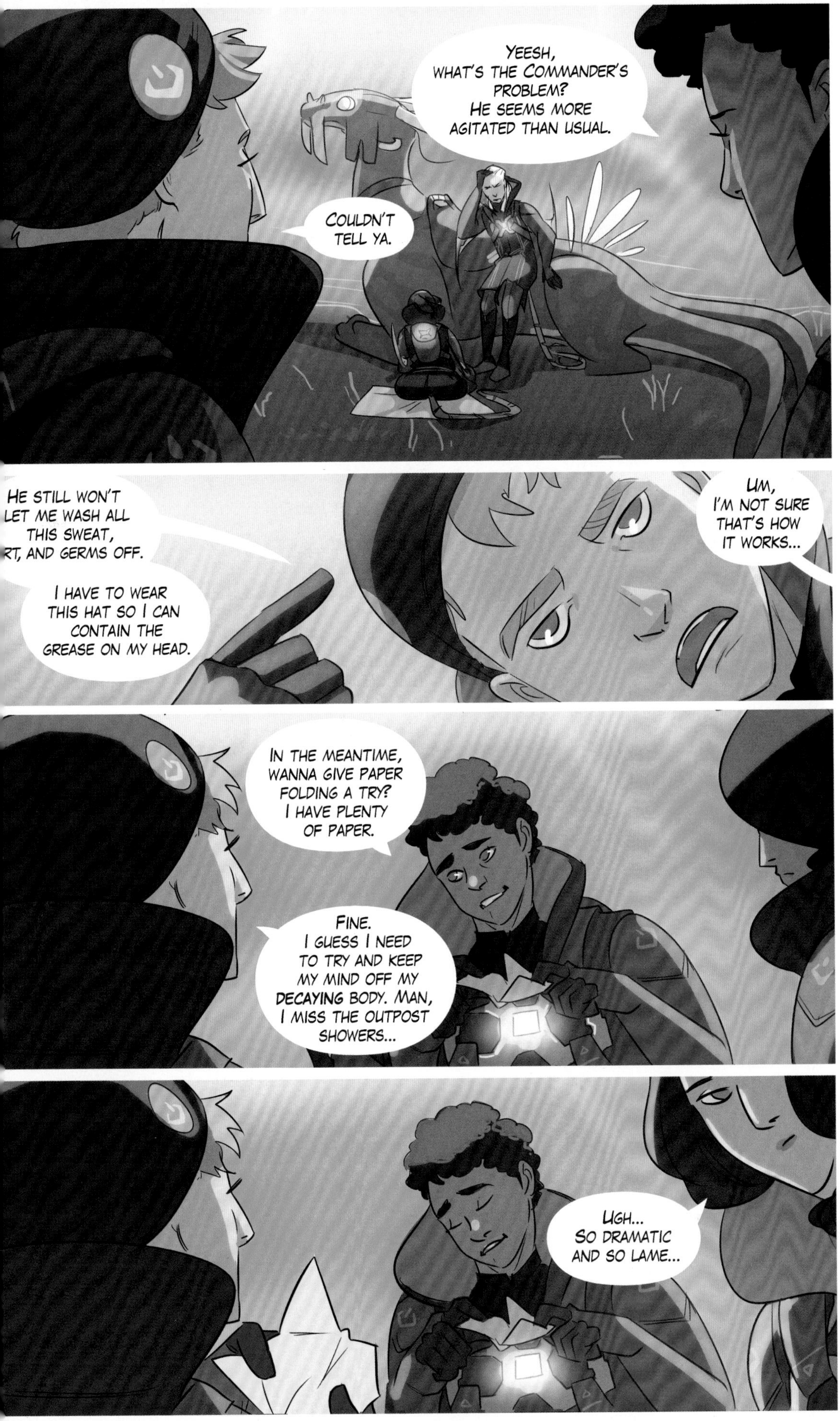
YEESH, WHAT'S THE COMMANDER'S PROBLEM? HE SEEMS MORE AGITATED THAN USUAL.
COULDN'T TELL YA.
HE STILL WON'T LET ME WASH ALL THIS SWEAT, RT, AND GERMS OFF.
I HAVE TO WEAR THIS HAT SO I CAN CONTAIN THE GREASE ON MY HEAD.
UM, I'M NOT SURE THAT'S HOW IT WORKS...
IN THE MEANTIME, WANNA GIVE PAPER FOLDING A TRY? I HAVE PLENTY OF PAPER.
FINE. I GUESS I NEED TO TRY AND KEEP MY MIND OFF MY DECAYING BODY. MAN, I MISS THE OUTPOST SHOWERS...
UGH... SO DRAMATIC AND SO LAME...

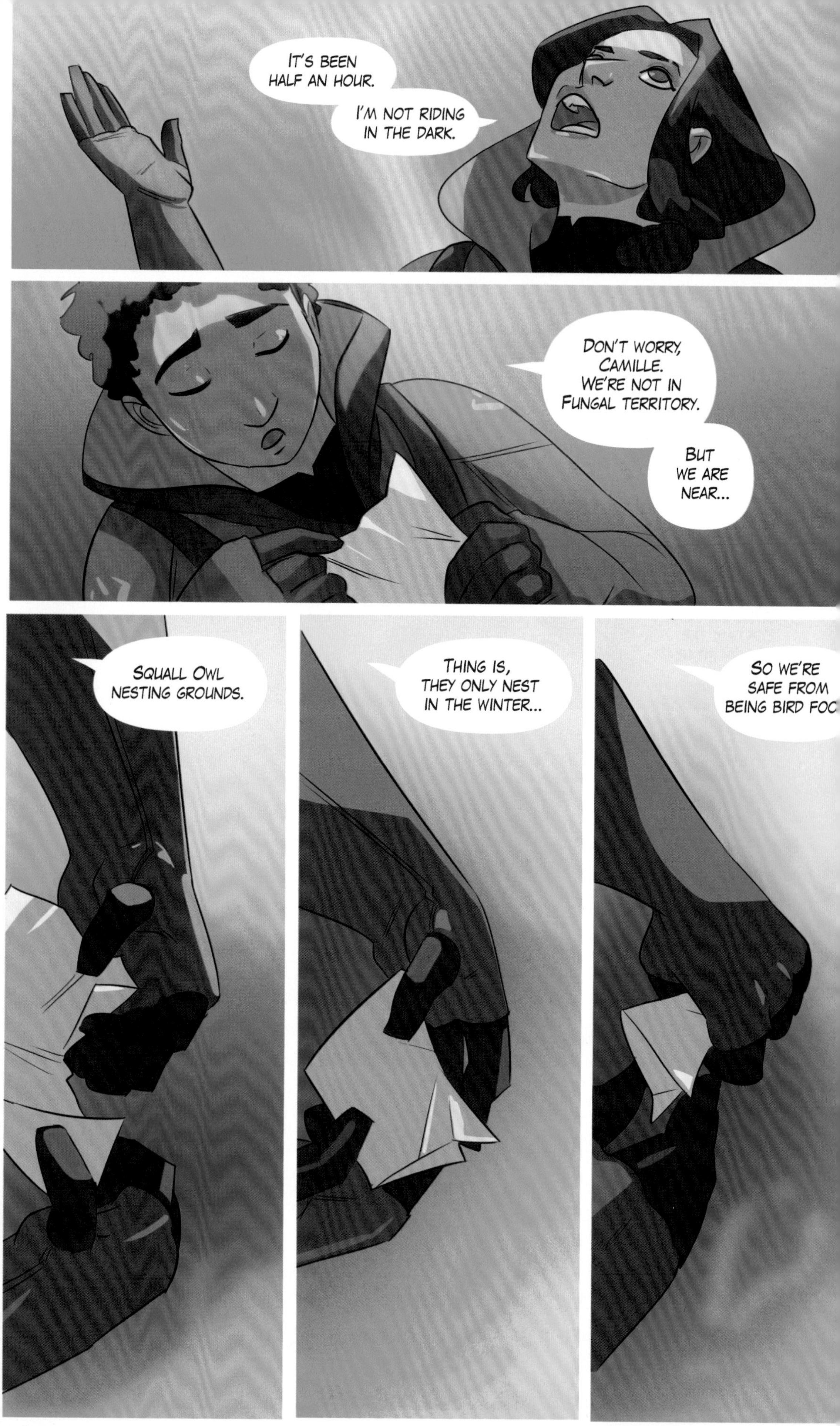

IT'S BEEN HALF AN HOUR.
I'M NOT RIDING IN THE DARK.
DON'T WORRY, CAMILLE. WE'RE NOT IN FUNGAL TERRITORY.
BUT WE ARE NEAR...
SQUALL OWL NESTING GROUNDS.
THING IS, THEY ONLY NEST IN THE WINTER...
SO WE'RE SAFE FROM BEING BIRD FOC

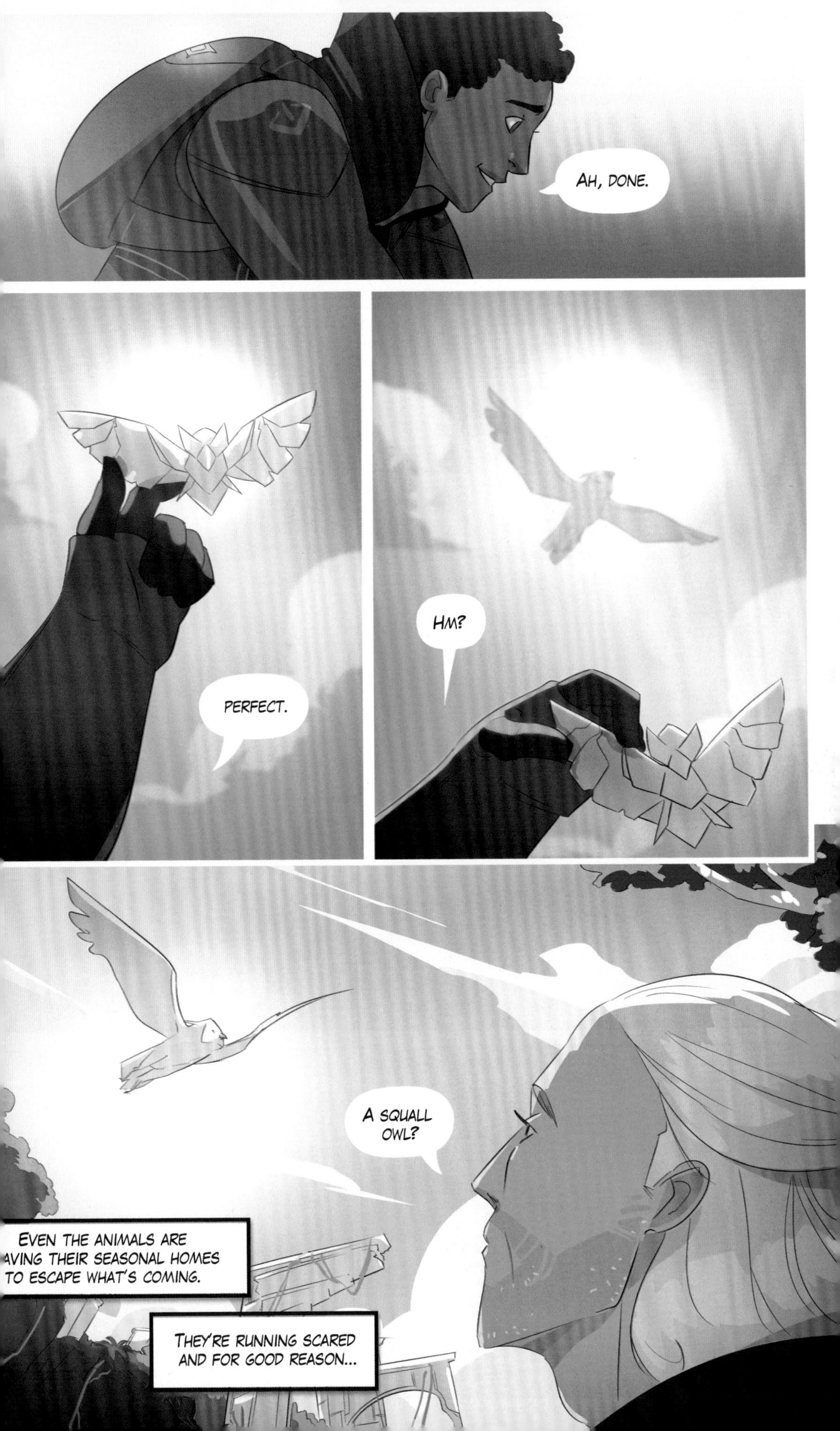
AH, DONE.
PERFECT.
HM?
A SQUALL OWL?
EVEN THE ANIMALS ARE
AVING THEIR SEASONAL HOMES
TO ESCAPE WHAT'S COMING.
THEY'RE RUNNING SCARED AND FOR GOOD REASON...

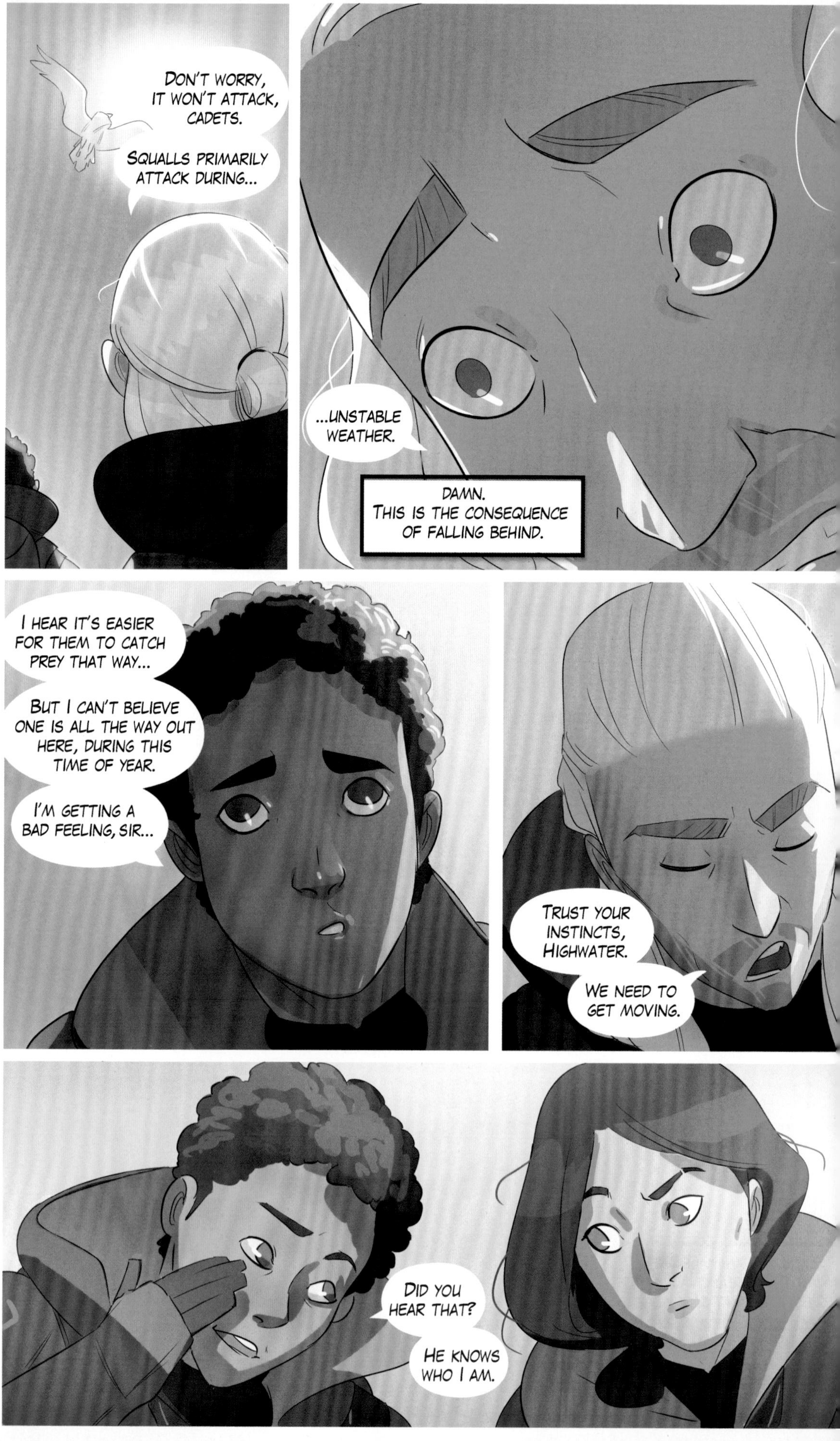
DON'T WORRY, IT WON'T ATTACK, CADETS.
SQUALLS PRIMARILY ATTACK DURING...
...UNSTABLE WEATHER.
DAMN. THIS IS THE CONSEQUENCE OF FALLING BEHIND.
I HEAR IT'S EASIER FOR THEM TO CATCH PREY THAT WAY...
BUT I CAN'T BELIEVE ONE IS ALL THE WAY OUT HERE, DURING THIS TIME OF YEAR.
I'M GETTING A BAD FEELING, SIR...
TRUST YOUR INSTINCTS, HIGHWATER.
WE NEED TO GET MOVING.
DID YOU HEAR THAT?
HE KNOWS WHO I AM.

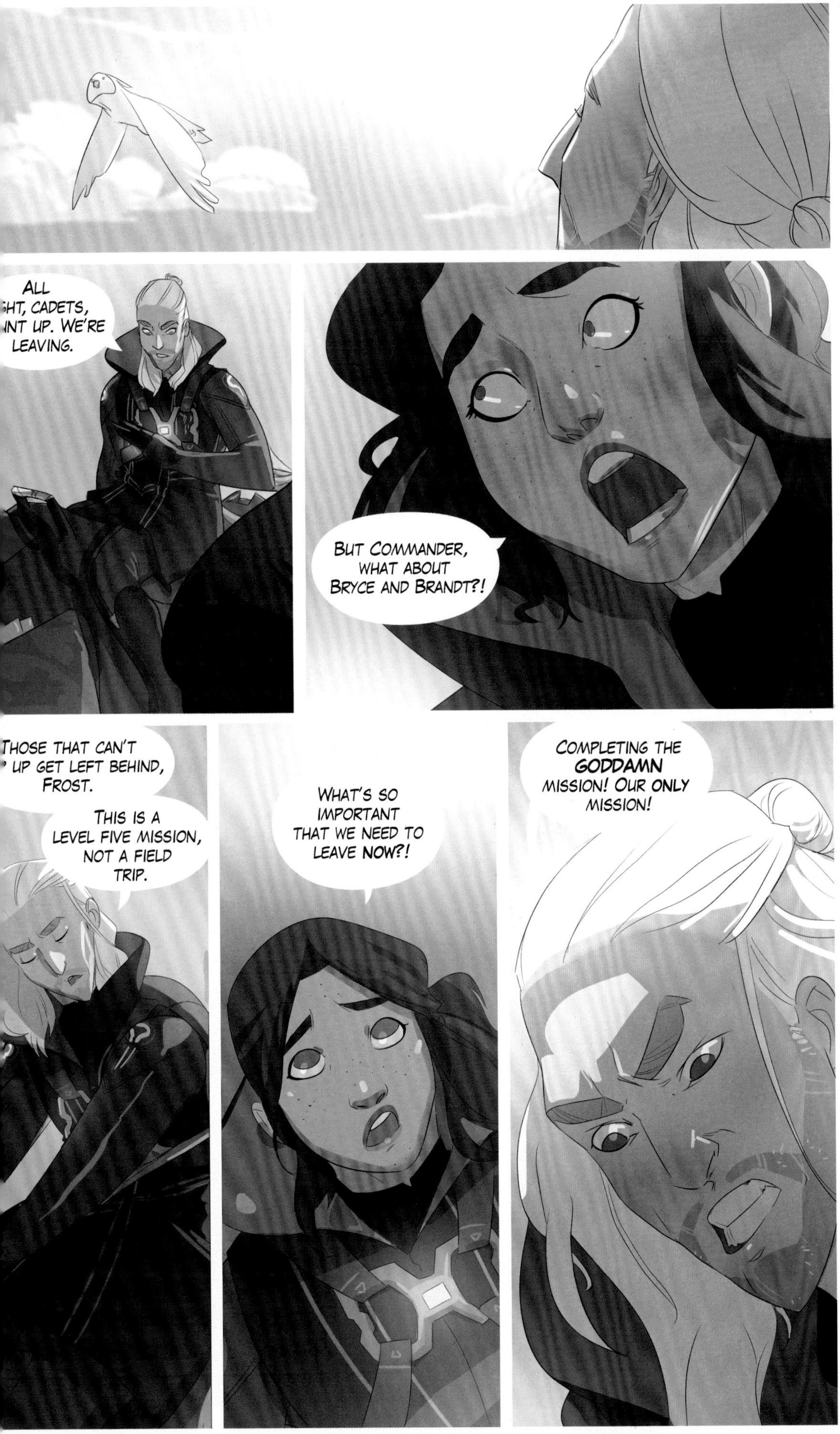
ALL HT, CADETS, INT UP. WE'RE LEAVING.
BUT COMMANDER, WHAT ABOUT BRYCE AND BRANDT?!
THOSE THAT CAN'T UP GET LEFT BEHIND, FROST.
THIS IS A LEVEL FIVE MISSION, NOT A FIELD TRIP.
WHAT'S SO IMPORTANT THAT WE NEED TO LEAVE **NOW**?!
COMPLETING THE **GODDAMN** MISSION! OUR **ONLY** MISSION!

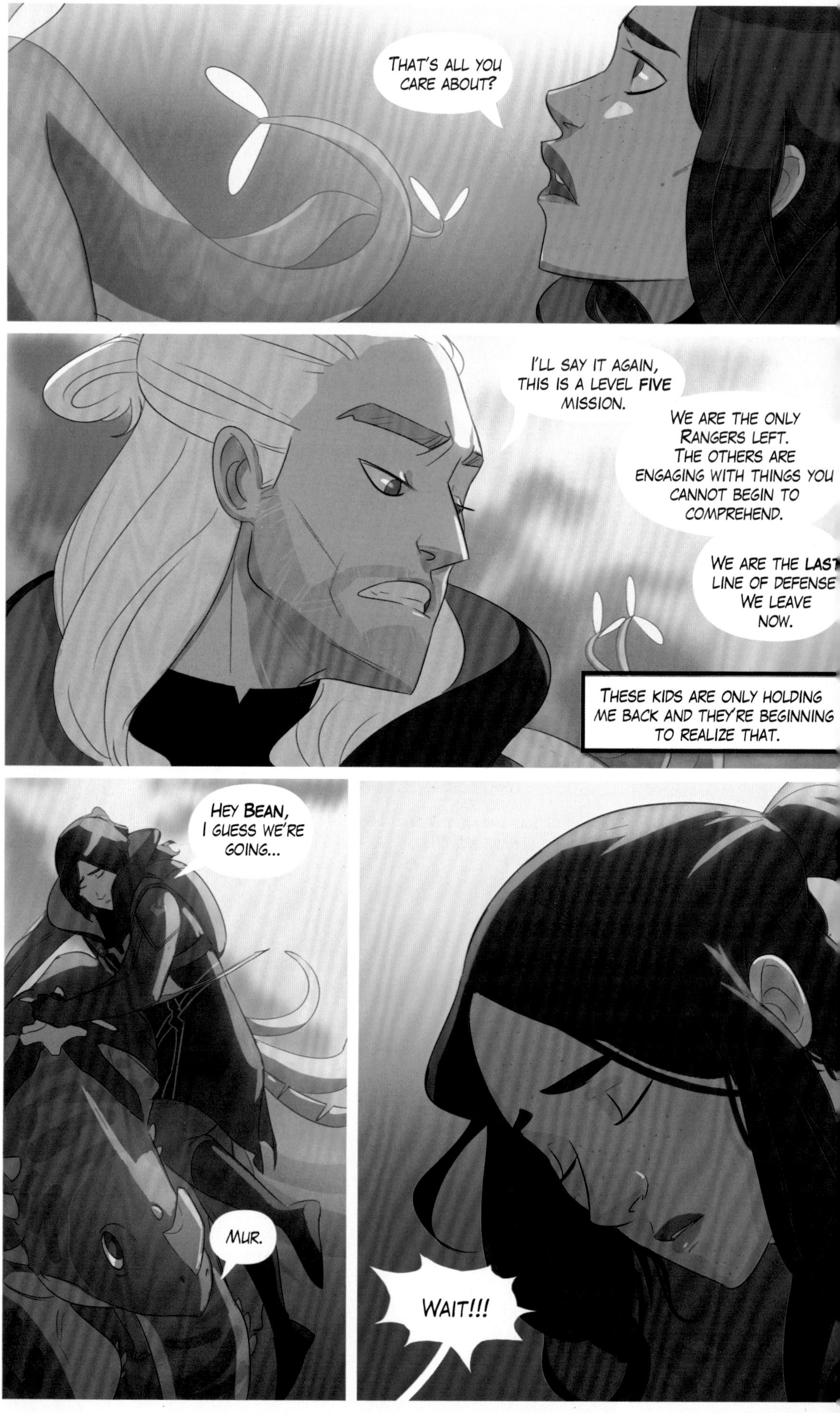

THAT'S ALL YOU CARE ABOUT?
I'LL SAY IT AGAIN, THIS IS A LEVEL **FIVE** MISSION.
WE ARE THE ONLY RANGERS LEFT. THE OTHERS ARE ENGAGING WITH THINGS YOU CANNOT BEGIN TO COMPREHEND.
WE ARE THE **LAST** LINE OF DEFENSE. WE LEAVE NOW.
THESE KIDS ARE ONLY HOLDING ME BACK AND THEY'RE BEGINNING TO REALIZE THAT.
HEY **BEAN**, I GUESS WE'RE GOING...
MUR.
WAIT!!!

WE'RE COMING!

WE HAD TO BRING BACK THESE ARCHAEOLOGICAL FINDS.

THIS ISN'T A GAME!

THERE'S NO TIME FOR A LECTURE.

OH SIR, I CAN GUARANTEE--

KLING!

KLANG!

SHOVE!

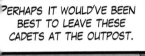

PERHAPS IT WOULD'VE BEEN BEST TO LEAVE THESE CADETS AT THE OUTPOST.

THEY'RE NOT READY, AND I DOUBT THEY'LL SURVIVE WHAT'S TO COME.

THIS ONE IN PARTICULAR.

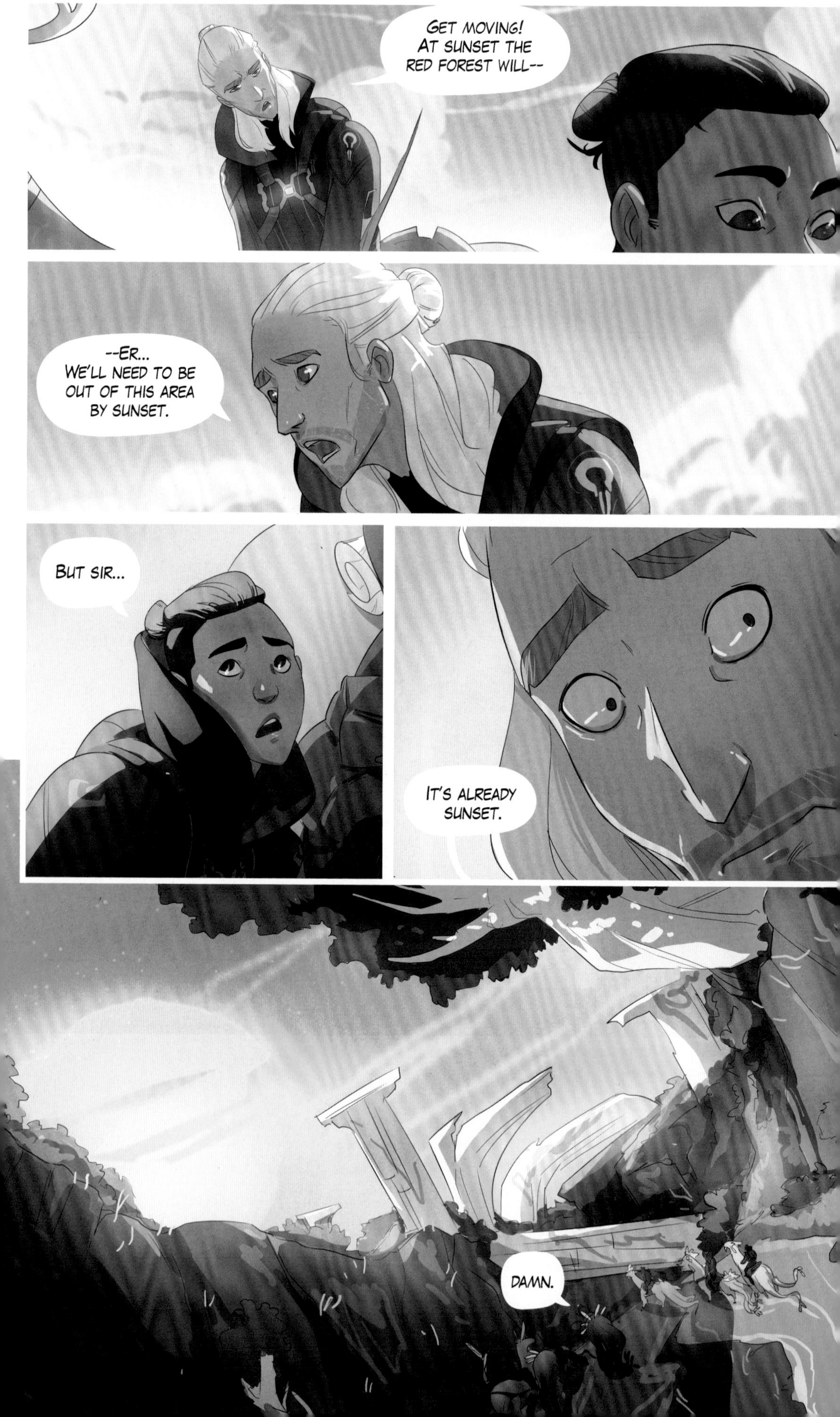
GET MOVING! AT SUNSET THE RED FOREST WILL--
--ER... WE'LL NEED TO BE OUT OF THIS AREA BY SUNSET.
BUT SIR...
IT'S ALREADY SUNSET.
DAMN.

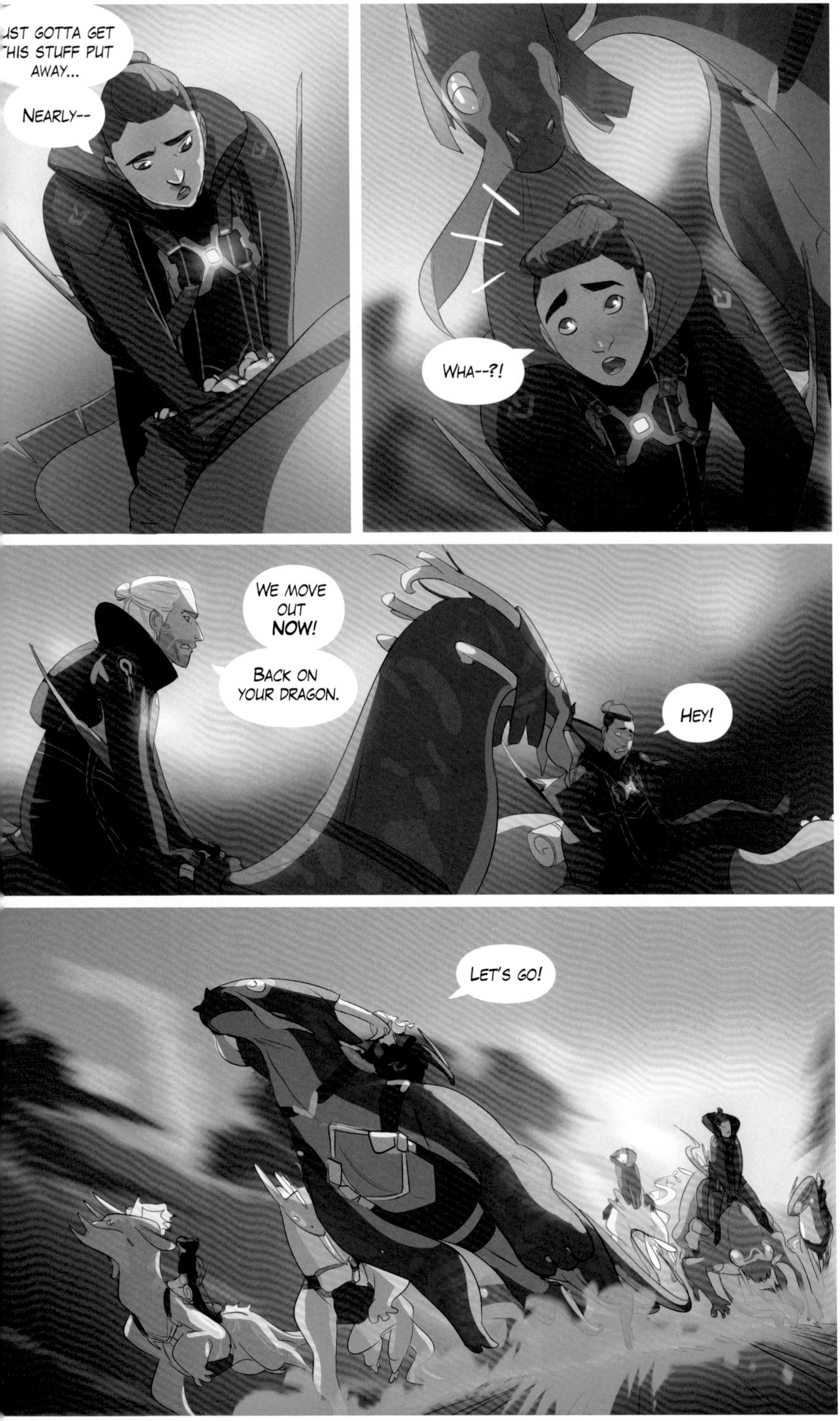
UST GOTTA GET
THIS STUFF PUT
AWAY...
NEARLY--
WHA--?!
WE MOVE OUT NOW!
BACK ON YOUR DRAGON.
HEY!
LET'S GO!

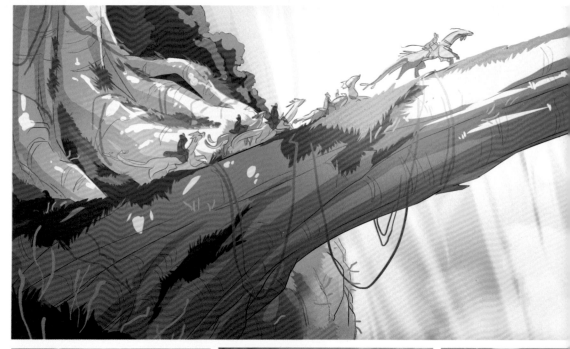

UH, SIR...
THE SQUALL OWL'S
FOLLOWING US!

IGNORE IT.

KEEP MOVING!

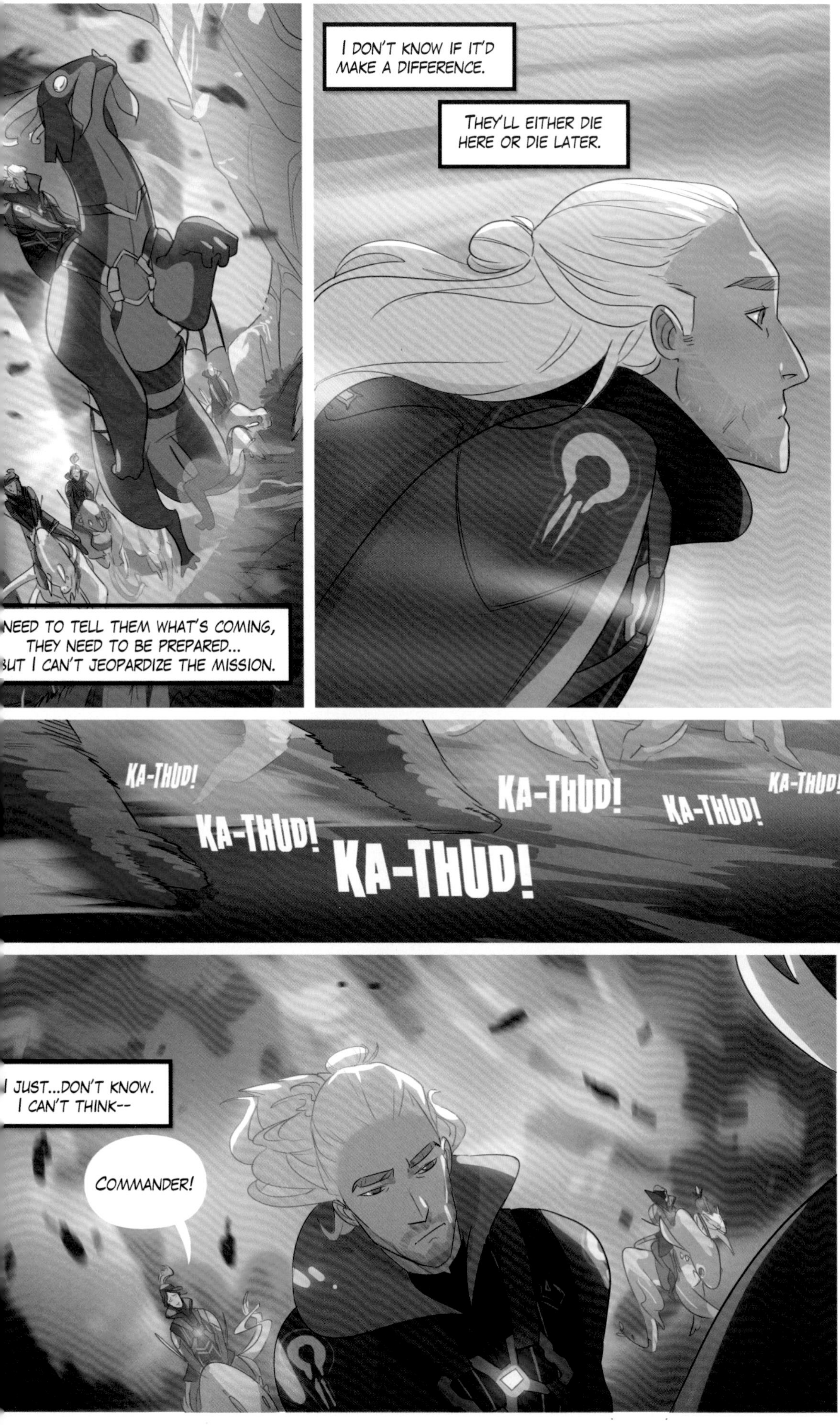
NEED TO TELL THEM WHAT'S COMING,
THEY NEED TO BE PREPARED...
BUT I CAN'T JEOPARDIZE THE MISSION.
I DON'T KNOW IF IT'D MAKE A DIFFERENCE.
THEY'LL EITHER DIE HERE OR DIE LATER.
KA-THUD!
KA-THUD!
KA-THUD!
KA-THUD!
KA-THUD!
KA-THUD!
I JUST...DON'T KNOW. I CAN'T THINK--
COMMANDER!

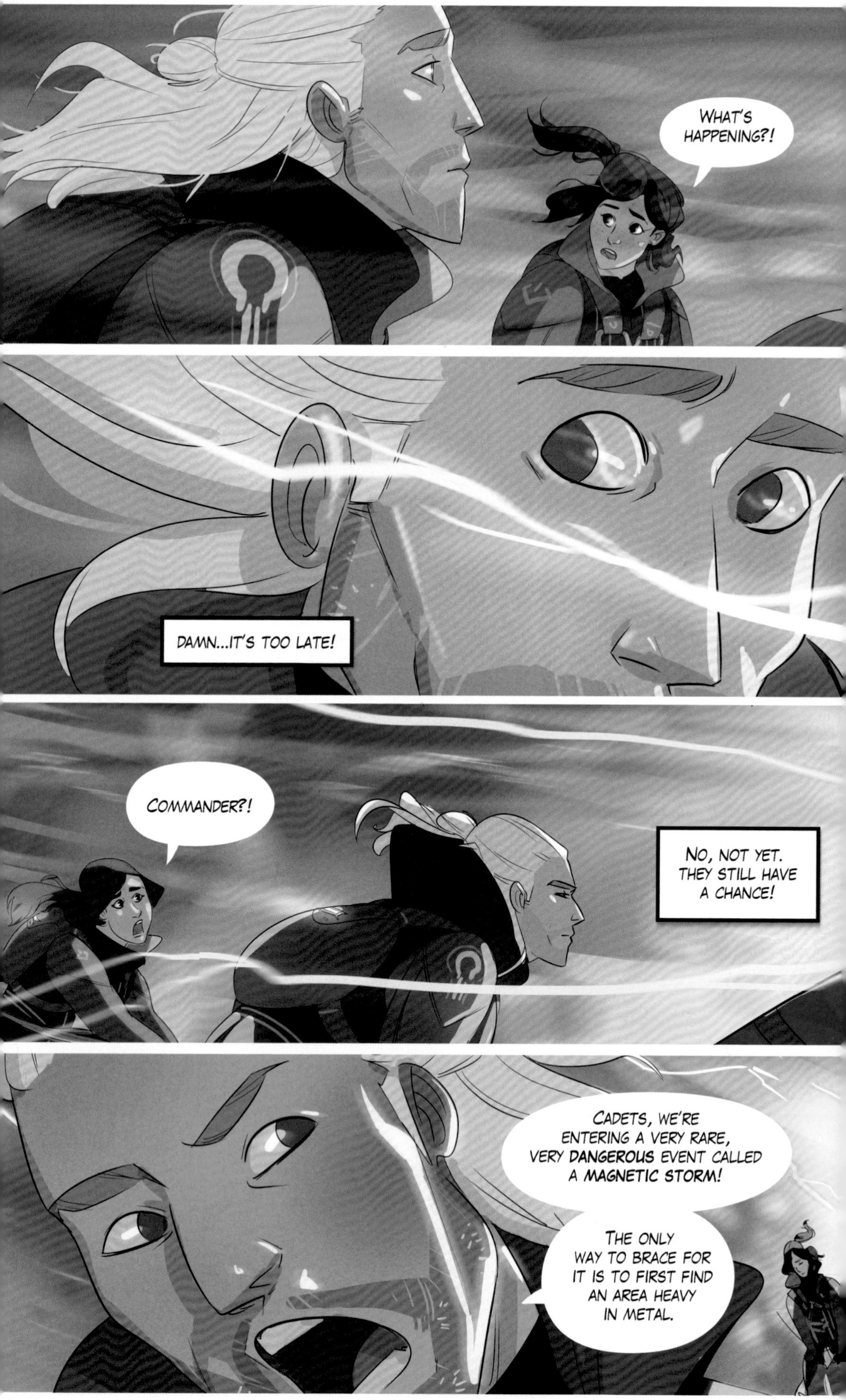
WHAT'S HAPPENING?!
DAMN...IT'S TOO LATE!
COMMANDER?!
NO, NOT YET. THEY STILL HAVE A CHANCE!
CADETS, WE'RE ENTERING A VERY RARE, VERY DANGEROUS EVENT CALLED A MAGNETIC STORM!
THE ONLY WAY TO BRACE FOR IT IS TO FIRST FIND AN AREA HEAVY IN METAL.

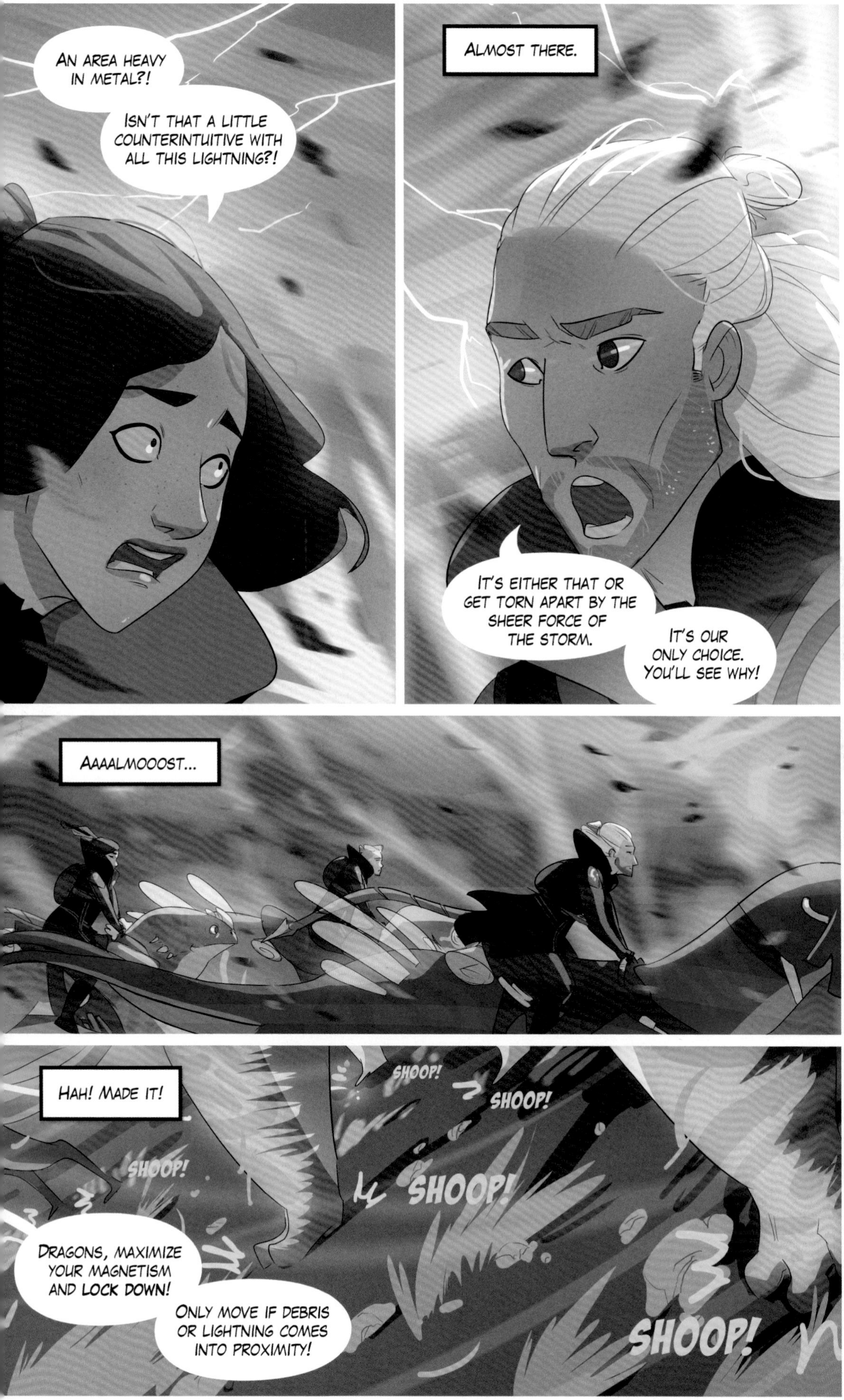
AN AREA HEAVY IN METAL?!
ISN'T THAT A LITTLE COUNTERINTUITIVE WITH ALL THIS LIGHTNING?!
ALMOST THERE.
IT'S EITHER THAT OR GET TORN APART BY THE SHEER FORCE OF THE STORM.
IT'S OUR ONLY CHOICE. YOU'LL SEE WHY!
AAAALMOOOST...
HAH! MADE IT!
SHOOP!
SHOOP!
SHOOP!
SHOOP!
DRAGONS, MAXIMIZE YOUR MAGNETISM AND LOCK DOWN!
ONLY MOVE IF DEBRIS OR LIGHTNING COMES INTO PROXIMITY!
SHOOP!

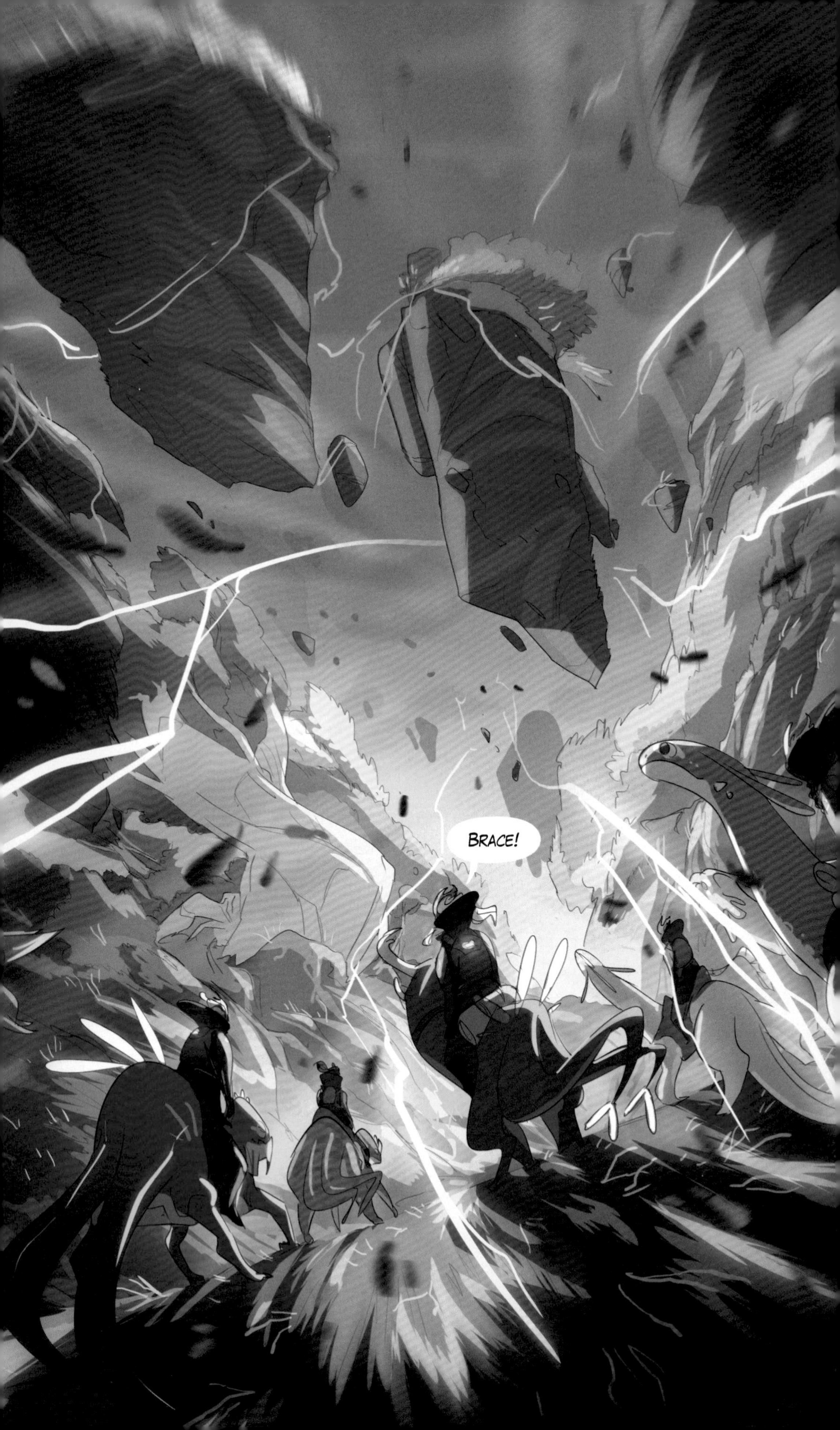
BRACE!

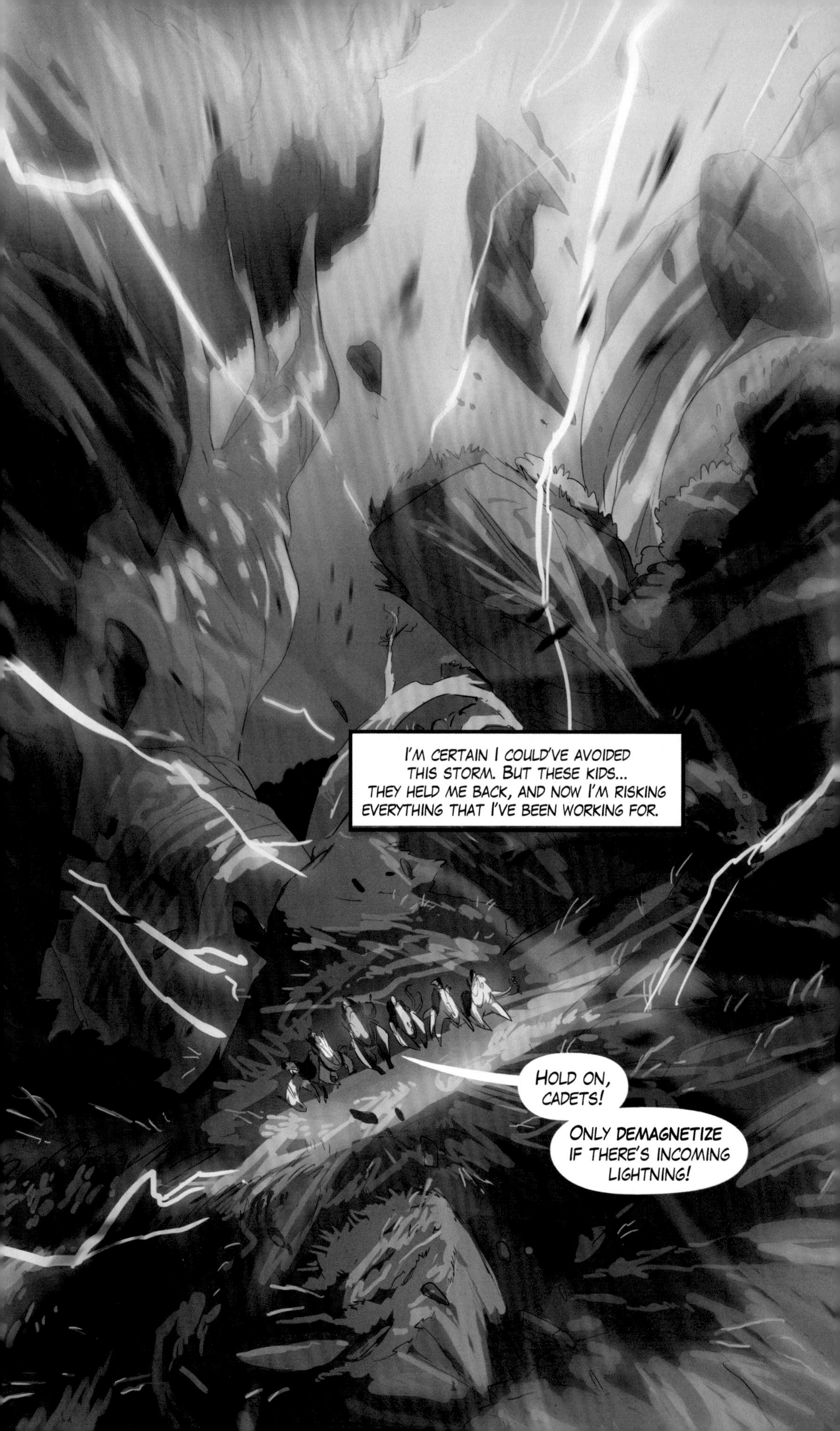
I'M CERTAIN I COULD'VE AVOIDED THIS STORM. BUT THESE KIDS... THEY HELD ME BACK, AND NOW I'M RISKING EVERYTHING THAT I'VE BEEN WORKING FOR.
HOLD ON, CADETS!
ONLY DEMAGNETIZE IF THERE'S INCOMING LIGHTNING!

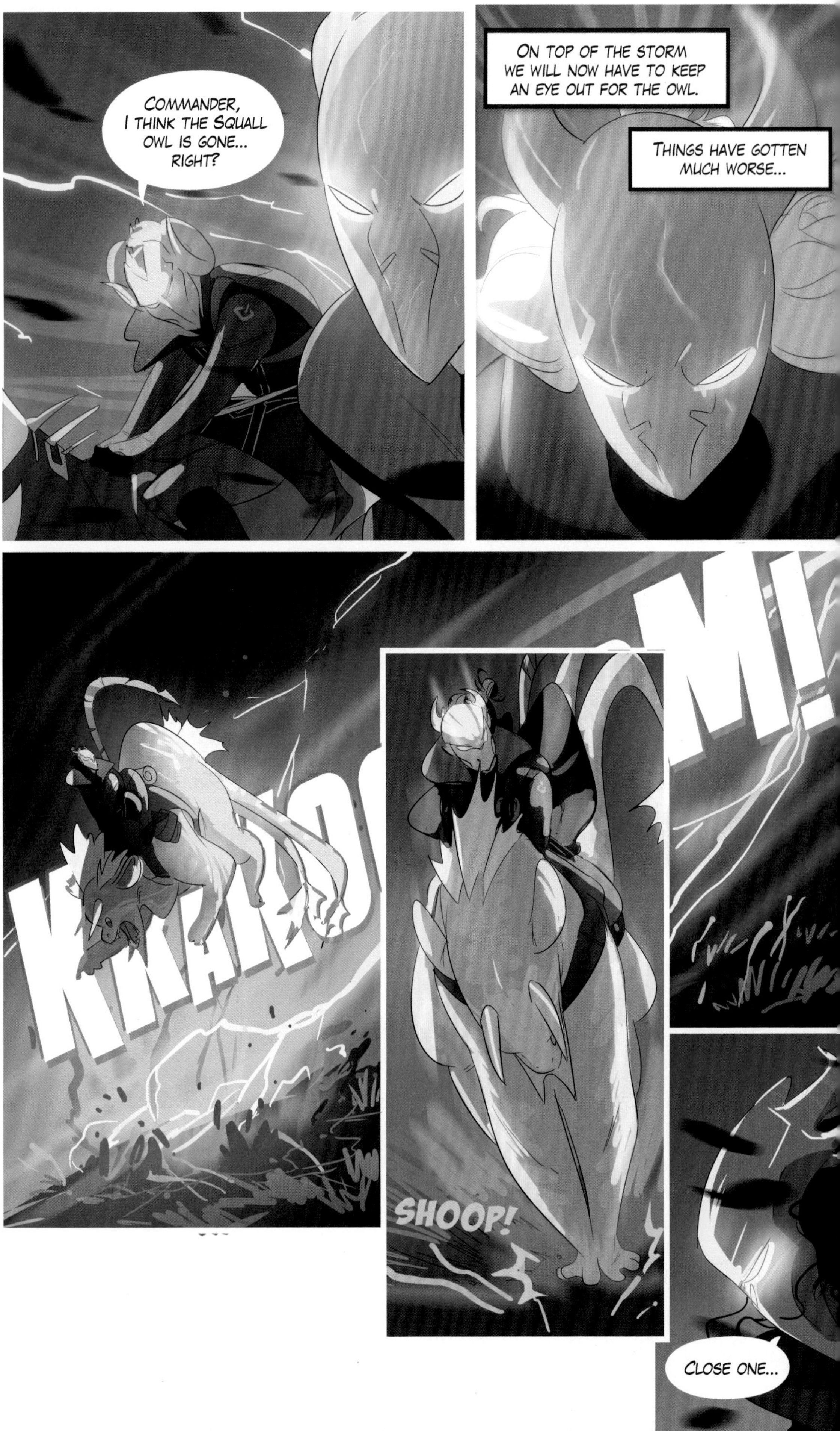
COMMANDER, I THINK THE SQUALL OWL IS GONE... RIGHT?
ON TOP OF THE STORM WE WILL NOW HAVE TO KEEP AN EYE OUT FOR THE OWL.
THINGS HAVE GOTTEN MUCH WORSE...
SHOOP!
CLOSE ONE...

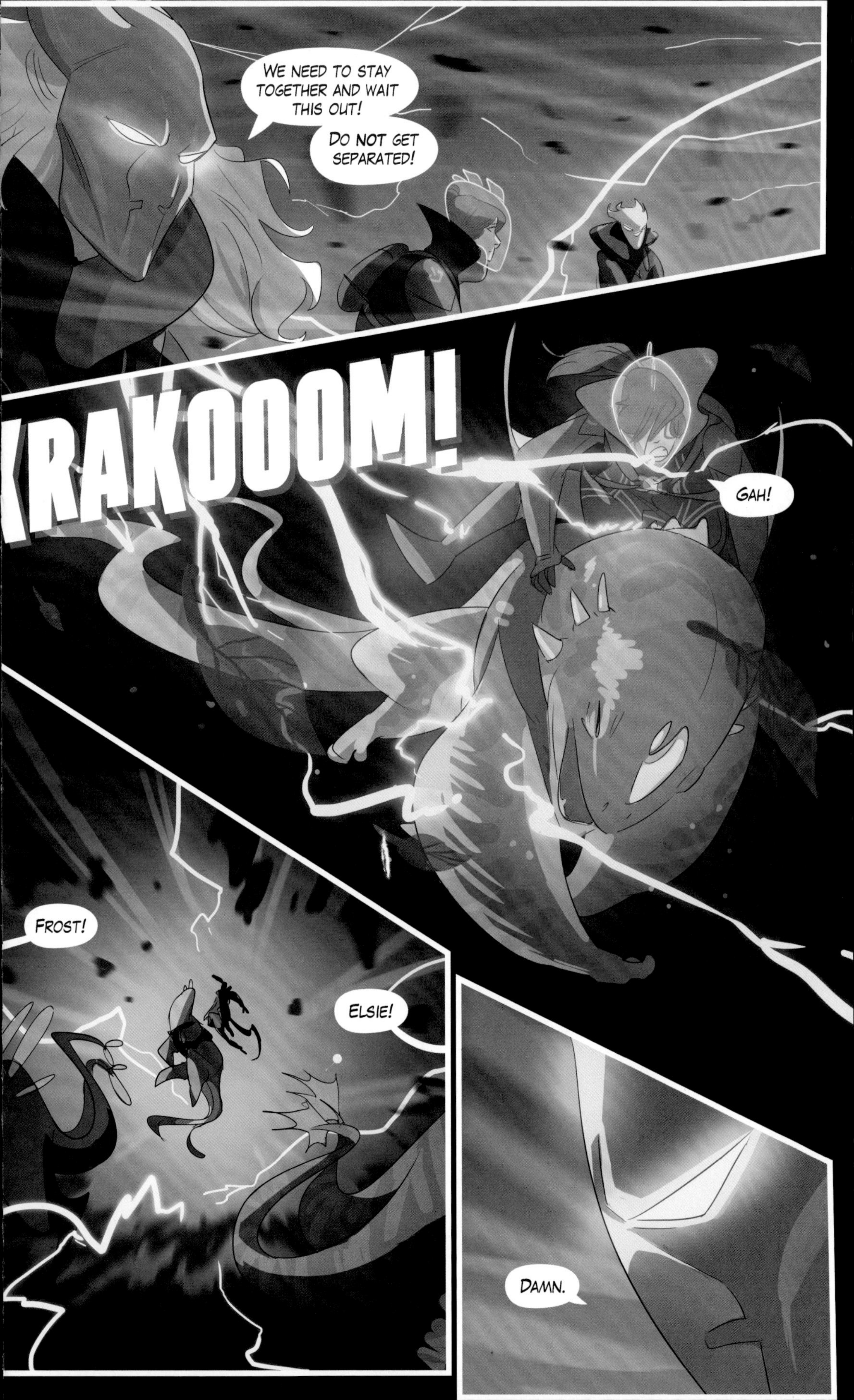
WE NEED TO STAY TOGETHER AND WAIT THIS OUT!
DO NOT GET SEPARATED!
KRAKOOOM!
GAH!
FROST!
ELSIE!
DAMN.

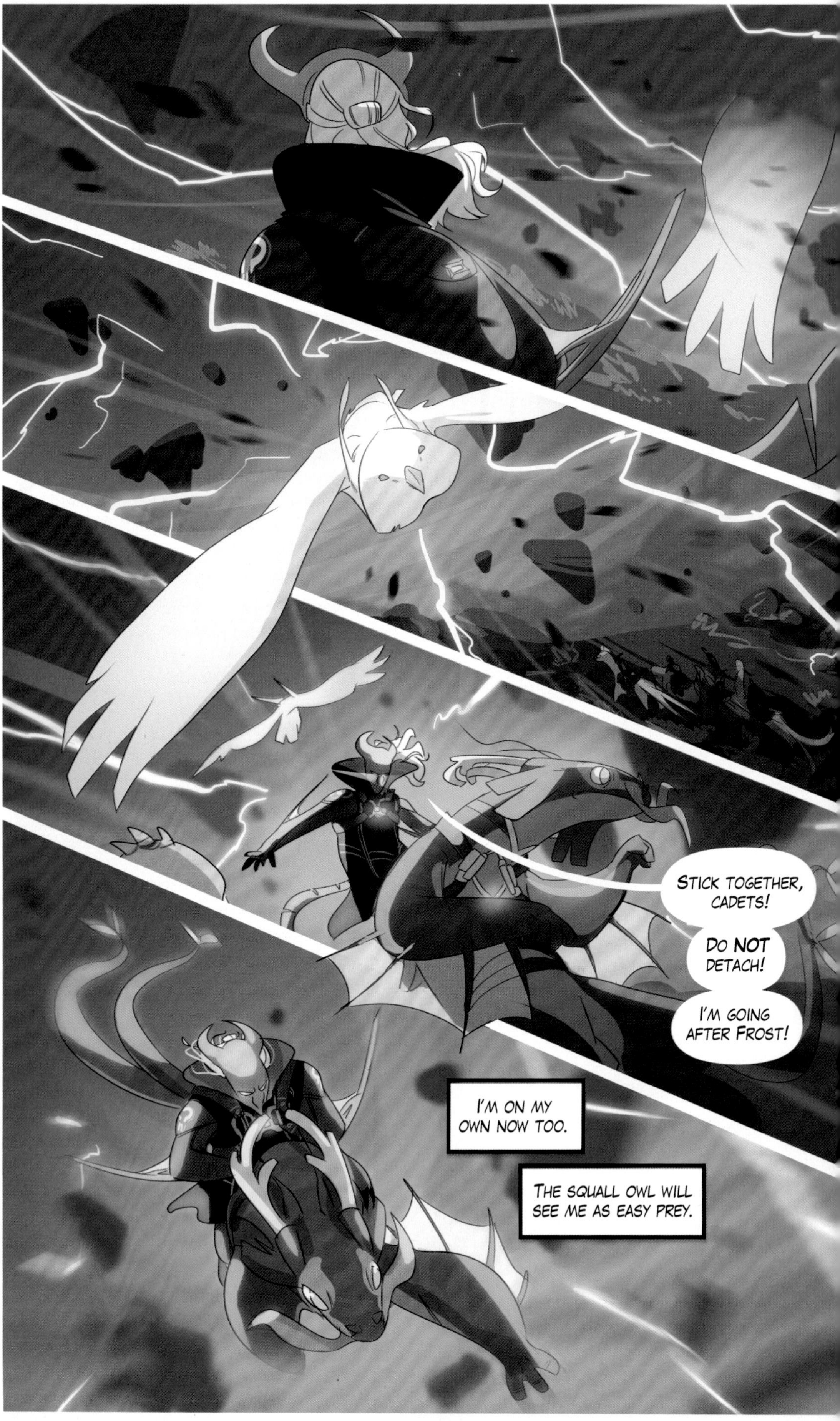
STICK TOGETHER, CADETS!
DO **NOT** DETACH!
I'M GOING AFTER FROST!
I'M ON MY OWN NOW TOO.
THE SQUALL OWL WILL SEE ME AS EASY PREY.

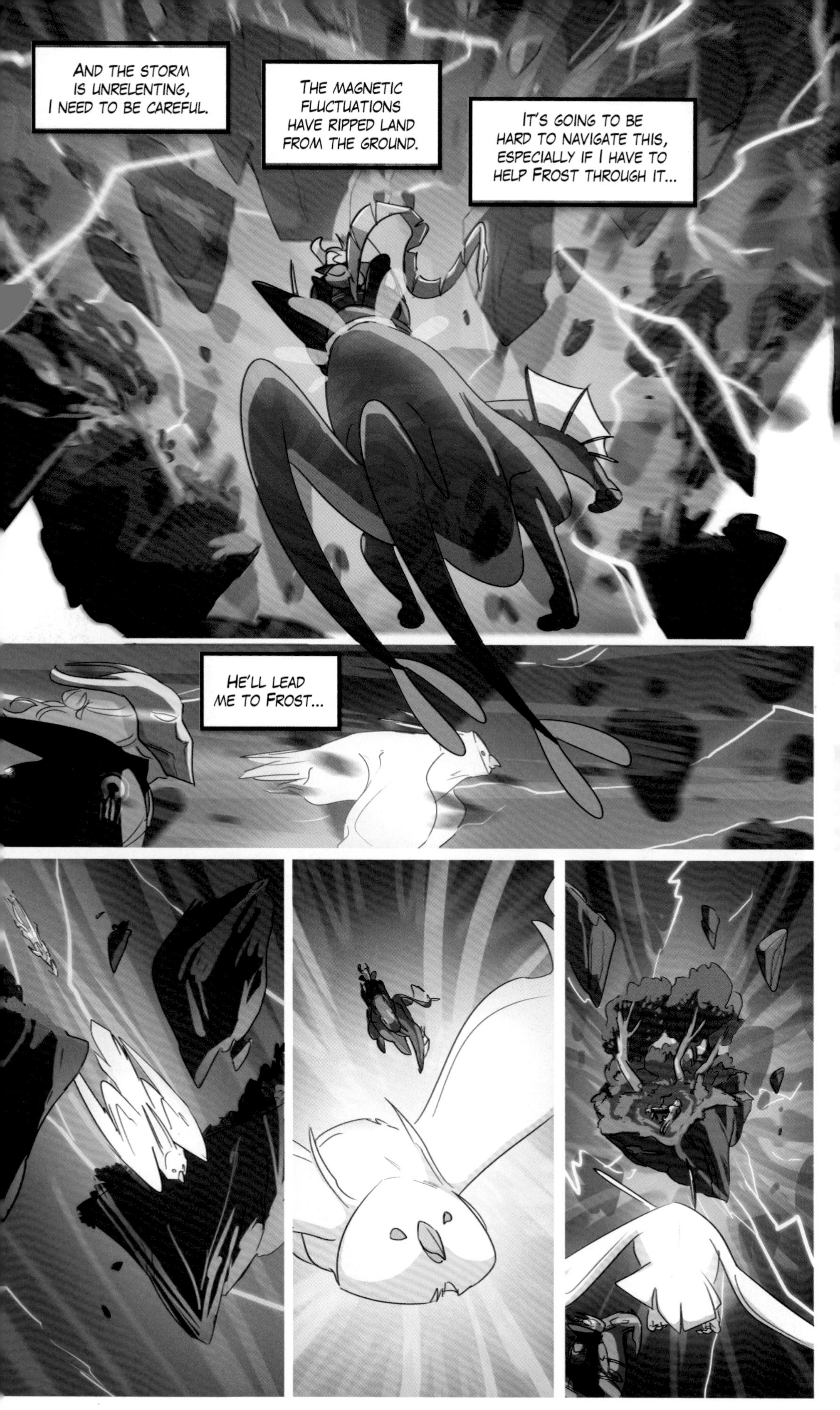
AND THE STORM IS UNRELENTING, I NEED TO BE CAREFUL.
THE MAGNETIC FLUCTUATIONS HAVE RIPPED LAND FROM THE GROUND.
IT'S GOING TO BE HARD TO NAVIGATE THIS, ESPECIALLY IF I HAVE TO HELP FROST THROUGH IT...
HE'LL LEAD ME TO FROST...

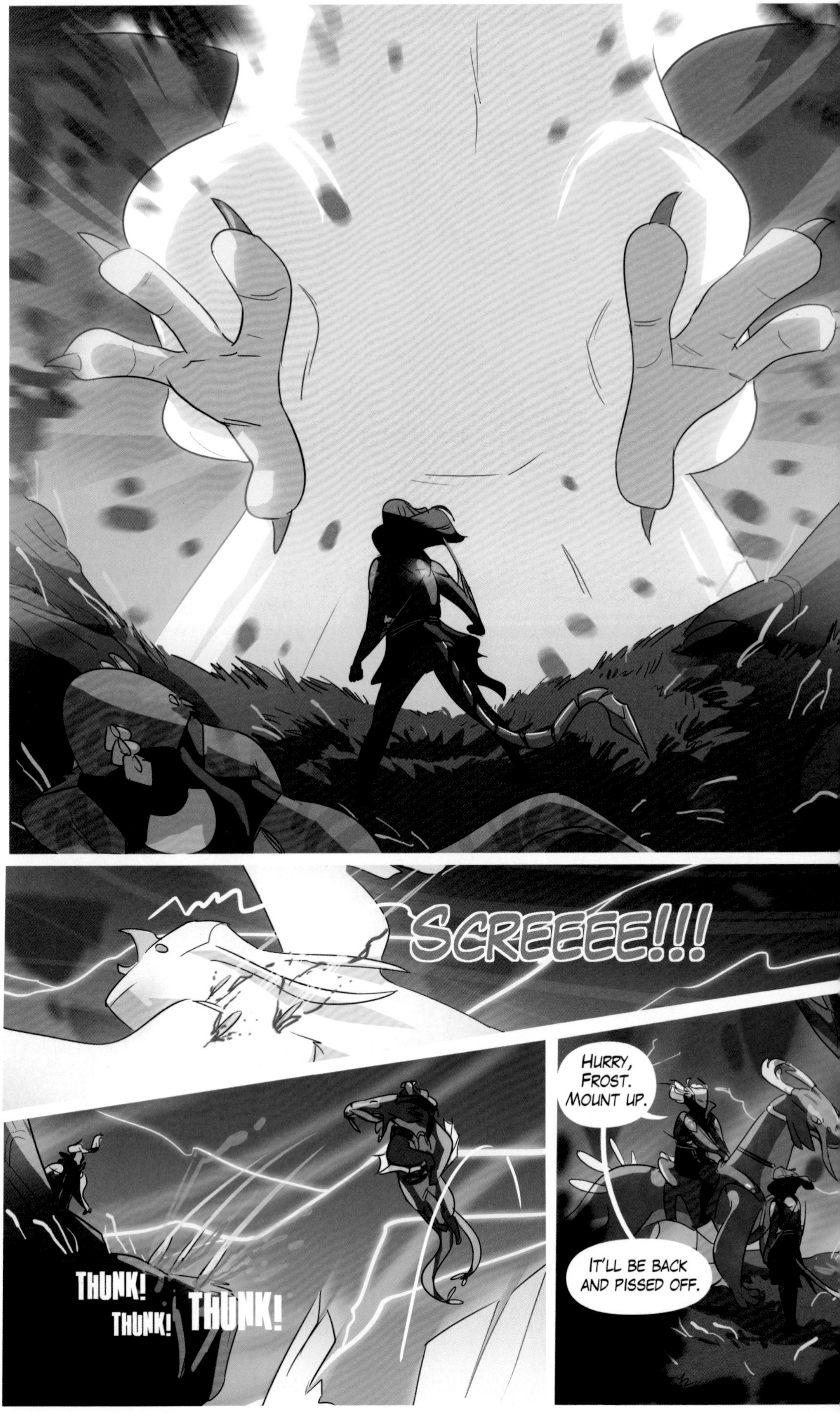
SCREEEEE!!!
THUNK!
THUNK!
THUNK!
HURRY, FROST. MOUNT UP.
IT'LL BE BACK AND PISSED OFF.

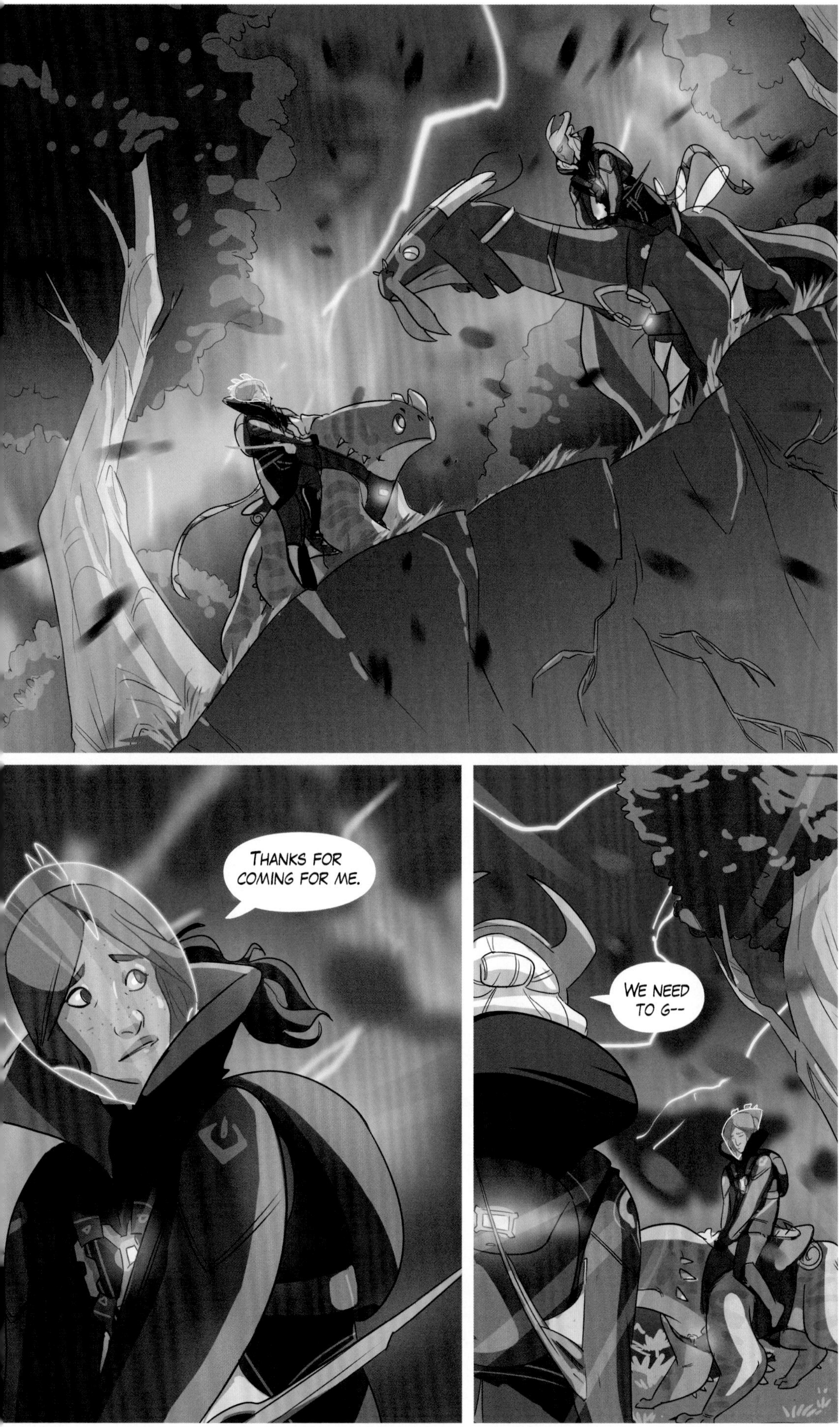
THANKS FOR COMING FOR ME.
WE NEED TO G--

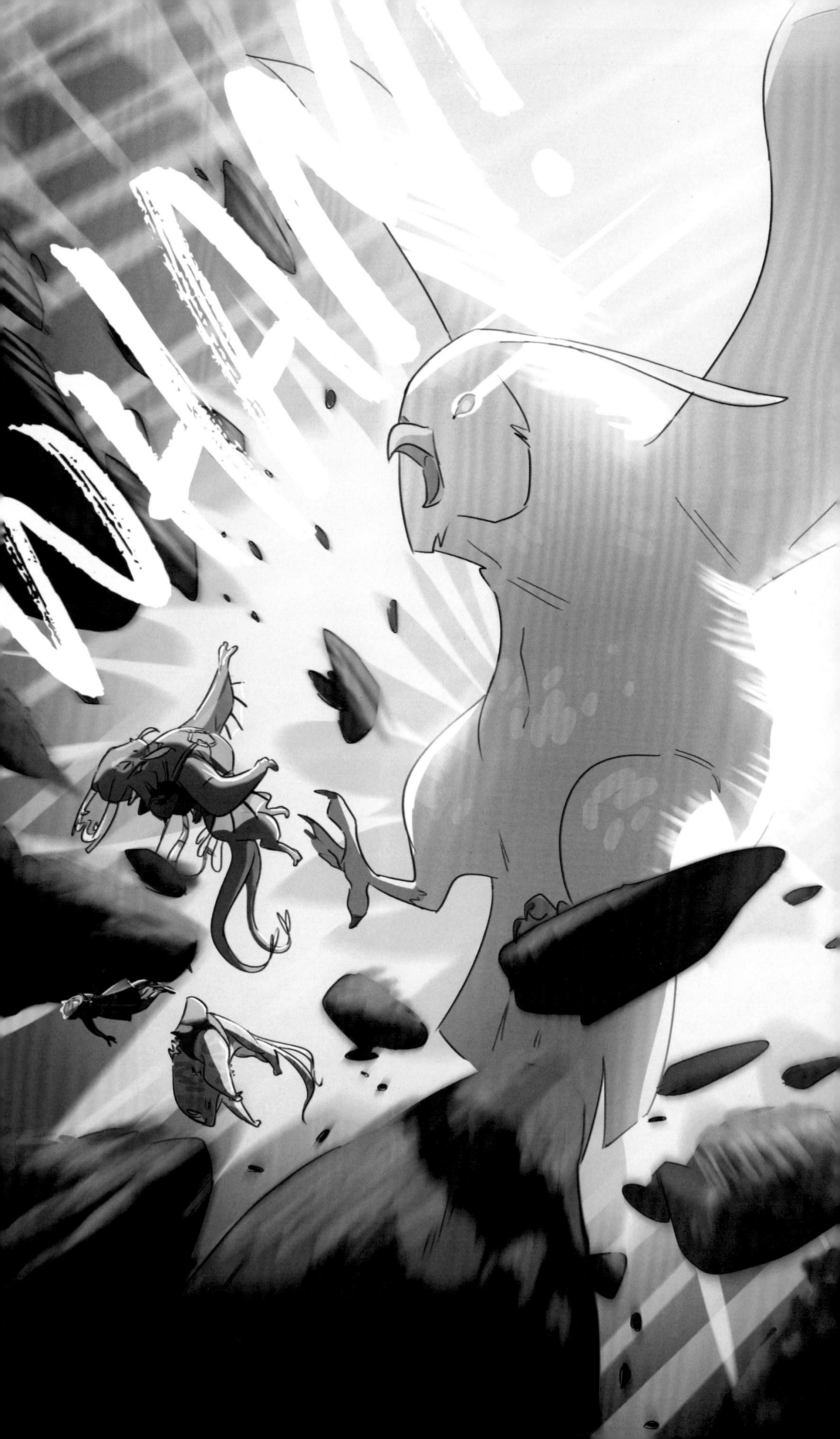

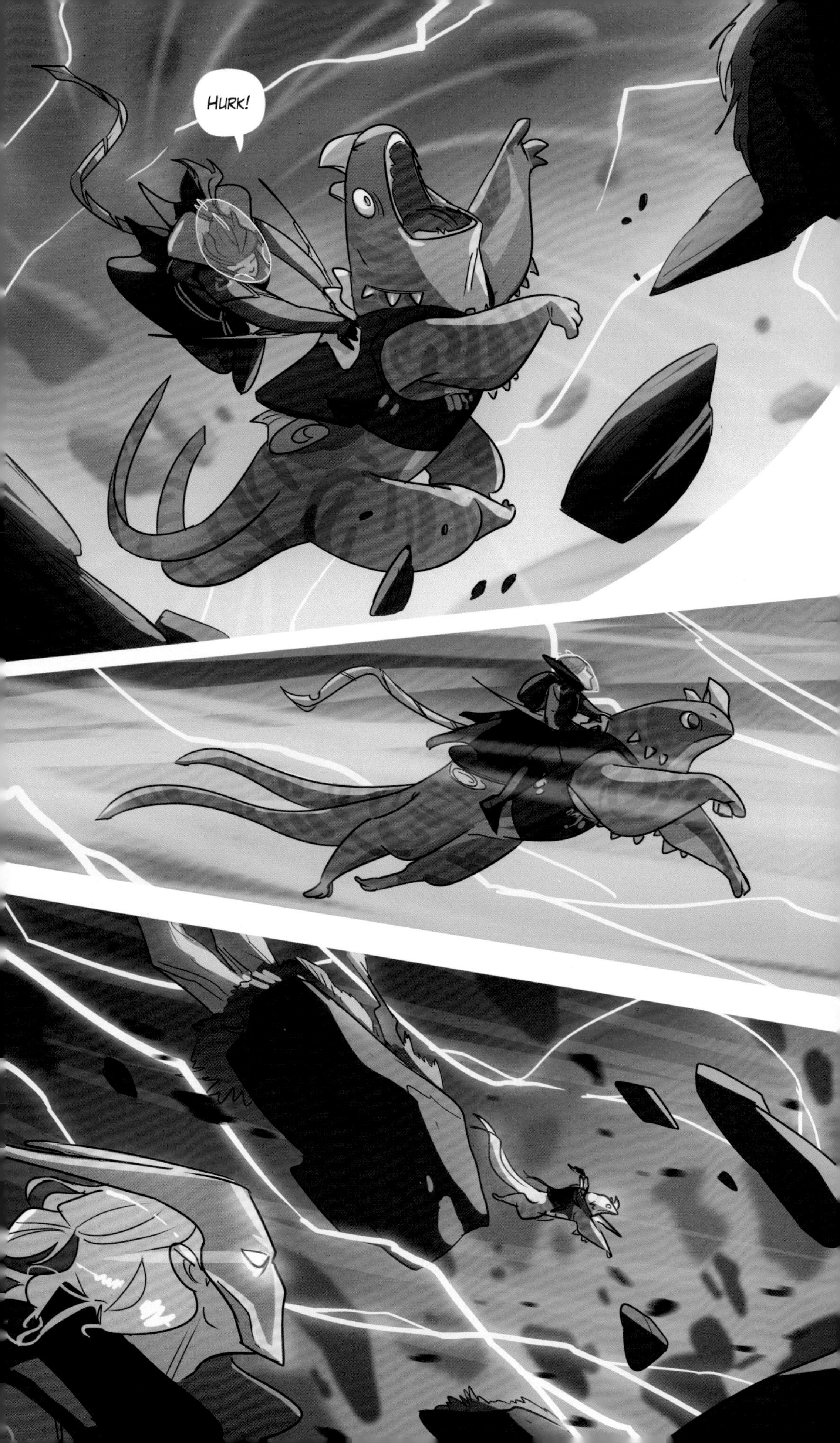
HURK!

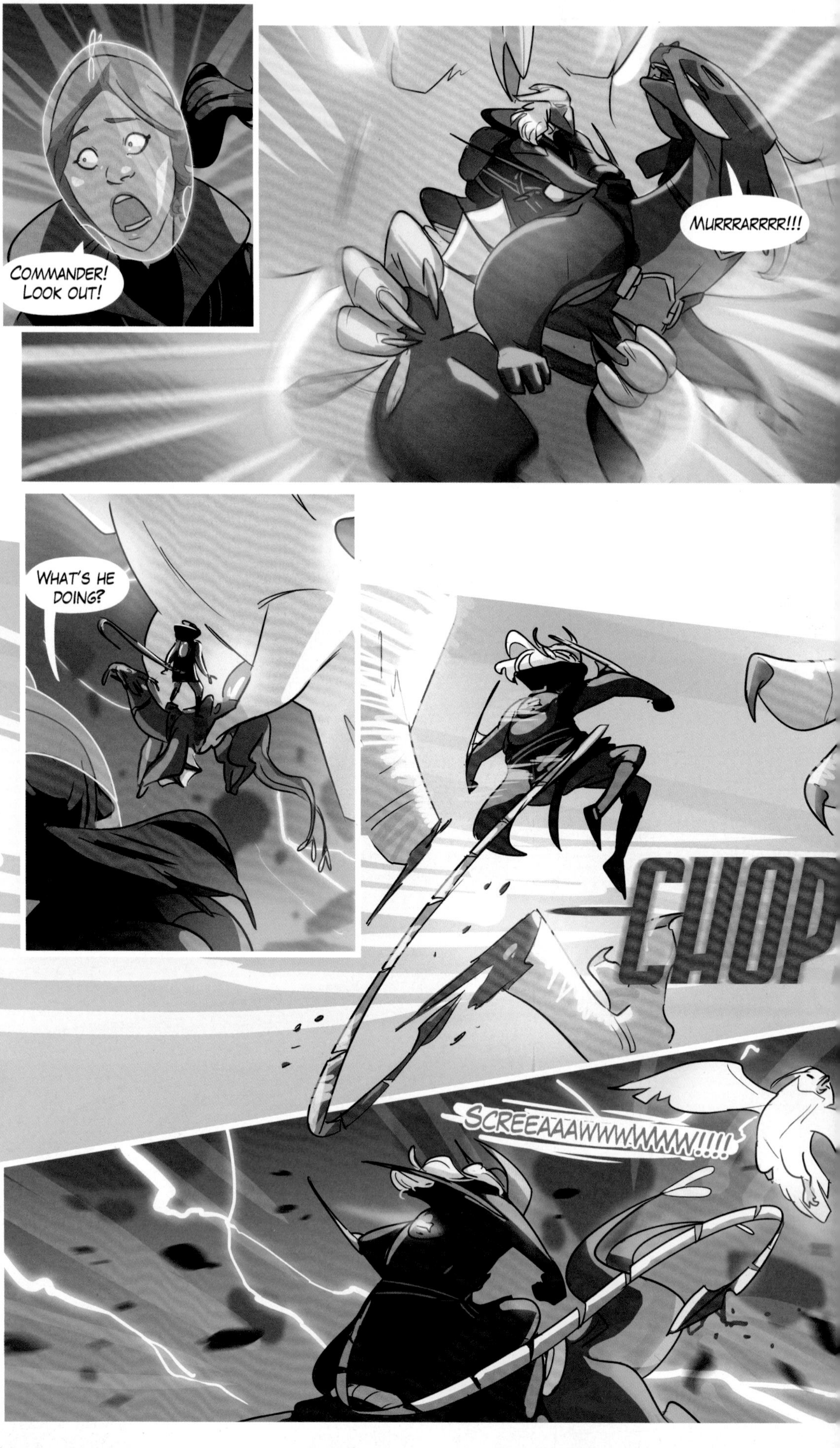
COMMANDER! LOOK OUT!
MURRRARRRR!!!
WHAT'S HE DOING?
CHOP
SCREEAAAWWWWWW!!!!

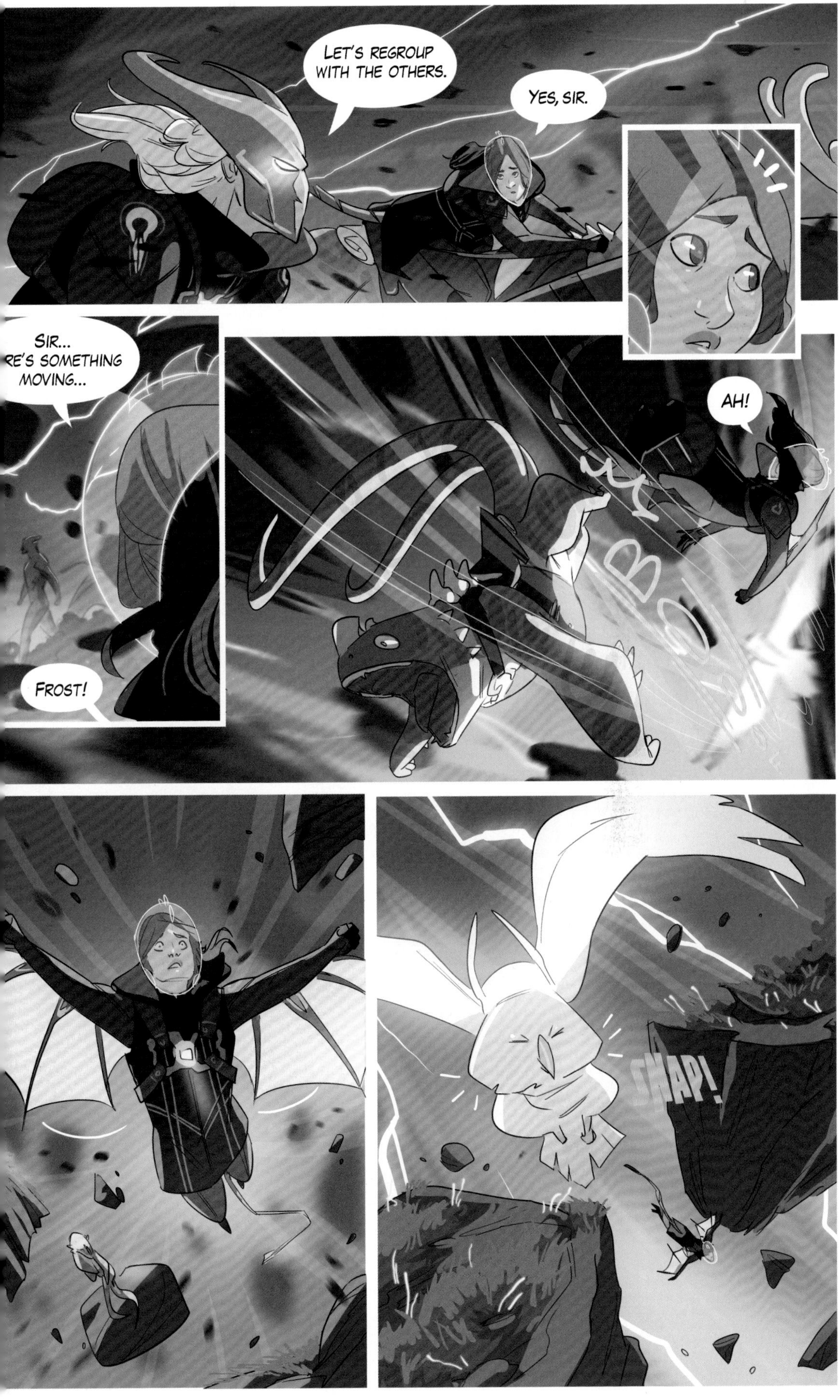
LET'S REGROUP WITH THE OTHERS.
YES, SIR.
SIR... RE'S SOMETHING MOVING...
FROST!
AH!
SNAP!

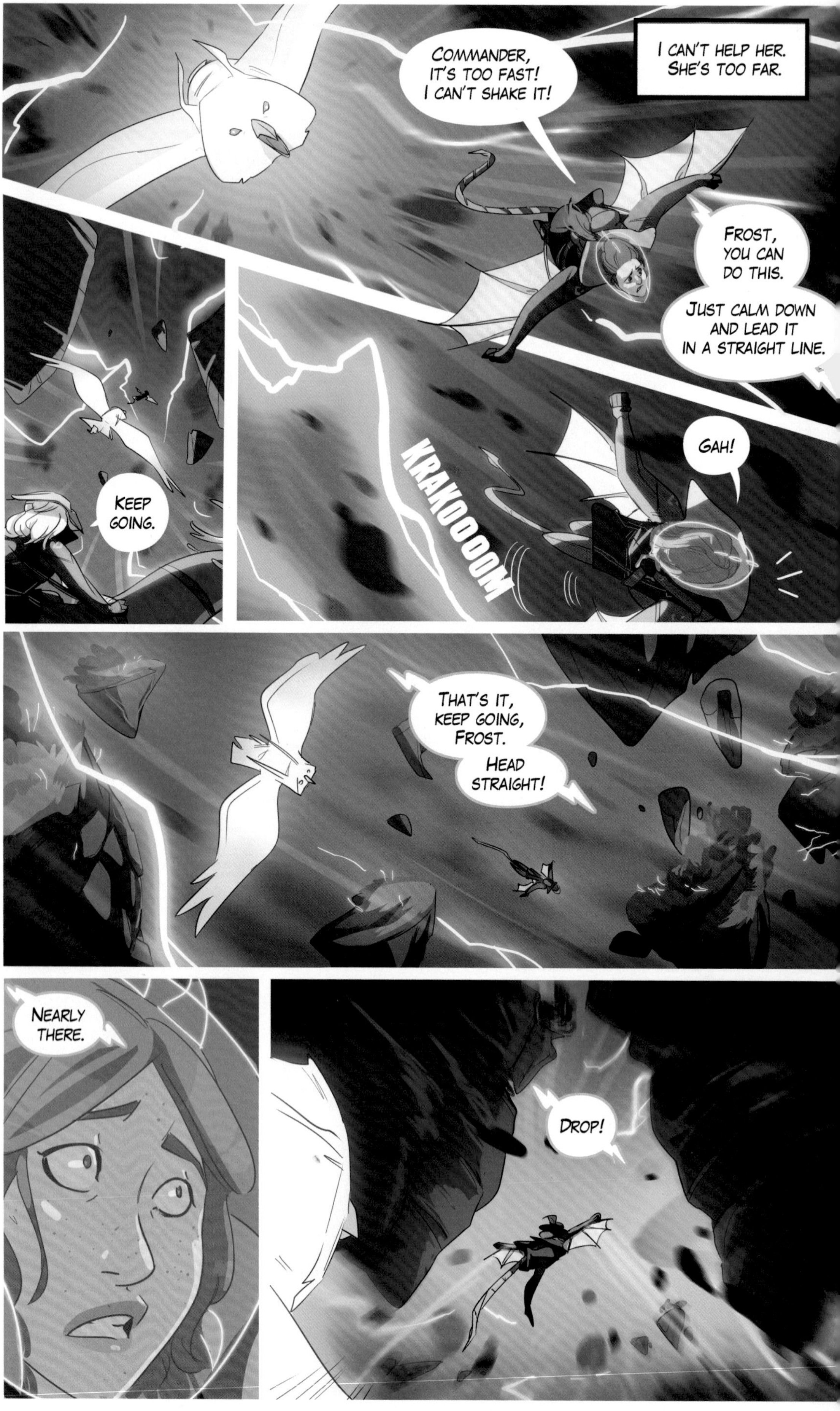
COMMANDER,
IT'S TOO FAST!
I CAN'T SHAKE IT!
I CAN'T HELP HER.
SHE'S TOO FAR.
FROST,
YOU CAN
DO THIS.
JUST CALM DOWN
AND LEAD IT
IN A STRAIGHT LINE.
KEEP
GOING.
KRAKOOOOOM
GAH!
THAT'S IT,
KEEP GOING,
FROST.
HEAD
STRAIGHT!
NEARLY
THERE.
DROP!

DROP?

DO IT NOW, CADET!

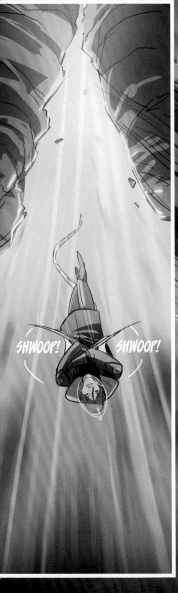

SHWOOP! SHWOOP!

WHA-BOOM!

SCREEEEAAW!!!

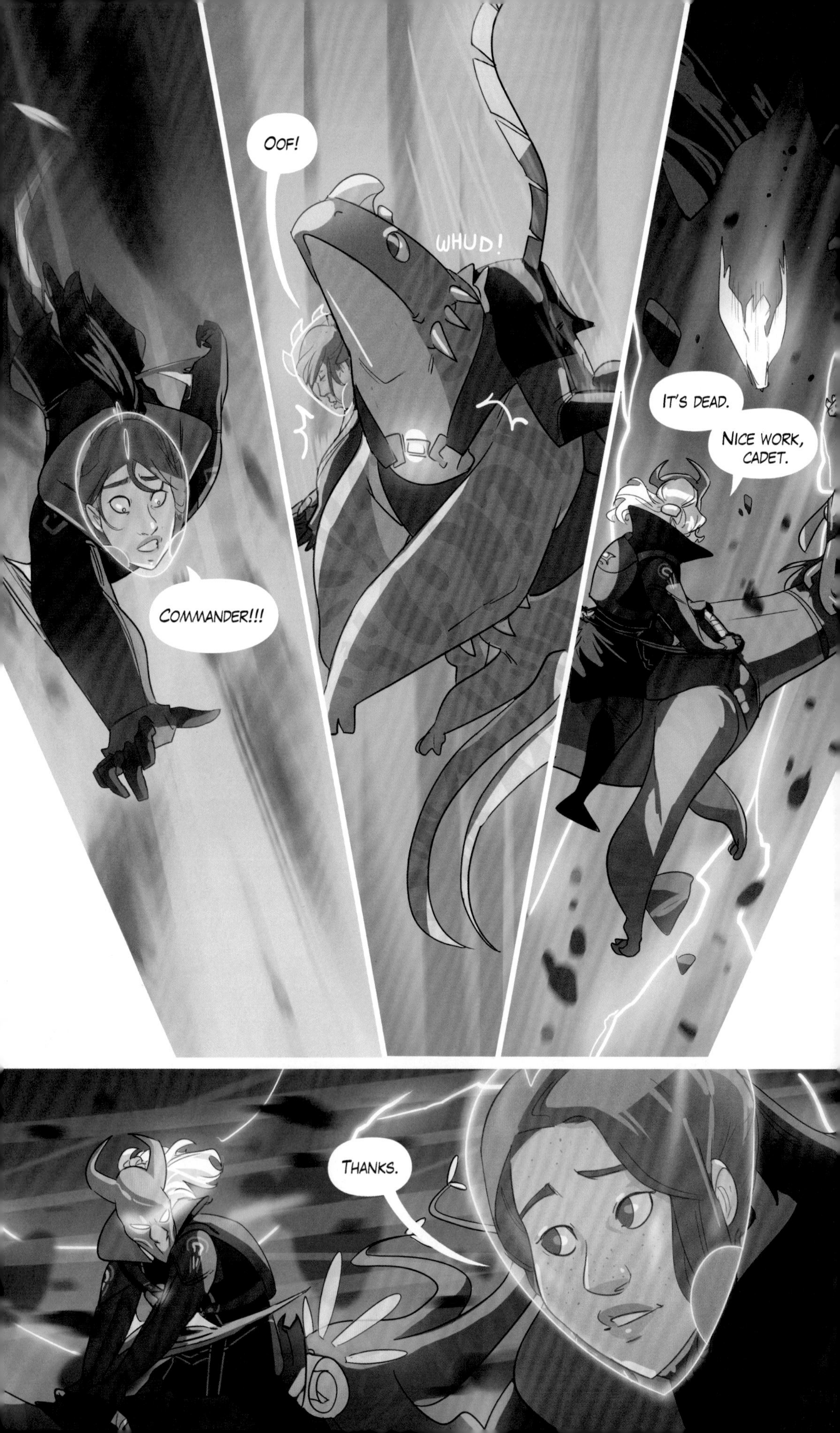
COMMANDER!!!
OOF!
WHUD!
IT'S DEAD.
NICE WORK, CADET.
THANKS.

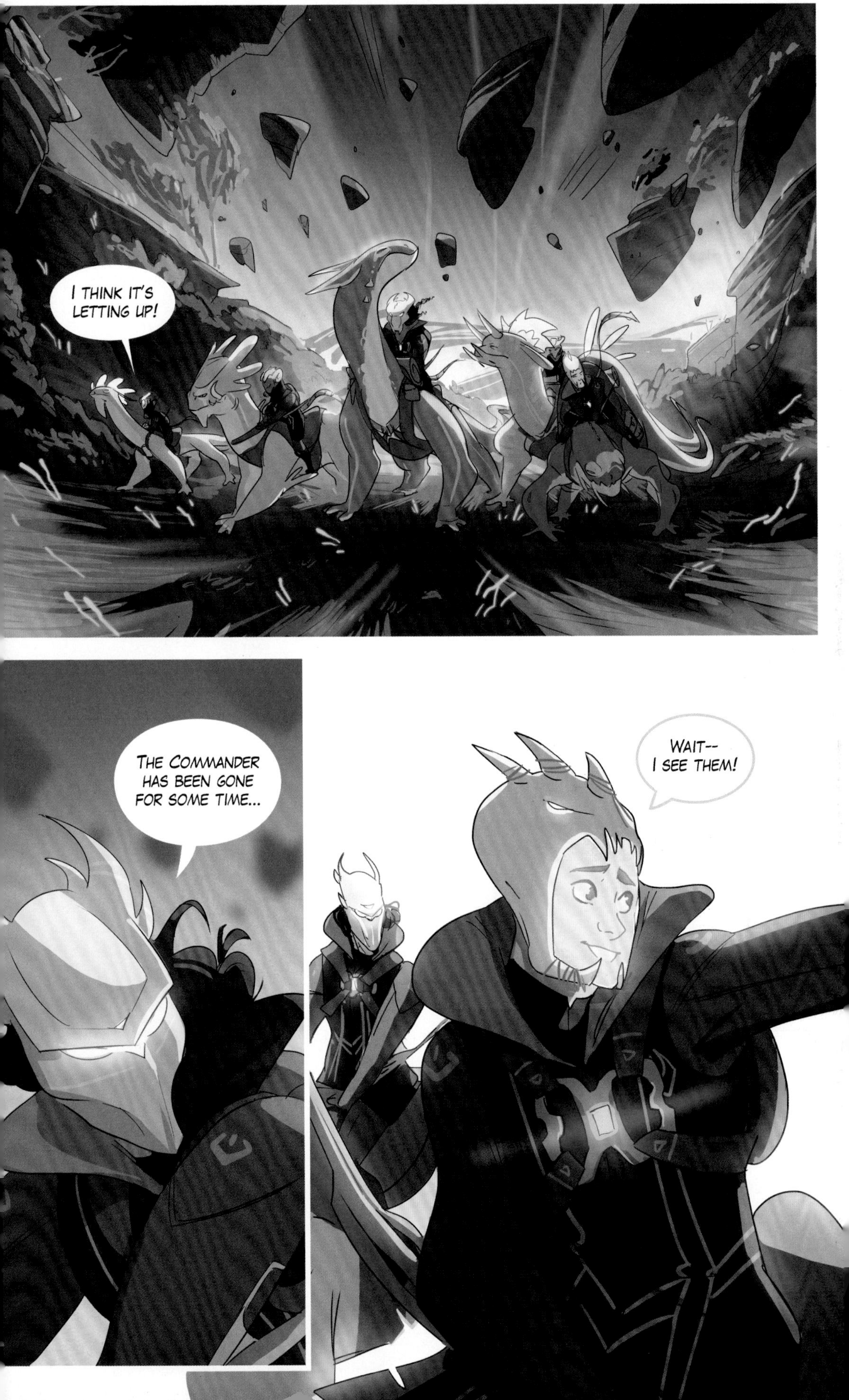
I THINK IT'S LETTING UP!
THE COMMANDER HAS BEEN GONE FOR SOME TIME...
WAIT-- I SEE THEM!

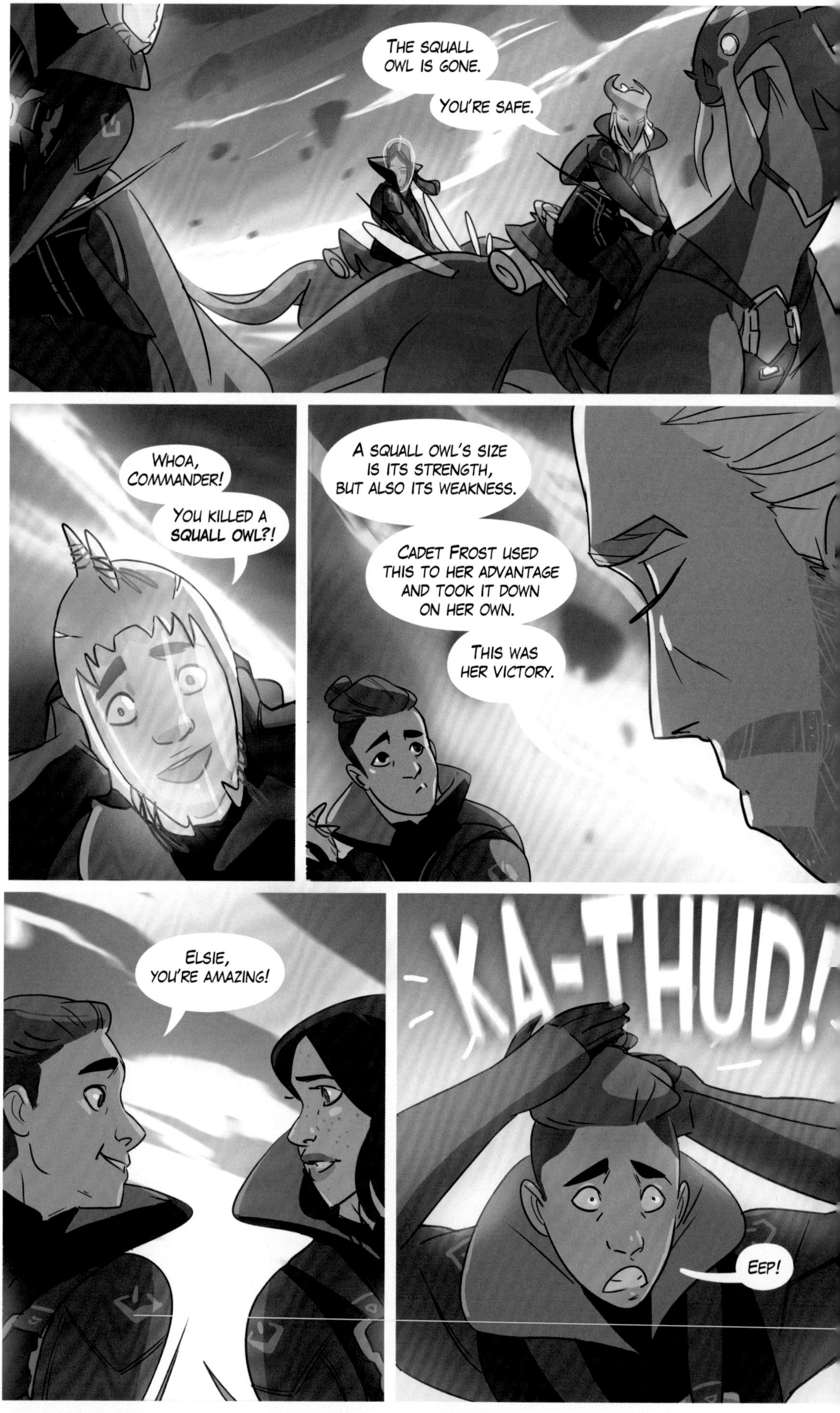
THE SQUALL OWL IS GONE.
YOU'RE SAFE.
WHOA, COMMANDER!
YOU KILLED A SQUALL OWL?!
A SQUALL OWL'S SIZE IS ITS STRENGTH, BUT ALSO ITS WEAKNESS.
CADET FROST USED THIS TO HER ADVANTAGE AND TOOK IT DOWN ON HER OWN.
THIS WAS HER VICTORY.
ELSIE, YOU'RE AMAZING!
KA-THUD!
EEP!

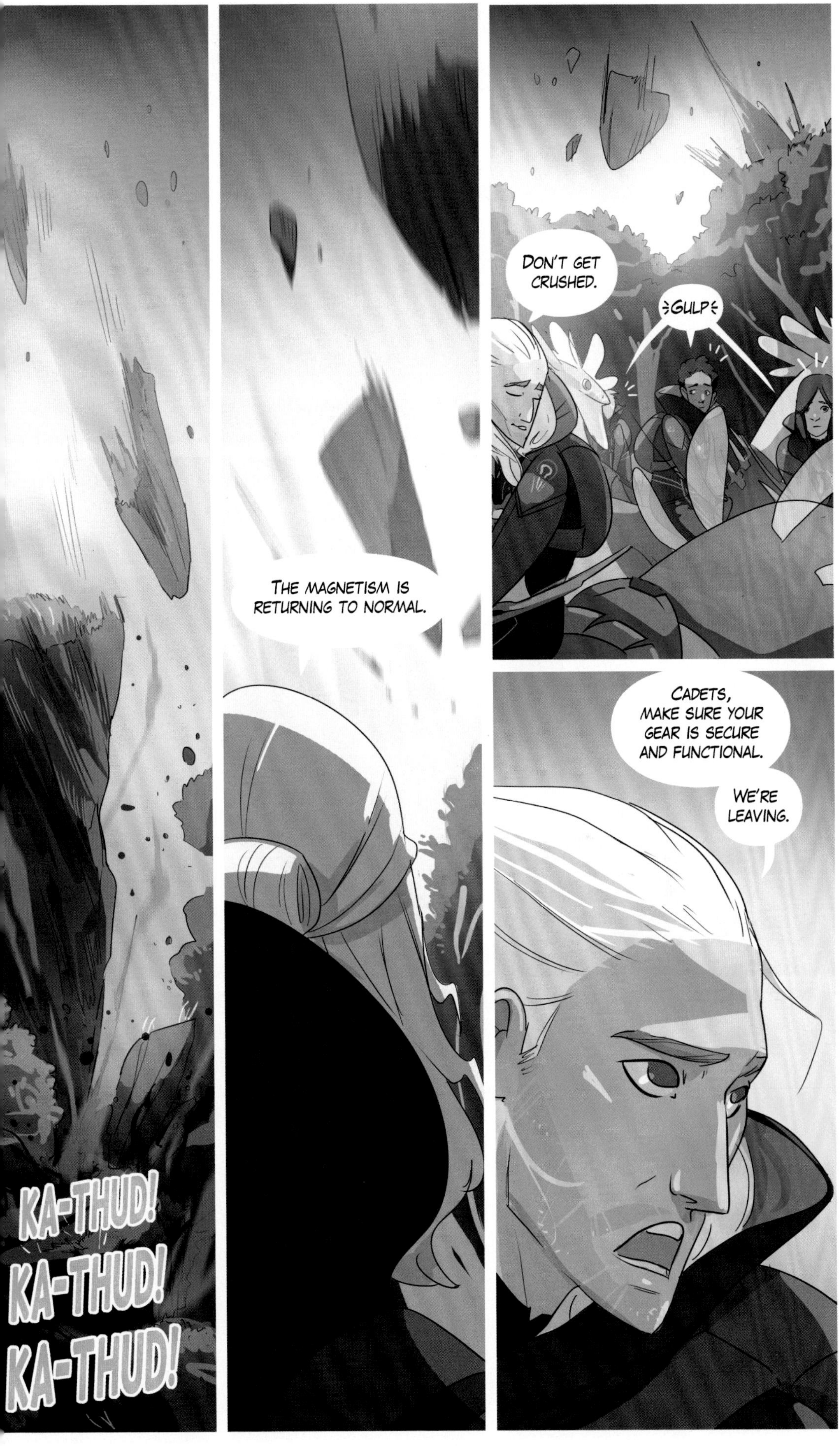
KA-THUD!
KA-THUD!
KA-THUD!
THE MAGNETISM IS RETURNING TO NORMAL.
DON'T GET CRUSHED.
GULP
CADETS, MAKE SURE YOUR GEAR IS SECURE AND FUNCTIONAL.
WE'RE LEAVING.

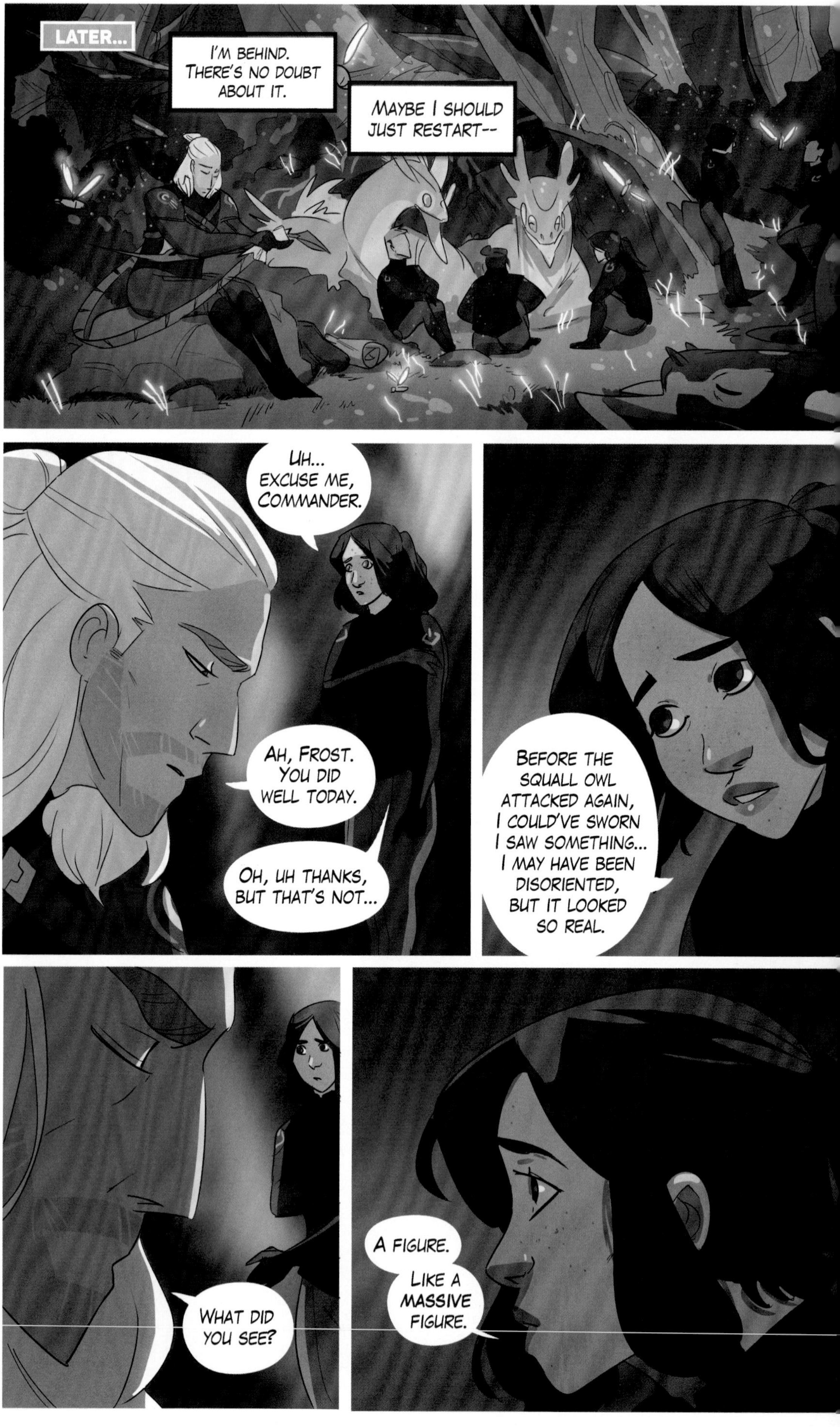
LATER...
I'M BEHIND. THERE'S NO DOUBT ABOUT IT.
MAYBE I SHOULD JUST RESTART--
UH... EXCUSE ME, COMMANDER.
AH, FROST. YOU DID WELL TODAY.
OH, UH THANKS, BUT THAT'S NOT...
BEFORE THE SQUALL OWL ATTACKED AGAIN, I COULD'VE SWORN I SAW SOMETHING... I MAY HAVE BEEN DISORIENTED, BUT IT LOOKED SO REAL.
WHAT DID YOU SEE?
A FIGURE.
LIKE A MASSIVE FIGURE.

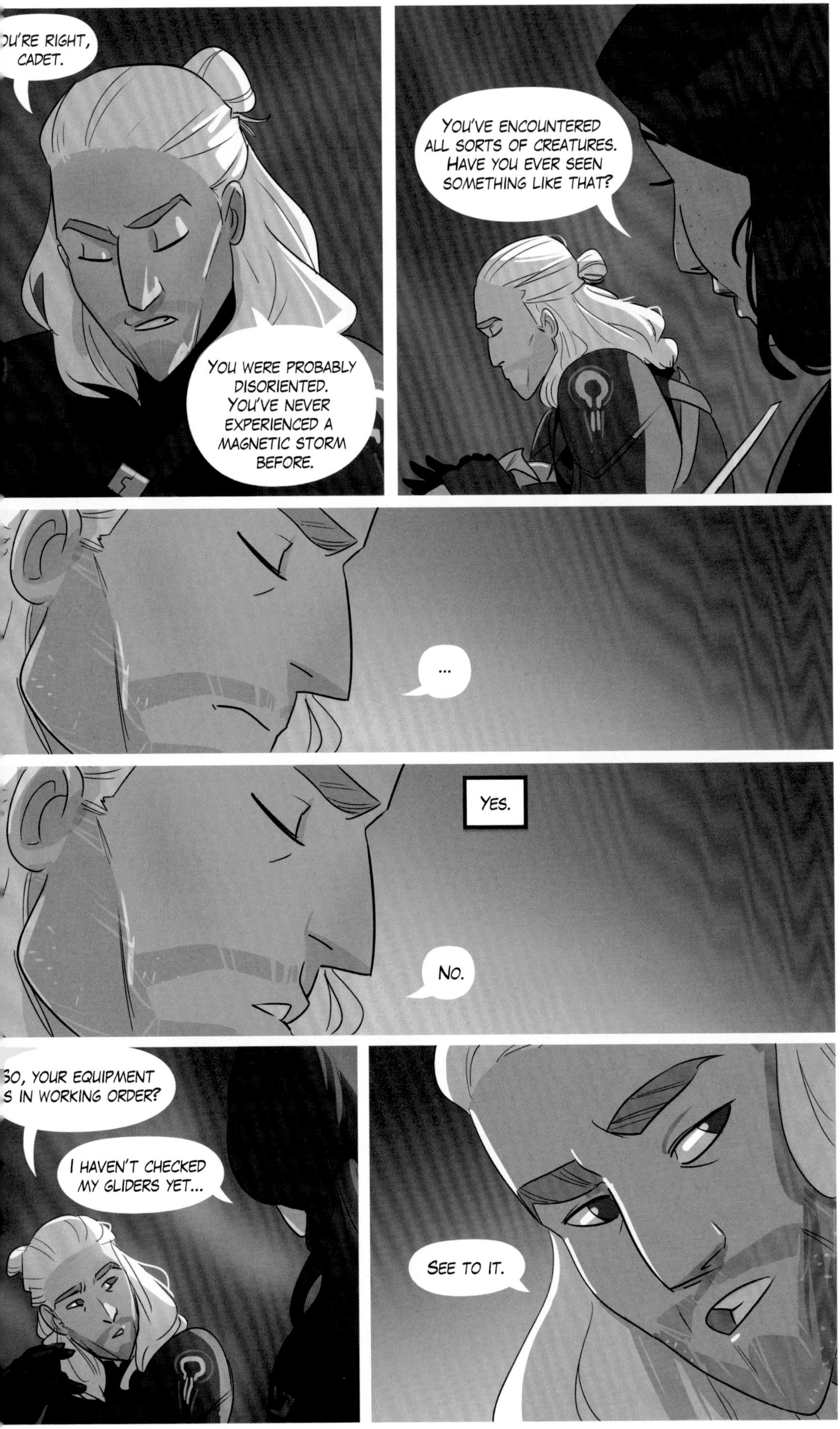

OU'RE RIGHT, CADET.
YOU WERE PROBABLY DISORIENTED. YOU'VE NEVER EXPERIENCED A MAGNETIC STORM BEFORE.
YOU'VE ENCOUNTERED ALL SORTS OF CREATURES. HAVE YOU EVER SEEN SOMETHING LIKE THAT?
...
YES.
NO.
SO, YOUR EQUIPMENT S IN WORKING ORDER?
I HAVEN'T CHECKED MY GLIDERS YET...
SEE TO IT.

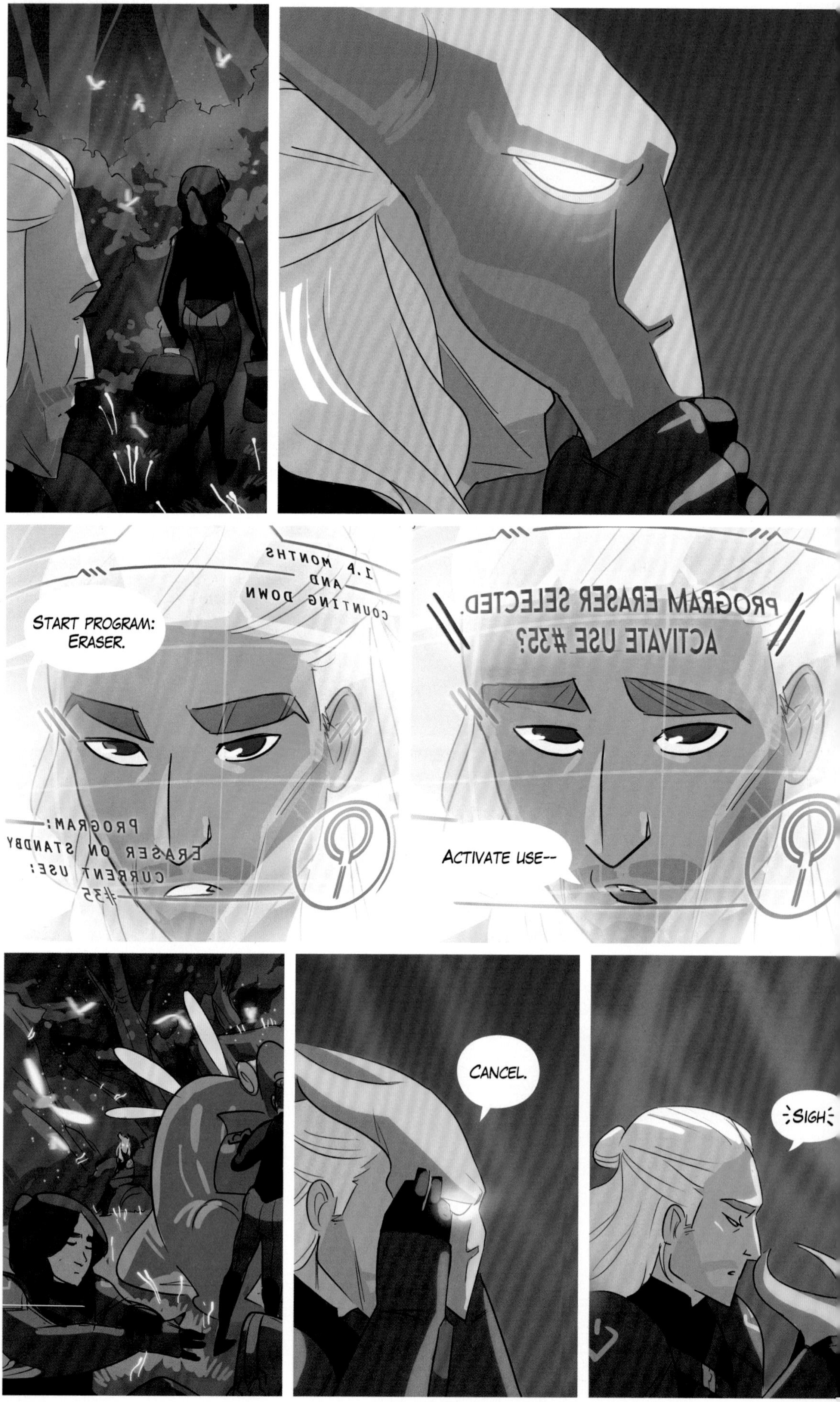
1.4 MONTHS
AND
COUNTING DOWN
START PROGRAM: ERASER.
PROGRAM:
ERASER ON STANDBY
CURRENT USE:
#35
PROGRAM ERASER SELECTED.
ACTIVATE USE #35?
ACTIVATE USE--
CANCEL.
SIGH

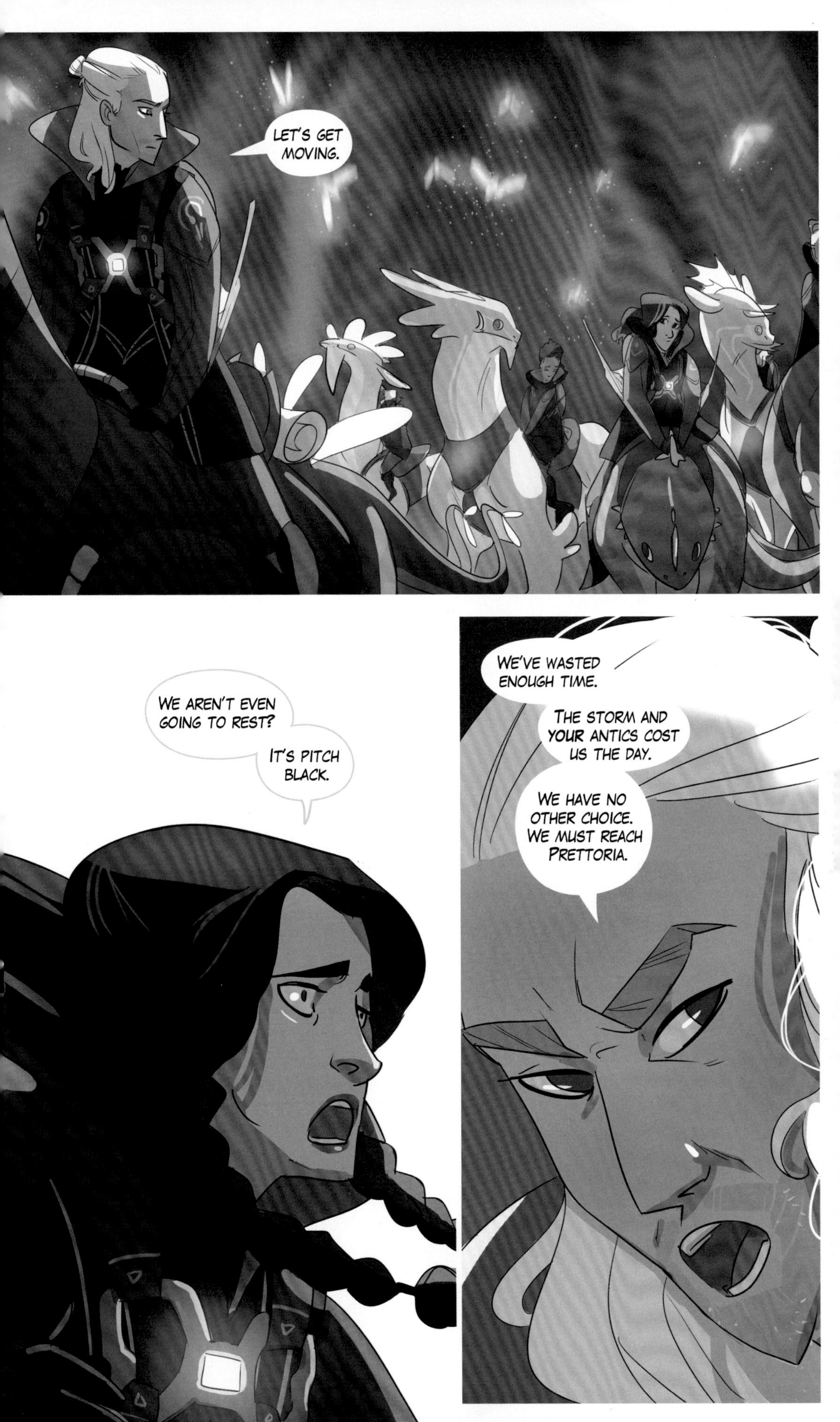
LET'S GET MOVING.
WE AREN'T EVEN GOING TO REST?
IT'S PITCH BLACK.
WE'VE WASTED ENOUGH TIME.
THE STORM AND YOUR ANTICS COST US THE DAY.
WE HAVE NO OTHER CHOICE. WE MUST REACH PRETTORIA.

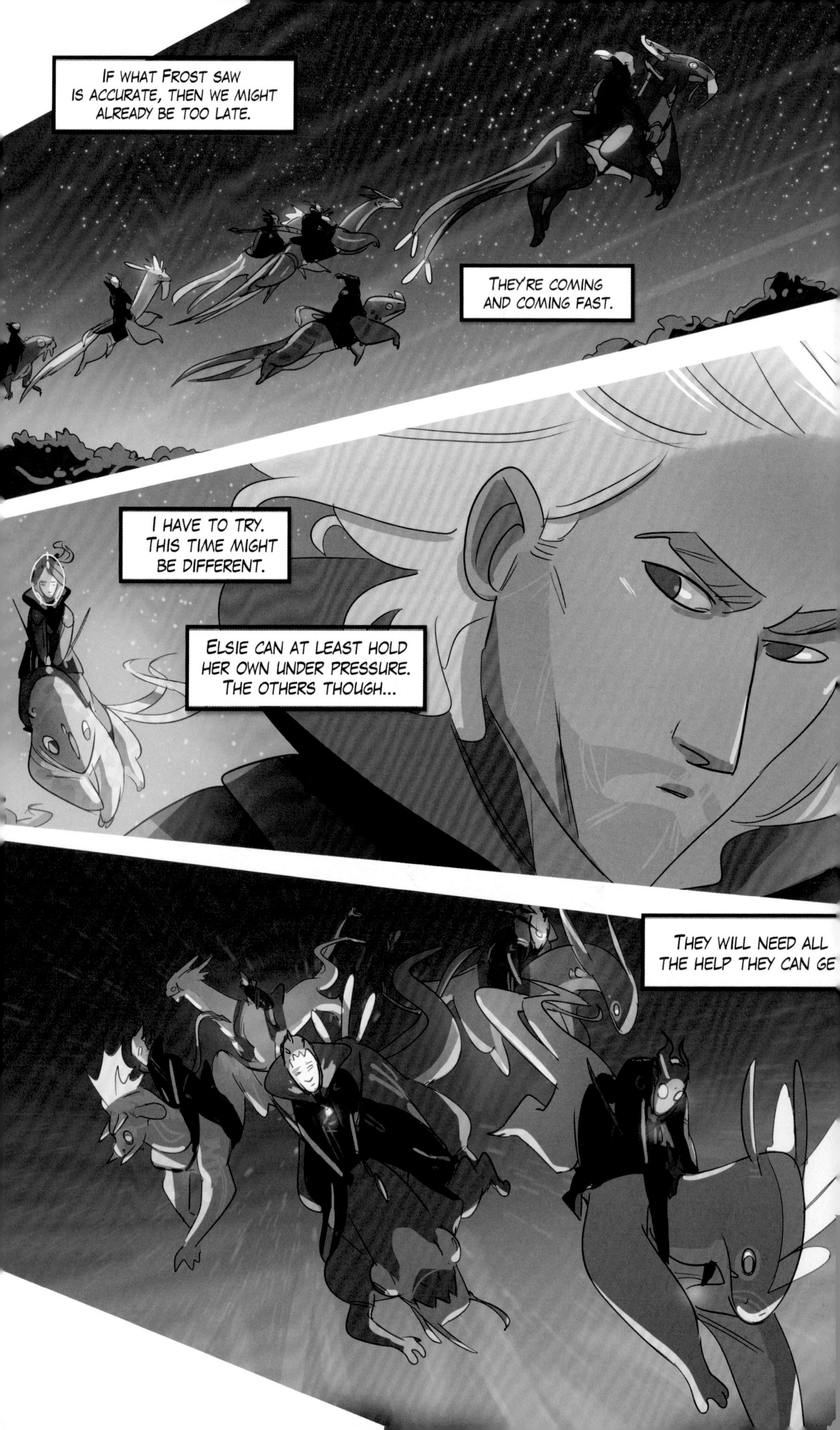
IF WHAT FROST SAW IS ACCURATE, THEN WE MIGHT ALREADY BE TOO LATE.
THEY'RE COMING AND COMING FAST.
I HAVE TO TRY. THIS TIME MIGHT BE DIFFERENT.
ELSIE CAN AT LEAST HOLD HER OWN UNDER PRESSURE. THE OTHERS THOUGH...
THEY WILL NEED ALL THE HELP THEY CAN GE

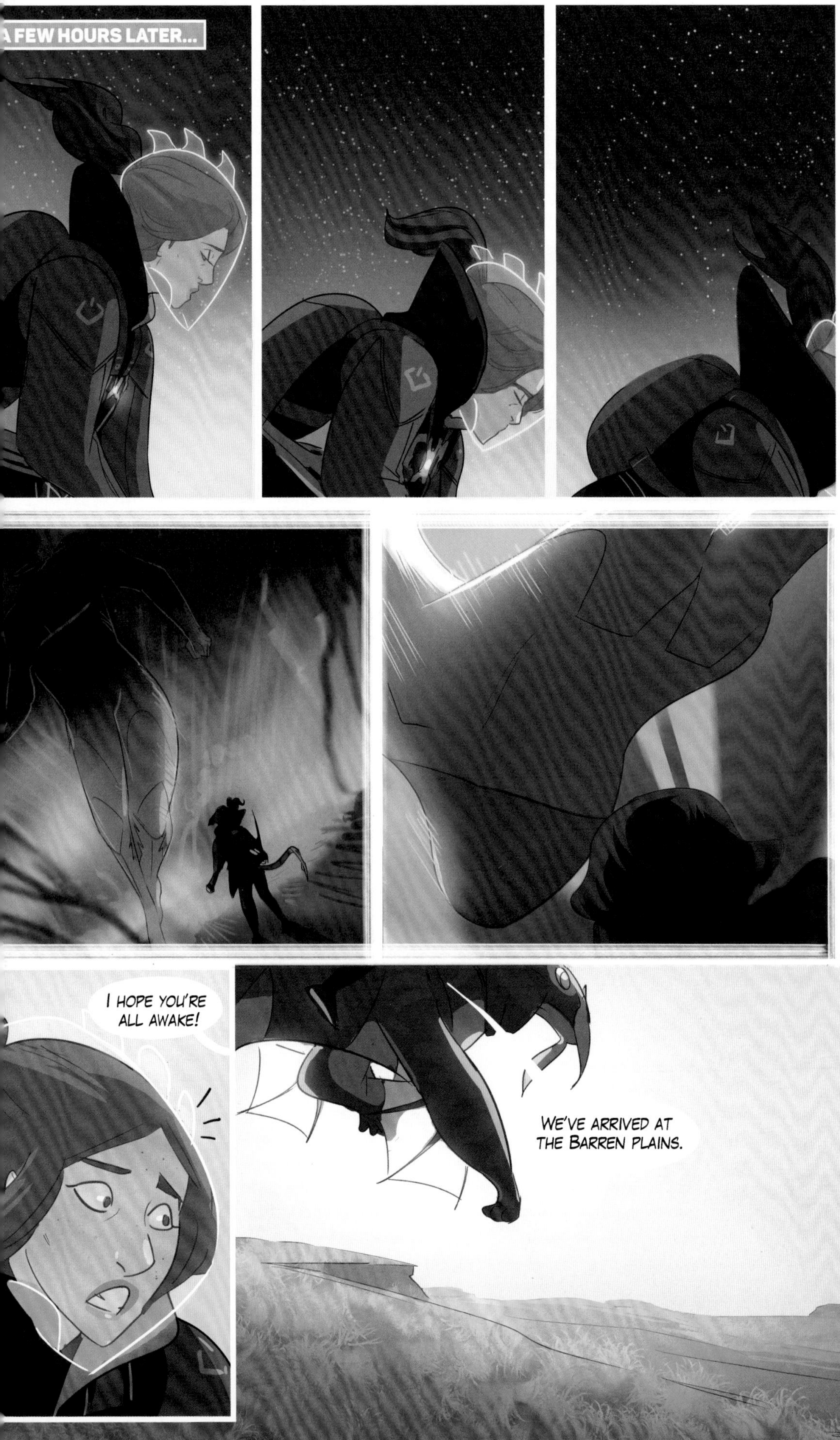
A FEW HOURS LATER...
I HOPE YOU'RE ALL AWAKE!
WE'VE ARRIVED AT THE BARREN PLAINS.

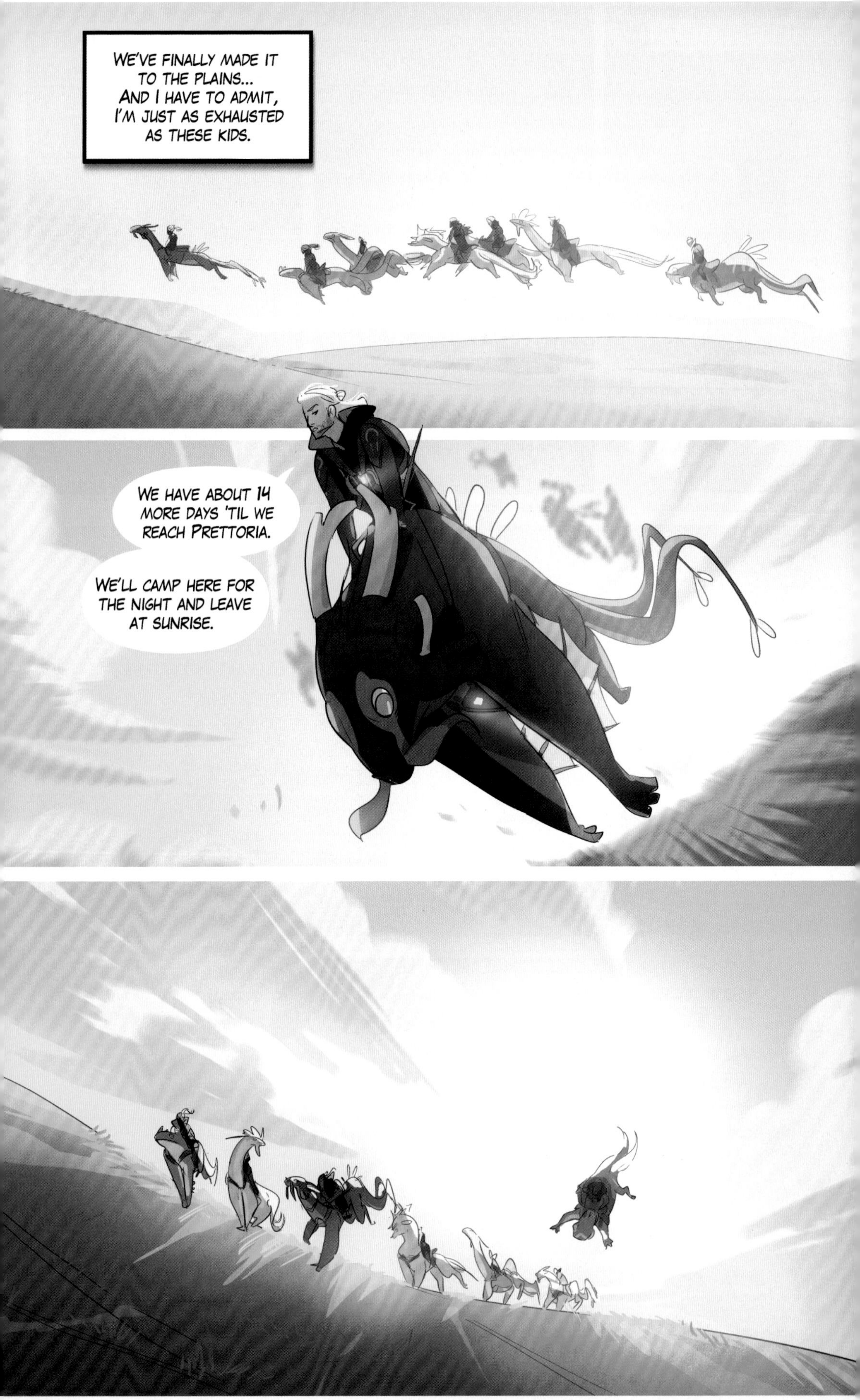
WE'VE FINALLY MADE IT TO THE PLAINS... AND I HAVE TO ADMIT, I'M JUST AS EXHAUSTED AS THESE KIDS.
WE HAVE ABOUT 14 MORE DAYS 'TIL WE REACH PRETTORIA.
WE'LL CAMP HERE FOR THE NIGHT AND LEAVE AT SUNRISE.

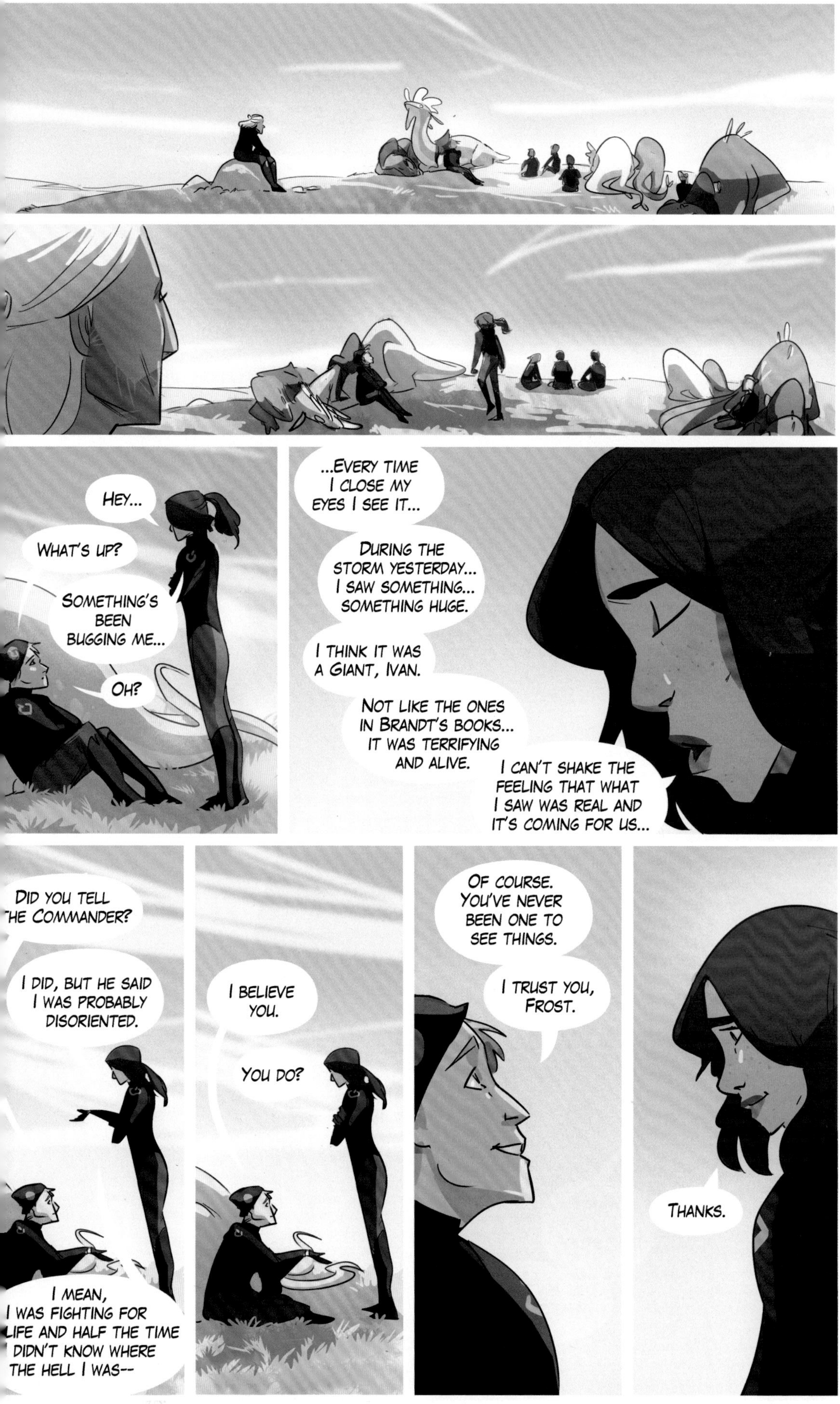
HEY...
WHAT'S UP?
SOMETHING'S BEEN BUGGING ME...
OH?
...EVERY TIME I CLOSE MY EYES I SEE IT...
DURING THE STORM YESTERDAY... I SAW SOMETHING... SOMETHING HUGE.
I THINK IT WAS A GIANT, IVAN.
NOT LIKE THE ONES IN BRANDT'S BOOKS... IT WAS TERRIFYING AND ALIVE.
I CAN'T SHAKE THE FEELING THAT WHAT I SAW WAS REAL AND IT'S COMING FOR US...
DID YOU TELL THE COMMANDER?
I DID, BUT HE SAID I WAS PROBABLY DISORIENTED.
I MEAN, I WAS FIGHTING FOR LIFE AND HALF THE TIME I DIDN'T KNOW WHERE THE HELL I WAS--
I BELIEVE YOU.
YOU DO?
OF COURSE. YOU'VE NEVER BEEN ONE TO SEE THINGS.
I TRUST YOU, FROST.
THANKS.

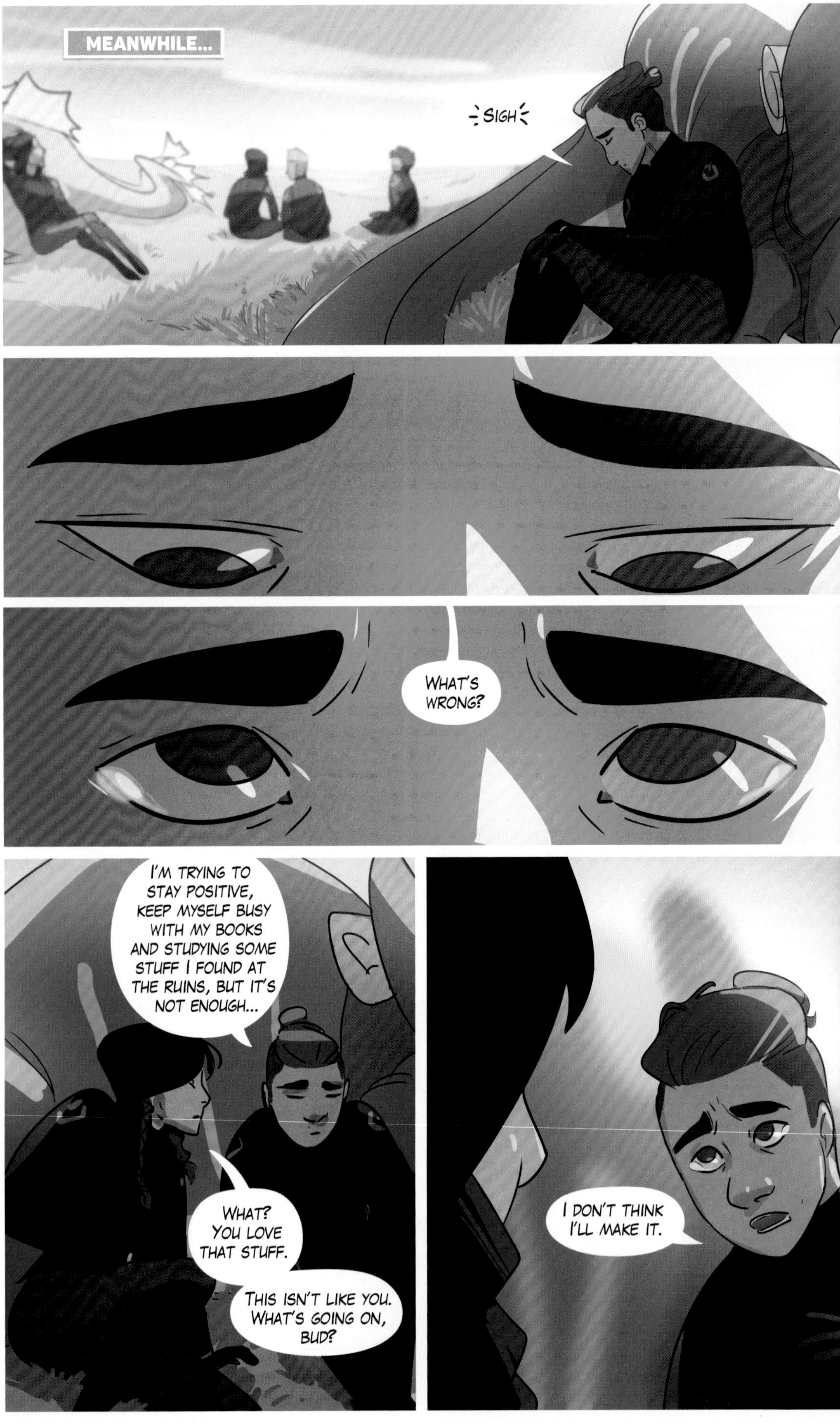
MEANWHILE...
SIGH
WHAT'S WRONG?
I'M TRYING TO STAY POSITIVE, KEEP MYSELF BUSY WITH MY BOOKS AND STUDYING SOME STUFF I FOUND AT THE RUINS, BUT IT'S NOT ENOUGH...
WHAT? YOU LOVE THAT STUFF.
THIS ISN'T LIKE YOU. WHAT'S GOING ON, BUD?
I DON'T THINK I'LL MAKE IT.

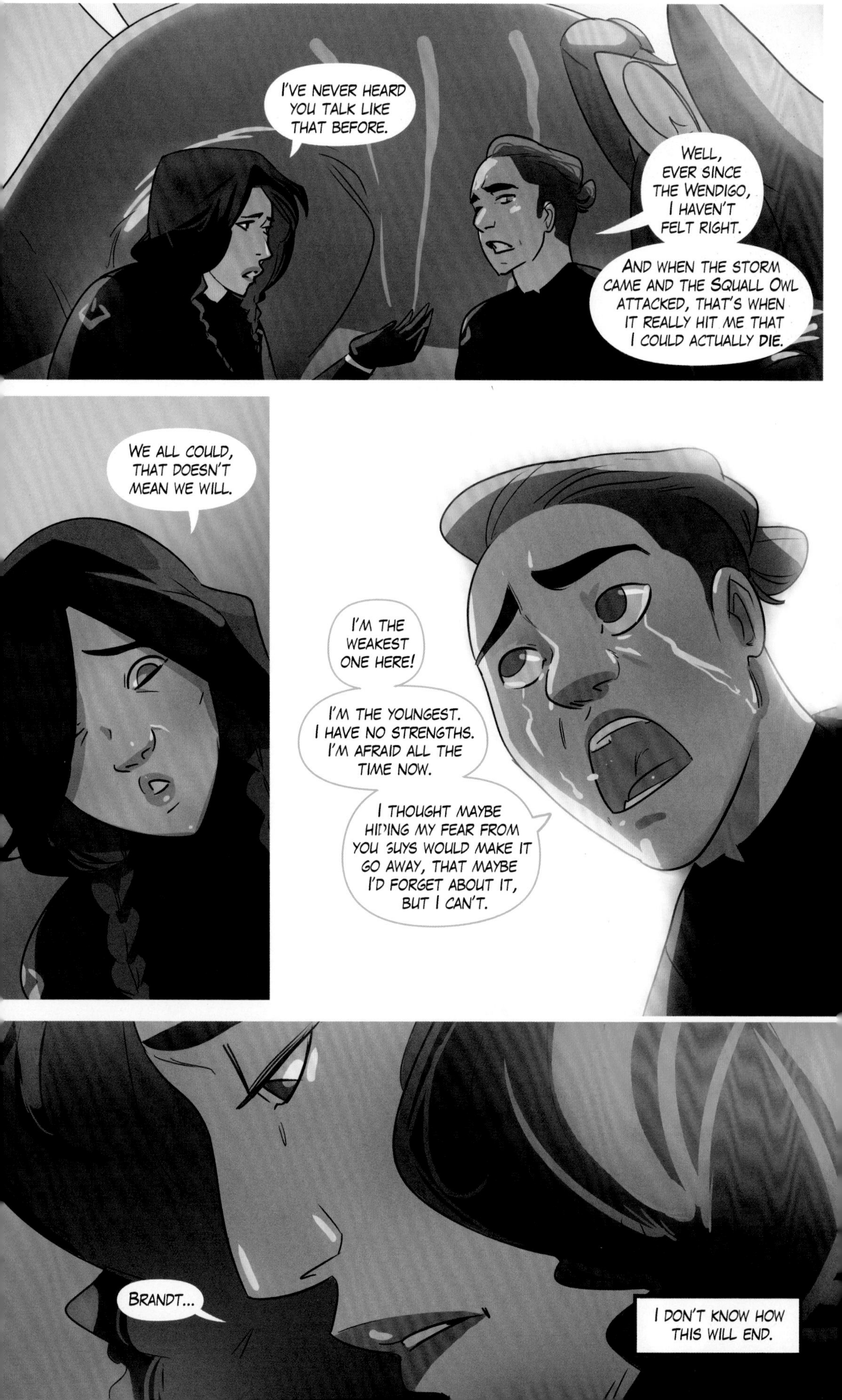
I'VE NEVER HEARD YOU TALK LIKE THAT BEFORE.
WELL, EVER SINCE THE WENDIGO, I HAVEN'T FELT RIGHT.
AND WHEN THE STORM CAME AND THE SQUALL OWL ATTACKED, THAT'S WHEN IT REALLY HIT ME THAT I COULD ACTUALLY **DIE**.
WE ALL COULD, THAT DOESN'T MEAN WE WILL.
I'M THE WEAKEST ONE HERE!
I'M THE YOUNGEST. I HAVE NO STRENGTHS. I'M AFRAID ALL THE TIME NOW.
I THOUGHT MAYBE HIDING MY FEAR FROM YOU GUYS WOULD MAKE IT GO AWAY, THAT MAYBE I'D FORGET ABOUT IT, BUT I CAN'T.
BRANDT...
I DON'T KNOW HOW THIS WILL END.

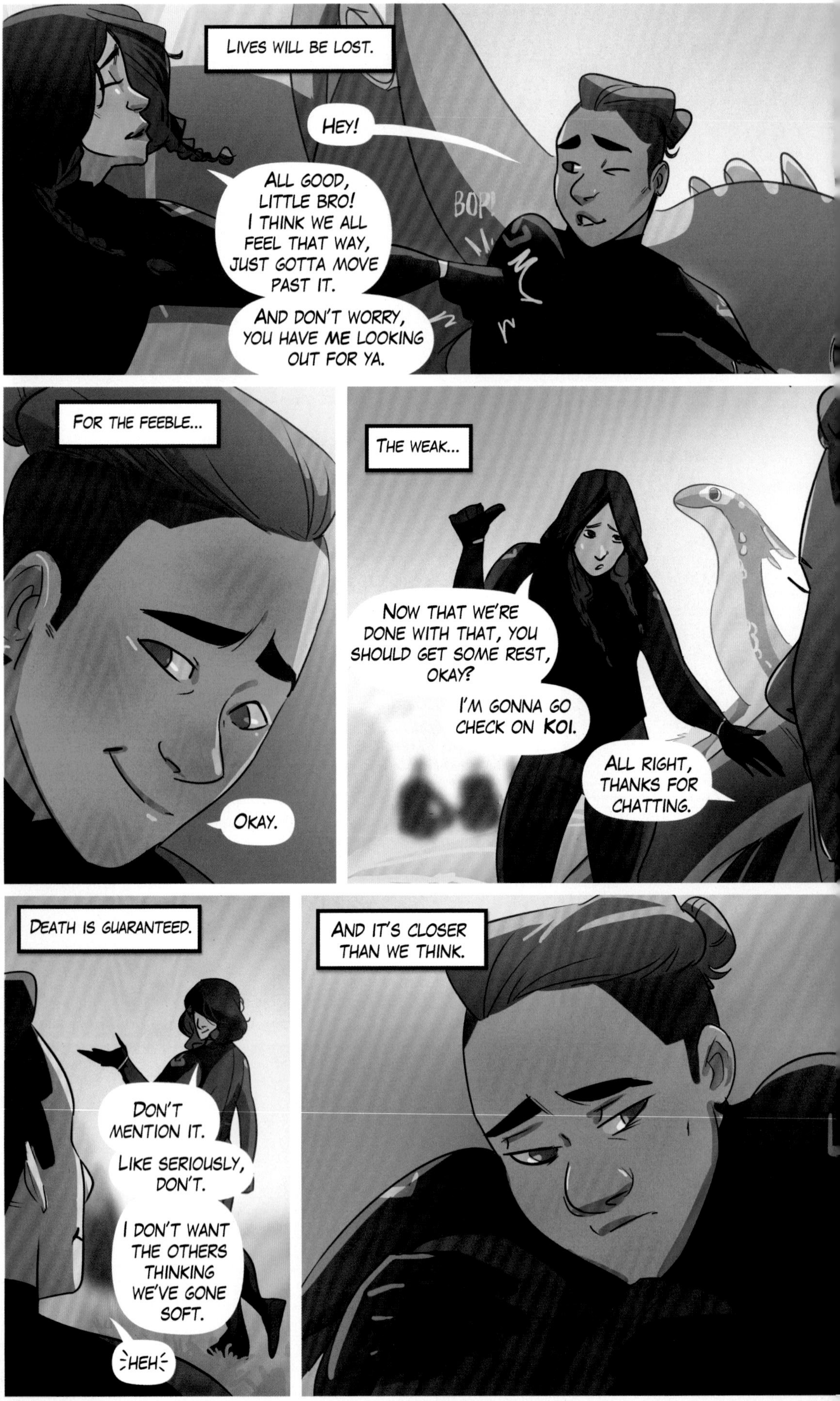
LIVES WILL BE LOST.
HEY!
ALL GOOD, LITTLE BRO! I THINK WE ALL FEEL THAT WAY, JUST GOTTA MOVE PAST IT.
BOP!
AND DON'T WORRY, YOU HAVE ME LOOKING OUT FOR YA.
FOR THE FEEBLE...
OKAY.
THE WEAK...
NOW THAT WE'RE DONE WITH THAT, YOU SHOULD GET SOME REST, OKAY?
I'M GONNA GO CHECK ON KOI.
ALL RIGHT, THANKS FOR CHATTING.
DEATH IS GUARANTEED.
DON'T MENTION IT.
LIKE SERIOUSLY, DON'T.
I DON'T WANT THE OTHERS THINKING WE'VE GONE SOFT.
HEH
AND IT'S CLOSER THAN WE THINK.

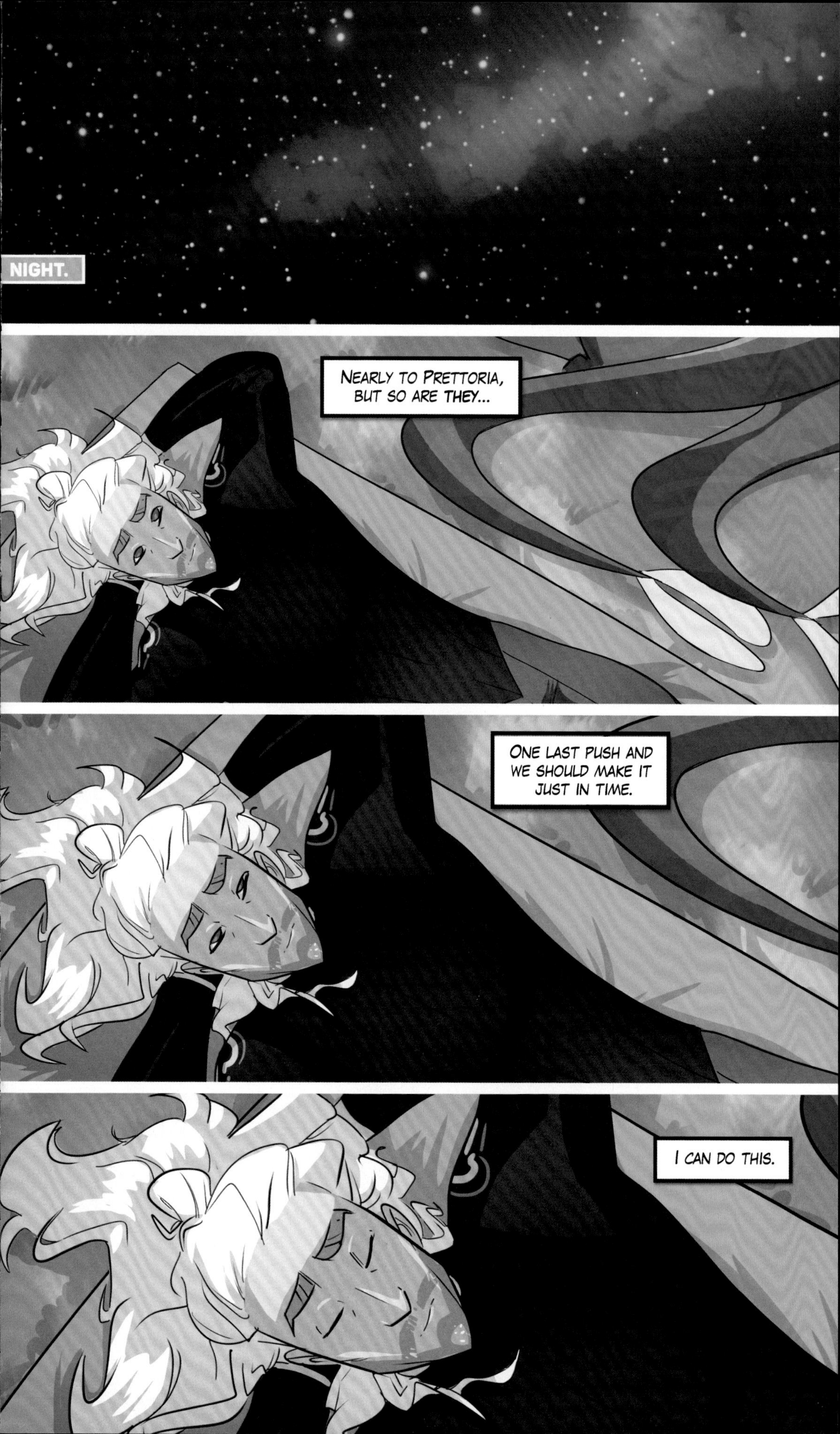
NIGHT.
NEARLY TO PRETTORIA, BUT SO ARE THEY...
ONE LAST PUSH AND WE SHOULD MAKE IT JUST IN TIME.
I CAN DO THIS.

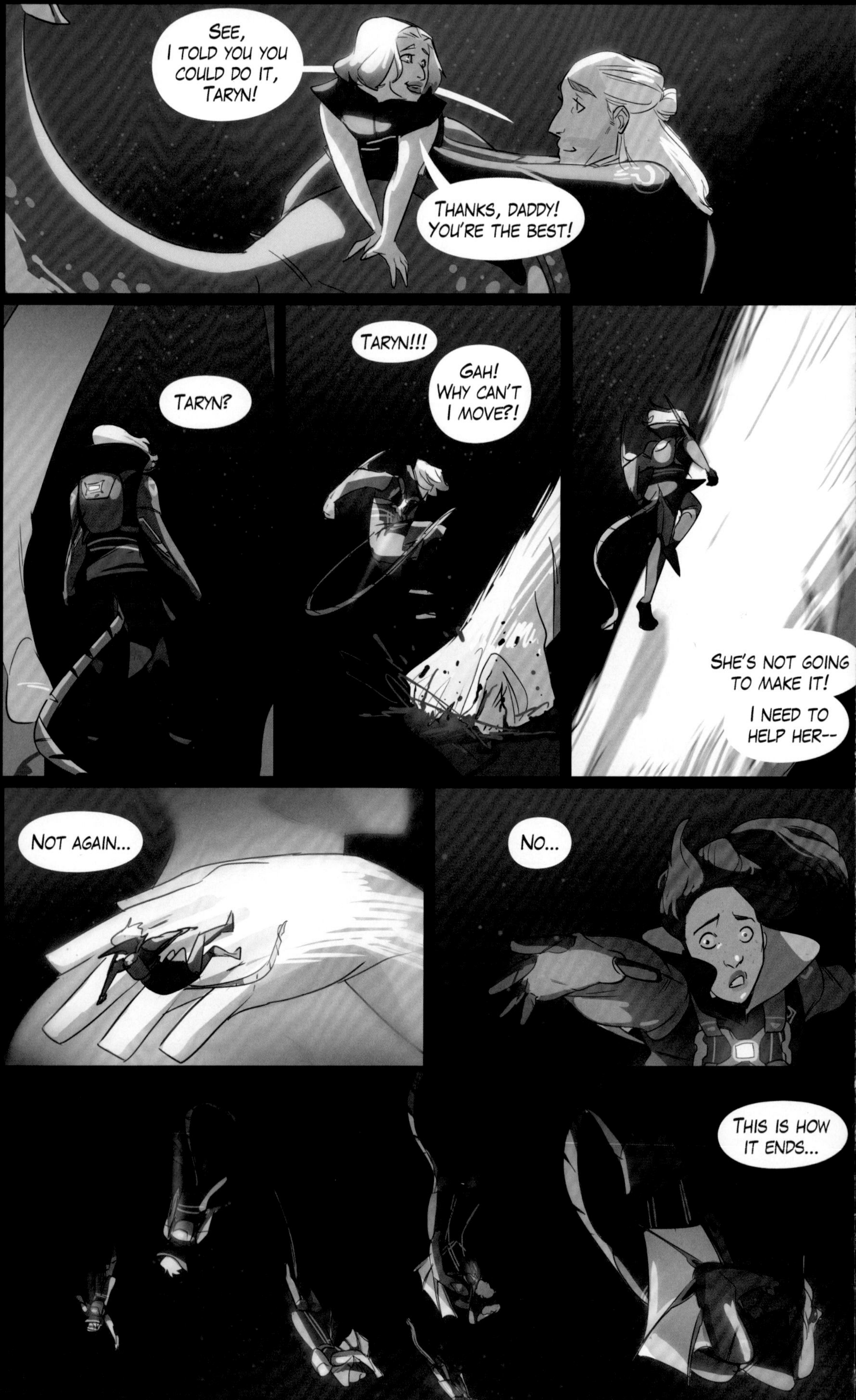

SEE, I TOLD YOU YOU COULD DO IT, TARYN!
THANKS, DADDY! YOU'RE THE BEST!
TARYN?
TARYN!!!
GAH! WHY CAN'T I MOVE?!
SHE'S NOT GOING TO MAKE IT!
I NEED TO HELP HER--
NOT AGAIN...
NO...
THIS IS HOW IT ENDS...

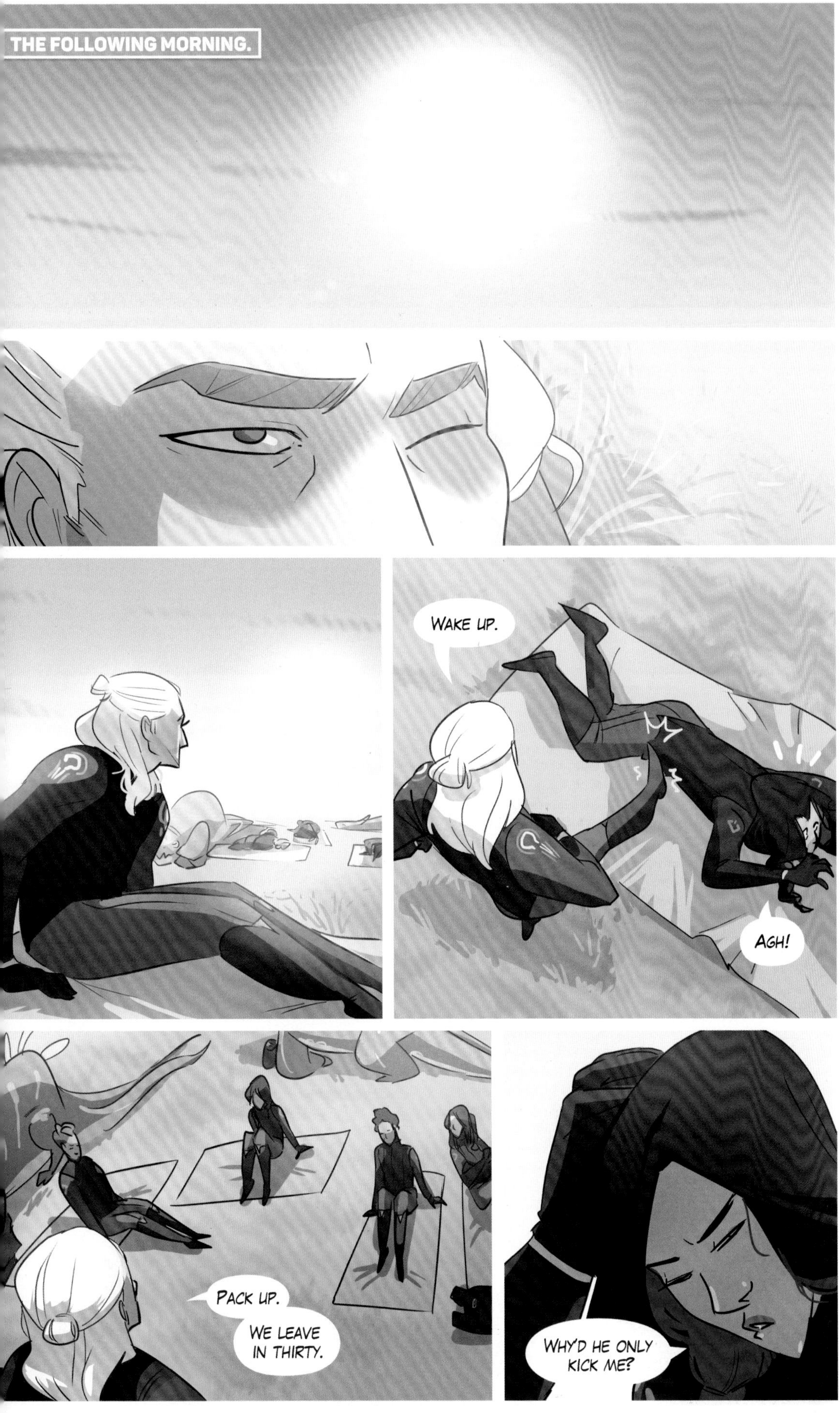
THE FOLLOWING MORNING.
WAKE UP.
AGH!
PACK UP.
WE LEAVE IN THIRTY.
WHY'D HE ONLY KICK ME?

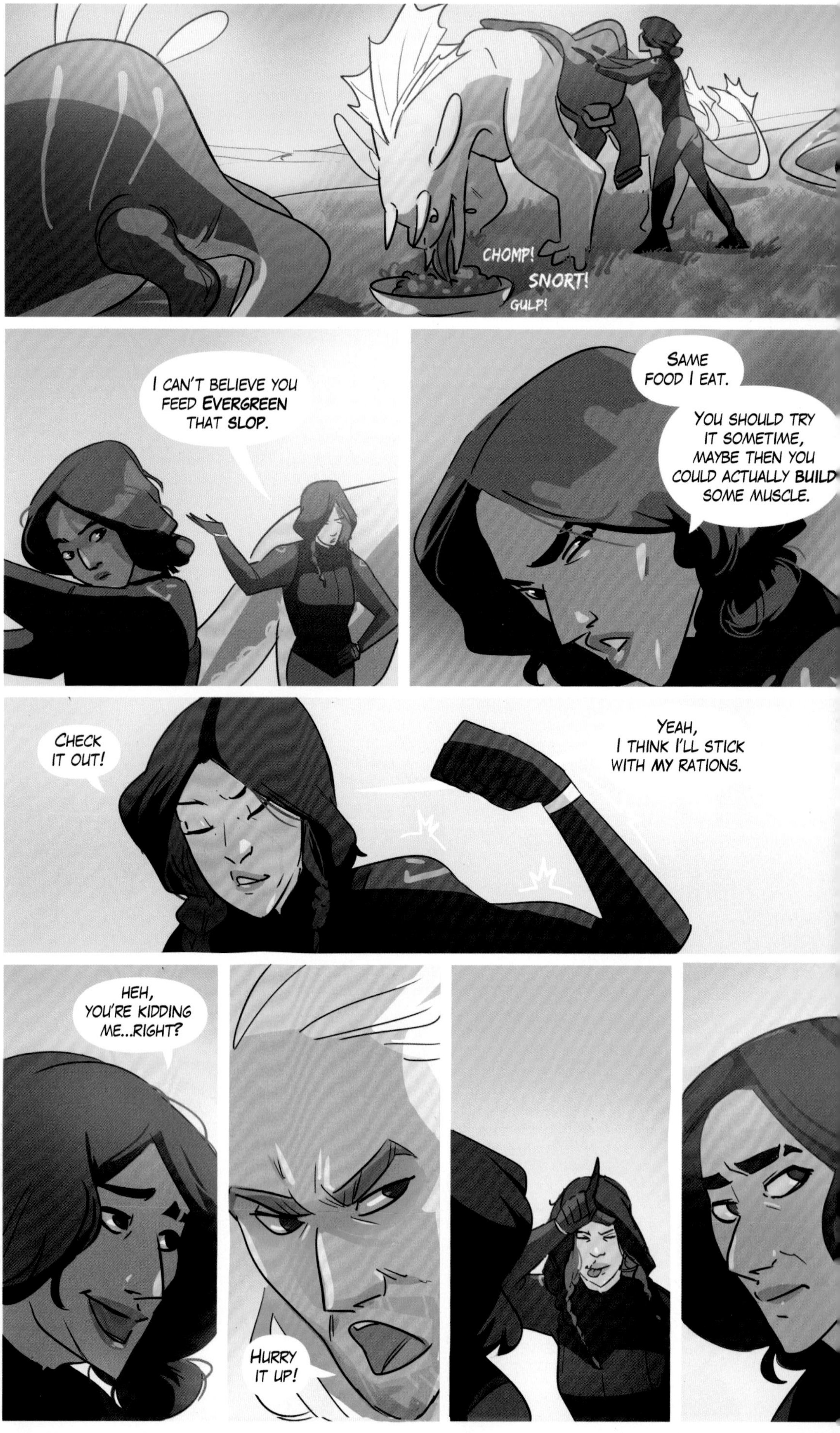
CHOMP!
SNORT!
GULP!
I CAN'T BELIEVE YOU FEED EVERGREEN THAT SLOP.
SAME FOOD I EAT.
YOU SHOULD TRY IT SOMETIME, MAYBE THEN YOU COULD ACTUALLY BUILD SOME MUSCLE.
CHECK IT OUT!
YEAH, I THINK I'LL STICK WITH MY RATIONS.
HEH, YOU'RE KIDDING ME...RIGHT?
HURRY IT UP!

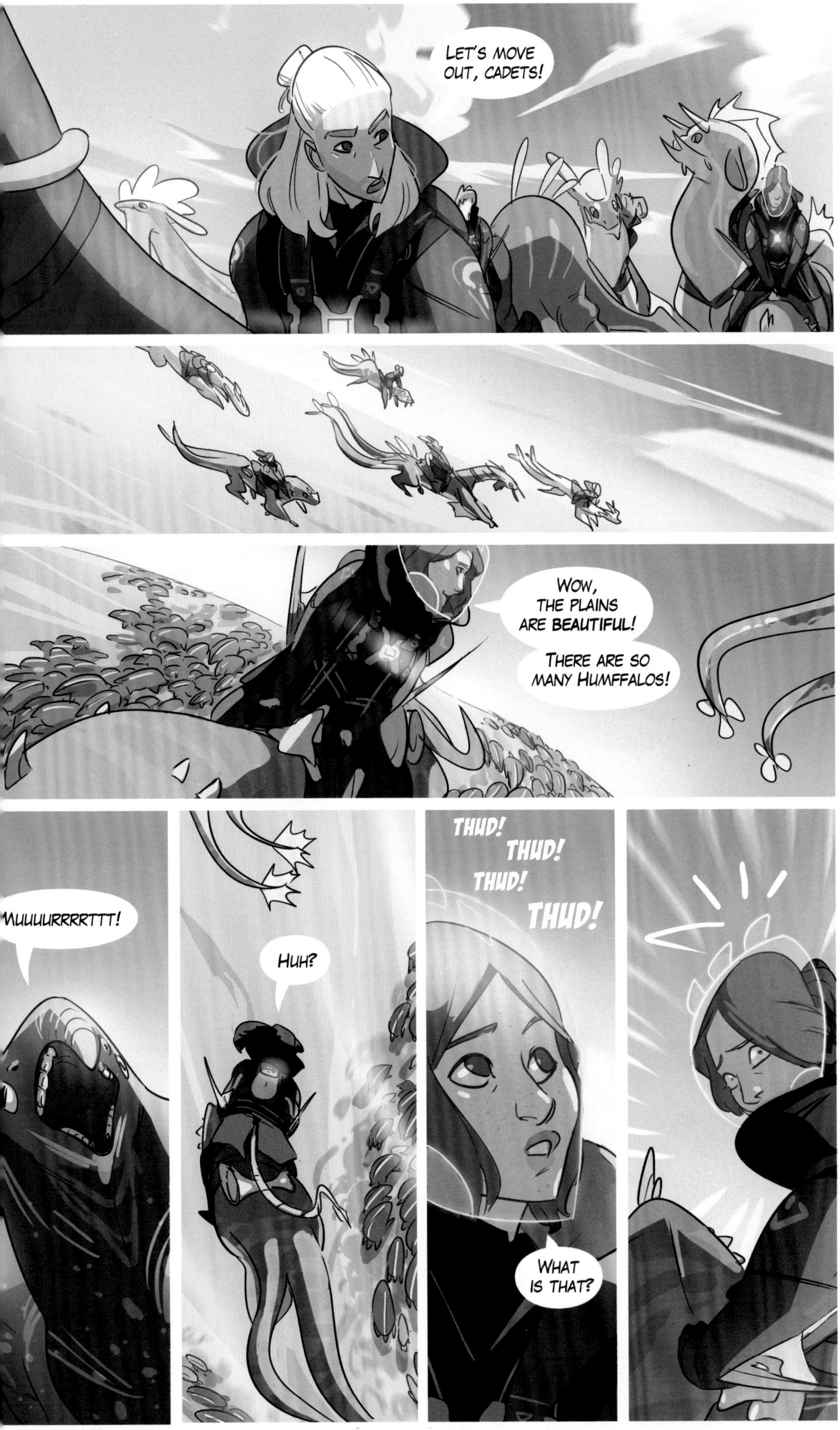
LET'S MOVE OUT, CADETS!
WOW, THE PLAINS ARE BEAUTIFUL!
THERE ARE SO MANY HUMFFALOS!
MUUUURRRRTTT!
HUH?
THUD! THUD! THUD! THUD!
WHAT IS THAT?

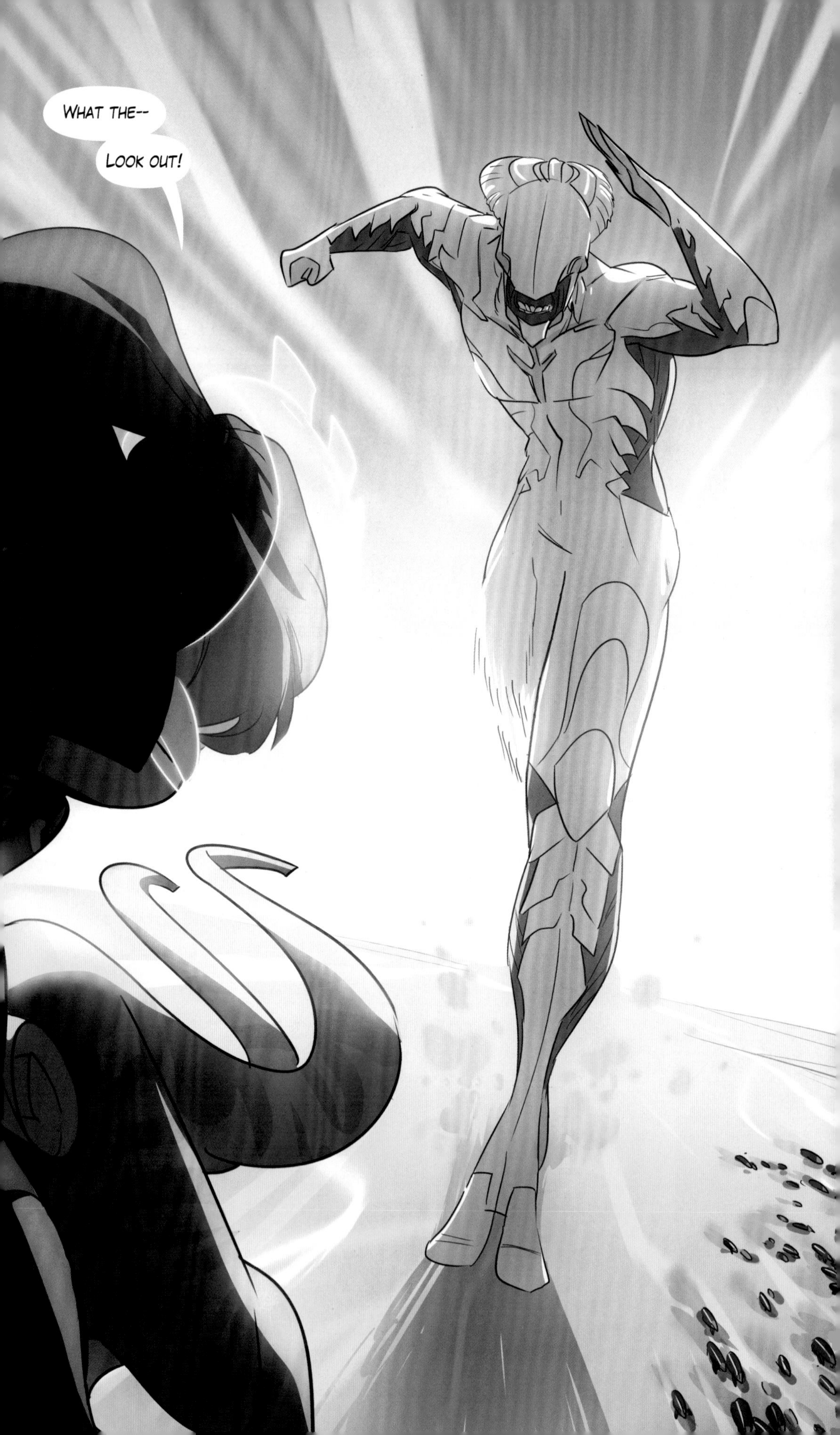
WHAT THE--
LOOK OUT!

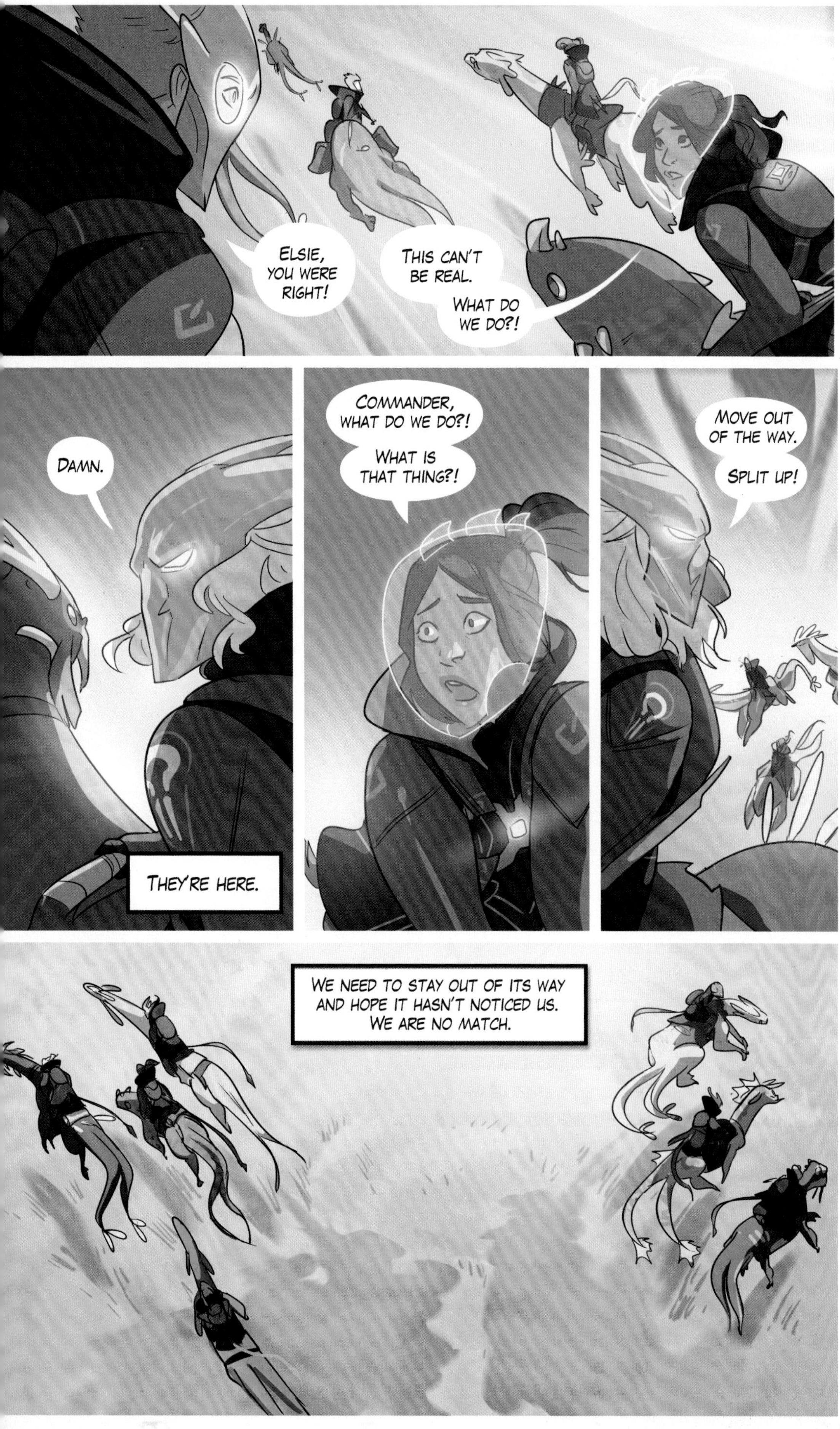
ELSIE, YOU WERE RIGHT!
THIS CAN'T BE REAL.
WHAT DO WE DO?!
DAMN.
THEY'RE HERE.
COMMANDER, WHAT DO WE DO?!
WHAT IS THAT THING?!
MOVE OUT OF THE WAY.
SPLIT UP!
WE NEED TO STAY OUT OF ITS WAY AND HOPE IT HASN'T NOTICED US. WE ARE NO MATCH.

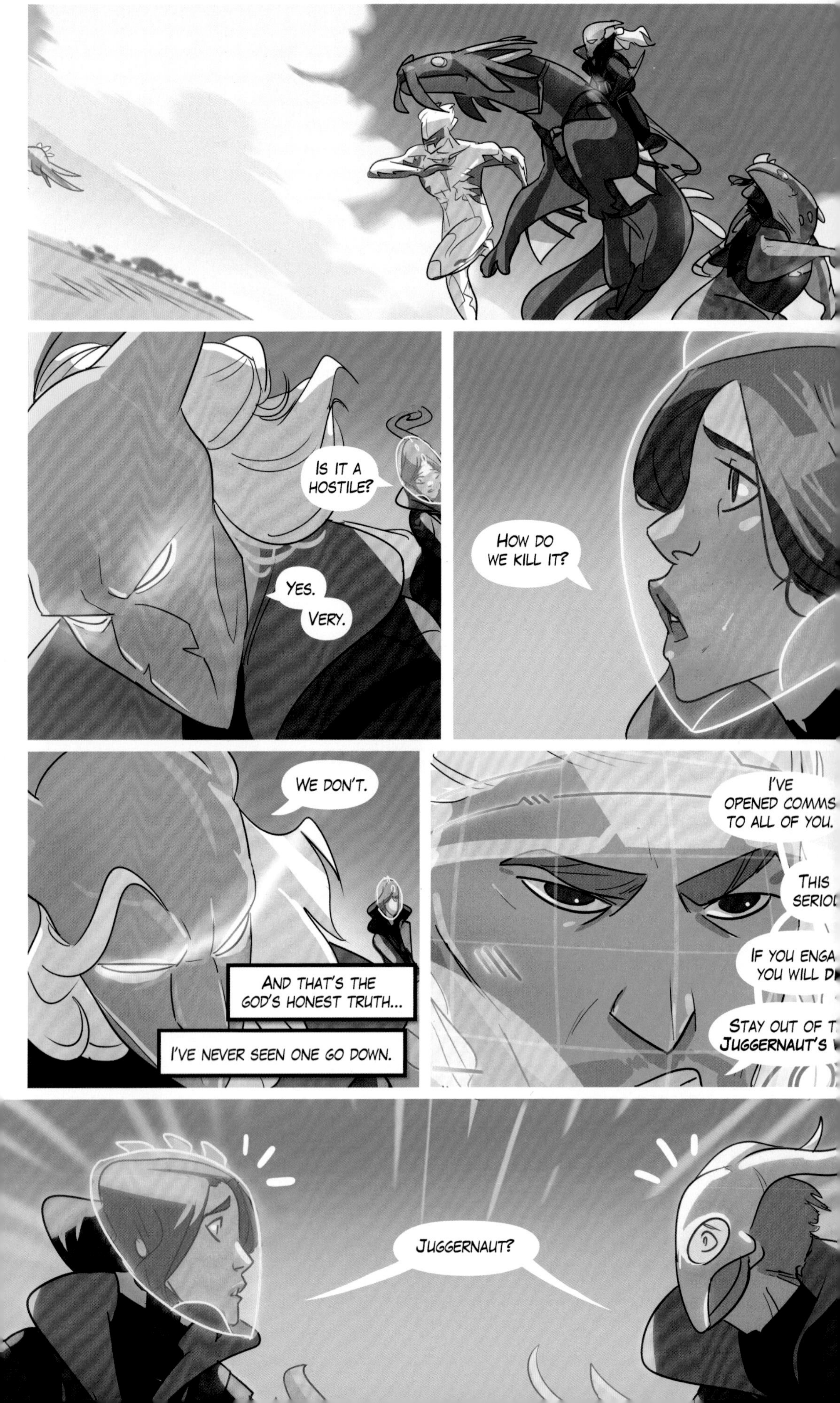

Is it a hostile?
Yes.
Very.
How do we kill it?
We don't.
And that's the god's honest truth...
I've never seen one go down.
I've opened comms to all of you.
This
If you
Stay out of
Juggernaut?

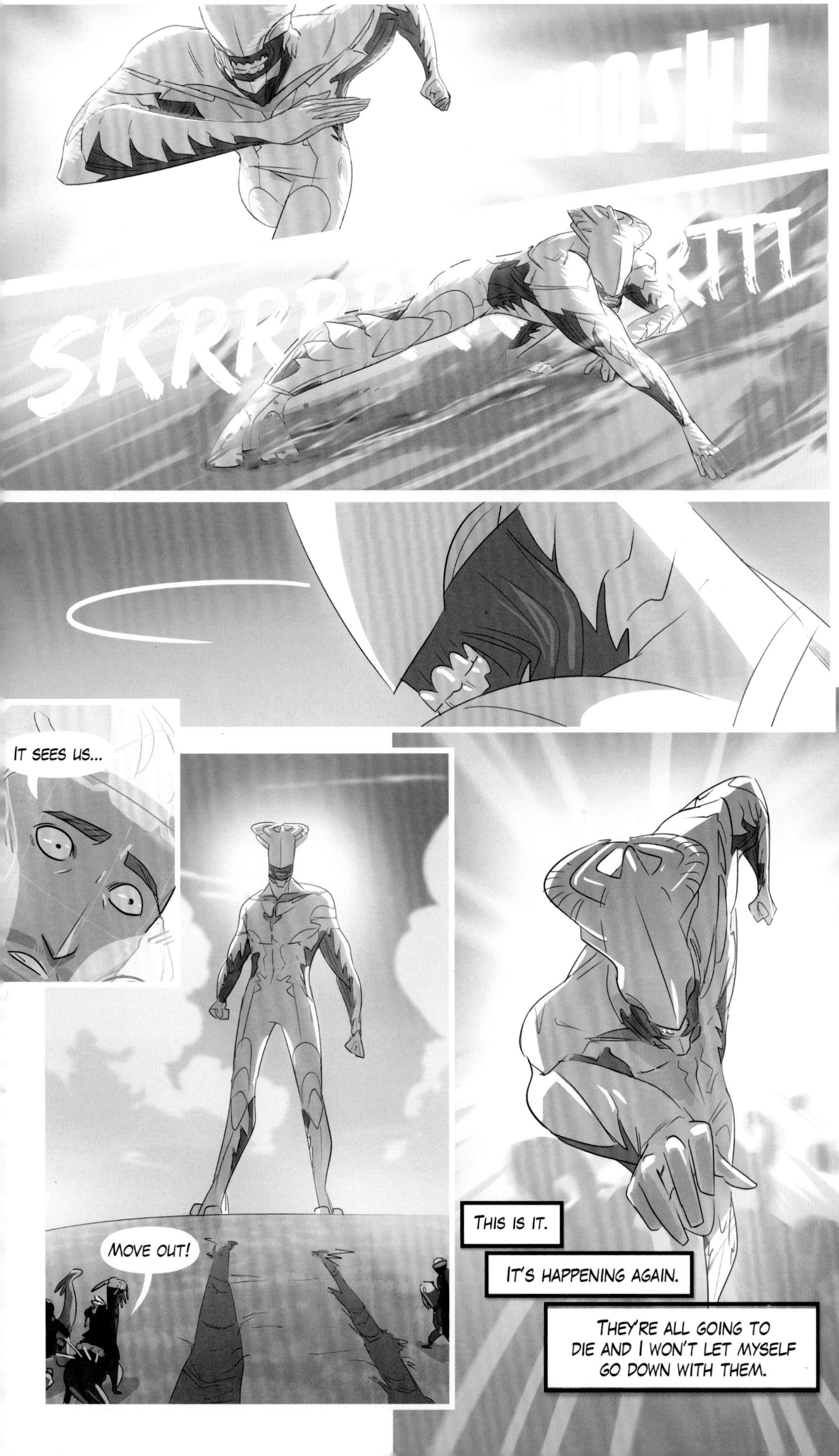
OOSH!
SKRR
RTTT
IT SEES US...
MOVE OUT!
THIS IS IT.
IT'S HAPPENING AGAIN.
THEY'RE ALL GOING TO DIE AND I WON'T LET MYSELF GO DOWN WITH THEM.

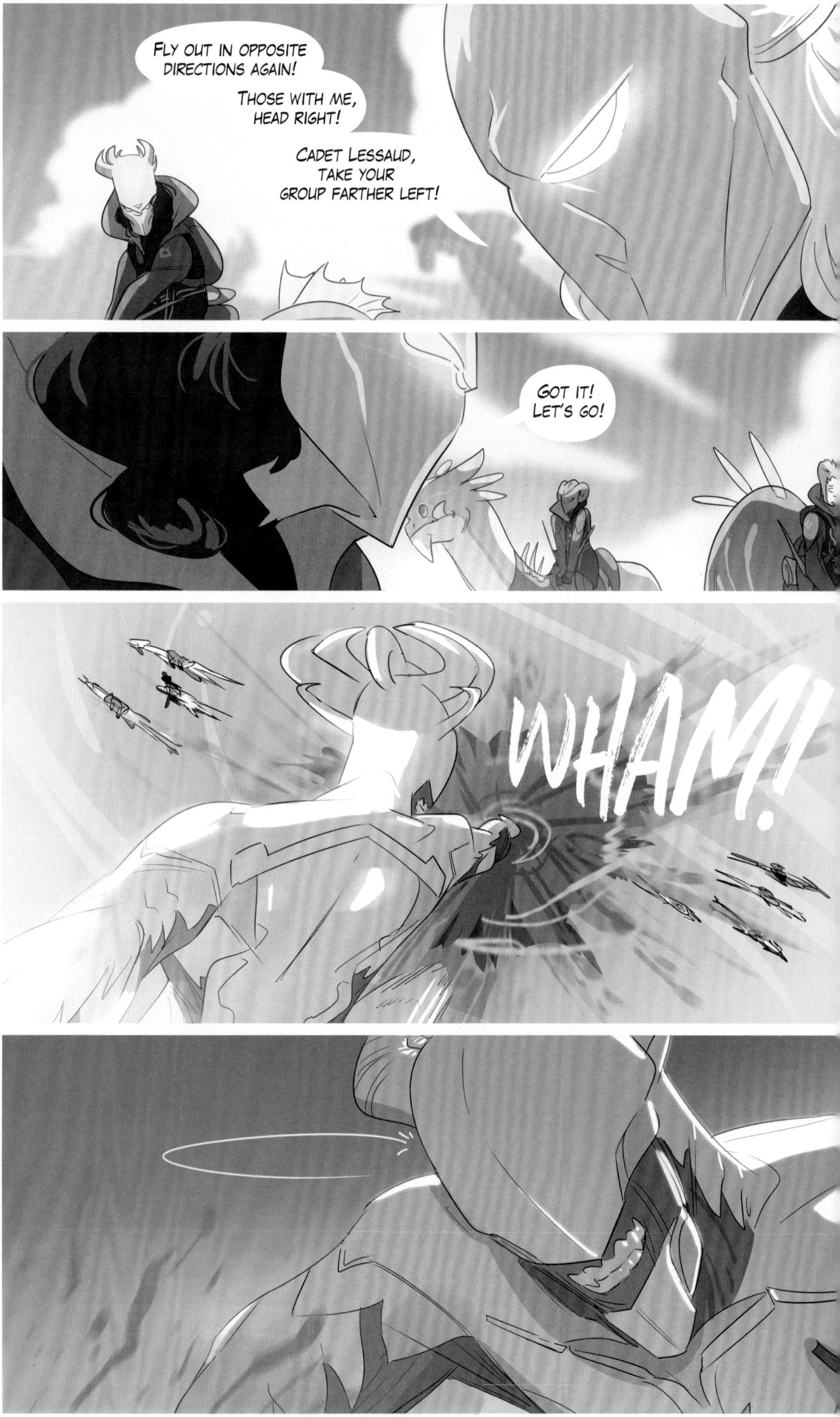
FLY OUT IN OPPOSITE DIRECTIONS AGAIN!
THOSE WITH ME, HEAD RIGHT!
CADET LESSAUD, TAKE YOUR GROUP FARTHER LEFT!
GOT IT! LET'S GO!
WHAM!

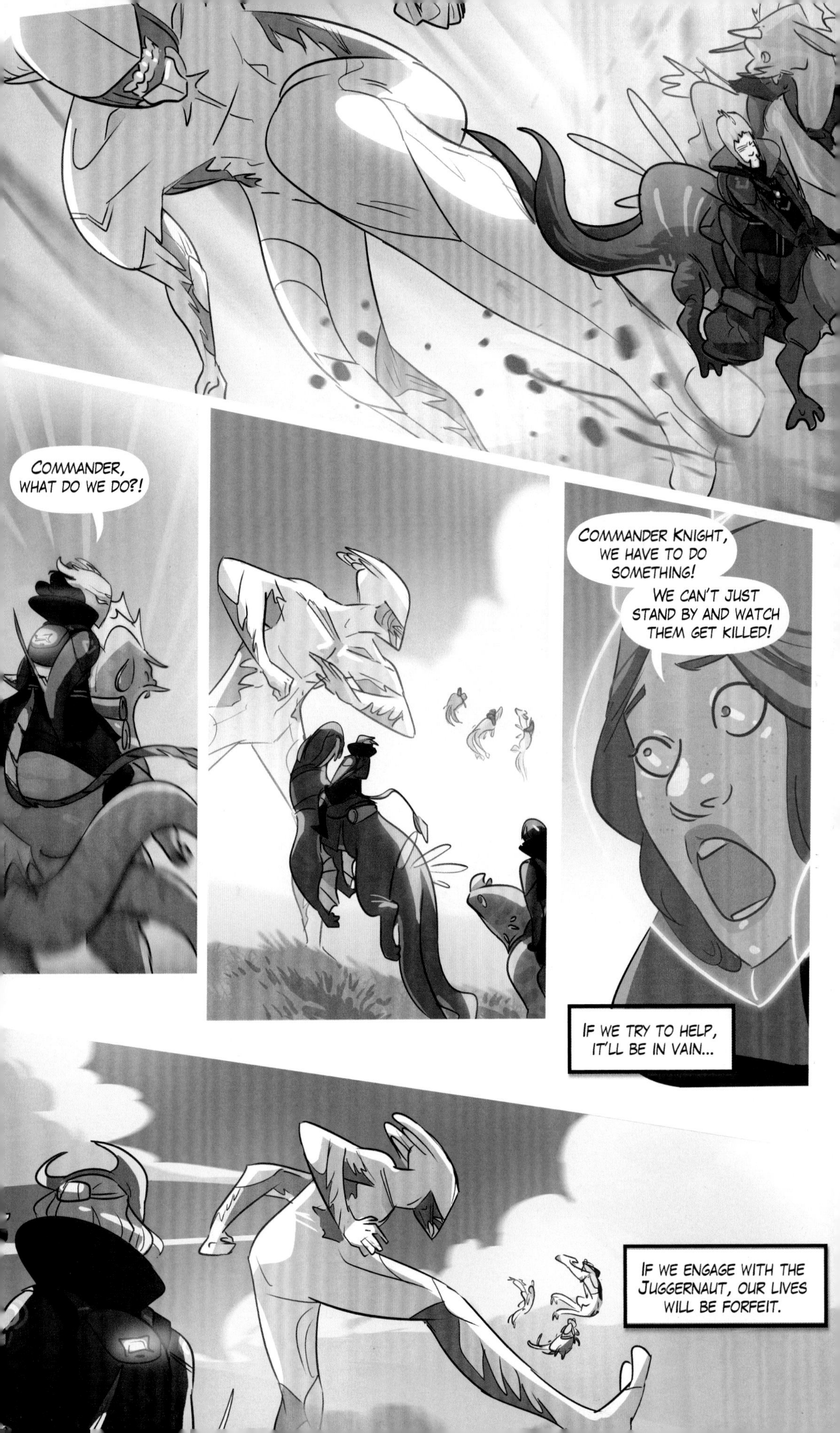
COMMANDER, WHAT DO WE DO?!
COMMANDER KNIGHT, WE HAVE TO DO SOMETHING!
WE CAN'T JUST STAND BY AND WATCH THEM GET KILLED!
IF WE TRY TO HELP, IT'LL BE IN VAIN...
IF WE ENGAGE WITH THE JUGGERNAUT, OUR LIVES WILL BE FORFEIT.

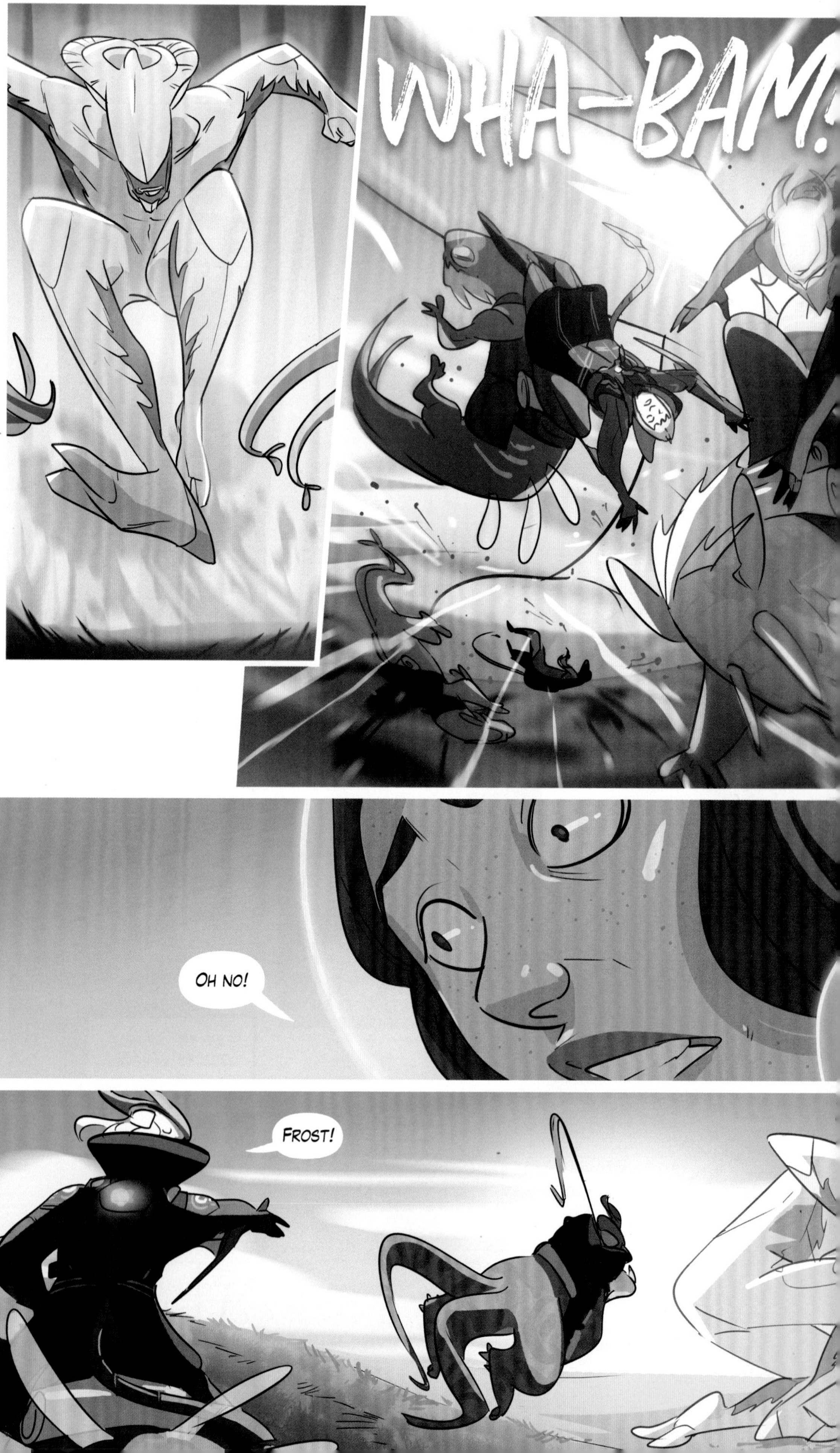
WHA-BAM!
OH NO!
FROST!

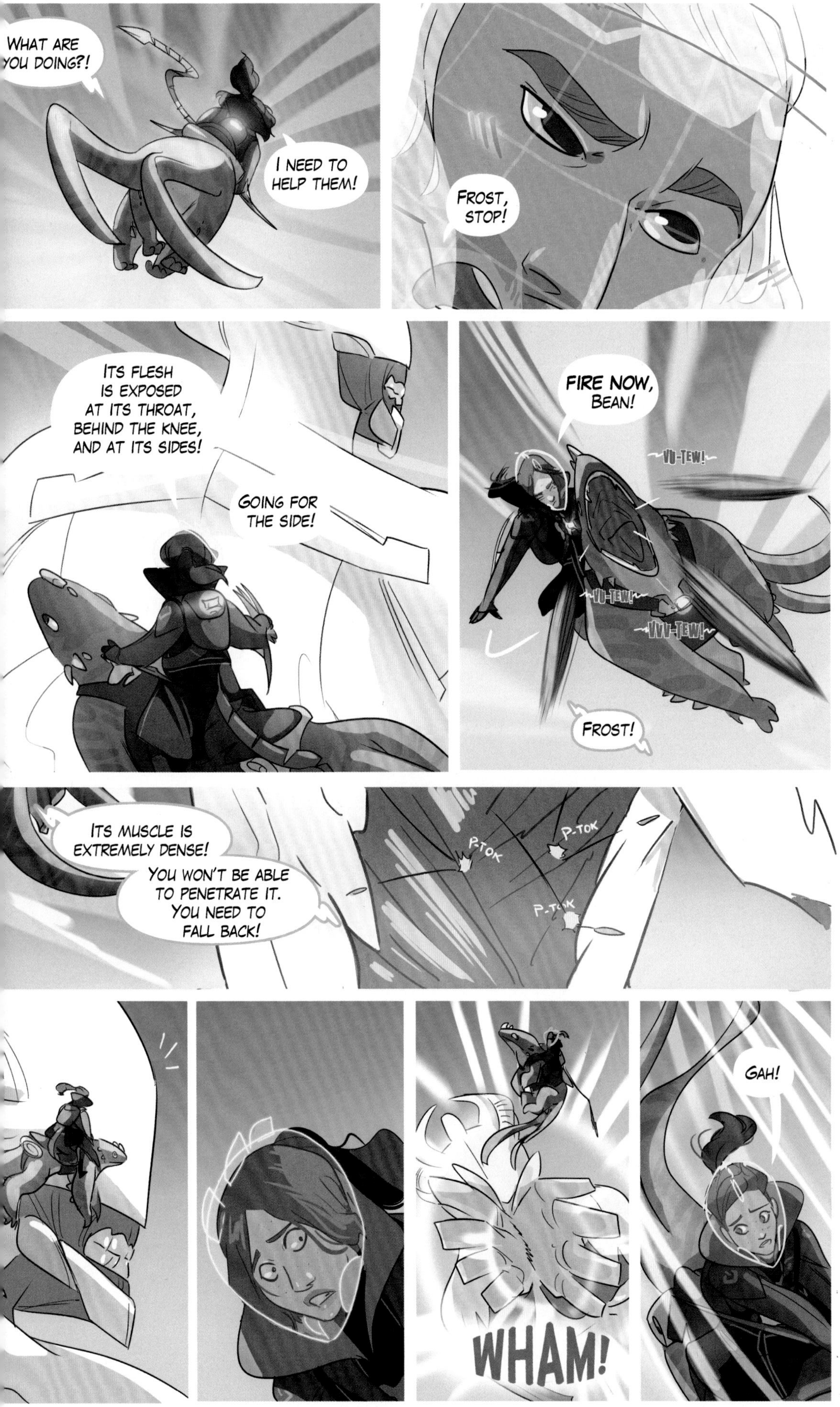
WHAT ARE YOU DOING?!
I NEED TO HELP THEM!
FROST, STOP!
ITS FLESH IS EXPOSED AT ITS THROAT, BEHIND THE KNEE, AND AT ITS SIDES!
GOING FOR THE SIDE!
FIRE NOW, BEAN!
VU-TEW!
VU-TEW!
VVV-TEW!
FROST!
ITS MUSCLE IS EXTREMELY DENSE!
YOU WON'T BE ABLE TO PENETRATE IT. YOU NEED TO FALL BACK!
P-TOK
P-TOK
P-TOK
WHAM!
GAH!

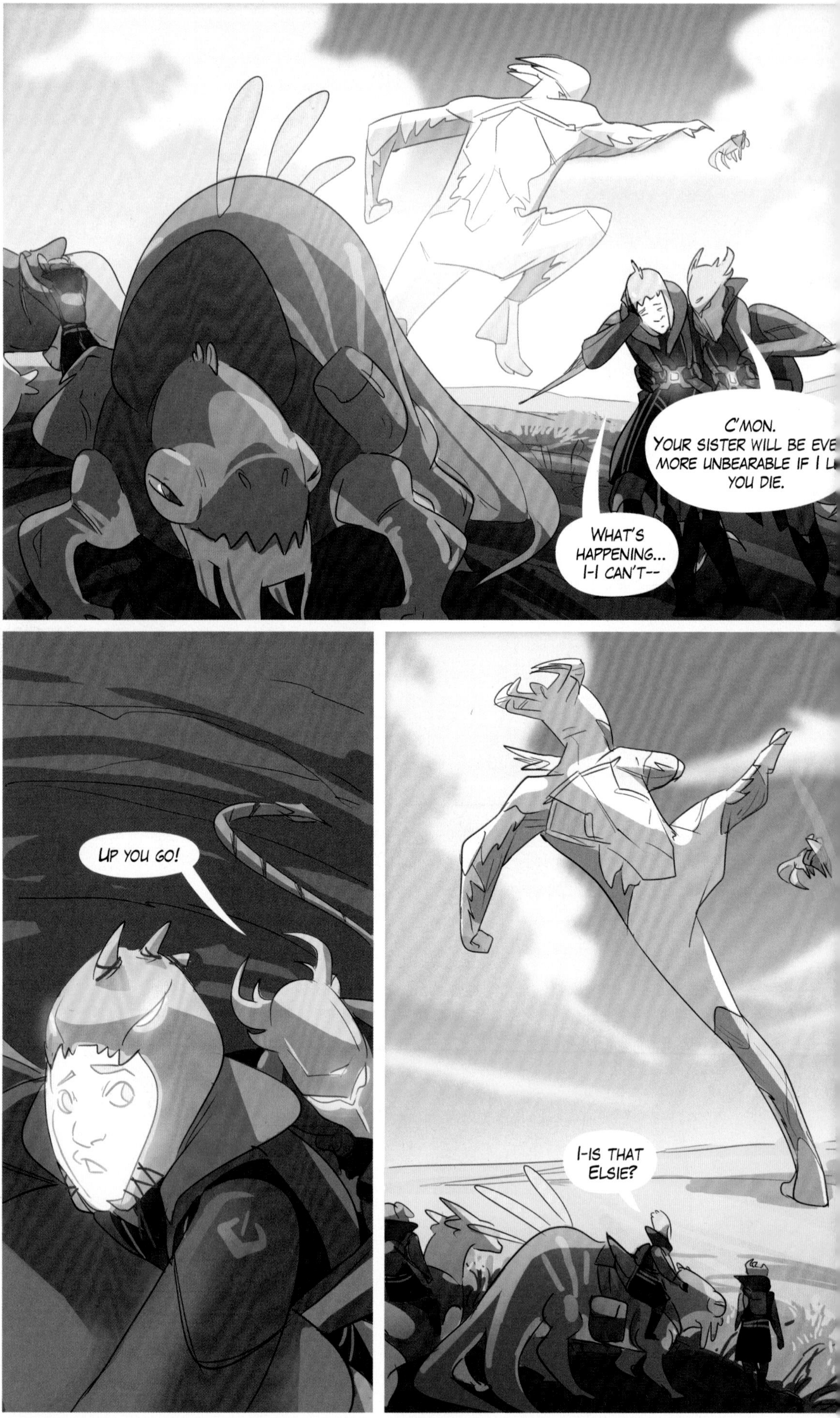
C'MON.
YOUR SISTER WILL BE EVE
MORE UNBEARABLE IF I L
YOU DIE.
WHAT'S HAPPENING... I-I CAN'T--
UP YOU GO!
I-IS THAT ELSIE?

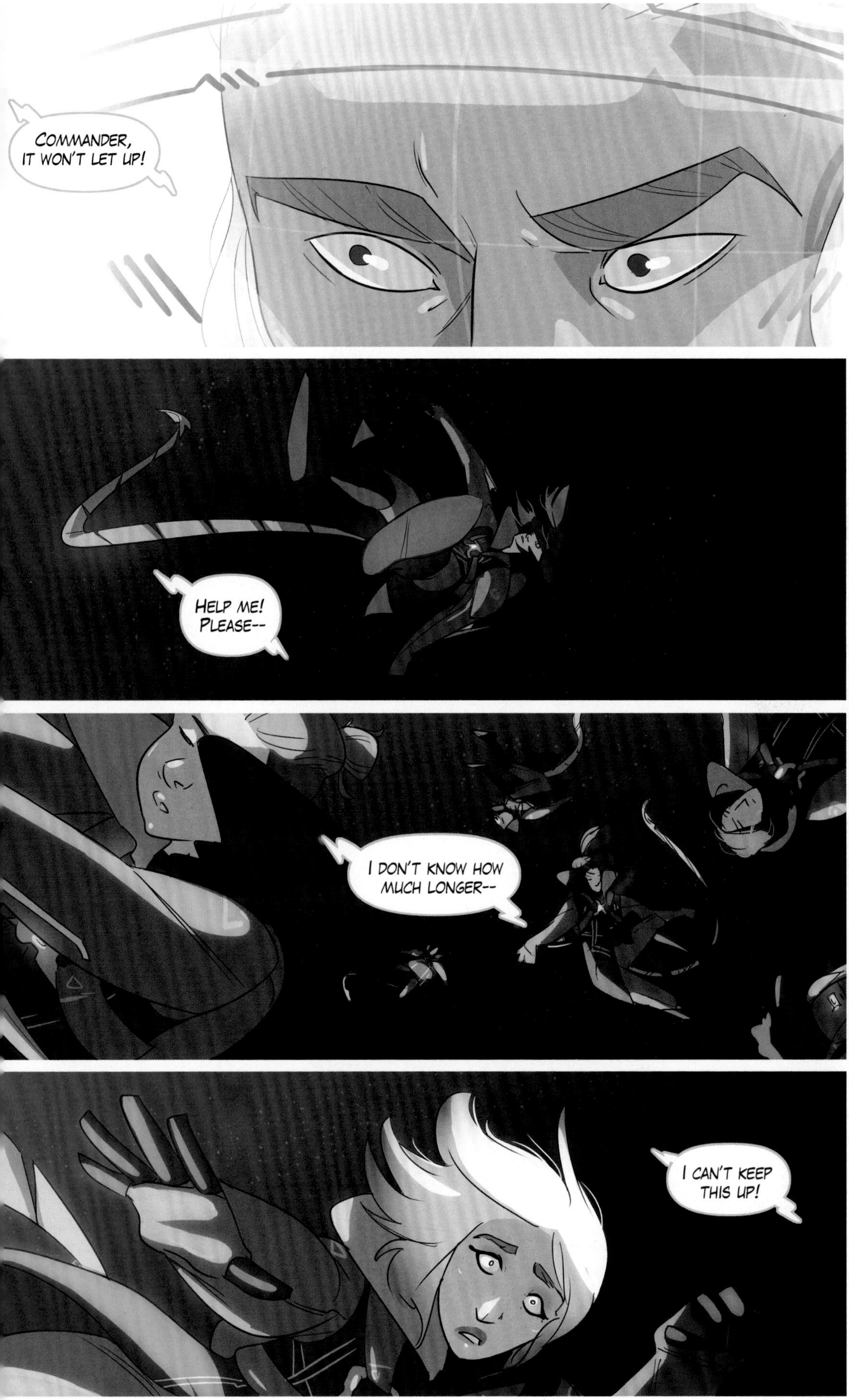
COMMANDER, IT WON'T LET UP!
HELP ME! PLEASE--
I DON'T KNOW HOW MUCH LONGER--
I CAN'T KEEP THIS UP!

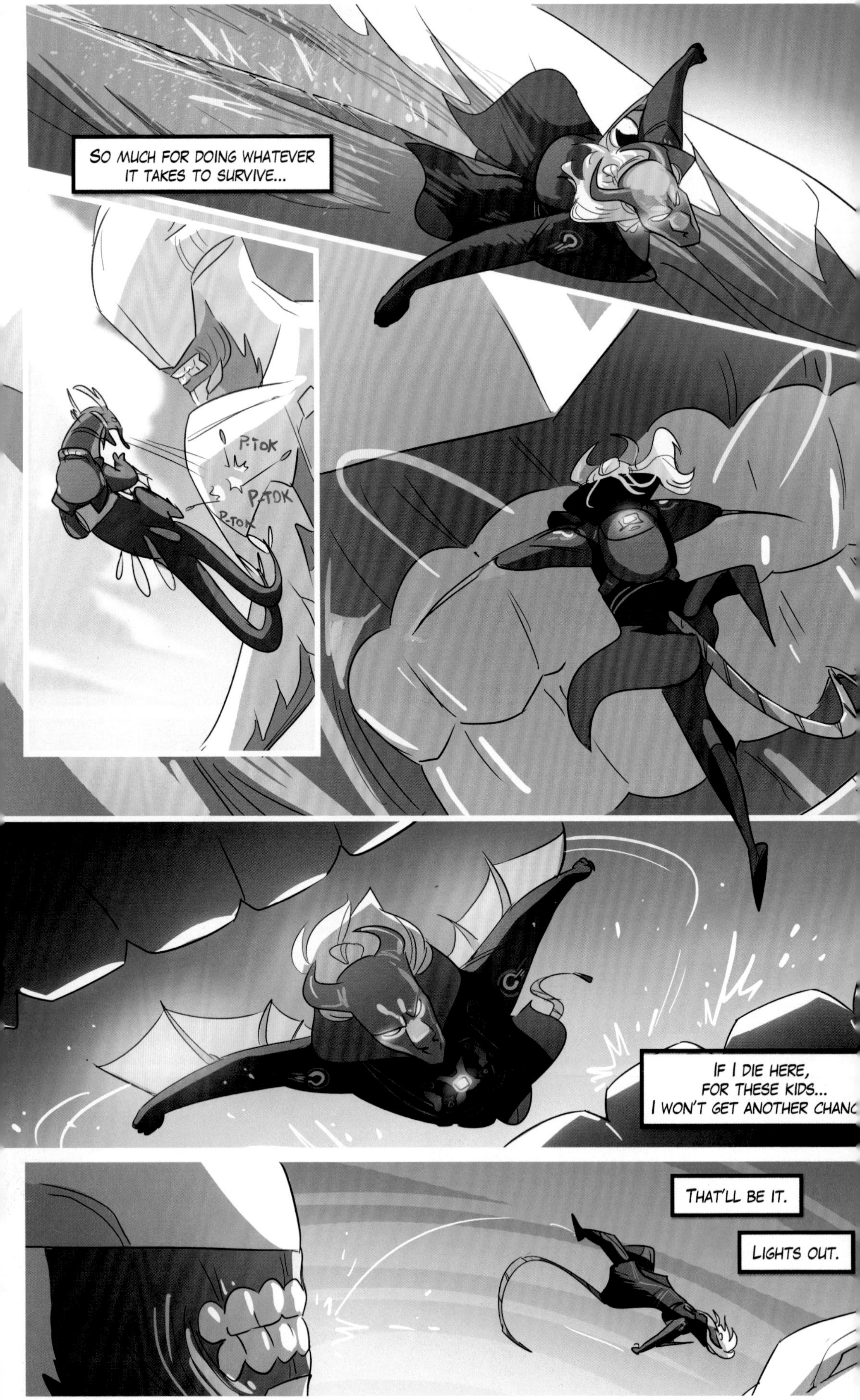

SO MUCH FOR DOING WHATEVER IT TAKES TO SURVIVE...
P-TOK
P-TOK
P-TOK
IF I DIE HERE, FOR THESE KIDS... I WON'T GET ANOTHER CHANC
THAT'LL BE IT.
LIGHTS OUT.

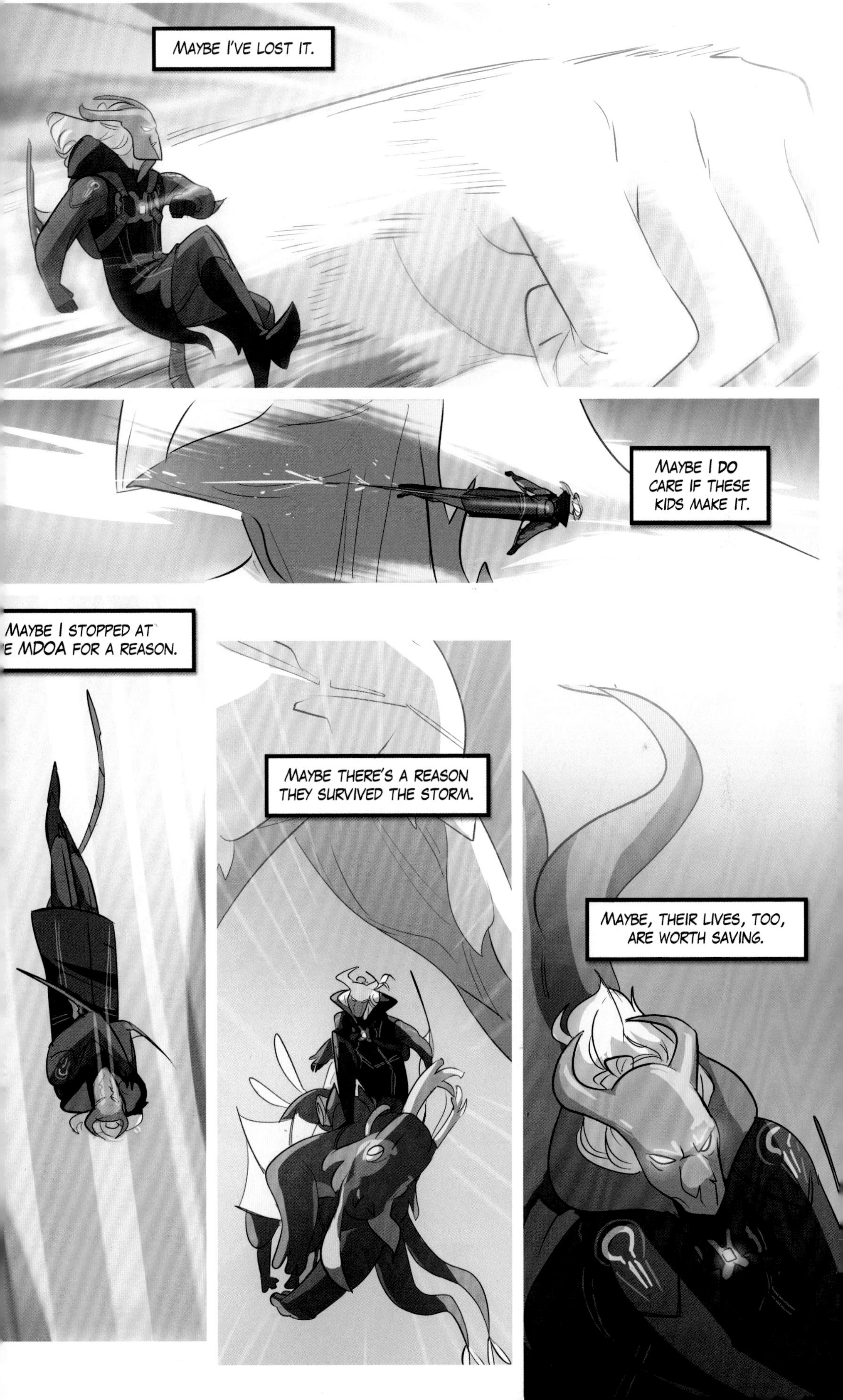
MAYBE I'VE LOST IT.
MAYBE I DO CARE IF THESE KIDS MAKE IT.
MAYBE I STOPPED AT
E MDOA FOR A REASON.
MAYBE THERE'S A REASON THEY SURVIVED THE STORM.
MAYBE, THEIR LIVES, TOO, ARE WORTH SAVING.

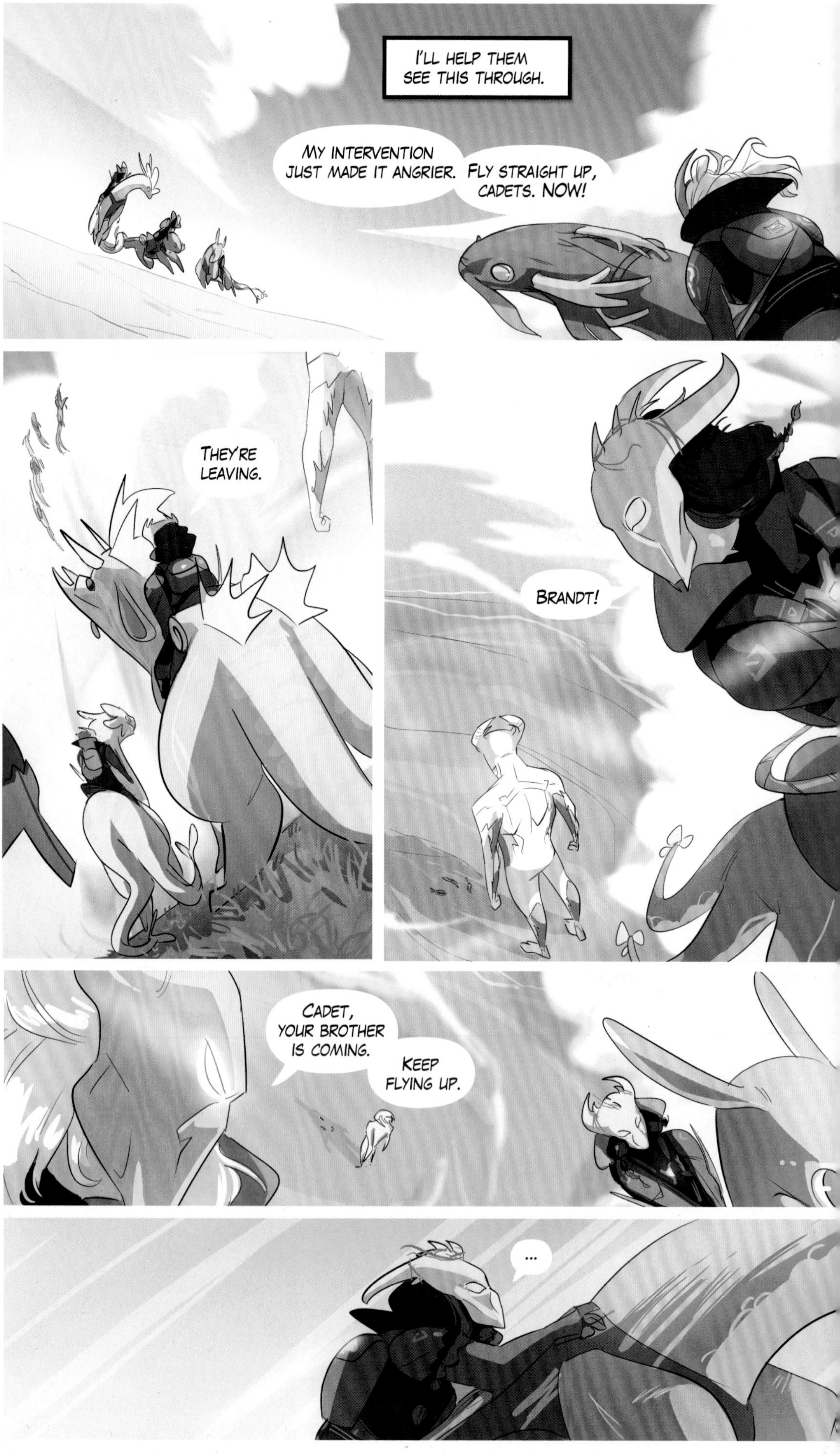
I'LL HELP THEM SEE THIS THROUGH.
MY INTERVENTION JUST MADE IT ANGRIER.
FLY STRAIGHT UP, CADETS. NOW!
THEY'RE LEAVING.
BRANDT!
CADET, YOUR BROTHER IS COMING.
KEEP FLYING UP.
...

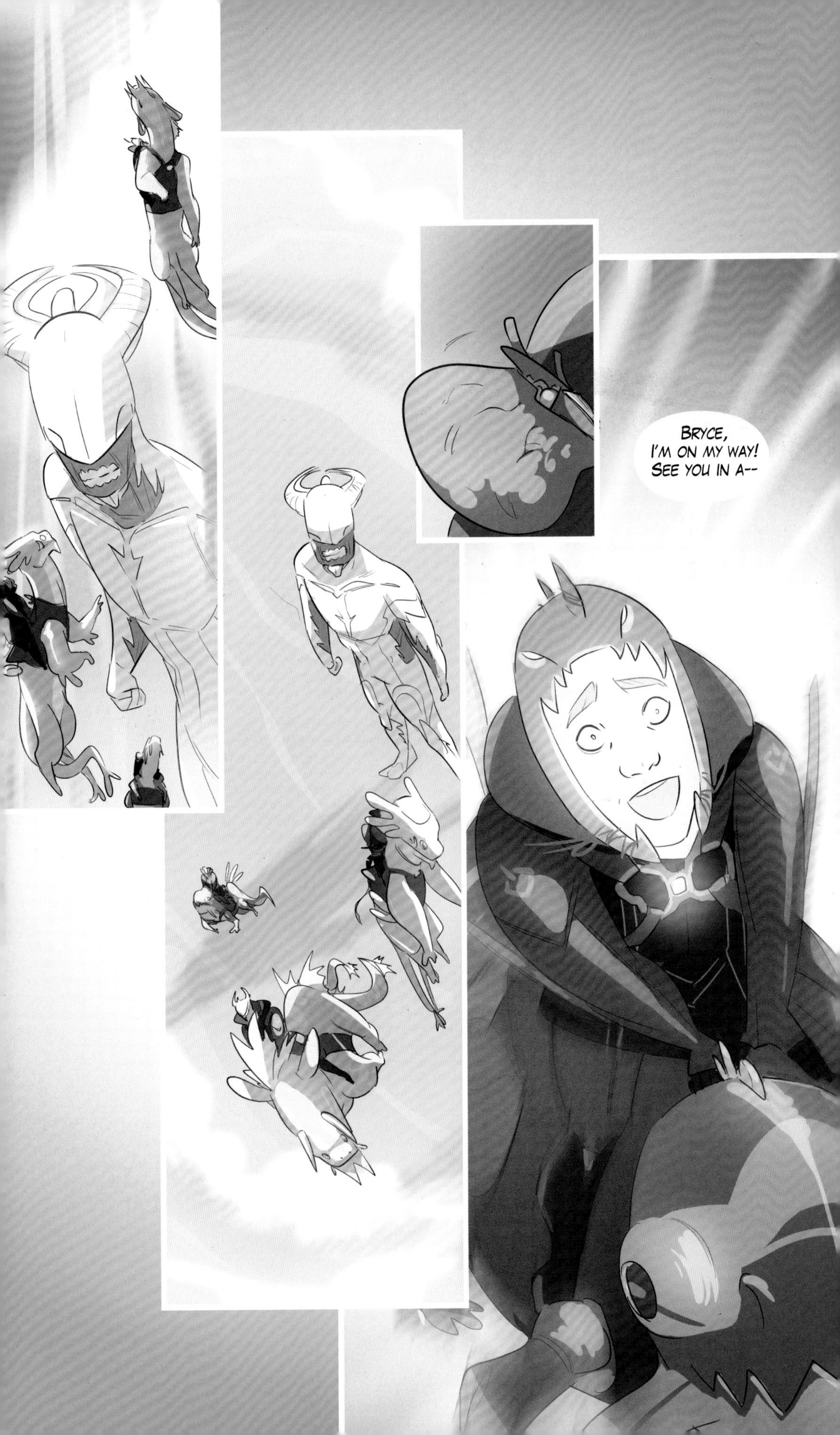
BRYCE, I'M ON MY WAY! SEE YOU IN A--

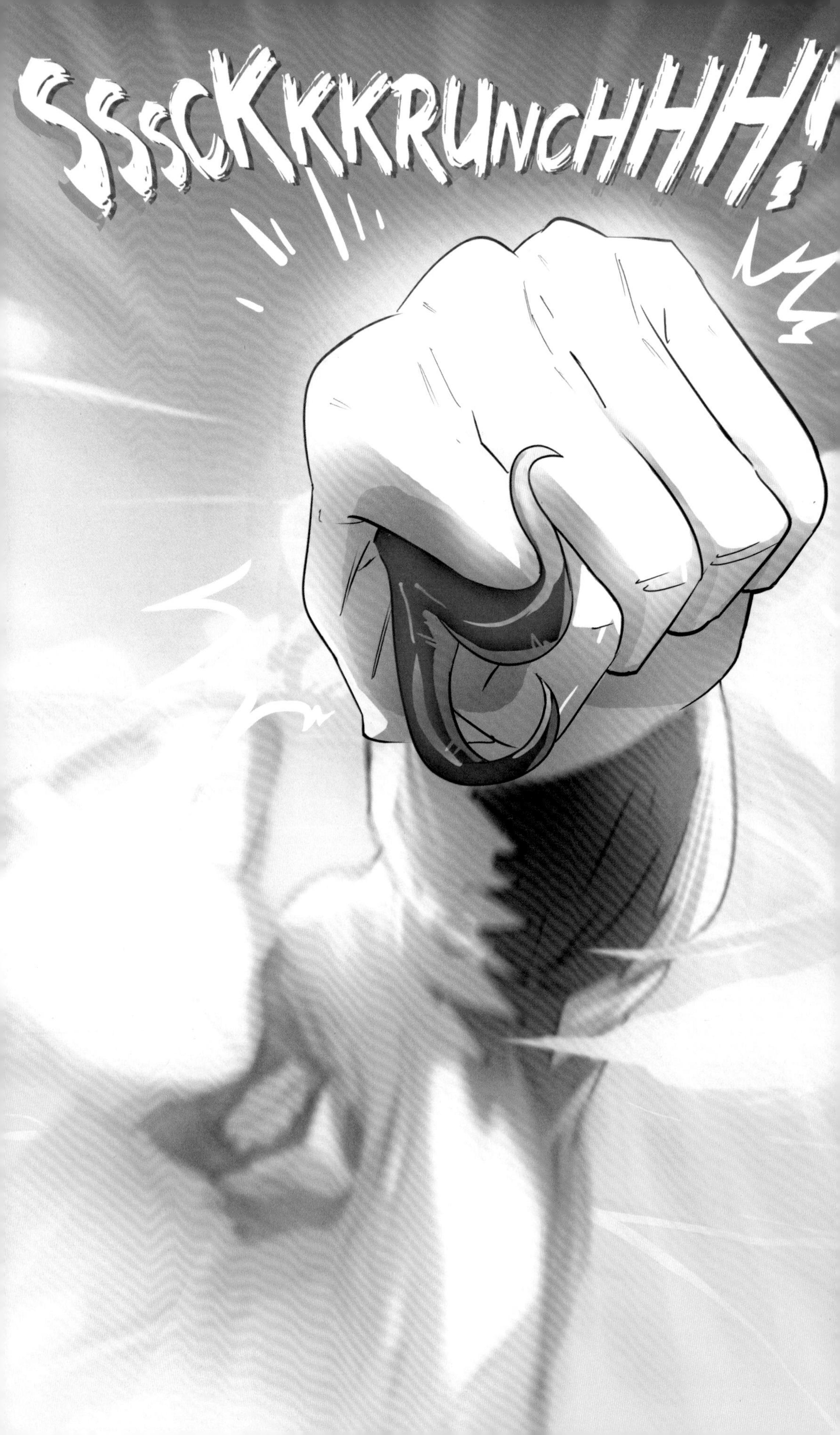
SSSCKKKRUNCHHH!

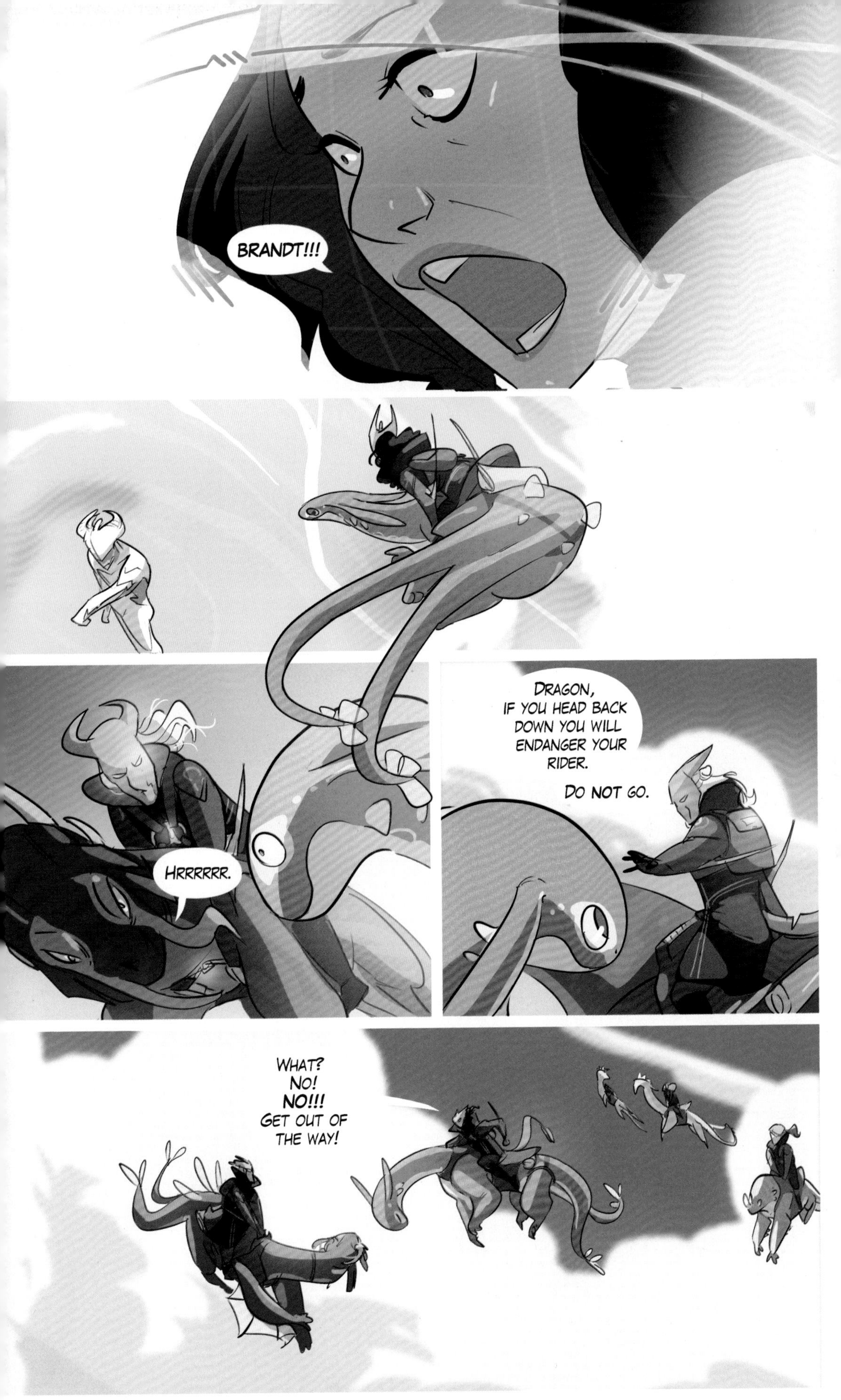
BRANDT!!!
HRRRRRR.
DRAGON, IF YOU HEAD BACK DOWN YOU WILL ENDANGER YOUR RIDER.
DO NOT GO.
WHAT? NO! NO!!! GET OUT OF THE WAY!

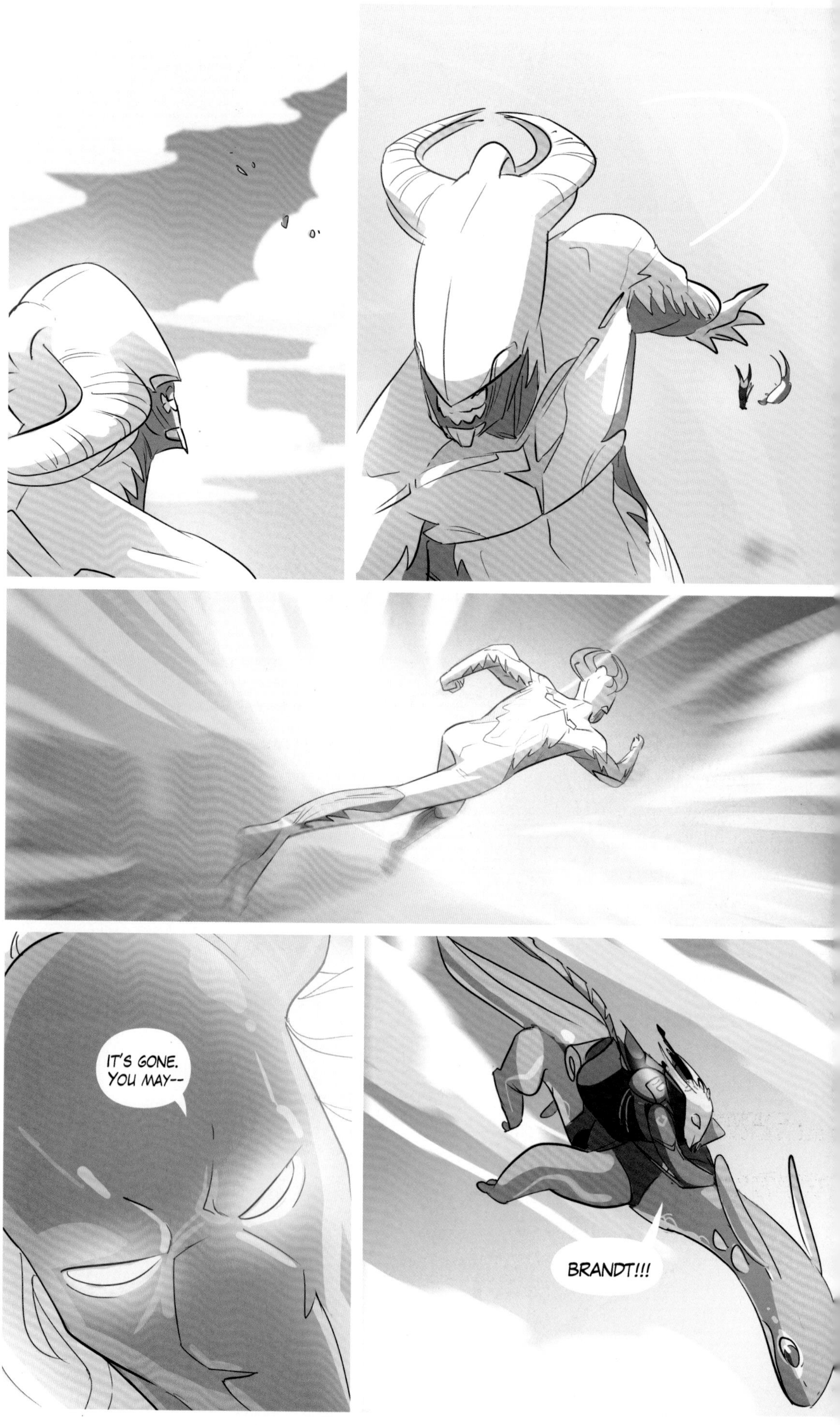
IT'S GONE. YOU MAY--
BRANDT!!!

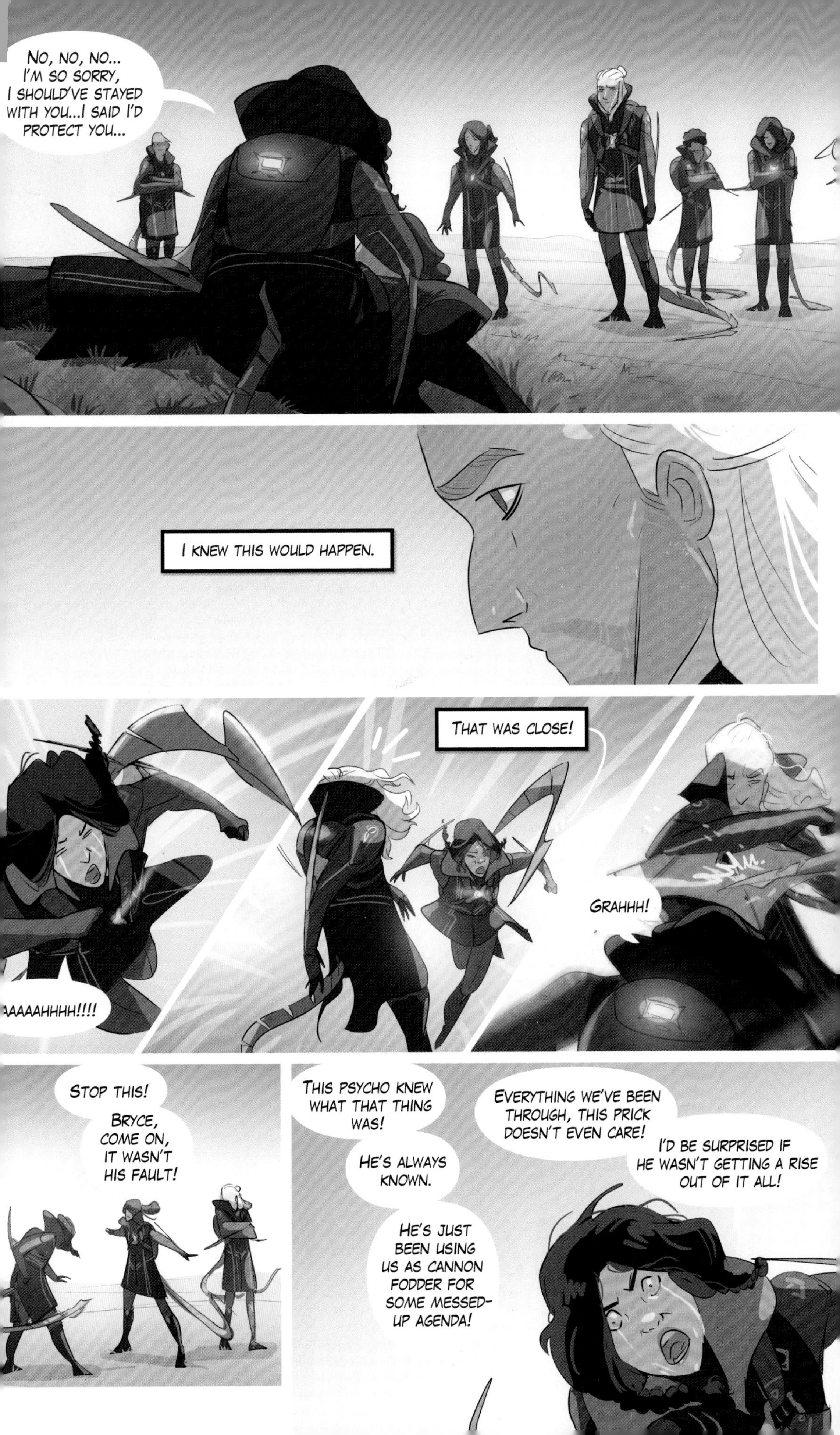
No, no, no... I'm so sorry, I should've stayed with you...I said I'd protect you...
I knew this would happen.
AAAAAHHHH!!!!
That was close!
Grahhh!
Stop this!
Bryce, come on, it wasn't his fault!
This psycho knew what that thing was!
He's always known.
He's just been using us as cannon fodder for some messed-up agenda!
Everything we've been through, this prick doesn't even care!
I'd be surprised if he wasn't getting a rise out of it all!

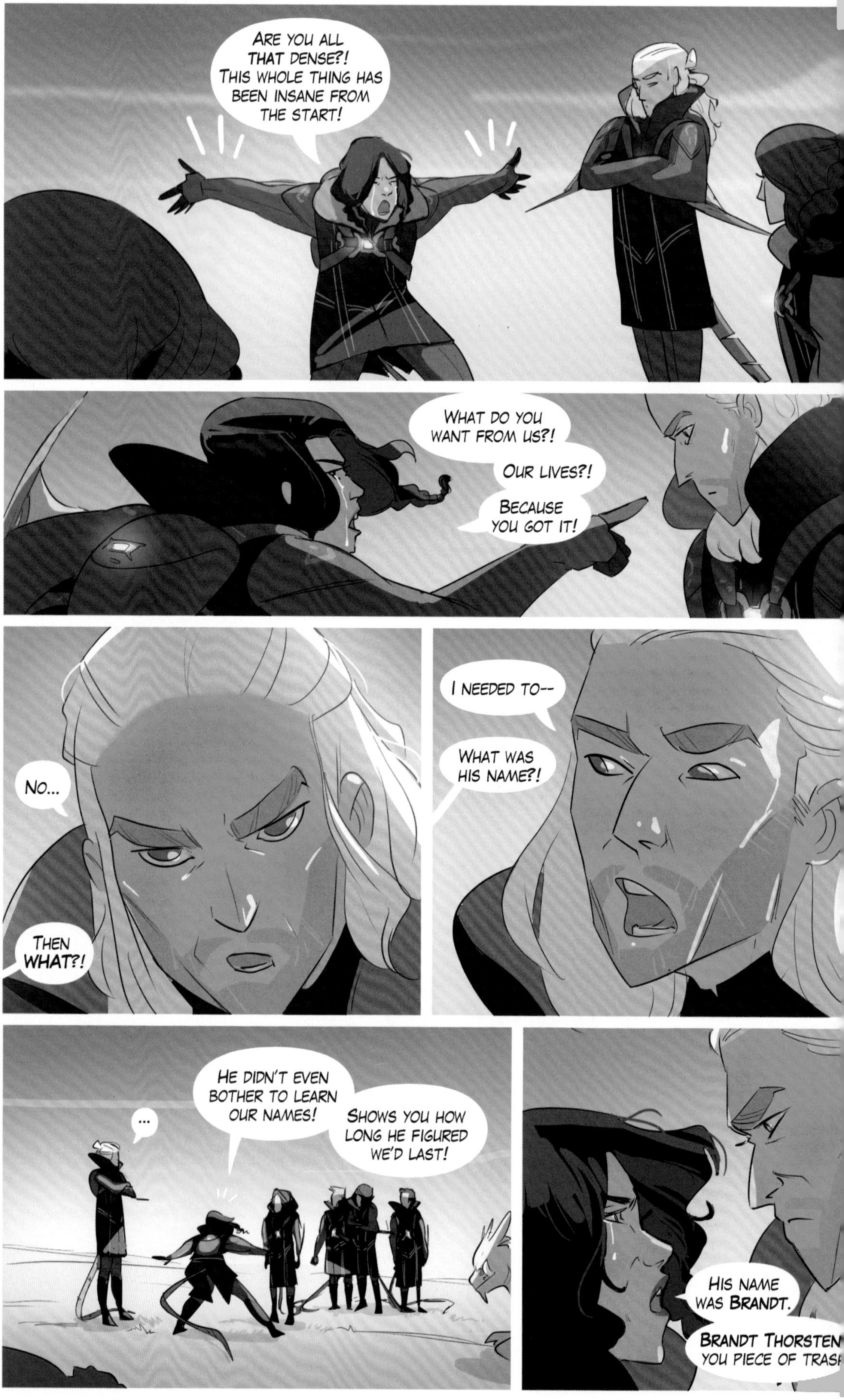
ARE YOU ALL THAT DENSE?! THIS WHOLE THING HAS BEEN INSANE FROM THE START!
WHAT DO YOU WANT FROM US?!
OUR LIVES?!
BECAUSE YOU GOT IT!
NO...
THEN WHAT?!
I NEEDED TO--
WHAT WAS HIS NAME?!
...
HE DIDN'T EVEN BOTHER TO LEARN OUR NAMES!
SHOWS YOU HOW LONG HE FIGURED WE'D LAST!
HIS NAME WAS BRANDT.
BRANDT THORSTEN YOU PIECE OF TRAS

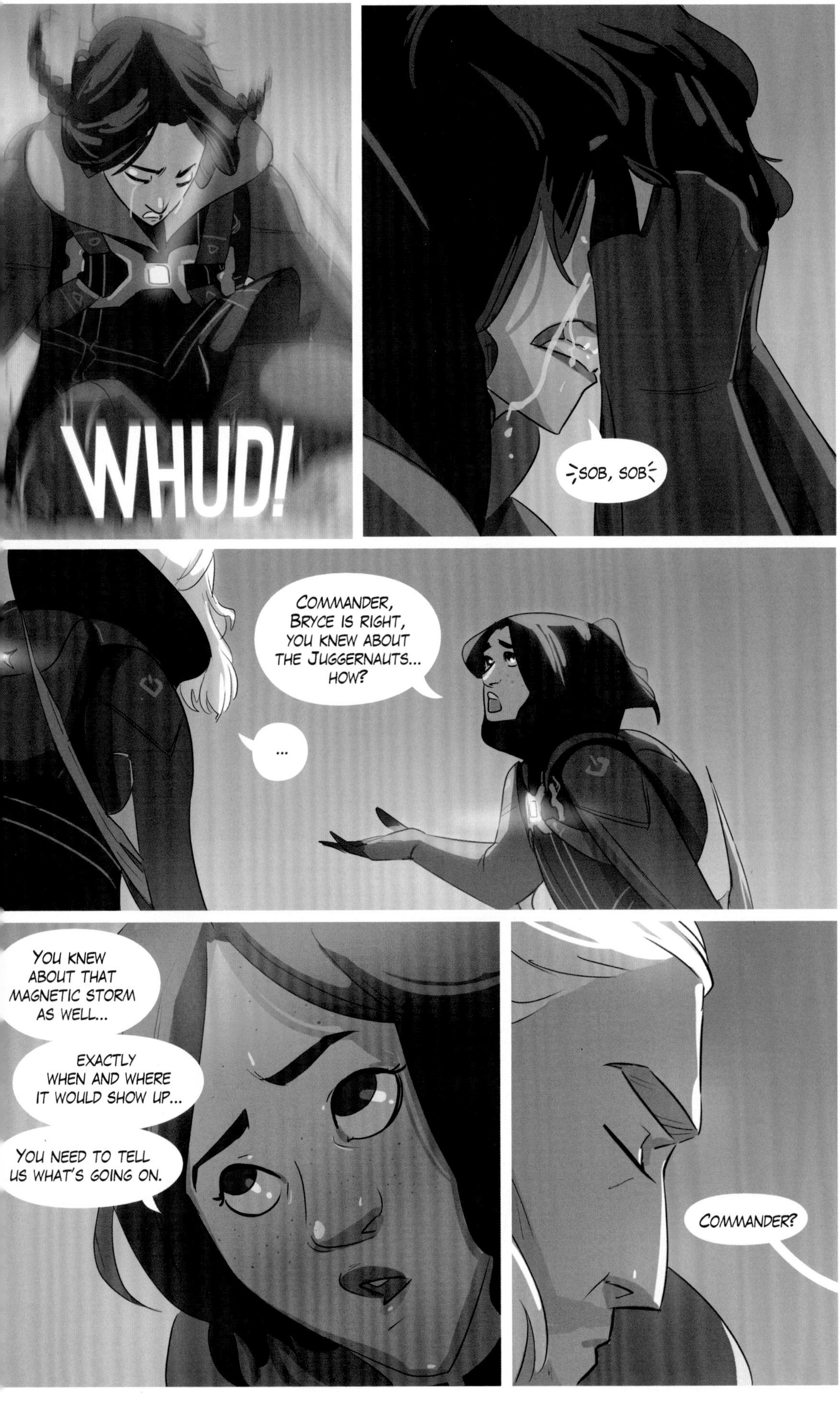
WHUD!
SOB, SOB
COMMANDER, BRYCE IS RIGHT, YOU KNEW ABOUT THE JUGGERNAUTS... HOW?
...
YOU KNEW ABOUT THAT MAGNETIC STORM AS WELL...
EXACTLY WHEN AND WHERE IT WOULD SHOW UP...
YOU NEED TO TELL US WHAT'S GOING ON.
COMMANDER?

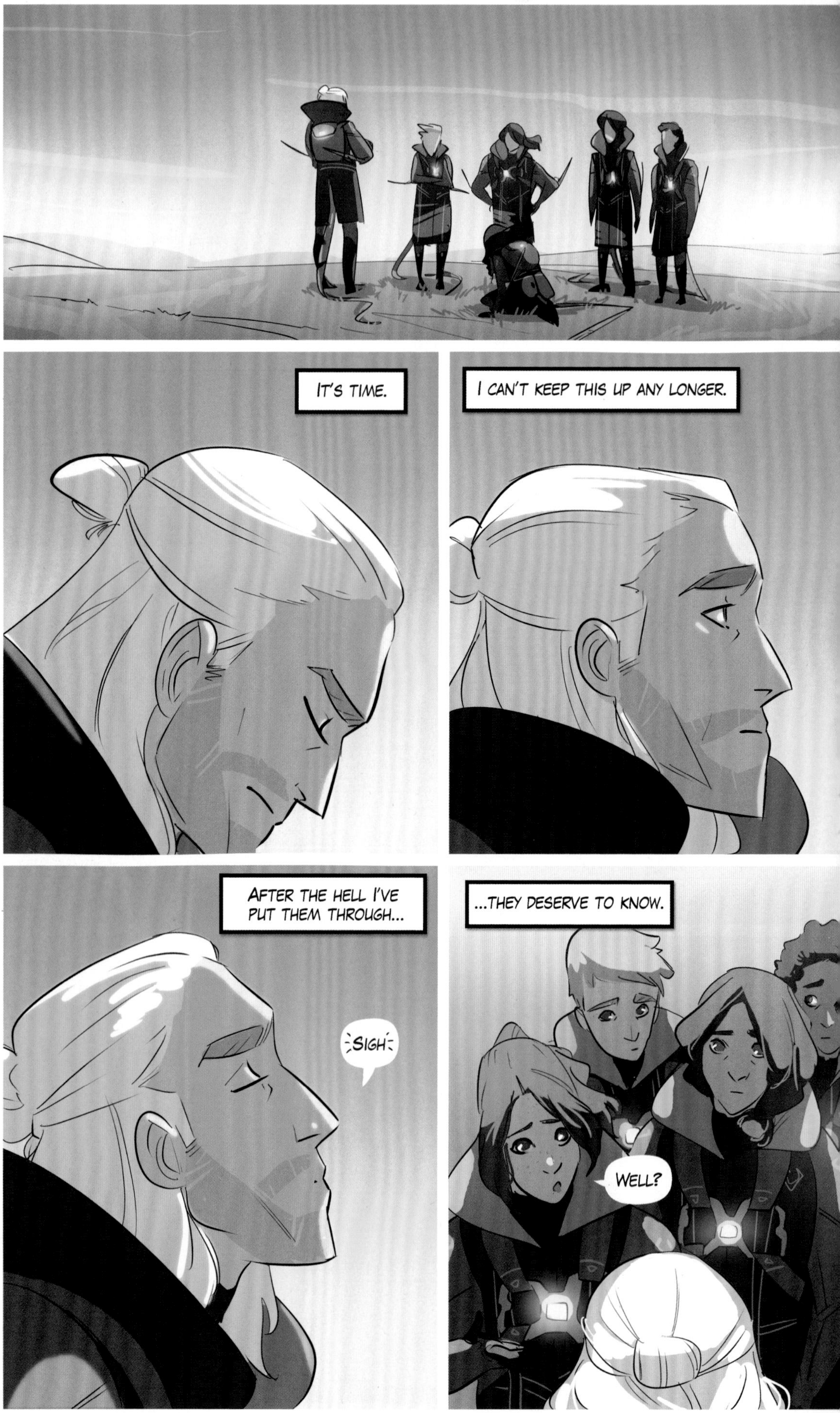

IT'S TIME.
I CAN'T KEEP THIS UP ANY LONGER.
AFTER THE HELL I'VE PUT THEM THROUGH...
SIGH
...THEY DESERVE TO KNOW.
WELL?

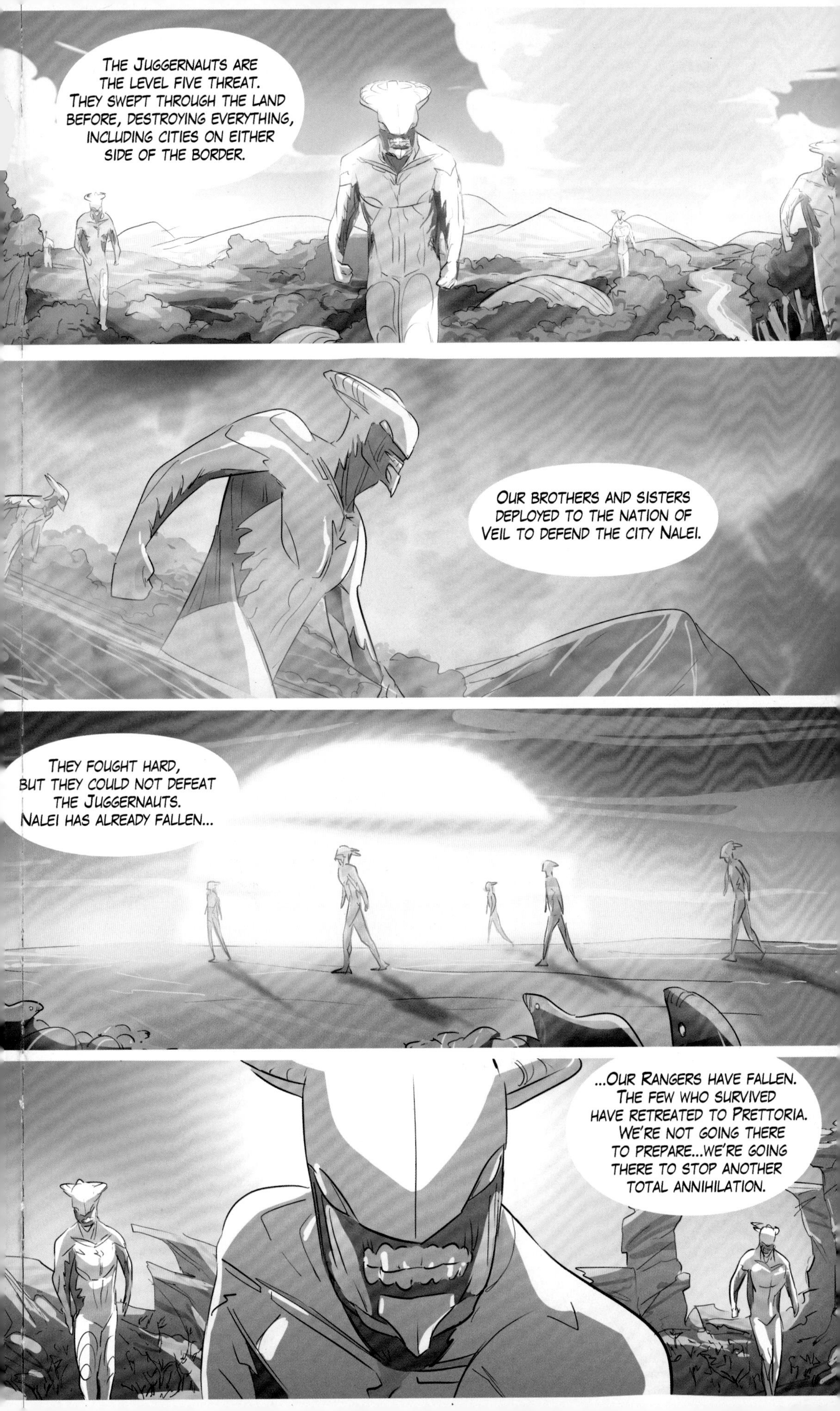
THE JUGGERNAUTS ARE THE LEVEL FIVE THREAT. THEY SWEPT THROUGH THE LAND BEFORE, DESTROYING EVERYTHING, INCLUDING CITIES ON EITHER SIDE OF THE BORDER.
OUR BROTHERS AND SISTERS DEPLOYED TO THE NATION OF VEIL TO DEFEND THE CITY NALEI.
THEY FOUGHT HARD, BUT THEY COULD NOT DEFEAT THE JUGGERNAUTS. NALEI HAS ALREADY FALLEN...
...OUR RANGERS HAVE FALLEN. THE FEW WHO SURVIVED HAVE RETREATED TO PRETTORIA. WE'RE NOT GOING THERE TO PREPARE...WE'RE GOING THERE TO STOP ANOTHER TOTAL ANNIHILATION.

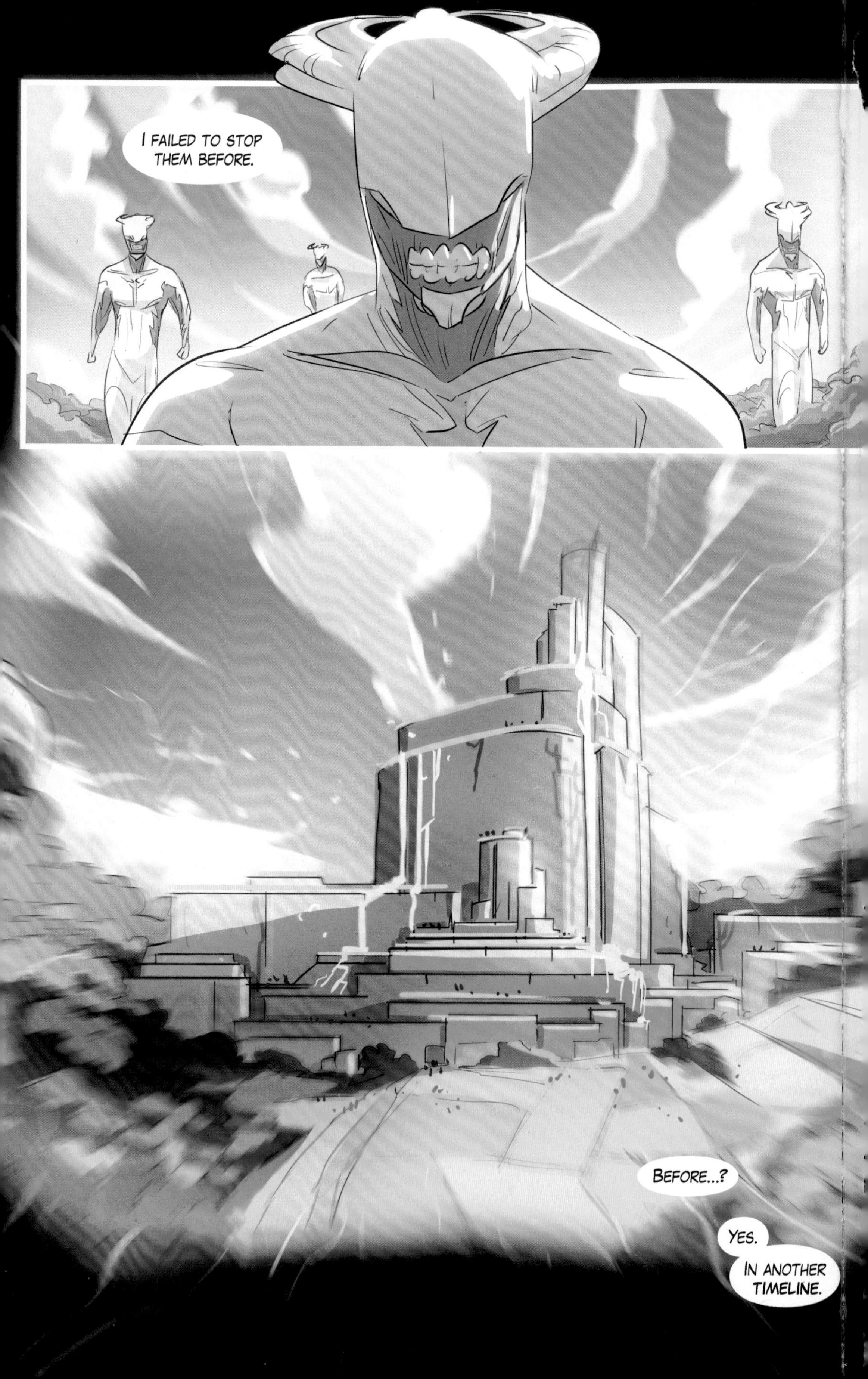
I FAILED TO STOP THEM BEFORE.
BEFORE...?
YES.
IN ANOTHER TIMELINE.

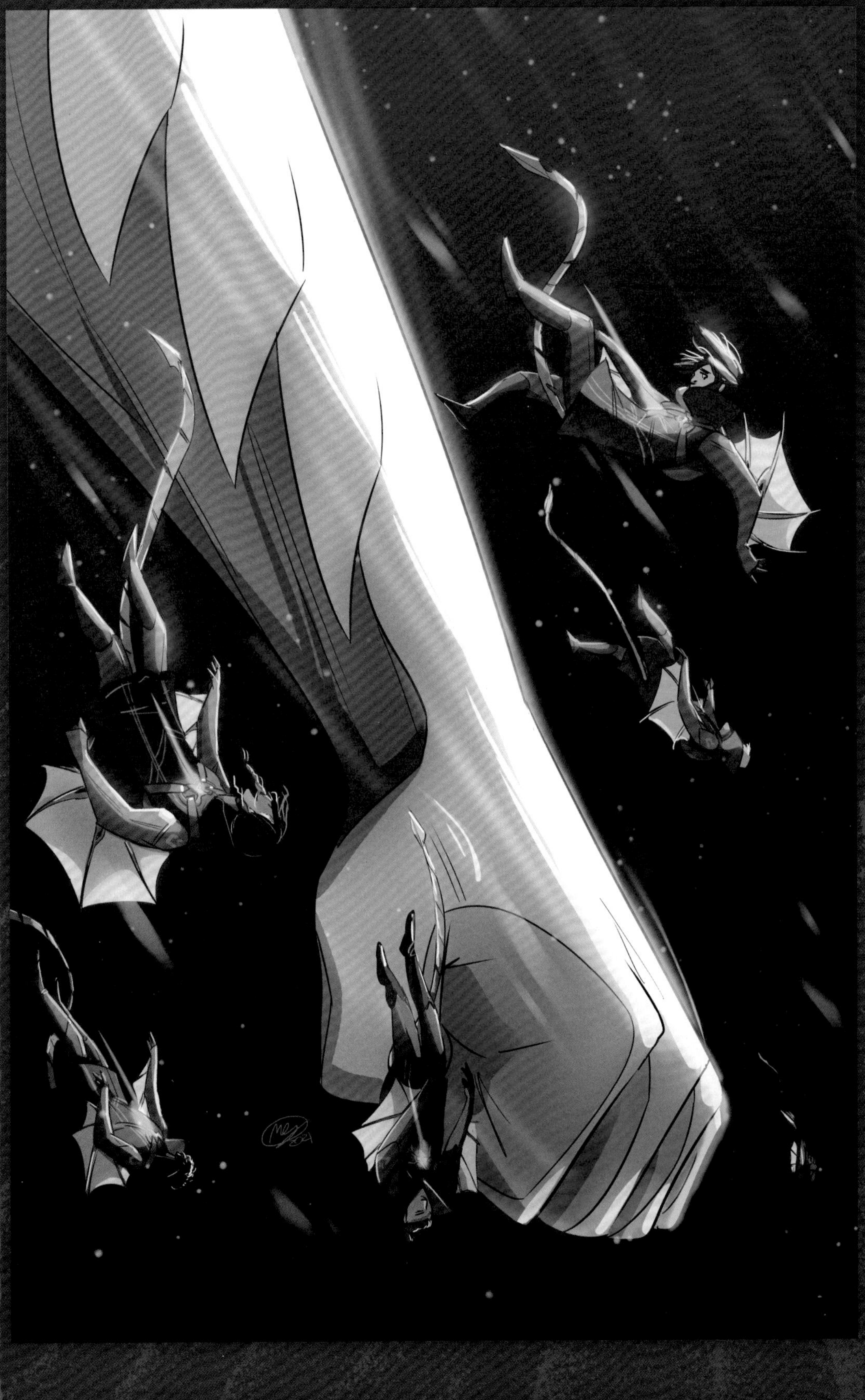

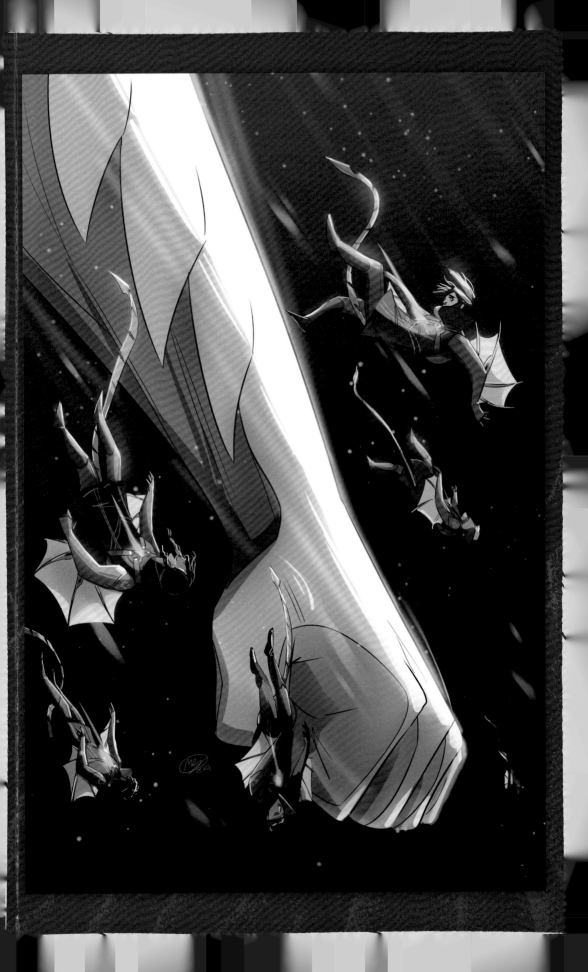

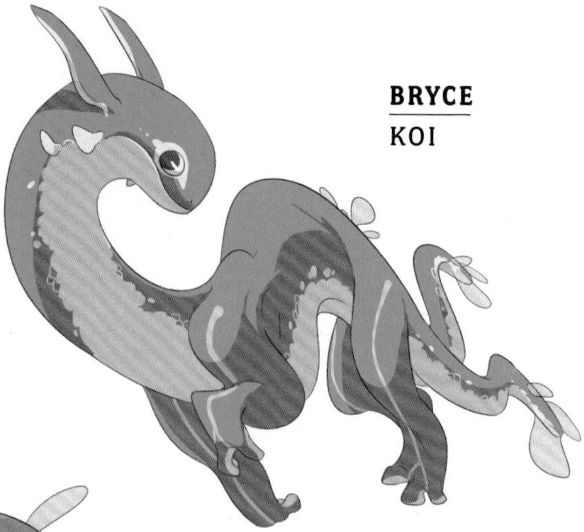

BRYCE
KOI

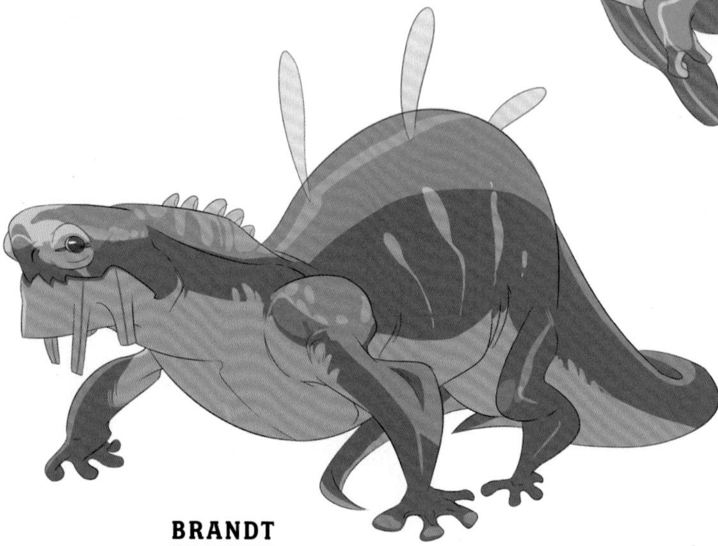

BRANDT
SLOG

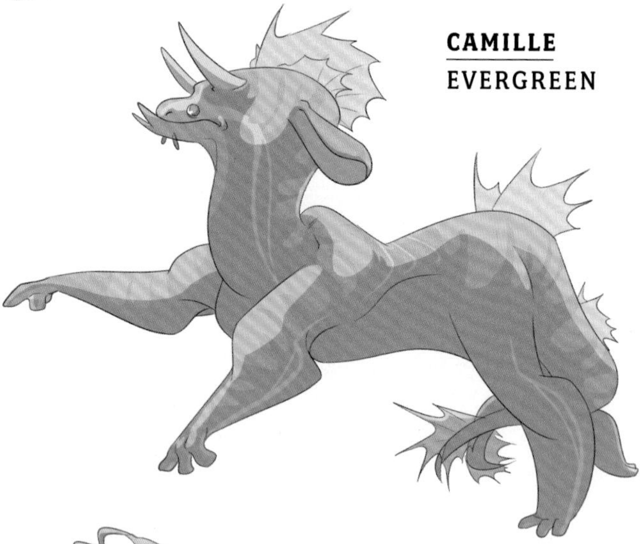

CAMILLE
EVERGREEN

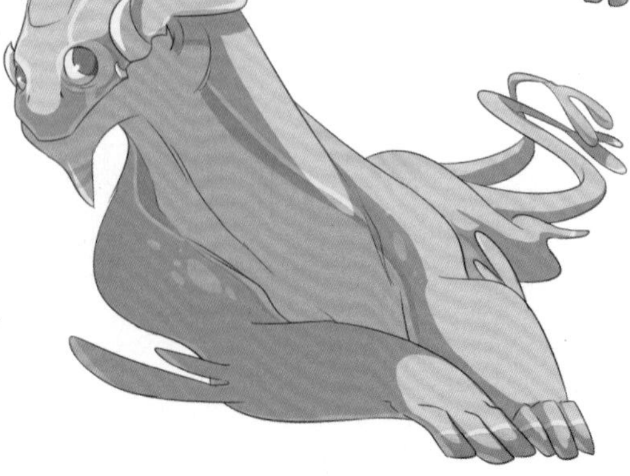

ARNO
PASTEL

ELSIE

BEAN

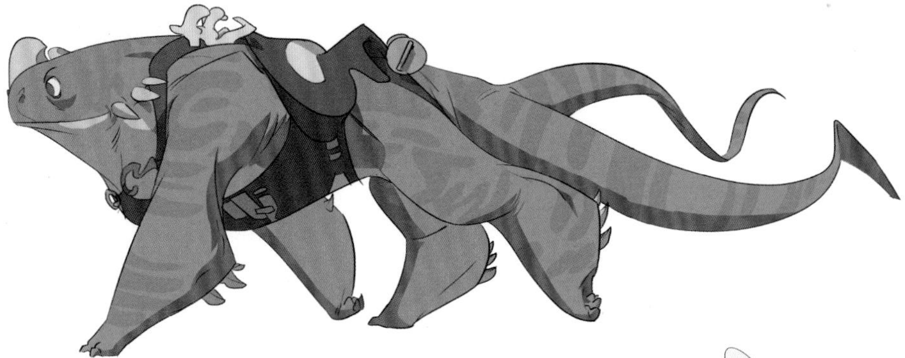

IVAN

ROOSTUR

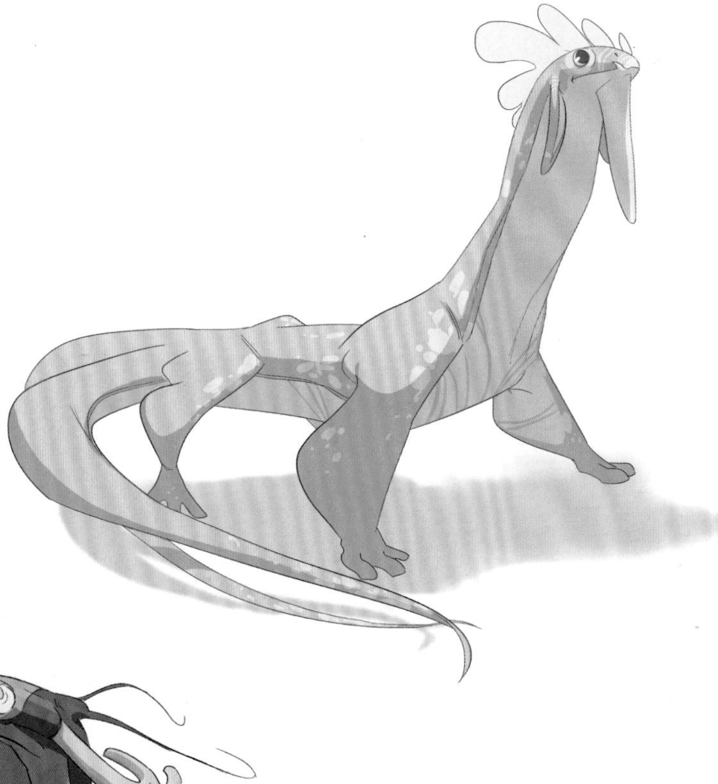

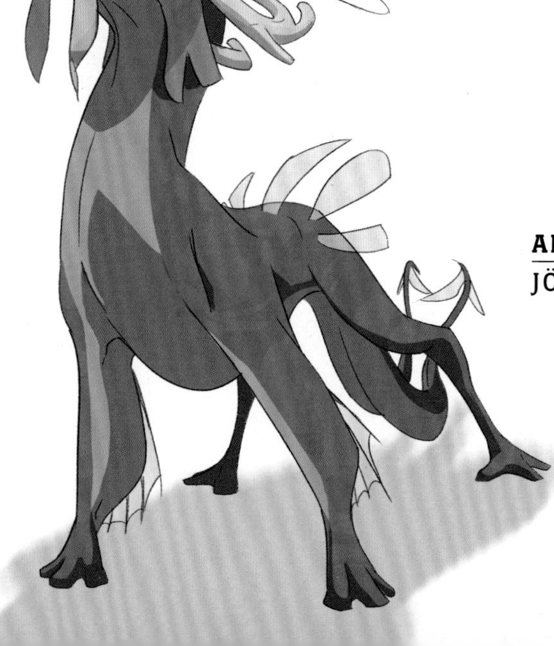

ARICK KNIGHT

JÖRMUNGANDR

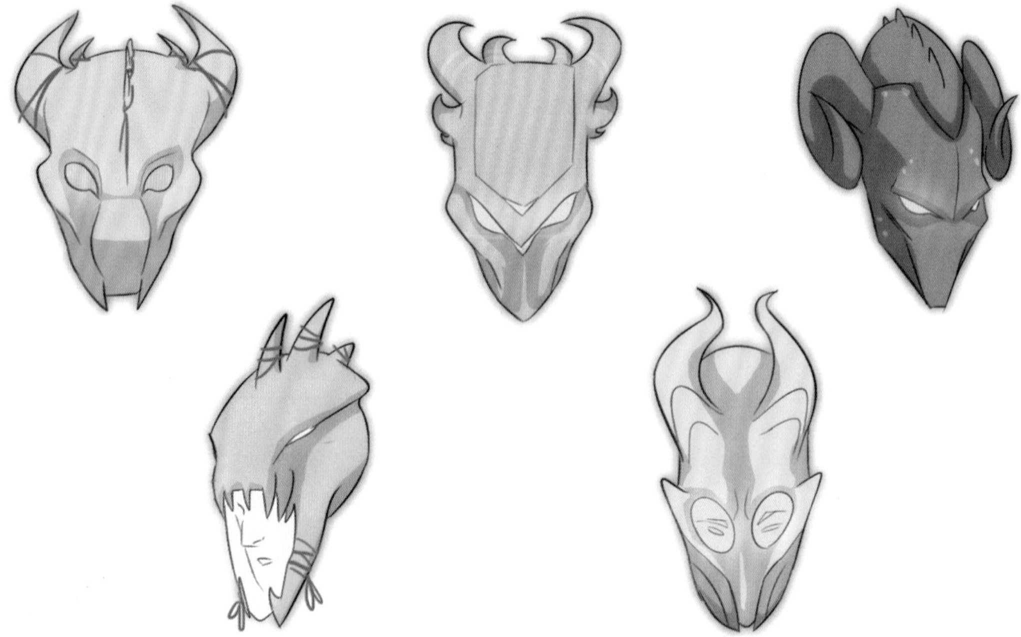

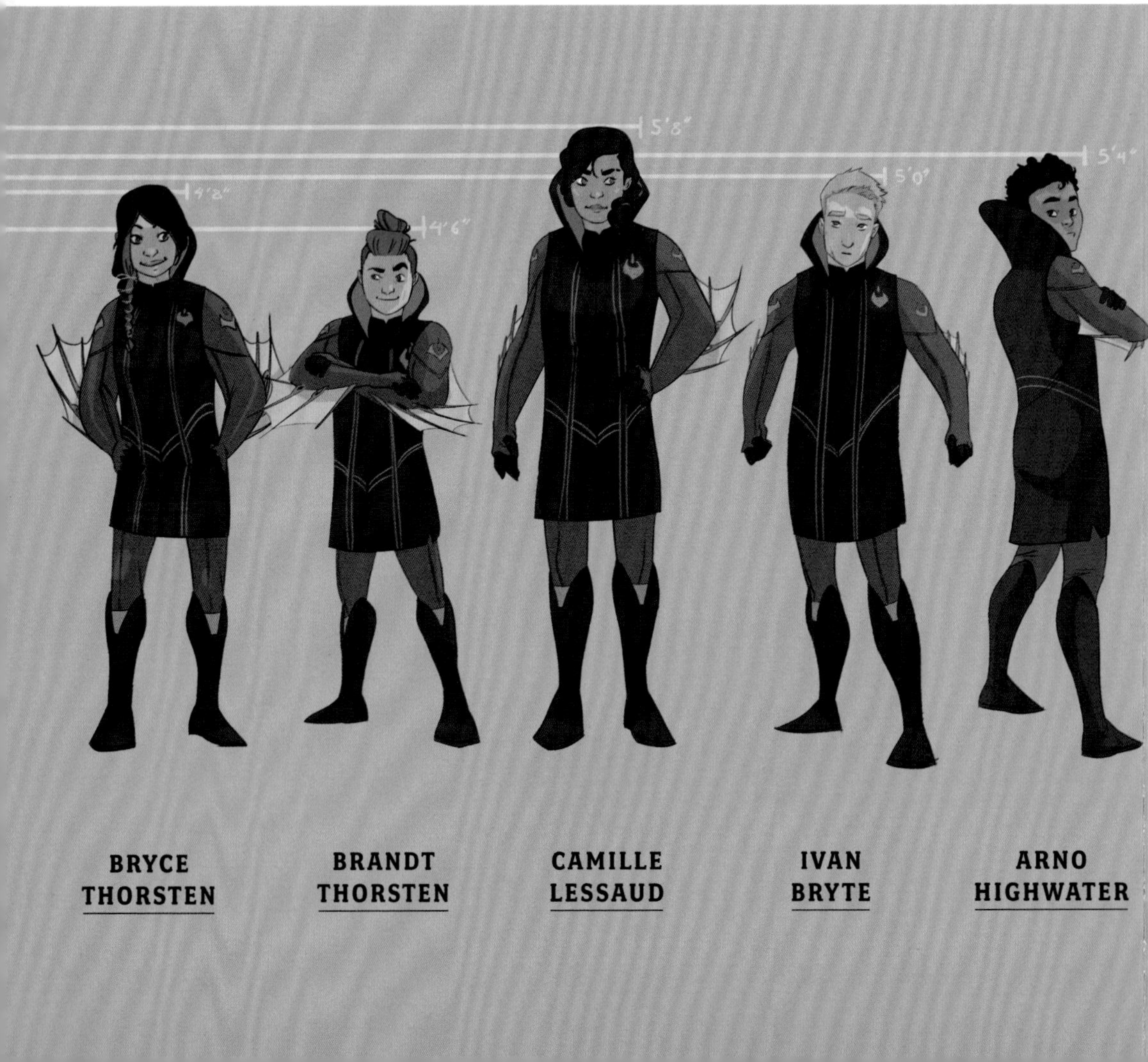
5'8"
5'4"
5'0"
4'8"
4'6"
BRYCE THORSTEN
BRANDT THORSTEN
CAMILLE LESSAUD
IVAN BRYTE
ARNO HIGHWATER

CADET ELSIE FROST

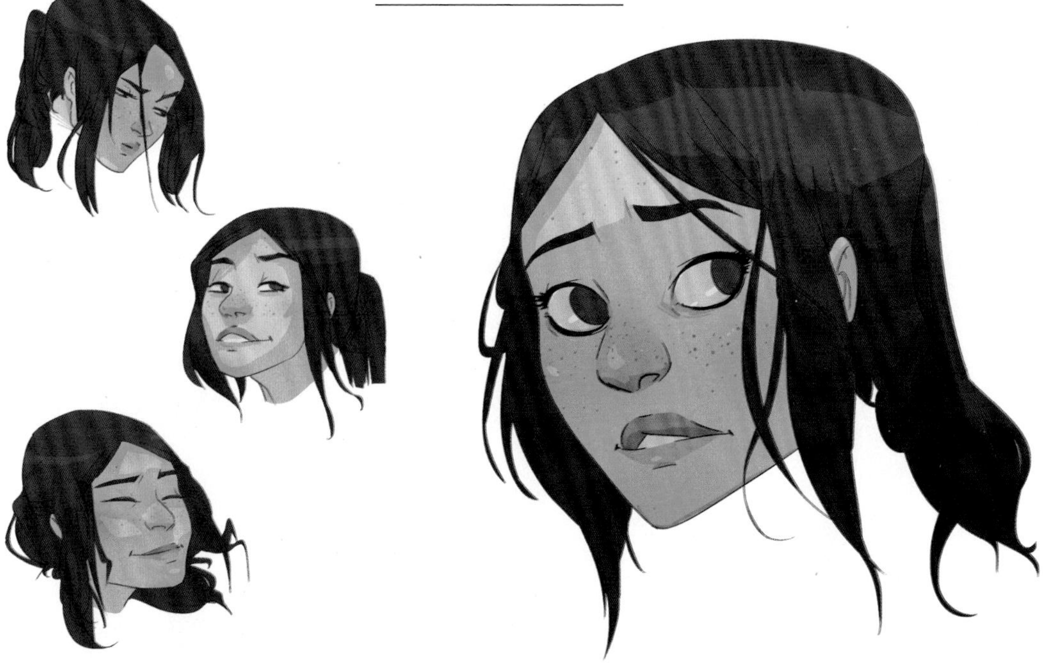

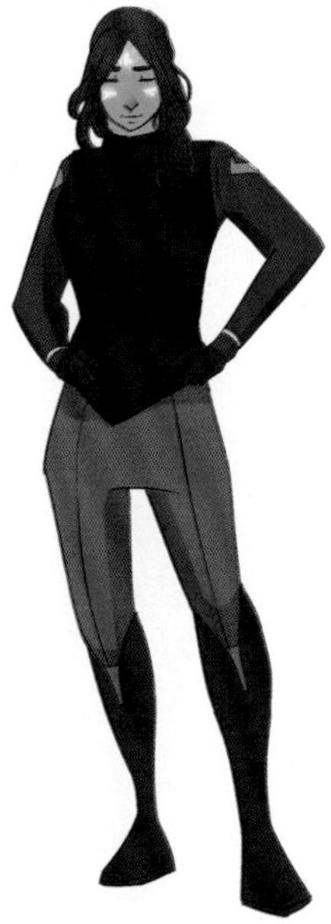

Casual

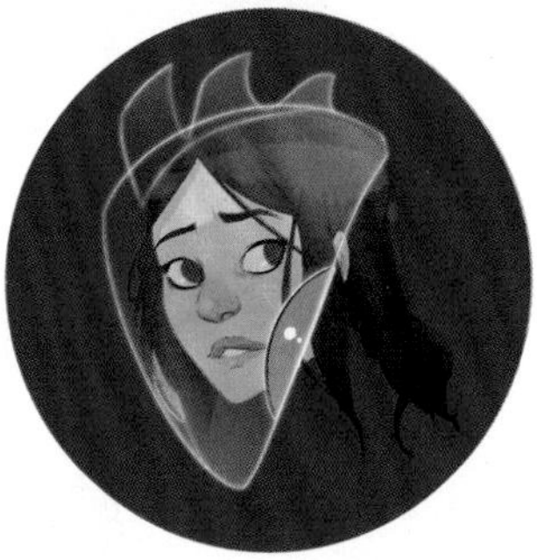

Collapsible Advanced Helmet

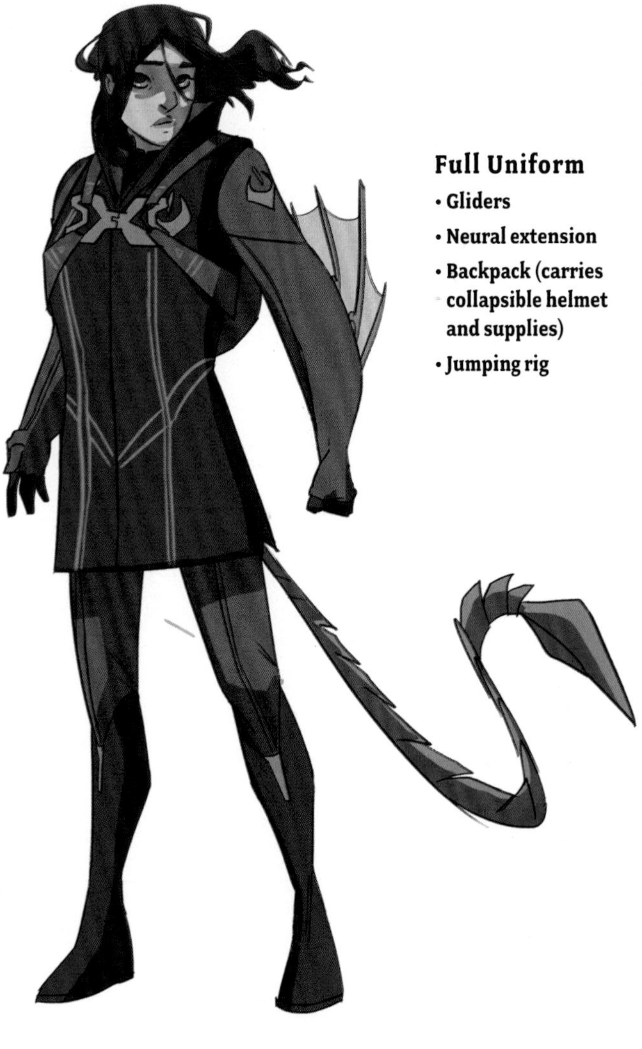

Full Uniform

- Gliders
- Neural extension
- Backpack (carries collapsible helmet and supplies)
- Jumping rig

COMMANDER ARICK KNIGHT

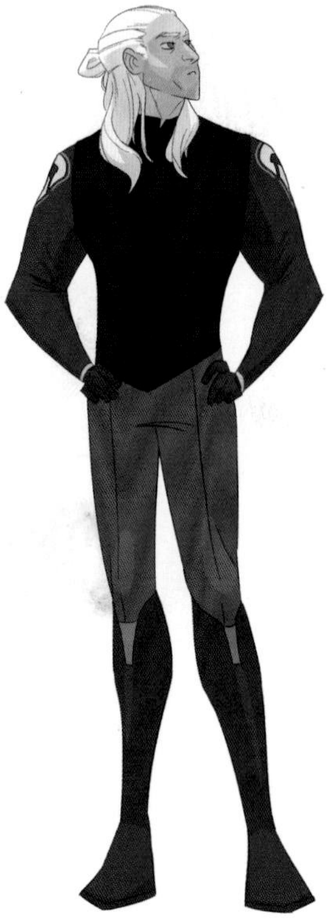

Casual Military

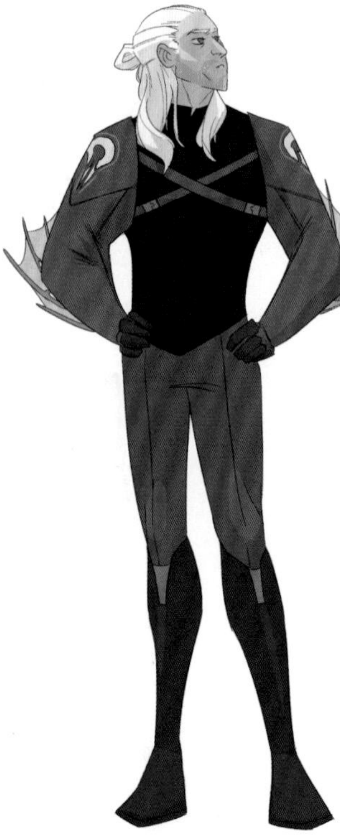

Blades / Flight Rig

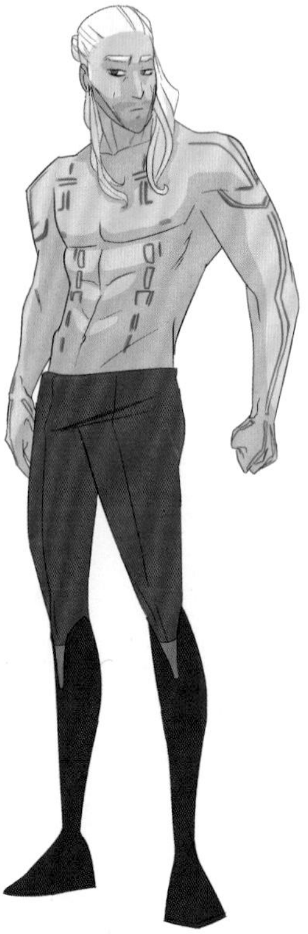

Physique

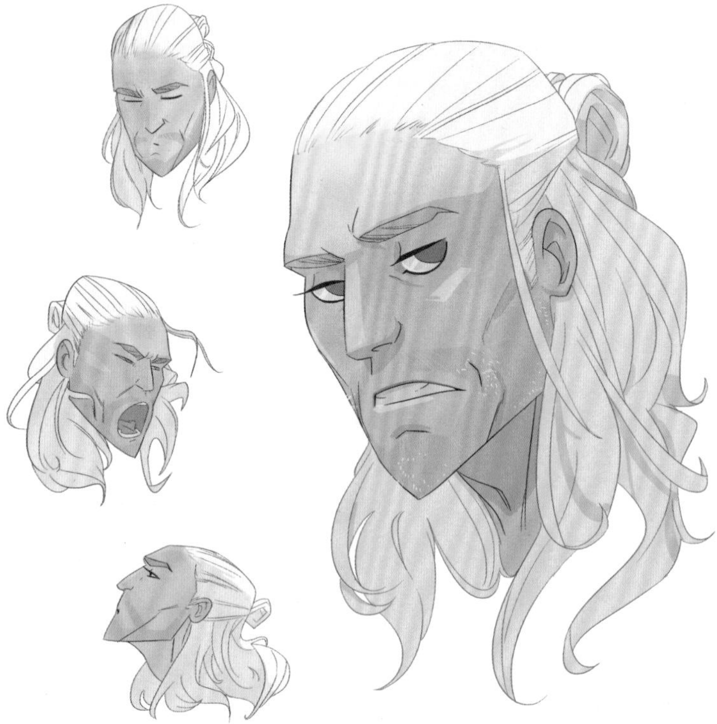

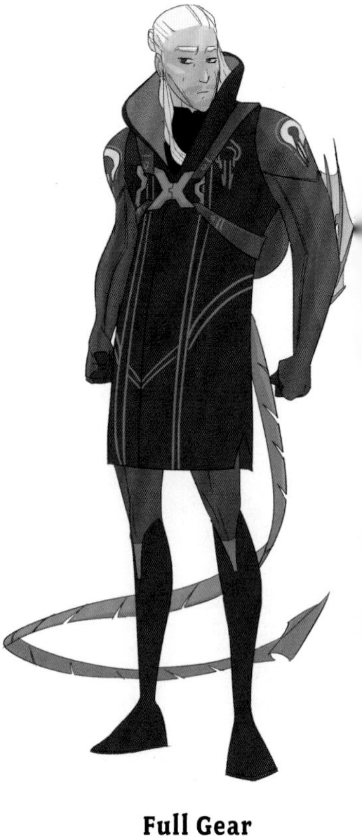

Full Gear

FINAL OUTFIT FUNCTIONALITY AND DESIGN

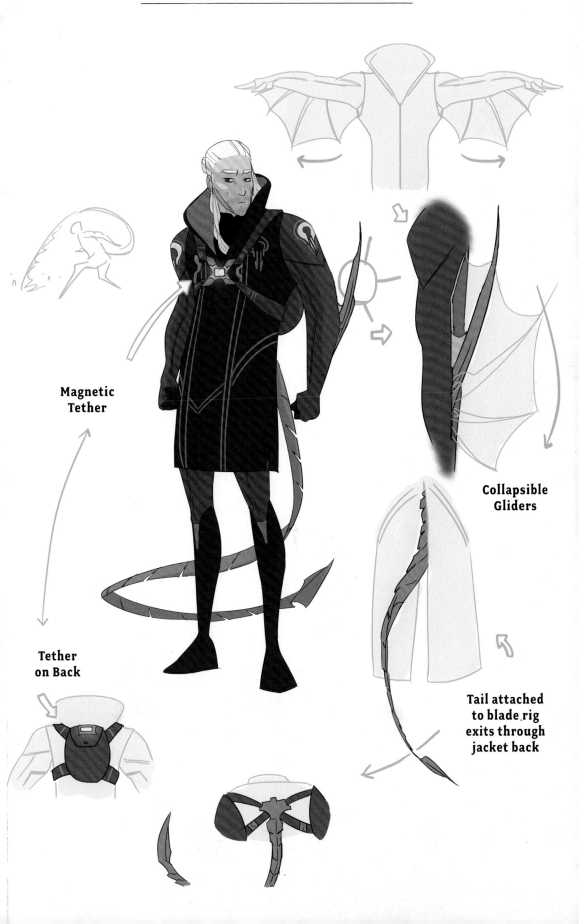

Magnetic Tether

Tether on Back

Collapsible Gliders

Tail attached to blade rig exits through jacket back

SQUALL OWL

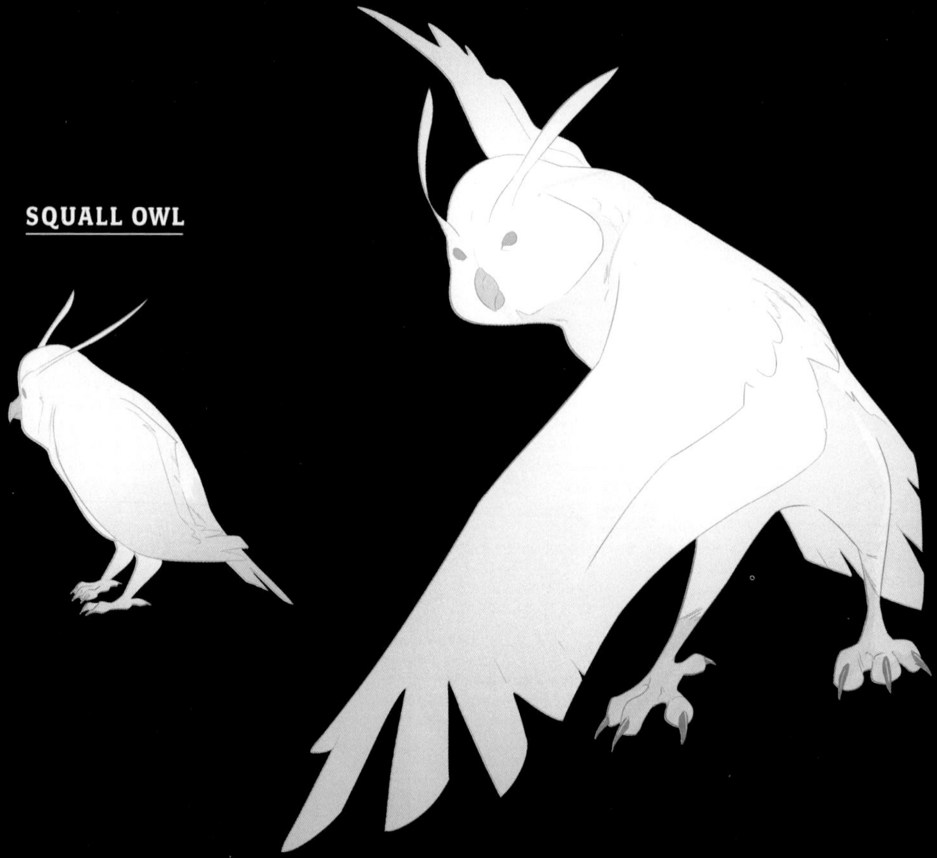

WENDIGO

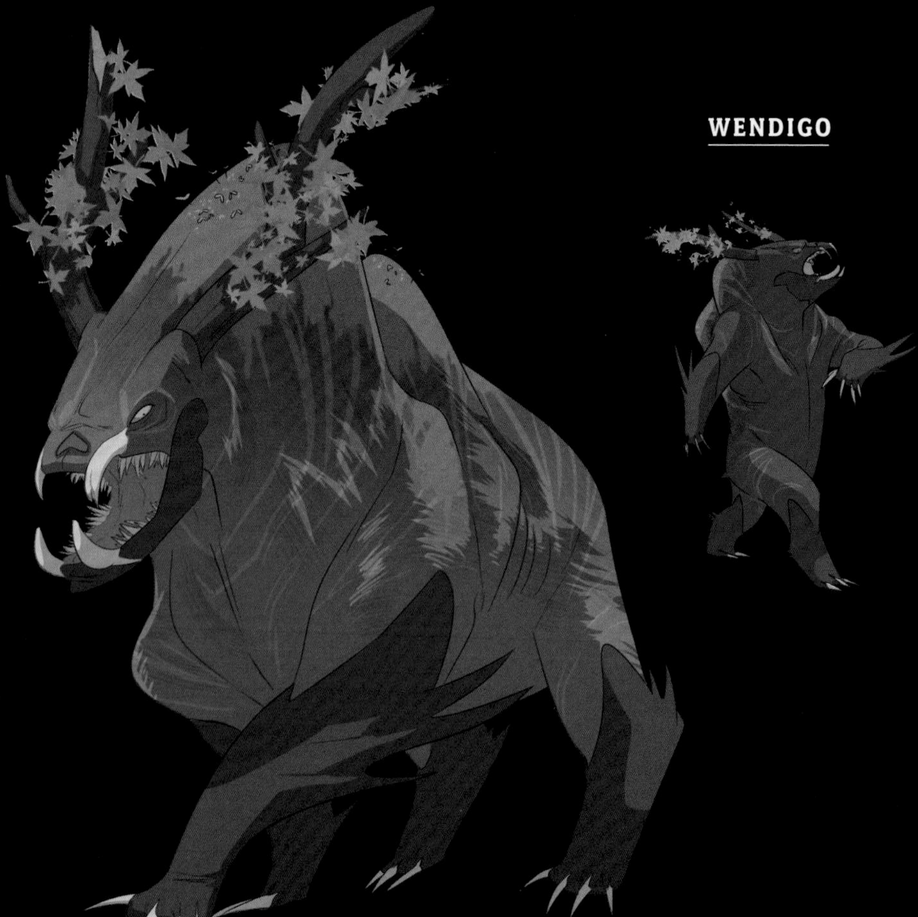

JUGGERNAUT

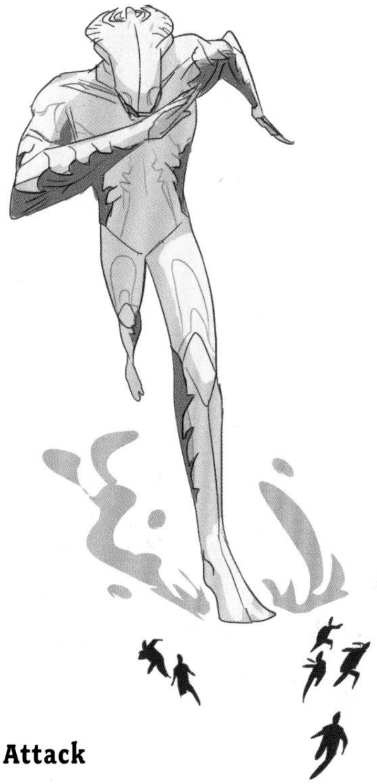

Attack

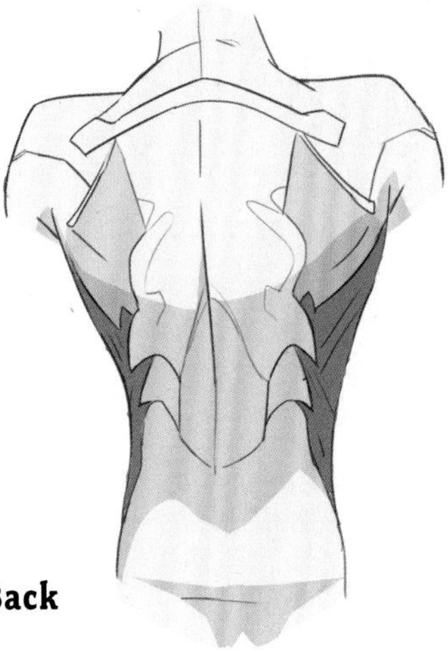

Back

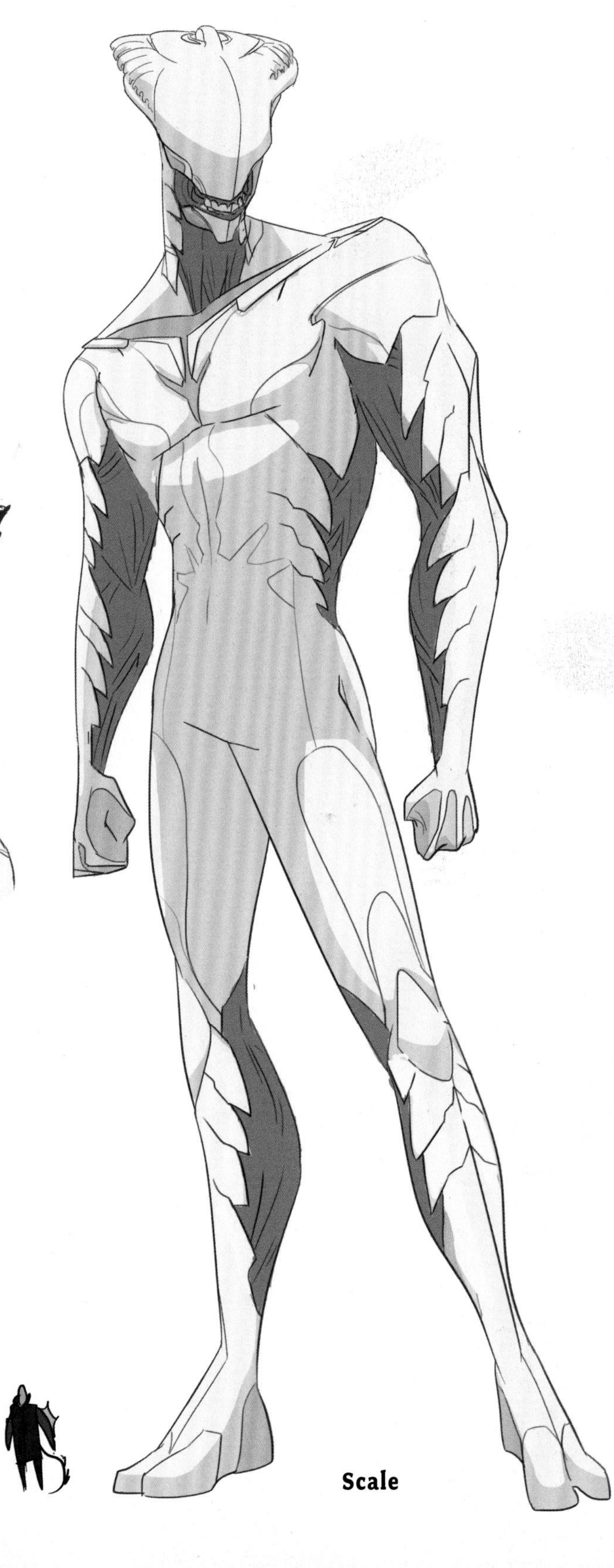

Scale

ABOUT THE AUTHOR

Megan Huang is a Canadian comic artist and writer. She has worked as a cover artist, interior artist, and colorist for various publishers, including Z2 Comics, Action Lab Comics, IDW, Image Comics, Oni Press, and Dark Horse Comics. She illustrated All Time Low's *Young Renegades* graphic novel for Z2 Comics, colored the comic series *Double Jumpers*, and illustrated *Princeless*, both for Action Lab Comics. Megan also illustrated the graphic novel *Jia and the Nian Monster* and worked as a colorist on the comic series *Jenny Zero* with Dark Horse Comics. Her debut comic series as a solo creator, *Rangers of the Divide*, was published by Dark Horse Comics in 2021. She strives to create an otherworldly feel in her stories. In her free time, Megan enjoys gaming, sleeping, and eating: the holy trinity. She currently lives in Ontario, Canada, with her dog, Ripley (a.k.a. her Alien-killing BFF), and a bunch of dragons.